THEY ALL FALL DOWN

RACHEL HOWZELL HALL

A TOM DOHERTY ASSOCIATES BOOK
NEW YORK

This is a work of fiction. All of the characters, organizations, and events portrayed in this novel are either products of the author's imagination or are used fictitiously.

THEY ALL FALL DOWN

A Forge Book
Published by Tom Doherty Associates
120 Broadway
New York, NY 10271

www.tor-forge.com

Forge® is a registered trademark of Macmillan Publishing Group, LLC.

ISBN 978-1-250-22461-3

Our books may be purchased in bulk for promotional, educational, or business use. Please contact your local bookseller or the Macmillan Corporate and Premium Sales Department at 1-800-221-7945, extension 5442, or by email at MacmillanSpecialMarkets@macmillan.com.

First Edition: April 2019
First Mass Market Edition: August 2020

Printed in the United States of America

0 9 8 7 6 5 4 3 2

For that one English professor who didn't want me to interpret precious English things as something darker and American.

Best of an island is once you get there—you can't go any further . . . you've come to the end of things.

AGATHA CHRISTIE, *AND THEN THERE WERE NONE*

THEY
ALL
FALL
DOWN

The blue scarf caressed my ear as it dipped beneath my head and pulled me down into the water.

It wanted to kill me.

I could have let the scarf go, but I'd won it. It was mine.

I was alone, drifting in the warm waters of the Sea of Cortez, floating on my back. Numb. My arms and legs felt so far away . . .

It was the first time this week I was truly resting. The first time ever that I'd floated in the ocean.

So many firsts.

My cracked lips parted. "I don't like it here."

Jagged rocks poked through my T-shirt and scraped the skin on my back. Salt water dribbled into my mouth, and I swallowed it. The sea tasted alive, tasted like tears. Morgan's tears. She had cried so many times, and I'd held her, wanting to cry, too, wanting to cry now, but no, I didn't. I wouldn't. Crying would be admitting that they were right. Crying would frighten me into accepting the hurt. I didn't feel hurt. No, not at all. I had to resist. Resistance was like the coral now scraping against my back and my arms and my neck. Resistance hurt. Resistance protected.

I blinked—salt water was burning my eyes.

The big sky had darkened into oranges and purples, juices and bruises, dragons and sunsets.

Pretty. So pretty.

I should've climbed out. Should've swum to the

shore to join the others back at the house. If I stayed in the ocean, though, I'd still . . . join the others back at the house, just meeting up on the other side. No difference. Not now. Not anymore.

A wave crashed over me. Pain burst and banged near my eyes. The world brightened, and I winced, and then the bright world spun. Dizzy, I closed my eyes.

Morgan, swaddled in her nursery blanket, smelled of sunshine and love.

Mother held my shoulders, so proud of me, then tapped the honor society pin on my collar.

Daddy had stopped running beside me as wind stung my face, as the spokes on my bicycle's wheels click-click-clicked as I rode faster and faster down Duncan Avenue.

Bright light shone above me and made me close my eyes. Desi's scarf wrapped tighter around my wrist, pulling me down as something behind my heart slipped past my ribs, through my skin, and drifted toward the light.

There she stood, way up on the cliff, prettier than the sky. Her dark hair blew across her face. Those dark welts on her neck looked like tattoos. She'd torn a hole through a pair of pink tights. Had slipped them over her head and slipped her arms through the legs. Ballerina forever. There she stood, the fairest of them all, way up there, looking way down here at me. Always looking down . . .

WE HAVE
A WINNER!

FROM: A. Nansi
TO: Mimi Macy
SENT: 4:45 a.m., Friday July 8
SUBJECT: Your Arrival

Congratulations! We are so excited and look forward to the journey you are about to take. It will be truly magical! As promised, we have a car, provided by Alpha Luxury Coaches, scheduled to pick you up at 7:00 a.m. and we have booked for you first-class air to Puerto Peñasco, Sonora, Mexico. There, you will take a luxurious yacht across the tranquil Sea of Cortez to the exclusive Mictlan Island, a Tropical Paradise! Attached please find the ticket for the short cruise, courtesy of Molinero Ocean Charter Services.

Thank you again for replying to our earlier email—we are always interested in personalities and how certain types of people interact. This *is* a television show, and we want viewers to tune in and to never look away. As a result, we look for personalities that may not work well together, types of people who wouldn't seek each other out for friendships. You don't have to get along with the other contestants—just let Nature take its course. Also, during your journey to Puerto Peñasco, we ask that you refrain from approaching others—we want to be sure to capture all interactions while also ensuring confidentiality. None of this should surprise you since you returned the signed contract agreeing to these conditions.

Upon your arrival, you and six other contestants will enjoy five-star accommodations at the beautiful Artemis estate.

Since this is a private island, Wi-Fi and internet connections will be intermittent. Further, the use of telephones is prohibited due to the nature of this competition. Do not worry, however. Satellite phones and radios will be available for dire emergencies. You have previously shared your emergency contact information should the need to reach someone arise. We have on record WILLIAM MACY, DDS, SPOUSE.

Miriam, your days and nights will be filled with challenges and enchantment. There will be times you will cry and times you will celebrate. You will meet the REAL YOU during your short time with us.

This is unlike any competition the world has ever seen! Congratulations again and good luck!

1

The Los Angeles International Airport was the worst place to lose your mind in post-9/11 America. Especially if you were a person of color. Especially if you perspired like Kobe Bryant in Game 7 of the NBA Finals. Especially if you popped Valium twice a day to combat anxiety. And there I was, standing in the TSA security clearance line at LAX, a sweaty, anxious black woman wearing sweaty green silk, sipping air and blinking away tears.

Miriam, keep it together. They're gonna pull you out of line if you keep on. Calm down. But "calm" was slipping further away, an iceberg on a quick current being pushed by a pod of enthusiastic killer whales.

And so I closed my eyes and I prayed again. *God, don't let them kick me out of LAX today. Please help me stay calm.*

"Next."

In my mind, I said, "Amen," then opened my eyes. I forced myself to smile at the gray-eyed TSA agent seated behind the little podium, and hoped that she thought I was a slow blinker and not a terrorist praying one last time before setting one off.

The agent flicked her hand at me and said, "ID and boarding pass, please."

I handed her both without saying a word.

She glanced at me, glanced at my passport—*Miriam Macy, Los Angeles, forty-five years old*—then she stamped, scribbled, and handed me back each document. "Have a nice trip."

I croaked, "Thanks," just as a teardrop bubbled to the rim of my right eye. I swiped it away, dropped my bag, shoes, and phone into a gray bucket, then set the bucket onto the conveyor belt. With panic punching at my gut, I stepped into the full-body scanner. Clamped my lips together as imaging beams searched my body for weapons.

"Step through, please." Another TSA agent, this one male and bearded, flicked his hand at me. He waited for the all-clear from the agent at the monitor, then said to me, "Thanks."

I snatched my bag, shoes, and phone from the gray bucket and hurried away from the security clearance area. I'd kept it together. But my prayer had met its expiration date and that calm I'd prayed for was now wearing away like sandcastles at high tide.

You have to respond to her.

You can't get on a plane and leave it like this.

Breathless, I tottered to the nearest bathroom, *thisclose* to 405 freeway levels of hysteria. I hid in the farthest stall, then shoved my hand deep into my bag. Shaking, I popped off the Valium's cap, then slipped a tablet beneath my tongue, not caring if enough time had passed between this and my last dose just two hours before. I closed my eyes and waited for the drug to untangle the bundles of nerves along my shoulders and neck. Didn't have to pretend for cameramen capturing B-roll here. I could be a loser in the privacy offered only in a bathroom stall.

Outside my cubby, women washed their hands at the sinks, then convinced children to wash their hands, too. They pulled paper towels from dispensers and made the air blowers roar.

So loud.

Loud enough?

Yes.

So I wept and rocked on the toilet and waited for the drug to work, for the drug to make the world softer.

How long would it take?

How long would I have to wait?

. . .

Valium became a part of my life on the afternoon I lost it on the westbound 10 freeway. It had been last New Year's Eve, and I'd had enough, and I'd stopped the car to wail in the far-left lane. Traffic had built around me, but I didn't care. I'd called my husband Billy, he'd called 911, and I rode in an ambulance for the second time in two months (the first time after I'd confronted Billy about his affair but left his girlfriend's apartment without killing him). Dr. Sandoval, a kind man and Cesar Romero look-alike, diagnosed me with post-traumatic stress disorder and wrote me a prescription for Valium.

A week later, I took a leave of absence from my job as the marketing and communications director for Hidden Treasures, a luxury goods consignment store. I'd loved my job—spinning stories about a second-hand Gucci satchel (*Indy stowed that simple cup here without worry . . .*) or a Chanel brooch (*She always said you had Coco's overactive imagination . . .*) or Louboutin stilettos (*At the stroke of midnight, you chose the shoe over the prince . . .*). Sartorial creativity made me swoon.

But I hadn't been able to create, not with all the drama swirling around me. My boss, Lola, lost all patience and told me that it was best that I left. No more creating something out of nothing for a living. After my departure, the copy read flat, like a bad first draft of an M.F.A. novel set in Nebraska. There were rumors that Hidden Treasures would file for bankruptcy—no one was inspired enough to buy other people's crap (or, as I'd called it, "luxury shared between friends") and no one ordered the catalogs just to read my product descriptions. Their loss—the company *and* its customers.

. . .

Five minutes of hiding in the bathroom stall had passed—but the world still hurt.

So tired. Last night, after fleeing from my ex-husband's house, after popping ibuprofen to banish the pain in my head, I hadn't slept. There had been cracking and snapping twigs outside my bedroom windows. Slowing cars rumbling too close to my driveway. Shadows lurking up and down my street, some stopping to lean against the palm tree in front of my house. In a state between dozing and awake, I had crept to my living room and perched in the armchair, eyes burning, iPad and cell phone on my lap. Flinching. Tight.

My heartbeat had ticked in my head and I'd tasted sour milk and I'd tried to swallow it but my throat and stomach were too tight, and so whatever it was pooled in my mouth.

A tub of Valium sat on the dining room table.

Drugs would smooth me out, but I didn't want to be smooth then. I had a game to win.

And so, I sat there in the living room, forcing down bile and fighting back dizziness, until a shaft of copper light broke past the wooden shutters.

This morning, the show's producer had sent a Town Car to drive me to the airport, and as I strode to the sedan, I ignored the state of my raggedy house and watched a flock of green parrots circle the glossy blue sky. Airplanes glinted like silver bullets en route to someplace better.

That will be me, I'd thought. *In Someplace Better. Soon . . .*

A half hour later, though, here I was, hiding in an airport bathroom.

In Someplace Better.

. . .

Ten minutes.

It had taken ten minutes for the Valium to work.

And now I felt nothing.

Smoothed out. Empty. Void of emotion.

And that hollowness lived solidly next to my heart and my lungs, that hollowness as useful as my appendix.

I took a deep breath, then found my phone in my purse. I took another breath, then reread my daughter Morgan's text message, the same message that had sent me flying into a toilet stall.

It was a short message.

Just three words.

I hate you.

2

I stayed in that toilet stall a little longer, until my bloodshot eyes were no longer puffy. Until the eye drops whitened my whites again. Until my knees could withstand gravity. Until the Miriam Macy who had sashayed into the airport found her way back into my soul again.

That took a moment. More like thirty minutes. But then, after that half hour, I was ready to face the world.

I studied my reflection in the bathroom mirror. Sea-green silk tunic *(airy)* and matching silk slacks *(luminous)*; and a signature jade and onyx necklace *(At an ancient temple in the lost city of Ping Yao, your hand brushes against a crumbling wall...)* that complemented my green eyes and elongated my short neck. A little lipstick, a little powder...

Boom. *You look like a boss again.*

Satisfied, I grabbed my black leather bag *(They will wonder if this same classic handbag hid Janet Leigh's stolen cash in Psycho...)* and my vintage suitcase *(Cuba meets Egypt...)*, then strolled out to the gates.

Like a boss.

I placed a final call to my attorney, Phillip Omeke. His phone line rang once... twice... and then hit voicemail. Phillip's pretty Somalian paralegal's voice told me that I'd reached the law offices of Omeke Squire and Pierce, that I should leave a message, and that he'd soon return my call. A lie—I'd left six messages in six weeks, and I'd only spoken to his machine, not even pretty Fazia, because Phillip Omeke no longer cared one flip about me.

Still, I obeyed, because I had no other lawyer to call and because I knew in my heart of hearts that he really did care about me. "It's Miriam again. You know what? I'm gonna press charges against Prudence McAllister once I get back to L.A. So ignore my other message, the one I left a little after midnight. That's it. Talk to you soon. Wish me luck."

The invitation to participate in a reality television competition had appeared in my in-box just a month ago. *New game show . . . filming pilot . . . all expenses paid . . . Mexico . . . Nothing like this has ever been filmed . . . Interested?* I needed money—legal bills wouldn't pay themselves, and now that I no longer received disability checks, I needed a source of income. So, in my reply to the show's producer, I'd told him that I never flew anywhere coach and that I required monetary compensation for my participation. He had responded with "Of course," and had then informed me that I'd take home at *least* ten thousand dollars for being on the show. In my excitement, I'd neglected to ask about the grand prize. If I'd receive ten thousand dollars for losing, though, the winner *had* to take home half a mil. Right?

Throughout the flight to Mexico, I scanned the faces of the other passengers. Who would I be competing against? The pit-faced steroid junkie in the Ed Hardy graffiti shirt? The vacuous big-boobed blonde with more paint on her face than the Berlin Wall? Or the Ryan Seacrest wannabe with the frosted blond tips and the down-market Italian loafers? These were the types of people who bothered me—fake and frosted, wannabe hotties with more air between their brains than the space between heaven and earth.

But no one associated with the game show approached me—not on the plane nor at the taxi stand in

front of the Sonoran airport. Guess we were all obey-
ing the order to avoid interaction before arriving to the
port. No one associated with the Los Angeles Police
Department approached me, either. Good. Cool.

While I had been in the air, though, Detective Gior-
gio Hurley had left me a voicemail: *"Ms. Macy, hi.
Just checking in with you. We need to talk, either at
your home or here at the station. Sounds like there was
some type of altercation last night? Sounds like folks
were hurt, you included? Sounds like—"*

I hung up before finishing his message.

Detective Hurley would not destroy my fire, nope,
not today.

I tapped the camera icon and snapped a selfie of
me crossing my eyes with a silly smile. I sent it to my
daughter with a text message. *The Krazy Lady landed
safely in Mexico.* A way to say, "No hard feelings, I will
always love you no matter what." I shoved my phone
into my bag, lifted my chin, and forced light onto my
face. Pictured myself on-screen, with that reality-TV
synthesizer music bopping as I wandered about town
wearing green silk. Sharp eyes, soft smile, and perfectly waxed eyebrows, I was now Black America's
representative—hardworking and stylish, persevering
against all odds, a believer in fairness and faith and
directness . . . *You can win* combined with *lift ev'ry
voice* meets *power to the people*. Yeah, I saw myself on
TV, and that vision of me, strong me, had now carried
me from one country to the next, from plane to taxi,
and soon, onto the Sea of Cortez.

The world didn't know what was coming, what to
expect from Miriam Macy.

Like the two Mexicans working behind the desk at
Molinero Ocean Charter Services. They didn't know
what to expect, either. The older man with slicked-
back hair and the skinny college-age kid with skinny

arms inked up to his knobby shoulders were studying a piece of paper. Both wore name tags—"Raul" was the older man, and "Andreas" was the kid, and both assumed that I didn't speak a lick of Spanish.

They didn't know that I'd taken two years of required public school Spanish. Yeah. *Hablo un poquito de español.* Enough *español* to figure out that they had just said something about three Americans, that something-something was "dead," and something about cocaine and *narcos.* Couldn't hear much more than that, not over accordion music now blasting from speakers mounted beneath a taxidermied blue marlin. Didn't bother me, that loud music—I was still riding the diazepam wave.

The waiting area smelled of fresh-brewed coffee, seaweed, and the sour body odor of sweaty *hombres* who hadn't bathed in days. And two of those sweaty *hombres* wore bulletproof vests with POLICIA stenciled in white letters. They roamed the dusty sidewalk holding the laziest-looking Uzis in the world. One slowed in his step, tossed me a glance, then looked away . . . and then at me again. Classic double take.

Had he been stunned by my beauty, or . . . ?

Shit.

My mouth dried and the smile I'd prepared for him froze on my face as I thought of the other possibility. The possibility that Detective Hurley had somehow found a way to reach me all the way in Mexico. The possibility that he had asked the Mexican *policía* for their help in detaining me.

I shook my head. *No. Impossible.* Silly, even. Last night, I'd done nothing wrong. *Technically.* There'd be no reason to spend resources and time to find me and drag me back to America. *Let me finish the game at least*—that was my prayer.

With weaker legs, I wandered back to the check-in

counter. Tried to look natural as I looked back over my shoulder at the *policía*.

"*Estoy leyendo este derecho?*" the older man asked the kid.

Am I reading this right?

The kid ruffled his sun-bleached brown hair. "*La Serenata* took the food and provisions yesterday," he said in English. "Didn't seem like enough for that many people."

I assumed they were talking about the competition—there *wouldn't* be a lot of food since folks would be voted out of the house. So I cleared my throat and said, "*Un momento, por favor.*"

Both men swiveled toward me. A .45 lived in a holster strapped around the older man's hip. "*Sí,* how can I help you?"

"*Soy el primero aquí?*" Am I the first one here?

"You're sailing over to Mictlan?" Andreas asked.

I glanced back at the cops—could they hear this conversation? I glanced at the rotting ceiling tiles in search of hidden cameras—was I breaking a rule by answering his question?

"Mictlan, *sí?*" Andreas asked again. His eyes also flicked over to the officers.

A nervous smile found its way to my lips. "If that's where Artemis is, then *sí.*"

Raul blinked at me, then glanced at the paper in his hand.

"A few others are around town, shopping," the kid said. "You can relax for now."

I flapped my hands at my face. "Relax? It's hot as hell out here, not that I'm complaining." I chuckled. "Ha. Yes, I *am* complaining. It's hot as hell out here."

The two men stared at me and said nothing.

I chuckled again—my attempted wit had failed on two men who didn't speak English . . . *well.* Or . . .

good? Whatever. I shrugged and smiled. "Could you tell me who the other guests are?" Since I was already breaking the rules.

The kid plucked the paper from the older man's hand. "There's Wallace Zavarnella; Eddie Sweeney; Desirée Scoggins; Evelyn Pemstein, R.N.; Franklin Clayton; Javier Cardoza; and . . . you are Miriam?"

My stomach hardened—no use in lying, so I grinned and said, "Miriam since 1970."

The old man darkened, muttered in Spanish, then snatched back the manifest.

I leaned forward on the counter. "I heard you two talking earlier, about three dead Americans?"

The kid grinned and his gold molar twinkled. "I hear it was drug-related. That Felix Escorpion was responsible even though he's in jail. Do you hear of him?"

"Oh, *sí, sí,* of course." Heck, yeah, I'd heard of Felix Escorpion. He was today's Pablo Escobar, killing thousands while smuggling millions and millions of dollars' worth of guns, heroin, meth, and cocaine into America. He now sat in a heavily guarded jail cell in Fort Worth, Texas.

"I hear that he had a room in the big house with hungry dogs," Andreas said. "Dogs who were fed the limbs and intestines of his enemies. I hear that he had marijuana plants and opium poppies growing all over the forest, and that there were men carrying AKs hiding in trees, taking out *narcos* and *federales* and—"

"Andreas!" the older man barked. Raul turned to me with a grin that was closer to a grimace. His face was a mixture of glee and gloom, a study in light and shadow. "These were simply rumors, *señora*." The older man patted, then squeezed the kid's shoulder. "All that *narcóticos* was a long time ago. Before you *yanquis* came."

The kid's head waggled. "*Sí*. A very rich man owns the island now. Bought it for *nada,* then built the *new* big house. No more *narcos,* they say. It is truly paradise now." He nodded and smiled.

And now, us *yanquis* were playing silly survival games on that same island. Maybe *that's* why there were police wandering the harbor—protecting *Americanos* from something far heavier, more dangerous than a dance mom who'd gotten into a silly little skirmish back in L.A.

Yeah, *that* made more sense.

I thanked the two men and wandered over to the vinyl chairs beneath the salt-flecked windows. This was not Monterey Bay and Cannery Row with its charming pastel-colored buildings and ordered disorder, and the ghost of John Steinbeck lording over it all. Here in this part of Puerto Peñasco, flies swarmed over fish carcasses left behind by the gulls. The vendors looked as shaggy as the stray dogs sniffing through the trash, and their tables had been crammed to the edges with wooden totems, pottery, and seashell jewelry. Delirious seabirds were the port's guardians. The peaks of the choppy green sea glinted with light sometimes, and at other times something like red kelp made the water look bloody.

Vicious dogs. Men with guns. Drug dealers. Danger, danger, dangerous. Dangerous like the Crips in my neighborhood. Dangerous like skinheads wearing Doc Martens.

I snorted and said, "Cute." Because I felt no fear—only that hollowness near my heart and my lungs.

The Valium was working.

FROM: MorganDancer
TO: Mimi Macy
SENT: 1:08 p.m., Friday, July 8
SUBJECT: <none>

Mom, did Prudence really hurt you? I asked her today and she said that she came over just to talk to you. I know she's lying. But I also know that you lie, too. But I can't blame her. I can't blame you, either. At least not yet. So, what happened last night? Because Detective Hurley came by this morning, looking for you. He was not happy. But he's never happy.

Remember when you asked me what I needed to make things right between us again? I didn't know then but I know now. You need to go back to therapy with Dr. Gail. You need to take your meds like you're supposed to. You need to GROW UP and stop comparing yourself and stop comparing me to other people. Stop being so JEALOUS of Ashlee and Daddy. I know it's weird and a little gross, but they really love each other. She really loves me, too, and she's going to get me back to ballet.

I want everything to be like it was. I want my old life back. Because people think I'm bad. I'm not. People think I hated Brooke. I didn't. I just want to dance again and hang out with my friends and just be 17. But you can't always get what you want. Daddy says that all the time. We can come close though. You say that all the time.

That's why Ashlee and Daddy are taking me to Disney

World next week, just to be a kid!! I'll think about you during Fantasmic—you always cry during Fantasmic!!

Mom, I don't hate you. I shouldn't have sent that text. I'm sorry.

I don't hate you.

But I don't like you, either. Not who you are now. You can change, though. I know you can. You are very smart. You are very strong. You just need to focus. Ha-ha, you also used to say that to me all the time about EVERYTHING!!!

See U in 7 days. Please don't embarrass me on TV. My life is hard enough.

Love,
Mo

P.S. That was a cute pic u sent Krazy Lady. Can you please bring me a sweatshirt? A purple one if possible.

P.P.S. I'll bring you something back from the happiest place in the world.

P.P.P.S. Slay KWEEN and bring home dat $$$!!!!

3

Disney World.

No one asked *me* if taking my daughter to the other side of the country was fine. Also? I wasn't jealous of Ashlee—being jealous meant that I wanted what she had. And I'd had Billy, and he wasn't that great. He smelled like Novocain, didn't like *Star Wars,* sighed more than he laughed, and would never order chicken or use hot sauce in public. He criticized my clothes *(too flashy)* and lamented that I never cooked quinoa and couscous and sushi *(your food is so boring).* I needed to exercise more *(140 pounds, what a cow)* and wear less makeup *(no thinking man likes all that war paint).*

William Macy had killed my spirit with his own lack of imagination and his surplus of criticism, even before the Bad Times. Let the dance teacher *(Morgan's* dance teacher, of all the women in the world to cheat on me with), let *her* have him and his tiny . . . Billy.

My next act would involve a larger man—in every way. A man who enjoyed hot wings on one night and a dry-aged rib eye the next. A man who ran the trail beside me and realized and accepted that the layer of fat around my belly was neither offensive nor an accessory that I could put on or take off. My next act would involve a man with a lot of commas on his bank statement—because I'd married for love already and it had left me poor and alone.

For the most part, dating after my divorce had been depressing. Daniel had thought he was funny, so funny that, at fifty, he'd quit his job as an IT senior vice president to pursue a career in stand-up comedy. His three jokes about computers had made me laugh, but the thirteen remaining minutes of his routine ... Yeah. No. And Ethan the fireman had scared me. Literally. One date in, he snapped at me after I'd said, "Thank you" to our waiter. "Because you smiled as you said it," he had explained. "Like you wanna sleep with him or something." My last two dates had been with Josh, a showrunner for a cable series. He made me laugh, he didn't kiss with his teeth, and he liked chili cheese fries *and* porterhouse steaks—and last month, his job had taken him to New York for who knows how long. Distance killed something that could've been.

My next act? Would be with someone like the older white man now wandering the waiting area. He moved with confidence and had the stride of a powerful attorney or a neurosurgeon or a minister. And now, his head of luxurious gray hair was bent over a stand of Mexican pottery.

Before going over to introduce myself, I checked my reflection in a makeup compact. My layered bob hadn't moved—but my makeup ... *Gah!*

The woman at the Estée Lauder counter had *promised* me that this foundation wouldn't run, even in the most humid conditions. That was then. This was now, and now, butterscotch soup trickled down my temples and neck, then dripped onto the neck of my silk tunic. *Melting, I'm melting, what a world, what a world.* It was three hundred degrees with 100 percent humidity in Puerto Peñasco—I'd been here all of twenty minutes and I was already breaking the first rule of competition: letting them see me sweat.

Couldn't save the blouse, but I dabbed at my face with a cosmetic sponge. Better. So much better.

The posh-looking white man didn't buy any Mexican pottery from the tiny brown vendor. Tchotchke-free, he crossed the lobby with his Louis Vuitton tote bag and matching suitcase *(no story needed—it's an LV)* and sat near the door. He looked rich, yes, but he also looked sick. His slate-gray sports coat *(He wore this jacket after he won America's Cup . . .)* looked like he'd borrowed it from a bigger man, and the eggplant-colored shirt *(His consumption is conspicuous, he'd have it no other way)* bunched at his shrinking waistline. That beautiful silver hair on his head . . . must've been a terribly expensive representation of his original head of hair. His yellow-tinged skin brought out the color of his eyes. Those eyes . . . they were the same violet hue as Elizabeth Taylor's, and they now burned into me as I stood before him.

"Hi," I said with my hand outstretched. "I'm Miriam Macy."

"Ah. Yes. Wallace Zavarnella." He gazed at my hand, then took a slow inventory: my face, silk slacks, the blouse stained with melted makeup, and my chunky necklace. "Dearest, did Dalí do your makeup? Because it's very . . . melting clocks. Just being honest." He finally took my outstretched hand with his fingers, barely pumped it before he dropped it. He sniffed, then lifted an eyebrow. "Do you smell eggs cooking? I smell eggs. That's not you, is it?"

Don't embarrass me on TV.

Anger flared in my gut and my grip tightened around my suitcase handle. So much for that cool jazz Valium high. So much for sharing a glass of wine with this man, and a kiss or two on a balcony overlooking the Sea of Cortez.

"I don't smell anything," I said, sweetly. "And yes, I know that my face is dripping—thank you for sharing that with all of North America. Anyway, I'm sailing to Mictlan Island, too."

"Wonderful. Glad you could make it." He took out an iPad from his tote, then glanced at his Patek Philippe titanium timepiece (Billy had a Patek Philippe and refused to call it a "watch"). He didn't move his tote from the only available seat.

"Have you seen the others?" I asked. "I hear there are seven of us going over right now."

Wallace grimaced and swatted at a fat horsefly buzzing near his hair. Old scars, pearly and faint, zigzagged across the life line and the meaty part of his right hand. "I've seen a few here and there, and between me and you and the flies? They look like they all belong on the short bus. But then, we'll be joining them, which means that we also belong . . ." He gasped, then chuckled.

The device on his lap chimed. "*There* she is, finally." He swiped at the iPad's screen. "Miriam, I need to finish with last-minute arrangements. Reaching the island will take a few hours—forty miles of ocean. There's no reliable Wi-Fi over there, so could you please excuse me? We'll have *hours* to get to know each other, to talk each other's heads off over old fashioneds and share stories of the good ol' days back when Times Square was nothing but sex shops and drug dens and whatnot. It'll be a blast. Promise. Thanks. You're a doll." And then, he crossed his legs and shifted away from me.

I had been dismissed.

Wow. Okay. So much for him being a part of my next act. So much for esprit de corps and camaraderie. Fortunately, after some skillful editing of this episode, Wallace Zavarnella would come off as The Bitch.

Chin high, I returned to my spot near the registration desk as heat and humidity, and the stink of old fish and dirty men, crushed me from all sides.

Over near *los baños,* a muscular, middle-aged white guy wearing vintage khaki cargo shorts and a vintage Red Sox baseball cap *(Dad tossed it high in '67 after the Sox won the pennant . . .)* rummaged through each of his big black bags. He was a cop or a fireman, I knew that for sure. Random Red Sox like him had ticketed me for speeding or jaywalking, and a whole posse of Red Sox had investigated me for . . . *that.*

Nope. Move forward. Positive thoughts. *I am the underdog.*

I took several deep breaths, then forced a smile.

That's when I spotted my *real* competition: a twenty-something-year-old brunette dressed in a blue stretch knit dress *(Billie Holiday smiled at you from the stage and asked, "Where did you get that dress?" . . .)* and a shades-of-blue scarf *(When you waved good-bye to him at the port that day, you didn't know that you'd never see him again).* She plopped down in the seat next to Wallace Zavarnella—he had moved his tote bag for *her.* She wore perfume—I could smell it way over here. Smelled like cherry Laffy Taffy mixed with Johnson's baby powder.

"I'm Desirée Scoggins," she said to Wallace in a super-sweet, twangy voice as sickening as her scent. "But you can call me Desi."

She'd only said her name, but I already hated her. The scarf around her neck, though, was gorgeous—it would go great with the yellow pantsuit now packed in my suitcase.

Desirée Scoggins glanced over at me and smiled. Pale skin. Lips too big for her face. Tiny eyes set close together. Almost double chin. Not pretty, not really. But America would root for Desirée Scoggins. They'd call her "America's Sweetheart" or "America's Darling," anything with "America" in it. And she was still smiling at me.

So I tossed a smile back, then mouthed, "Hi."

Ugh.

At the end of the day, I didn't come to make friends

and swear that I'd be buddies with these people after the show wrapped. Nor had I come to play the stereotypical Angry Black Woman. Because I wasn't angry. I was just over it. Even before reaching Mictlan Island and eating grubs as big as my head and standing on one foot atop a pole and competing in—and winning—other ridiculous challenges, I was already over it. Still, I'd smiled at Desirée Scoggins and had mouthed, "Hi," and thrown in a wave because I'd made a promise to my daughter.

Don't embarrass me on TV.

I wouldn't give America one reason to root against me. Nope. I came here to win.

FROM: Ashlee Macy
TO: Mimi Macy
SENT: 1:42 p.m., Friday, July 8
SUBJECT: <none>

Miriam, I know you're in Mexico right now, preparing for some bizarre challenge with fire ants or quicksand, but I needed to email you. I don't KNOW what you are up to BUT DON'T EVEN TRY IT!! Just STOP!! I've been SO patient with you and I GET IT. You and Bill were married for almost 20 years and you have a child together. Bravo. That's something special. No sarcasm.

But you FUCKED IT UP!!!

You did.

I am NOT sorry we happened. I'm just a symptom of what was wrong in the FIRST PLACE.

He can't have your brand of crazy in his life anymore.

And Morgan can't have your crazy in her life either. Police showing up at our house at all times of the day? NOT. COOL. What did you do to Prudence??? Again with THIS??!!

We almost lost Mo how many times last year??? I AM NOT blaming you for any of those times!!! You did what was right. Brooke was a bully. I remember girls crying after class because she'd made fun of their bodies, their clothes, their technique. But THAT IS THE WORLD OF BALLET. BULLIES AND BITCHES. We don't sit. We don't chat. We DANCE. Some girls can't handle that. I'm sorry Morgan wasn't better prepared for this reality. And please believe me. I NEVER told her to stop eating. I said she should WATCH what she ate. Big difference.

None of this is the point. The point is YOU.

Why are you doing this?? Morgan couldn't win every role. It's been a year now, but your jealousy and anger over Brooke taking the lead was immature and ridiculous. And really? I don't think it's even that. You're competing against her mom. *Phoebe.* You don't want *Phoebe* to win. And because of that, all hell's broken loose. I told Detective Hurley the truth, that you were *unhinged* last night. Because you were.

Miriam. Okay. I actually APPLAUD you, to be honest. Brutal, but Brooke was brutal. She was a CANCER. You exposed her and only light can clean out darkness. Ballet class is almost pleasant again. BUT YOU HAVE TO STOP THIS!!!

Coming over here last night was PATHETIC.

Billy's over you. Okay? You LOST. And yes, I'm aware that a cheating man cheats. Once he gets tired of my callused feet scratching him at night, once he gets tired of the way I stand, I'll grand allegro out of that house and OUT OF HIS LIFE.

Until then tho?

MOVE DA FUCK ON.

Ashlee

P.S. You can stop using MRS now. I know you're still claiming him. Again: MOVE. DA. FUCK. ON.

4

So big of Ashlee to tell me that she under-
stood me. So *self-aware* of her to recognize her tem-
porary status as Billy's wife, especially since Morgan
had so many pretty female teachers in her life. Like
Ms. James, the math teacher, and Ms. Howard, the
college counselor. Ms. Sparks had a boob job done
over Christmas break and Ms. Cotton had lost thirty
pounds doing months of extreme cleanses, and both
women were ready for some lovin'. And Ashlee telling
me to drop "Mrs."? This was the twenty-first century
in America—I could use whatever the hell prefix I
wanted to use.

So glad that there'd be no internet on Mictlan Island.

No Prudence. No calls or emails or text messages
from Billy. No cops. No questions. I could ignore that,
all of that, for three days. No Wi-Fi? Not my fault.

As the time to board neared, our small group—com-
prised of Desirée, Wallace, Red Sox, and me—moved
outside and closer to the gangway. The sun had traveled across the sky, and the smooth turquoise sea had
turned choppy with whitecaps. The frothy mess made
my gut frothier, even though I still stood on land.
Didn't help that those police officers with the laziest
Uzis in the world had taken an interest in our little
group, especially an interest in *me*. They kept staring at
me, then whispering to each other, staring, whispering.

Sometimes they looked at their wristwatches with concern on their faces. What had they planned?

"Can we get going now?" I asked Andreas, a little light-headed. "Some of us have been traveling all damned day."

"*Un momento, señora,*" the college kid said. "We are still needing a few more passengers."

Beads of sweat, these different from the beads of sweat that come from heat, prickled across my skin and beneath my arms. Another apprehensive look at those cops—they had gained two more, for a total of four. One of them now talked into his shoulder radio. *What was he saying?*

Andreas must have detected my anxiety, and said, "Don't fear, *señora*. Captain will get you there in plenty time. No worries."

We would be gliding over on *La Charon,* a 182-foot yacht, gleaming white, three stories high and with enough radio equipment in its communications tower to eavesdrop on water-cooler talk in the Kremlin.

"She has a cinema room, a swimming pool, private balconies, and a sun lounge," the college kid was telling Red Sox. "She also can accommodate up to seventeen people in seven cabins."

"Ooh," Desi cooed. "So we each get a room? Cuz there's gonna be seven of us, right?"

Great. Desi Scoggins could count.

Andreas shook his head. "Sorry. The rooms are locked since we are simply sailing you over to Mictlan. Don't worry, though. There's plenty of space to relax—the Italian builders made sure of that."

"And how big is this island?" Desi asked.

"Around ninety acres," Wallace said. "That's about . . . two miles around. Lots of vegetation, and it slopes up, up, up to about 328 feet—thirty stories or so high. That's where Artemis sits and looks over the rest of the island. Really, the view is just breathtaking. Clear waters, six white-sand beaches on one half, and rocky shores on the other."

"Great. Wonderful. Are there refreshments on board the boat?" I asked, already in need of every margarita being made around the world at that moment.

Red Sox rolled his eyes and shook his head. "She's about to board a bajillion-dollar yacht but asking for hot wings and beer. Really?" He chuckled. "That's my *homegirl.*"

I ignored him, then said to Andreas, "So. Refreshments?"

"There will be margaritas on board," the kid said, smiling, "as well as fresh fruit and sandwiches."

My stomach growled when I heard "sandwiches." "Sounds wonderful. *Gracias.*" I turned to Desi and whispered, "Watch: Red Sox is gonna be the first one attacking those hot wings and beer."

Desi didn't hear me—she was too busy gaping at the blond, red-faced man as he picked up one of his heavy black bags. His biceps flexed and popped beneath the sleeves of his basic black T-shirt. "Ain't seen nothing like *that* in a long time," Desi said, thumbing her blue scarf.

"You get his name yet?" I asked.

"Eddie Sweeney, and lemme tell you: it's hot as blue blazes out here and it ain't cuz of the sun."

"In L.A.," I said, "you can find muscle-bound men in every shade on the way to the mailbox. We're the main hub, the *Costco,* of muscle-bound men."

"Not where I'm from," Desi said. "West Virginia ain't got nothing like *him* around."

I knew nothing about West Virginia, or what they had a lot of besides coal mines and the Appalachian Mountains. Not that I'd spotted or flirted with any muscle-bound men in my new neighborhood. In my new neighborhood, scrap-metal-recycling businesses crammed beside ratty duplexes smashed against party supplies rackets hugging liquor stores wedged between apartment buildings and abandoned pet hospitals. There were late-night vendors cooking bacon-wrapped hot dogs on stainless steel carts. Spaced-out addicts stumbling on sidewalks or sleeping on bus benches.

Billy had remained in our two-story Spanish-style on Corning Avenue in Ladera Heights. Rich. Affluent. Powerful. A black Angeleno's utopia, with palm trees, clean gutters, and a grocery store that sold edible produce and didn't have to keep razors, baby formula, and cold medicines in locked acrylic cases.

I let Desi gape at Red Sox and turned my attention elsewhere. Like to the creature sitting in the shade of the building. She was a chubby, older white woman with wiry brown and gray hair and skin as beaten as ginger root. She unwrapped a stick of gum and stuck it in her mouth. Was she the nurse? Evelyn something?

In the parking lot, a black Ford Escalade roared to a stop. The driver's-side door opened, and reggaeton music and a fat Latino wearing an orange guayabera (*She thought you were kidding when you purchased this shirt...*) poured out from behind the steering wheel. He shouted, "Wait up!" then grabbed bags from the Escalade's trunk and ran over to the dock. With sweat pooling in the pockmarks of his face, he said something in fast Spanish to Andreas, then pointed back to the truck. To us, he said, "Let's get this party started *right*," then fished a silver flask from the shirt's pocket. It was a beautiful, elegant flask. A flask that Ernest Hemingway or Teddy Roosevelt would've taken on safari or to the front lines of the revolution. A flask fought over between the long-suffering wife and the ... *secret boyfriend. Yes!*

What had he filled it with? And could I get a taste?

With eyes shinier than the flask's silver finish, Orange Shirt shouted, *"Salud, mis amigos,"* then toasted himself and drank.

"Olé, my *amigo!"* Desi shouted.

"I got lost," Orange Shirt said as he wiped his mouth with the back of his hairy wrist. "The streets, man, they're freakin' twisty and go in circles and shit, and this cat, man, he told me about this li'l stand that sells roasted armadillo and peppered prawns, and it took forever, know what I'm saying, tryna find this place but I found it, took fuckin' forever, and lemme tell you, it was worth it."

"Oh, yeah?" I grinned—a cokehead had joined us.

Wallace sighed, then inched closer to the gangway.

"I'm *stoked,* man," Orange Shirt continued. "I've done some researchin' on Mictlan and they got all *kinds* of seafood over there." He laughed, then waggled his big head. "I'm Javier Cardoza, the executive chef. That's why I'm goin' on and on 'bout food, so don't think I'm some random weirdo, just excited, man. Oh, hey, I think there's one more of us!" He pointed over to the parking lot, and shouted, "Over here, *amigo!"*

A round dark-skinned black man had just climbed out of a chauffeured gold Bentley. He had sweat through his lemony linen shirt *(The revolutionaries saw you coming a mile away)* even though the luxury car probably boasted the best air conditioner in the country. He pushed up his wire-rimmed glasses, then waved at us.

"Who's *that?"* Desi asked, bored now with Eddie's muscles.

He was only too happy to tell us: Franklin D. Clayton. "Mea culpa for my tardiness," he said. "I've lost track of time. What day is it? Ha. Not to proffer excuses, but I've been in meetings—Texas, Arizona, Cali—since Wednesday. My secretary is having a root canal and my wife, Celeste, is in the South of France, so I'm the one currently managing my life. Forgive me now and in advance. Ha."

Had anybody asked him all that?

"So, are you a lawyer?" Desi asked.

"Goodness, no," Frank said, chuckling. "I'm a financial advisor in Dallas. One of the most successful, I must add."

Oh, brother, Brother.

As we strode up the gangway (finally!) to board *La Charon,* Frank continued to dazzle Desi with recaps of his meetings with Buffett's people and Greenspan's people and Soros's people. As we strode up the gangway, Eddie ignored us and fretted over his big black bags of nuclear weapons. The chef tottered beside Wallace as he described his dream to open another restaurant, of becoming a traveling chef like Anthony Bourdain, with television shows and books on the bestseller lists and trips to the White House. As we strode up the gangway, the quiet woman with the leathery skin chomped her gum and talked to no one, bringing up the rear with her quilted handbag and ancient turquoise suitcase.

A sick man. A country chick. A shaggy nurse. A cokehead cook. An uppity banker. And a mass shooter. My competition, ladies and gentlemen.

I found a quiet place at the polished guardrail and watched smaller boats pull in and out of the harbor. The Valium was wearing off, and now I thought about falling into the sea and never coming out again. I thought about the apartment I'd found online in Cartagena, Colombia, on the coast of the Caribbean Sea. I thought about Ashlee being gone and Billy being gone and Morgan stuck, no, *embracing* her time with me in her new home country. I thought about winning and revenge and the better life awaiting me after I'd won this competition. I thought of how I looked at that moment, on television, and how I would appear ... pensive, reflective, *deep*.

Back on land, the *policía* now sat in the shade. Rifles lay across their thighs like guitars. Boys dribbled worn soccer balls between stalls, but stopped to watch *La Charon*. A deckhand covered in dirt and oil pulled the plank away from the yacht and grinned at me. The *policía* sat up in their chairs. Even one of the dogs paused to stare at the boat, to stare at *me*. They were all staring at me.

Let's go. Let's go right now. Before—

The wood railing beneath my arms rumbled—*La Charon* had come to life.

The anchor clank-clank-clanked as it rose from the bottom of the harbor.

Slowly ... slowly ... the yacht inched away from the dock.

On the other side of the ship, Desi cheered. "Woo-hoo! We're goin' to Me-hi-co!"

We were *in* Mexico already, but I didn't want to spoil the nitwit's fun.

Sea lions still barked from algae-covered boulders. Seabirds swirled above us squawking their good-byes.

A picture-perfect *adiós*—to the old and to the non-sense.

Someone tapped my shoulder.

I startled. *Crap.* Game over. Handcuffs. Perp walk.

But it was the college kid, with a strawberry margarita in his hand. "For you, *señora*."

"*Gracias.*" Before I took my first sip, I glimpsed the shore.

Oh—!

My breath left me again, and I stumbled back a few steps from the railing.

A teenage girl with straight black hair and eyes so

light they looked transparent stood on the dock. She clutched a basket filled with mangos and avocados in one hand, and waved at us with the other. Her smile was bright against her pale skin, and the way she brushed her bangs away from her forehead reminded me of . . .

I tried to swallow, but my throat had closed. *It's her.* My mind wheeled around those two words. *It's her. It's her.* I tore my gaze away from the girl and forced myself to stare into my cocktail at the shards of ice that had escaped the blender's blades. *It's her.*

La Charon gained speed and almost immediately boxed against the shining waves.

I kept my eyes down as I gulped half of my margarita. My hands were shaking and my chest was tight, so tight, but then . . .

The tequila made the crooked places straight and the rough places smooth. Weak knees? Not anymore. Twisty stomach? Not anymore. It was all "not anymore." Just my imagination. Just the booze, the drugs . . . just the sea. *It's not her. It can't be her.*

You got this. You ain't scared of nothing, of nobody.

Filled with liquid courage and the last molecules of Valium, I found the nerve to look up and out again.

By then, the Mexican shoreline was gone. The *policía* were gone.

And so was the girl with the straight black hair.

Excerpted from the *Los Angeles Times*
Wednesday, February 11

NO CHARGES FOR TEEN IN
CYBER-BULLYING CASE

"Morgan had nothing to do with this," the teen's mother said. According to Miriam Macy, her daughter Morgan is the true victim in this story. "Brooke had been her best friend before she turned on her. And then Morgan's school turned on her. She's only seventeen and has to deal with all of this, and it's simply unfair. Just leave my daughter alone. Just stop, okay? Please?"

But the parents of Brooke McAllister are demanding justice. "They all need to go to jail," said Phoebe McAllister, Brooke's mother. "Someone has to take a stand against all the bullies in the world. There's no excuse, you know. People stood by and did nothing. Morgan is a sweet girl, but she's complicit in everything that happened. If that means she has to go to jail, then so be it."

Excerpted from the *Los Angeles Times*
Wednesday, February 11

NO CHARGES FOR TEEN IN
CYBER-BULLYING CASE

Morgan had nothing to do with the threat, insisted Annadale's mother, Mrs. her daughter Morgan and the boy's mother in the story. "Brand" had been her best friend before she turned on her. And they "Morgan" school turned on her. She's only fourteen and hasn't dealt with it. "I'm not a perfect parent, but I have tried my hardest. Just ask anybody. Please?" But the parent of Brooke DeAlmeyda, the man in question. "They all need to do it all," said mother. McAllister, Brooke's mother. "Someone has to take a stand against online bullies in the world. There's no excuse, you know. Once people stand behind and do nothing. My name's never out but I don't know. Sometimes it's something that happens. If that's what she has to go to jail, then so well.

PURGATORY

5

Neither the skinny college kid nor the older man had left the yacht's wheelhouse to assure us that we weren't gonna drown today. Since sailing from Puerto Peñasco and boarding *La Charon,* I hadn't stayed in one spot. I kept searching for a calmer place, a dryer place—a place that also remained in sight of any hidden cameras. I'd found a seat in the middle of the deck, the best view for me, the best view for the cameras. With sunglasses hiding my frightened eyes and with a drink in hand, I was ready for this scene. But I wasn't ready for this voyage over to the island. Not at all.

How were we supposed to endure two hours of dipping and swaying, lurching and rising? How was it that this yacht had cost the owner a bajillion dollars and yet the damned thing couldn't sail straight? Why weren't there other boats on the sea? Why was it so damned cold out here? And where were the airplanes? Had we fallen into the Bermuda Triangle via Mexico? Worse: Did we have a Jonah on board? Someone bringing us bad luck and putting us all in danger? That was the only explanation for this nautical pandemonium.

Not that anyone else had noticed the walls of water that were threatening to knock us all into the Sea of Cortez. Wallace had reclined in a deck chair. He snored lightly, having only made it a few pages in the *Esquire* magazine now forgotten on his chest.

"Ohmygosh, another one!" Desi shrieked, pointing

at a sailfish that had just leapt out of the sea. "This is wonderful. Just like SeaWorld. A sight for sore—ooh, lookit that one!"

Another sailfish, iridescent blue and a million feet long, had burst from the water and hung in the air— *one Mississippi, two Mississippi*—before splashing back into the sea. Each time one leapt, I gasped. Not out of awe, but more, *This will be the end of me, this fish's nose will break the ship and we will all die, and then I will lose the million dollars and embarrass Morgan on TV.*

Why couldn't *I* be wide-eyed and constantly thrilled like Desi? "Ohmygosh" dripping from my mouth every time the sky changed. For me—*the Jonah?*—life sucked right then. Sucked like being trapped in Disneyland's crowded parking lot on a hot summer day with only ten dollars in my pocket and a lost debit card.

Another sailfish launched into the air.

Maybe I should try it. "Oh, wow, look—" But my stomach dropped to my ankles, bile burned up my throat and my cheeks had numbed from the stinging cold.

As Javier searched the boat for a fishing pole and muttered about all he'd do to a sailfish in a skillet, I settled into a deck chair next to Frank and beside the Cracker Jack box–sized swimming pool. A little calmer here and still a good spot to be seen.

"This boat's gonna roll over," I said, cramping myself into a ball. "And the way it's slamming back and forth like this? Can't be normal. I should go talk to the captain."

Frank snorted. "This *yacht* was manufactured for the open ocean. It's not one of those putt-putt watercrafts forced to wander about the crowded harbor during Sunday gospel brunch. Don't blame the yacht, Miriam. The ocean has swelled up and down since the beginning of time, and more people have worked on engineering this watercraft than the two people who created you. You're not used to adventure on the high seas—that's obvious—but I'm certain you'll eventually get there. Welcome to better living. Enjoy the ride. Try not to vomit."

My lips went numb. "You know, there's a time to say, 'Yeah, it *is* a little rocky out here,' and then there's a time to shut entirely the hell up, and since you don't think we're gonna sink, guess which time this is."

Frank's smirk slid off his face and plopped onto the deck alongside my inner ear.

Time to move again, time for ping-ponging between all six of my sailing companions, not saying much out of fear of vomiting. I hadn't been the only person moving from place to place, playing adult-size musical chairs. Eddie had moved away from Desi to sit with Wallace. Wallace had moved to nap on a chaise lounge. Every seat Evelyn chose was too small for her body. Desi moved to sit with me, then Frank, then Wallace. Javier jumped here and there, asking us about food allergies, lobster or crab, quinoa or vermicelli, whiskey or rum, dark chocolate or butterscotch, sushi or tempura, smoke or vinegar.

Now, my hair lay like a mat against my skull, wet from the freezing mist of pounding waves. The yellow bra I wore glowed beneath my silk tunic, which was also saturated with salt water. Water sloshed in my suede flats, too, and the wet leather kept rubbing against my raw feet. I could feel the blisters coming. That's when I said to no one in particular, "I can't. . . ."

Not caring about my storyline for the moment, and done with it all, I lurched into the living room with its dry couch, warmer air, and blue-and-white-striped carpet. The soft recessed lighting almost persuaded me into believing that I was resting in a hotel suite in

Malibu, not thirty-eight million miles away from the Mexican shore.

A platter of untouched sandwiches sat on a low-slung coffee table. My stomach gurgled—the thought of ham or tuna salad or mozzarella with sundried tomatoes made me gag. *Do not throw up on TV.* I skipped the sandwiches.

On Mictlan Island, there'd be plenty to eat—Javier would make that happen. He'd liked my answers to his culinary questions: lobster, vermicelli, rum, butterscotch, tempura, and smoke. But was there anything he could do about the sea?

"Gimme a minute," he said, scribbling into his tiny notebook. "I'll make you a cocktail that'll make you forget you're in the middle of the ocean." Then he winked at me and said, "Oh, one more question—foam or sauce?"

Ugh. No foam. I was surrounded by it. Hated it now more than sushi and quinoa.

Maybe I should throw myself overboard and find peace that *way.*

The *yacht* dipped.

Arms flailing, I staggered to the couch, knocking the top slice of bread from a ham sandwich onto the table. The crystal chandelier above me tinkled—it was laughing at me.

This wasn't good.

La Charon was gonna crack in half. The way it shimmied and those vibrations beneath my feet? Not normal. Not for a boat. Not for a yacht. Ask the *Titanic*. Oh, you can't? See? Vibrations.

Out on the deck, Desi laughed. Then Javier laughed. Then Frank *cachinnated*.

I was the only one having a bad time. I was the only one hating the shrieking wind and the pounding waves. I hated this fiberglass-hardwood floating death trap. I hated the way my heart pounded and my nerves jumped each time the yacht groaned. It sounded as miserable as me. Nauseous, I glanced at the sandwiches again and gagged. I was gonna do it this time. I was going to upchuck all over the coffee table.

I kicked off my flats, then crept to the bathroom, touching walls, touching rails, touching every solid thing to keep me here. As I crept, the dark wood corridor pressed me from all sides. *Good.* The boat plunged to the right. I hugged the wall and closed my eyes as my belly dipped. I prayed quickly—*please don't let me die*—and staggered an inch closer to the bathroom. Then the boat rolled to the left. I hugged the opposite wall. Prayed. Waited. Staggered. Prayed some more. Waited some more. Staggered some more.

Back in the living room, Desi said, "It's so cozy in here." Her hair looked like a bird's nest, and her eye makeup had run from all of her gawking in the mist. "Oh, lookit! A chan-dee-lee-yer! On a boat. How queer! I just rhymed now, y'all."

I threw myself farther down the corridor, finally arriving at the bathroom. As I reached for the handle, the boat dipped to the right. I grabbed the wall again as the bathroom door slid open. Gold light from the lavatory poured out into the hallway.

Eddie's reflection appeared in the bathroom mirror. His Red Sox cap sat on the sink, and a red scar ran across his hairline. That scar looked raw. Still angry. Still sore. He was examining a silver gun in his hand. It was the biggest handgun I'd ever seen. Like Dirty Harry's .44. Something else—*was that the wooden butt of a revolver?*—was shoved into the waistband of his shorts.

My heart shuddered.

Guns? Why did he have—?

The boat rolled left.

Bam! The bathroom door slid again and slammed shut.

Didn't matter.

Guns! He had guns. Why did he have—?

Forgetting my seasickness, I staggered back to the living room and leaned on the bar for support. Fear of drowning had taken a backseat to fear of dying by gunshot.

Wallace had awakened from his nap and now reclined in an armchair. Desi perched close to Frank on the love seat. "That Bentley you came in," she cooed, tapping his wrist. "Was that yours?"

Frank covered her hand with his. "No, babe. Car service—had to arrive in style. But I *am* the proud owner of a Maserati, a Ferrari, and of course, a Ducati. Not that I drive much—I prefer car service for any business. And my wife, Celeste, hates my bike—but lately, she doesn't understand me. Anyhow, there are more important things to think about than filling a gas tank and not making right turns on red."

Wallace noticed me clutching the bar. "My, my, Miriam. Someone else has now done your makeup. Let me guess: Elphaba? The Grinch? Uncle O'Grimacey?"

Frank laughed.

"Everything okay, girlie?" Desi asked. "You *do* look a little green."

I teetered over to the couches, and with a shaky hand, pointed back toward the hallway. "I just saw Eddie right now," I whispered. "I saw him in the bathroom, and he has two—"

"What's she whispering about? What's the big secret?"

We all turned to the voice—Eddie was now standing in the doorway. His hands were empty, and his black T-shirt had been pulled over the waistband of his cargo shorts.

"I believe we may have a troublemaker in our little group." Wallace's violet eyes shone like the sharpest knives.

Eddie crossed his massive arms. "Yeah? Who would that be?"

Wallace smiled at me. "That would be . . . *her*."

My blood chilled, and it took me a second to realize that he had just called *me* the troublemaker. "*What?*"

"Oh, don't choke yourself clutching your pearls, dear," Wallace said. "You and I both know that crying wolf is something you do, isn't that right? To be completely honest, I could *never* believe a single word that tripped off that forked tongue of yours."

Everyone was now staring at me as though I was the biggest, blackest spider on the whitest wall in the world.

Javier cleared his throat, then said, "Did I just miss something?"

"Drama," Eddie said.

Take control. Now. A boulder lodged in my throat and I swallowed and swallowed to force it up or to force it down. But it wouldn't move.

Wallace smiled at the others. "Helpful FYI. A little bird told me that *Mrs*. Macy cannot be trusted."

"Geez," Desi spat. "Can you give her a chance to speak? You ain't even let her complete a single sentence." Dismayed, she shook her head and sucked her teeth. "My gosh, Mr. Zavarnella. Wanna talk about trust? I don't even *know* you, and what I *do* know, I'm not liking one bit. I don't care *who* you are, but you're not the boss of this group, sir, and this ain't a good start to what's supposed to be a trip of a lifetime."

Wallace held up his hands. "No need to shout, dear heart. I'm gay, not deaf. *Today.* Tomorrow, that may all change and I'll wake up gay *and* deaf, who knows. Never thought I'd be *old* and gay, but alas, the universe has her own plans. So. I do apologize for interrupting. I didn't mean to be . . . *mean*. Just a hobby of mine. More of a bad habit, like, say . . . *lying*." He offered me a sly smile, then nodded. "Lying is an *awful* habit. You were saying, Miriam?"

"Go on, girlie," Desi said. "Tell us what you were gonna say."

I took a deep breath—that boulder had plummeted to my knees—then squared my shoulders. "Just a minute ago, I saw Eddie in the bathroom, and he was loading two giant handguns. And he was muttering something, but I couldn't make out what he . . . was . . . saying."

No one spoke. No one reacted. Wallace stared at me as the others stared at Eddie.

"Are you certain that's what you witnessed?" Frank finally asked.

"It was not a glimpse, nor was it in my imagination." Although the "muttering" part may have been . . . *flair*. "The guns were as real as . . . as . . . this boat—*yacht*—we're on right now."

"Dude," Javier said, eyes on Eddie, "why you got guns?"

"I have no idea what she's talking about." Eddie's arms were still crossed.

"They're hidden in his shorts," I said, pointing at his hips.

"Where? *Here?*" Eddie lifted his T-shirt to show a washboard-tight stomach but no guns.

Desi giggled, patted her neck, and said, "Goodness gracious."

My face flushed, and bile was now helping lift that boulder back up to my throat.

"Oh, dear." Wallace chuckled, then sighed. "There's a wolf, *where?*"

Eddie squinted at me. "Guess *I'm* the wolf. A wolf with two guns."

Frank rolled his eyes, and Desi gave me an apologetic smile before they both turned away from me. Even Evelyn, now seated near the door, found her raggedy cuticles more interesting.

So *this* was how Wallace Zavarnella planned to win.

Not the first time I'd been accused of crying wolf. Last month, I had thought someone was snooping around my backyard. The cops came and found no one there except a family of possums. There was also the time someone kept calling me and hanging up. Calling and hanging up, over and over again. I freaked out and texted Billy, who then got the phone company and the police involved. After a brief investigation, they discovered that those hangups had been robocalls that had taken a few seconds to start.

Was I a little sensitive? Prone to exaggeration and jumping at shadows a little too often? Probably. But none of those things had equated to "crying wolf." Because Brooke McAllister's sister Prudence *had* threatened me. And a few months ago, she *had* grabbed me that first time, maybe not hurting my left arm as bad as I'd claimed she had, but she *had* grabbed me. Well . . . she'd *pushed* me. Okay, bumped against me. Hard. Hard enough that I couldn't lift my arm for a while, not really, thus legitimizing my disability claim. Basically. And that disability money—it wasn't like I hadn't *worked* for it, it wasn't like I hadn't put into the system. It was *my* money.

But now, here I was, being mocked by people who'd only met me hours before, who didn't believe that I'd seen what I'd seen. Eddie had brought two guns on board. *He had!* The hidden cameras in the bathroom would ultimately prove me right.

"Baby, you need *this*." Javier handed me a glass tumbler filled with salmon-colored liquid. "Scotch, orange juice, club soda, and pomegranate-cherry juice. Blood and sand." He squeezed, then patted my shoulder. "Seriously—it'll help you chill the hell out."

The cocktail was a one-two icy-hot punch to my gut. "Chilling the hell out" in progress.

Evelyn darted over to the windows. "Look—there's the island! And there's the house." Her voice—the first time I'd heard it—was deep and bleating.

Enhanced now by the blood and sand, I floated over to the windows, squeezed into the middle of the group, and caught my first glimpse of Mictlan Island. A grand white house sat high on a hill, overlooking a canopy of thick elephant ear trees and wild grass. Tall palms dotted the shore to the island's south, and white water swirled around large craggy rocks to the north.

My ears buzzed, and I tried to smile—but Wallace Zavarnella ... Thinking about him kept my smile lumpy and lopsided. What did he know about me? What secret had he been sworn to keep and how had he learned it? Who was the secret-spilling little bird and why had this stranger called me a liar? Now, Americans would go onto the internet and search on my name. My past would be discussed in recaps and forums and during reunion shows. All of it would be thrown in my face. Yes—my life had been subject to public discussion, but only in Los Angeles County. This show was *nationwide,* and ...

Maybe you should've thought about that before agreeing to play the game.

Money, though—or the promise of it—was a helluva drug.

Still, I had to *do* something. I needed Wallace Zavarnella kicked off the island.

Bastard. He'd pay for embarrassing me in front of this group—and in front of all America.

And as I drained my cocktail and joined the others out at the rail, I tossed Wallace Zavarnella a look that wiped the smile off his smug, jaundiced face.

I will get you back, old man.

I had my ways.

6

For the moment, though, all plans of revenge against Wallace Zavarnella had to be stowed. The Sea of Cortez had turned golden, and I shaded my eyes to see . . . nothing. The sunlight had blinded me, and as we neared the rickety dock, the big white house disappeared behind a shimmering tree line.

"Ohmygosh, that's Artemis?" Desi asked with a wistful smile. "It's just about the most beautiful house I've ever seen."

Back in Los Angeles, I used to live in a beautiful home. But now I lived in a crappy house in the middle of crappy L.A., with police helicopters always thundering above my head. There were more weeds than grassy lawn, a puke-green paint-chipped porch, and sagging shutters. This house was not the house I'd dreamed of. This house was all cautionary tales and children beware . . . and I had become the wicked witch who ate them.

And now, the voice in my head whispered, *Watch out.* Something about Artemis, something about Mictlan Island made me breathless—and not in a thrilling way. So many trees were packed tight together. All that water sloshing, forever green, forever choppy. There were so many places to hide and to be hid, and I remembered Andreas's talk of drug dealers and man-eating dogs and opium poppies and fields of weed.

"It's so *far* from everything," Desi said to me.

So far from the police (a good thing), the fire department (a bad thing), from . . . America (good, bad, depended on the moment).

"Being far makes it an island," I said, my bravado as strong as foam.

Desi swiped at her chapped nose, red now as though she'd been crying. She rubbed her elbows and shook her head. "If something bad happens, it'll take forever for the cops or the paramedics to reach us."

"I'm sure they have helicopters, and like, high-speed catamaran-things."

"True," she said, brightening. "Hey—" She tapped my wrist. "Wallace Zavarnella is a jerk, okay? A jerk wearing a bad wig. Stuck-up little prick."

"Back at the port," I said, "he wouldn't even move his bags to let me sit down."

"*I* sat with him, and lemme tell you . . ." She wrinkled her nose. "The man is as old as the hills. He smells like my momma's medicine cabinet, if you really wanna know. Just don't let him spoil your adventure, Miriam. Next time, when he's all bitchy like that, tell him to stick it where the sun don't shine."

"Believe me, I'm trying very hard to be nice. Next time, I will let my true self run up one side of him and down the other." I blinked to try and glimpse Artemis again, but I still couldn't see it. Guess I could blame my blindness on Javier and his delicious red *drank*.

The closer we came to shore, the more the boat rocked . . . just like the putt-putt Sunday gospel brunch tugboats tooting around the harbor. I gripped the rail tighter. *Don't react. Be strong. Control your story.* My grip remained firm.

Desi's gaze turned from the sea and landed on Eddie, who now stood ramrod straight at the stern. She grinned as she fingered her blue scarf. "You see that guy's abs when you made him lift up his shirt? Hot *damn*. So he's a little grumpy—ain't seen him smile once today, but he's big, blond, and a *man*, make no mistake about it."

"You forgot crazy, Desi," I said. "Big, blond, and crazy."

"I ain't had crazy yet," she said, grinning. "I've done 'young,' and I just finished doing 'old'—Larry, my husband, rest his soul. He was ancient—almost sixty—and he was soft and he was a penny-pincher and he couldn't keep up with me in bed or anywhere else." She nodded at Eddie. "But Mr. Boston Strong? He'll do for a spell." She winked at me and wiggled her nose. "You'll be my wingman, won't you?"

Well, I'll be . . . America's Sweetheart was a horn-dog.

I cocked an eyebrow. "And those two guns I saw— those guns don't bother you?" Really: Where had he hidden the guns? In his back pockets? In ankle holsters beneath his socks?

Desi flicked her hand. "That's just part of the adventure, girlie. Maybe he's a Navy SEAL. Ooh—or with the CIA. Or the DEA. Something dangerous and secretive and sexy, know what I mean? This is so freakin' exciting—I ain't ever been out of the States before. Okay, no, I took a Disney cruise to the Bahamas for my honeymoon, but everybody there spoke English and it was clean and reminded me of Epcot Center in a way. You know, not a real place?"

"But Me-hi-co?" Her eyelashes fluttered as she lifted her face to the sky. "What a beautiful language. Pretty little native girls selling Me-hi-can pears and whatnot. Blue sky . . . Okay, yeah, we got big blue sky, too, but that's about all we have in WVA. I've never seen a kind of sky like this. The sky here is the color of a robin's egg, you know? Even Me-hi-can Coca-Cola tastes different.

"Back at the airport? I tried something new? Called

sir-vee-chay? Kinda like tuna salad but without the mayo and the fish is raw and there's lime and tomatoes and some other stuff? It was the most delicious—oof."

The yacht bumped against the dock and the anchor clank-clank-clanked until it splashed into the sea. No other boats were anchored at the barnacle-crusted pilings.

Desi shimmied, then elbowed me in the gut. "You ready for this, girlie?" Before I could answer, she clutched my arm and brought me close to her. "That other woman," she whispered. "You talk to her yet? She looks kinda dumb, don't she? Reminds me of my momma's dog, Princess? Kinda shaggy and smells like blinked milk? Not a good look for a lady. Not. At. All."

Well, I'll be again . . . America's Sweetheart was also a Mean Girl.

Evelyn sat at the back of the boat. Working that gum so hard that her jaw clicked and popped. She must have sensed my gaze, because she smoothed her wrinkled linen skirt *(Item Not Available Since 1979)* against her slabs of thighs. Then she nervously twisted the gorgeous turquoise ring *(This is the most beautiful thing that you will ever own . . .)* on her finger.

"I want that ring," I told Desi.

Desi snickered. "I'm sure she'll give it to you if you look at her wrong. Maybe we can stay up all night tonight and give her a makeover. What's that saying? She got the perfect face for radio?"

Someone tapped a wineglass. Desi and I stopped talking and noticed that Wallace was now standing in the middle of the living room.

"First," he said, "I hope everyone's having a wonderful time here on *La Charon*."

"Two words," Desi said. "Holy. Cow."

Some of us chuckled. Wallace simply gave her a patient, pleasant smile. "You are a doll, Desirée." He cleared his throat, then met each of our gazes. Then: "A magnificent joke has been played on you." To Desi, he said, "Your friend Alex did not invite you to stay on Mictlan Island." To Frank: "There is no business summit this weekend." To me: "This isn't a reality show competition and there is no million-dollar prize. All of what you've heard has been a lie."

"Excuse me?" I whispered.

"I'm so confused," Desi said.

"You fuckin' kidding me right now?" Eddie said.

"I'm . . . huh?" Frank chuckled. "What do you mean?"

Javier laughed, and said, "Am I still getting paid?"

And then we started shouting exclamations on top of each other, "what" and "huh" and "fuckin' kidding me," over and over again, until Wallace raised those scarred hands of his and shouted over the din. "Let me explain."

Javier whistled, then clapped his hands. "Shut up for a minute. Let him talk, jeez."

I crossed my arms and forced myself to breathe through my nose. "Okay. Talk. Please."

Wallace sighed, then met my gaze, then Frank's, Desi's, and finally Eddie's. "Someone we all cared about . . ." His voice broke and he cleared his throat again. "Someone we all cared about wanted to play one last practical joke and trick you into coming to something meaningful, something . . ."

"Who is 'he'?" Eddie demanded. "*Who* wanted to play one last joke?"

"Phillip," Wallace said. "Dear, dear Phillip."

I frowned at him. "Phillip . . . ?"

"Omeke."

My breath left my lungs. "My *lawyer*? The Phillip Omeke who hasn't returned my phone calls in six weeks?"

Wallace canted his head. "Yes, Miriam. Please understand. See: Phillip didn't want the entire world to know that he had a brain tumor. Glioblastoma. The cancer kept growing and growing until finally . . . Phillip died last month, and I'm *here* on this island to carry out his last wish: to sprinkle his ashes off the coast. This, my fellow travelers, is Phillip's memorial service. He wanted his friends and a few of his most unforgettable clients to gather at Artemis for a few days to remember him."

"Oh, no. Oh, no, no, no." I closed my eyes and covered my ears. "I wanna go home."

"Turn the boat around," Frank demanded. "Immediately."

"Phillip's *dead*?" Desi asked, bugged eyes fixed on the carpet.

"We all lead such busy lives," Wallace continued. "We all have so many things to do, and Phillip wanted to make sure . . . that you all attended the service. And he knew you all so well, he knew what would get you to come."

I shook my head. "I can't afford missing . . ." *Days off?* I had no job. *Seeing my daughter?* Yeah, she hated me right now and was on her way to Orlando. "If I'm gonna be honest, I was counting on . . ."

"The cash prize?" Wallace asked.

I blushed, then nodded.

"A time to get away?" Wallace asked Desi.

She blushed, then nodded.

"Landing new clients?" Wallace asked Frank.

"Of course," the banker said, lifting his chin.

Wallace offered each of us a weak smile. "Phillip knew that, too. He knew that you were in dire straits after your cases, Desi, Frank, and Miriam. That you needed work, Javier, Eddie, and Evelyn. He told me about each of your situations."

"Oh, no. Oh, Phillip." Sadness washed over me, and my knees, as weak as wet tissue paper, gave, and I plopped into a chair.

What would I do without him? What was gonna happen to me?

Desi squeezed my shoulder, and I placed my hand atop hers. "This is absolutely unbelievable," she whispered.

Wallace continued. "I've been directed to read his will at the end of his scattering ceremony, on Sunday afternoon. I can't be 100 percent certain, but each of you may be wealthier leaving Mictlan Island than when you came. So . . . any questions?"

"Phillip left me . . . ?" My mouth moved but no words came. I had no words. *Me. Speechless.*

"Money?" Frank said. "He left me *money?*"

Tears burned in my eyes—for many reasons. Because my hopes for winning millions had just been dashed. Because someone who'd become my savior had died. Because Phillip had considered me a friend and had possibly set aside money to help me after he'd passed.

"This is freakin' crazy," Eddie said, shaking his head.

"Wanna turn the boat around now?" Wallace asked Frank, his eyebrow high.

"No, no, no." Frank smiled, then clapped Wallace on the shoulder. "Phillip was a good man. A *great* man."

"What about our cases?" I asked.

Wallace held up a finger. "Phillip told me that he personally developed a plan for each of you. But we'll deal with all of that after this weekend. He said for me to tell you not to worry. All of your problems will be solved." Wallace waggled a finger at our group. "So let's do as the great man said and *not* worry—we don't want him haunting us, now, do we?"

A teardrop tumbled down my cheek. Poor Phillip. So smart, so crafty, so elegant in his custom Italian suits. He had been tall and slender, and his dark face reminded me of those African wood masks you'd see at an arts and crafts fair. He'd been persuasive, too, especially with his posh Oxford University accent. A remarkable attorney. A remarkable man.

And I'd cursed his name once he had stopped returning my calls. Little did I know . . . he had stopped calling me because he was *dying*. Why hadn't he told me so? And why had he tricked me into coming to Mictlan Island? If he'd asked, *of course* I would've come.

But he *did* have a great sense of humor. He had always been a joker, cracking on jurors, sometimes even the judge, and we'd laugh a lot, Phillip and I. We'd flirt some, too. He'd touch my elbow sometimes. Hold my gaze longer than usual. We'd make each other laugh. More of a man than Billy could ever be.

Desi rubbed my back as she said, "I'm honored just to be with y'all. Phillip was the best thing to come into my life."

"Mine, too," I said. "He cared about me when even my own family . . ." A sob choked me back into silence, and I clamped my hand over my mouth.

Frank and Eddie didn't speak.

Javier said, "I'm gonna make his favorite dishes, then. In his honor."

Wallace grinned, then said, "We'll have a gay old time." He paused, then added, "Well, at least, *I* will." He laughed, so we all laughed.

"All ashore to Mictlan Island," the college kid called from the communications tower.

"Maybe I'll stay in Me-hi-co after this," Desi said as we all separated to fetch our bags. "Start a new life. New friends, new food, new lovers." She futzed with her messy hair. "This is definitely gonna be a trip to remember. I've been waiting for this my whole entire life, and I'm glad Phillip is giving me a chance to spread my little wings and fly."

I, too, had waited for something magical to happen in my life. I thought it had been meeting Billy, then marrying Billy. I thought it had been giving birth to Morgan, but then . . . no. When would it happen, that something magical? On this island, maybe? Maybe.

"Woo-hoo!" Desi cheered. "We made it." Eyes wild, she shook me out of my wondering. "C'mon, girlie! The island's waitin' for us!"

I was the first person to rush off the boat onto the dilapidated gangway. For the ride back to the mainland, I'd have to pop three Valium chased with two blood and sands.

The heavy warm air quickly dried my silk tunic. The sun beat down on my face—magnificent heat melted the ice that had frozen every inch of my skin over the two-hour voyage.

Andreas and Raul carried our luggage off the boat and deposited it near a dockside boathouse that looked two tropical storms away from collapse. Not much here—just that toolshed-sized boathouse, no boats, not even a canoe, and the start of a jungle trail.

"Excuse me," I asked Andreas. "Where are the bellhops or the house staff?"

"I know we're not expected to lug our own bags to the house," Frank sniffed. "We're guests here. Wallace?"

Wallace's mouth opened, then closed. "Maybe there's a butler. I'm not sure. Phillip didn't say if he hired staff for the weekend. Let's call."

Eddie plucked a satellite phone from one of his bomb bags. "What's the number?"

Wallace shrugged. "Oops. No idea."

Raul didn't care—he moved from boat to shore with his eyes cast down, with his mouth in a tight line.

The kid said, "This is all we are to do."

"You're bringing more of my guests over tomorrow,

correct?" Wallace asked, "and then, retrieving us Sunday after the ceremony?"

Raul said, "If it's on my paper, then *sí*, I will do."

Once Raul had marched back onto *La Charon* for good, Andreas hopped onto the yacht and pulled up the boarding stairs. He waved at us and shouted, *"Buenos suerte, mis amigos!"*

And the seven of us stood on the dock as *La Charon* sped back to the open sea. Soon, it was just a swanky white dot on the graying horizon.

Eddie sighed. "Screw this. I'm not waiting here forever." He picked up his three black bags and one of Wallace's, and marched to the dirt trail that cut through the jungle.

"I guess that's that." Desi grabbed her bags and followed Eddie into the thick brush.

So did Wallace, Frank, and Evelyn.

I grabbed the handle to my suitcase and shouldered my bag. *You can do this.* Yes, I could, and I smiled up at the sun as it glided across the cloudless sky. As I started to follow the group, I looked behind me.

Javier stood on craggy rocks, looking down into a tide pool. "Hey, Miriam. Come look at this."

"We should go."

"Yeah, yeah, come look."

I groaned, then hurried over to the chef.

Swimming in the tide pool were fuchsia fish and yellow fish and sea urchins the colors of eggplant and rhubarb, tiny crabs and quick shrimp. So peaceful in that pool even as the ocean crashed around it.

"It's beautiful," I said—and it was. "But we should head to the house. We don't wanna get separated and lost." I glanced up at the sun. "It's gonna get dark soon."

"Yep." Javier leaned over the tide pool and tottered some. "Whoops!" He waved his arms for balance, then wedged his flip-flopped feet into the rocks' nooks. His silver flask fell out of his shorts pocket and landed in the sand.

"You're gonna fall, Javier," I warned.

"Nope. I got this."

I grabbed his flask from the sand, then stowed it in my bag. "C'mon. Let's go."

"Okay," he said, not moving.

The sun dropped lower in the sky.

My pulse spiked a bit and my eyes scanned the edges of the thick forest. Thick forest that hid monsters. *What kind of wildlife live on Mictlan Island? Cougars? Boar?*

I couldn't get eaten during my first ten minutes on this effin' island. But I didn't want to leave Javier and travel the jungle alone, either.

The cocktails and the Valium weren't working anymore. Worry had returned, and what now felt like an ice cream headache pounded in the center of my skull. "Javier," I snapped. "What the hell are you getting? What is so freakin' important?"

Javier teetered again, then smiled back at me. "Appetizers."

7

Javier promised (or threatened) the sea life in the tide pool that he would be back tomorrow—and that he wouldn't be leaving empty-handed. Then he and I hurried along the trail to catch up with the others. Not that anyone seemed to notice our absence or arrival.

Besides our huffing breath and the scuffing of our feet against the dirt trail, there was no sound in the jungle. It was as though we were the only human beings that existed on Mictlan Island. Desi had attempted to narrate everything she saw—*ohmygosh lookit that bird, ohmygosh lookit that flower*—but the exertion of talking while walking with luggage uphill, then downhill, then uphill again, and Eddie's refusal to answer her queries slammed her mouth shut.

Frank tired of the quiet. "Why are we traipsing through the wilderness? Where's our host? Wallace, where's the damned house?"

No one responded to his futile queries. Talking required superfluous breath. Which Frank acknowledged when he said, "I know no one wants to respond to my futile queries since talking requires superfluous breath."

I visualized the final edit as though this was a scene from the competition—time-lapsed close-up shots of Desi's mouth and Frank's mouth, moving . . . moving . . . moving . . .

My own throat was raspy—the blood and sand

cocktail should have killed any cold germs that had tried to swarm my immune system. But now I worried about Zika and malaria as mosquitoes hungrily bit at my bare arms and through my tunic. Maybe "airy" hadn't been the best choice in attire. Something "steeled" or even "seasoned" would've worked better. Too late. Every piece of clothing in my suitcase was "casually seductive," "breezy," or "delicious."

And we walked.

The sun's threat had been tempered by the canopy of island live oaks, their broad limbs curving down before shooting up to the sky. Back in Puerto Peñasco, it had been eighty-five degrees, but now, with the humidity, it felt like 130. The heat wasn't the worst of it. The dirt path we clomped on never widened, and so branches snapped and scraped against our faces. And finally, there *was* sound—something was rustling deep in the brush, walking along with us, keeping pace, but never presenting itself.

Fortunately, whatever it was left us alone.

Damn it all. I'd spent a month preparing for a reality game show. Walking ten thousand steps a day. Jogging. Eating spinach and egg whites. I'd purchased outfits on credit, had hyped up my trip to Morgan so that she'd talk to me more. I'd even bought a pack of chocolate ants to prepare my mind for insect-eating challenges. And just like that, it was over. *It's all a prank. None of this is real. Oh, by the way, your lawyer's dead and you'll also need to carry your own shit to the house.* My chest was tight, not because I couldn't inhale. I couldn't inhale because I'd been hoodwinked and because I could picture Morgan rolling her eyes and calling me lame or worse . . . a liar. Again.

I gritted my teeth and dragged my bag and my body over roots and vines. And I thought about Wallace Zavarnella. Memorial service or not, he had trashed my reputation. He had partnered with Eddie to ridicule me in front of the others.

How best to retaliate? *Snatch his wig.* But only after we'd all given our tributes to Phillip Omeke, only after he'd spelled my name correctly on the check Phillip had left for me. And *then* I'd snatch his wig. I was many things, but I wasn't stupid.

How would that play in front of the others, though? Would that make me the Mean Bitch picking on the Sick Old Man even though that Sick Old Man had come for me first? Had kept me from sitting in that seat back on the mainland?

Doesn't matter anymore, Miriam. There are no alliances, there is no strategy. Let. It. Go.

Couldn't let it go, though. Because this *always* happened to me—penalized, judged, and castigated for reacting to someone hurting and insulting me.

Just thinking about battling people's perceptions of me was exhausting, and a part of me, a *small* part, just wanted to surrender already. Surrender and plop down on the trail and let the boar and cougars come and tear me apart. It wouldn't be that much different from all that I'd endured since that *thing* with Brooke McAllister.

The seventeen-year-old had dug into her bullying campaign against my kid. And I'd said, "No, you will not badmouth my daughter, I don't care how old you are. No, you will not get to call Morgan a nigger, I don't care who your granddaddy is and who he marched with back in '63. Yes, I will call you on your shit, think I won't?" But for some, standing up on behalf of Morgan meant bullying.

But that was then.

This was now, and now, twenty minutes had passed, and we still hadn't reached Artemis. Sometimes we stopped in our step to watch a lime-green butterfly flutter around our heads. Sometimes a shaft of sunlight cut through the timber, reminding us that it was still daytime. We'd lift our sweaty faces to the sky. We'd smile, then sigh, then press on through the brush.

"We'll get there," Desi would say each time. "And it's gonna be incredible when we do."

I tried on her enthusiasm and positivity for a minute or two.

Morgan will be so proud of me.

I need this exercise, good for my heart.

Phillip left me at least a hundred thousand dollars in his will.

But then another mosquito bit my neck. Another blister popped up on my foot. And we trekked deeper and deeper into the bush, into thick, oppressive heat, into darker jungle with roots that tripped us and threatened to shatter our ankles and elbows.

How and why in the hell had Phillip chosen *this* place?

Then we broke through a glade of saplings, and we all gasped. There she was: Artemis. The house had come out of nowhere—God felt sorry for us, so He'd just . . . dropped it there. *Here you go. Satisfied?*

The two-story contemporary Mediterranean glowed in the coming dusk. It had a ceramic tile roof, a centered wrought-iron balcony, and at least four chimneys. It had windows of every size and shape: pictures, bays, and a tall arched window two stories high. About fifteen steps led from the tangled jungle up a wide porch and the glass and iron front door. There were no esplanades. No ornamental gardens or porte cocheres. Just a perfectly plastered white house. Beautiful.

Wanting to cry out of relief, I blurted, "It's like the Embassy Suites."

Desi, wide eyed, said, "It's just like Disneyland."

Frank's pink tongue licked his lips. "Phenomenal. I want one just like it."

Javier whistled, then asked, "How much you think it cost?"

"Twenty million," Frank estimated.

Wallace snorted. "Ridiculous. On a tiny Mexican island with nothing on it except trees and butterflies? Phillip had money, but not twenty million. The land cost four million, and then he spent another million to build."

"This is *Phillip's* house?" I asked.

Wallace smiled. "Surprise."

"I've dreamed of living in castles like this," Desi said. "And now, lookit. Just *lookit*. I've never been happier in my life than right now." She smiled up at the sky. "Thank you, Phillip."

I was first to climb the steps.

A seventy-inch monitor on a stand had been placed on the porch. Animated versions of the bright green butterflies that had traveled with us flitted on the screen around yellow letters.

TOUCH TO BEGIN

"Who's gonna mash the button?" Desi asked.

I reached out to touch the screen, but Eddie tapped the monitor first. I glared at him, but the activity on the television quickly distracted me.

The digital butterflies flitted away just as they had in the forest. And now we were treated to an aerial shot of Mictlan Island—greenery and bluffs, and a big white house in the middle of it all. A pleasant female voice, an older contralto ex-smoker, drifted from the monitor speakers.

Welcome to Mictlan Island. We are pleased that you've joined us.

Wallace said, "That's one of Phillip's clients, a voice actress. She's coming over on *La Charon* tomorrow.

She sounds just like my aunt Doris, owner of a thousand caftans, lover of Virginia Slims and cans of Tab soda mixed with gin."

Music boomed from the speakers. The score was grand and Wagner-ish, like "Ride of the Valkyries" or the "William Tell Overture." The shot dropped down to the ground, sped through the front door, up a staircase and down a bright hallway, then stopped at closed double doors.

Each of you has been assigned a room.

The double doors opened, and the orchestra played on.

Mr. Wallace Zavarnella, you will occupy the lavender suite on the second floor.

It was a bright room with purple bed linens, and a wall-in television above a wall-in fireplace.

"Two words," Desi said. "Gor. Jus."

Ms. Miriam Macy, we have prepared the green room for you.

Arias and strings now. Light green walls and matching sheer curtains. Floor-to-ceiling windows. Lots of light.

Mr. Javier Cardoza, as the island's executive chef, you will command a kitchen that has been designed to make your cooking a pleasurable experience.

The fancy kitchen had dark brown cabinets and stainless-steel appliances. The walls were painted cantaloupe and cinnamon, and the floors were light and dark hardwood. A breakfast bar glowed beneath four overhanging lights.

Eddie would sleep in the red room on the second floor, which was next to Frank's yellow room. Evelyn's room was light blue and on the first floor with Desi and me, who'd been assigned the navy-blue room.

The nerves beneath my eyes twitched. I frowned,

then murmured to Desi, "Okay, so why do the men get to stay on the second floor?"

Desi waggled her eyebrows. "Being on the first floor just means we're closer to that gorgeous kitchen."

Tomorrow, at quarter to seven, the voice continued, *please join us on the terrace for a cocktail reception in memory of Phillip Omeke. Dinner, prepared by Chef Cardoza, will be served afterward. For tonight, though, please rest and make yourselves comfortable. At twelve thousand square feet, you have luxury, privacy, and a beautiful view overlooking the turquoise-jeweled waters of the Sea of Cortez. Amenities include a hot tub, spa, media room, sauna, swimming pool, and tennis court. Indulge. Relax. Remember. Thank you again for coming to Mictlan Island.*

The lime-green butterflies bobbed back onto the screen. They flapped their wings twice and the monitor faded to black.

Javier shouted, "Thanks, Aunt Doris."

Desi said, "She sounds just lovely."

"There was no mention of house staff," Frank pointed out.

"Yeah," Desi said. "Who do we call if we run out of toilet paper?"

"Or vodka?" Javier said, then laughed.

"What if there's trouble?" Eddie said.

I squinted at him. "Like, what *kind* of trouble? Someone shooting and killing us? That kind of trouble?"

"Jokes. She's got jokes." Eddie shrugged. "I don't know. People lose their minds when they're away from home. And when they're at a funeral? Shit gets crazy. No lie—about nine months ago, I had to break up a gang fight. Listen to this: During the processional, one group of thugs saw another group of thugs and hopped out the funeral car. A beatdown right there in the middle of the fuckin' drive to the cemetery. During the freakin' processional, I kid you not. And then. *Then!* They smashed homie's skull open, hopped back into the limos, and headed to the cemetery. Unbelievable. Bunch of assholes."

"And . . . you think we're going to . . . *jump* people?" I asked.

Eddie shrugged again. "I'm just sayin' it happened, is all."

"You worry too much, my friend." Wallace clapped his shoulder. "Phillip always said you were wound a little tight. Relax. You're sounding a bit like our friend Miriam."

Right as I opened my mouth to respond, Desi squeezed my arm, then asked, "Can we go in now? It's getting late. And I gotta pee."

"Who'll do the honors?" Wallace asked.

Eddie said, "Me," then opened the front door.

We moved forward with lots of "oohs" and "wows."

Before stepping across the threshold, I glanced back over my shoulder. The jungle was so close. Ninety acres of wilderness right . . . there. I could run through those trees and never be found again.

The lights in the foyer's large iron and wood chandelier popped on. Soft yellow light.

"Hello?" Desi howled. "Anybody here? Aunt Doris? *Hell-ohhh!*" Her voice echoed across the two-story entryway and the sparkling parquet floors. Stained-glass windows candy-colored our faces. The house shuddered from the sudden noise of us.

No one answered. No one else was here.

There was a full-length window at the opposite end of the foyer that boasted a view of the terrace, and beyond that, blue sky and a sun the color of molten gold. There were thousands of pillows on the couches and armchairs in the living room. Two staircases led to the second floor.

No foul smells. No ugly angles. Perfect. Classy. Just like Phillip Omeke.

Awed, I gaped at the dramatic ceiling. "This lobby is just . . . it's incredible."

"Despite your earlier observation, Miriam," Frank said, "this is *not* the Embassy Suites." He paused, then added, "And it's a *foyer*."

I rolled my eyes. "Relax, Roget. Just used the wrong word. Gravity still works."

Frank puffed out his cheeks, then pushed out his chest. "I'm calling my Realtor as soon as I return to Dallas. I want an estate—no, a villa, no, a hacienda—similar to this one, but grander." He stroked his chin as he thought. "However, I want a better location. Not on a deserted island—what good is a mansion if no one sees it?" He nodded at Wallace. "No offense."

"No offense taken, friend. Phillip designed the house without too much input from me. Honestly? I wanted to build in the Maldives. Anyway, you can offend him when we all get to heaven. Or hell, if what Phillip said about you is true." He laughed.

Frank grinned and pointed gun-fingers at him.

"What's this?" Desi wandered to a round brown table that sat in the middle of the foyer.

Wallace stood over it and traced the edges of the table with his slender, yellow fingers. "Interesting. This wasn't here on my last visit."

The entire tabletop was a work of art. Literally. A painting of Jesus in the center of a large circle, and smaller circles of scenes from everyday Renaissance life. A man drinking wine. A man eating. A man asleep at a fireplace. Couples having a picnic. A woman gazing at her reflection in a mirror. A woman standing between two men fighting. A couple looking at a rich man who'd strapped a hawk to his wrist. A man listening to another man speak. Four panes spoked off those circles with depictions of an angel and a demon, heaven, angels awakening the dead, and a sinner in hell. Seven carved figurines, similar to chess pieces, sat atop seven slices of the circle. Finally, two banners filled with scripted Latin sat on the top and bottom of the Jesus circle.

"So, this is weird," I said, touching the figurine of a round man eating cake.

"Is it a game?" Desi asked. "Like old-timey Monopoly?"

Wallace tapped the table with one finger. "Hmm . . . I don't see a man shooting down six people." He glanced at Eddie. "Are you still planning to murder us like Miriam thinks?"

I smirked at Wallace. "Good one." To Eddie: "Are you, though?"

Eddie said, "Yep. Line you guys up in the parlor and just start shootin'. Then, collect two hundred dollars once I pass Go. I'm thinking that's painted on the other side of the table."

Frank snapped his fingers. "*The Seven Deadly Sins.* Hieronymus Bosch."

Wallace nodded. "Impressive, Franklin."

"I collect art," he said. "At my main home, I have a Degas, a Dalí, lots of Pollack. No Bosches—too weird, too busy. *Obviously.* Anyway, right now, I'm more interested in having a quiet moment in my room than further discussing this depressing table."

"Oh, dear Franklin," Wallace said with a sigh. "You *can't* own a Bosch. There are not that many, first of all, and second, they're all hanging in someone's museum."

Frank cocked his chin, then said, "Anything, including some weird painting, can be bought. Everything has its price."

"You must tell me, then," the old man said, "how

you would manage to get your hands on something as rare and precious as a Bosch."

Both men bid us farewell, then chatted about *good* art as they climbed the stairs to find their bedrooms . . . on the second floor. Which was higher than the first floor. And had better views of the jungle and the ocean than the rooms on the first floor. Where I would be staying.

Ugh.

Desi slipped her arm through mine because we were now besties. "Whaddya think so far?"

"About what? About being lied to? About not having staff around? About being alone on an island with six strangers and finding out that my friend died a month ago but only learning about it an hour ago?"

"No, silly. I don't need somebody cleaning up after me. And I think it's kinda funny and sweet what Phil did." She flicked her wrist. "No. What do you think about all of *this*? The house. The *men*." She dropped her voice. "I know he's married, but Frank is kinda cute. Sounds like he's got some money, too. He'll do for three days . . . unless *you* want him."

My skin crawled at the thought of Frank standing naked anywhere near me, and I gagged. "No. Have at it. Enjoy." I paused, then said, "You're not pissed off just a *little*?"

Desi shrugged. "I didn't come here for money, remember? I wanted to get away from the assholes and jerks and haters back home. And I'm gonna get to do that *and* take home some cash I wasn't counting on. I'm grateful, girlie. You should be, too. Now . . ." She licked her lips. "Who are *you* gonna hook up with? Not Wallace. If you couldn't tell, he's gayer than a piñata."

I blinked at her, then laughed. "Girl, bye. I have better shit to do. Like finding out who the hell made the room assignments."

Desi said, "Goodness gracious, relax, Miriam," then she gave me a raspberry.

"A word of advice, Desirée," I said. "You better get your head out of Frank's pants and hope your name's in that will."

She rolled her eyes. "Of *course* it's in the will. Phillip wouldn't have brought me all this way if he wasn't gonna hook me up." She playfully shoved me, then said, "Don't be so boring. This is our one chance to be free, to cut loose and not be judged for once in our lives." She waggled her hips, whipped off her blue scarf, and waved it in the air. "And that's exactly what I'm gon' do. Cut loose and get me some. Thank you, Phillip O.!" She threw kisses to the sky, then said, "This will definitely be a celebration of life. Cuz you only live once, right?"

8

Desi was right. You *do* only live once—and I
didn't want to spend too much of it talking to her or
hiding in my bedroom (on the first floor). I wanted to
find a quiet space to pen a tribute to Phillip.

But first, I found my room and quickly unpacked.
I barely glanced at the queen-size bed, the teak armoire, or the chaise lounge before I rushed back into
the foyer. It didn't take long to shed the unease I'd
felt earlier—it was like shedding a fur coat in Tahiti.
Just that quick, I'd been suckered and seduced by the
swimming pool that lapped out and out and beyond
the blue skies. I'd been charmed by the Mexican tile
work cemented against the house's stark whiteness,
lulled by the opium-poppy-sweet breeze lifting the
gauzy white curtains. The excitement of mansion-
living on someone else's dime brought out my inner
Desi Scoggins—ohmygosh lookit that fireplace in the
bathroom, ohmygosh lookit the laundry room, ohmygosh lookit the chan-dee-leer!

Standing out on the terrace, I took a deep breath—
no stink of sweaty men or dead fish or dead dogs left
to rot in dark alleys. The air smelled of ocean and
green, and no one smell lingered too long before it was
replaced by the scent of another living thing. Nothing
died here on Mictlan Island.

Now that we had arrived, fatigue tugged at my
limbs as though they'd been trapped in quicksand.
Complete thoughts sat unused like old furniture in the

dark shadows in my mind. Eat, drink, and sleep—my three directives for the rest of Friday night. I trudged to the kitchen to handle numbers one and two.

"I'll whip up something real quick for dinner," Javier announced to Desi and me. "How about . . . shrimp scampi?"

"Sounds good to me," I said, settling on a stool at the breakfast bar.

"Yum, yum, *yummy,*" Desi said, pulling a bottle of Corona from the fridge. "You got some crusty bread in them cupboards?"

Javier nodded. "And berries with fresh whipped cream?"

Desi giggled and hopped up and down. "Yes, yes, yes."

I flicked my hand. "I don't care. Just as long as there's alcohol nearby." The thought of talking to one more person, of casting another side-eye at Eddie or Wallace, the thought of all the mental gymnastics with anyone not in this room made me nauseous and clammy. Good food and a giant cocktail would thaw and soften parts of me that had turned hard and cold.

Wallace—it was his smugness that burned me up more than anything. The dismissive way he talked to me reminded me of the way Billy talked to me.

I'd seen my ex-husband late last night after being assaulted in my own front yard. Billy had called me a liar, had rolled his eyes, had told me to take my meds and . . .

Don't think about him right now. Enjoy the quiet. Enjoy the ocean. Don't let Bill Macy ruin your time here.

And so, I actively ignored all Billy-thoughts as Desi and I devoured the most delicious scampi we'd ever eaten. "West Virginia ain't known for its fine cuisine," Desi was saying with a full mouth. "No one ever says that word 'cuisine' in my neck of the woods. Squash casserole, pinto beans, and fried chicken ain't cuisine. Apple butter and pepperoni rolls? That ain't cuisine, either. And I've always wanted to say that word and have it to be true. To *eat* what that word—cuisine— means. And *hors d'oeuvres*: I want some of those, too."

I said, "Uh-huh," then offered her another piece of crusty bread from the basket. "So how did Phillip trick *you* into coming here?"

She gulped from her glass of sangria, then wiped her mouth with a napkin. "He emailed me, saying that he was Alex, one of Larry's college friends that I hadn't met. Said he was sorry that he'd missed Larry's funeral and everything, and that he'd heard how rough I was having it. So he wanted to fly me over for some peace and quiet." She shrugged. "Which was true. I mean, a trip away from the sadness and craziness? I woulda been a fool to turn that down. My momma didn't want me coming over here cuz she thought this Alex guy was gonna make a move on me.

"Honestly? I was surprised that one of Larry's friends was still talkin' to me—after the funeral, no one called on me, and a coupla people 'unfriended' me on Facebook. Folks at church and sometimes in the grocery store straight-out ignored me. *But!*" She lifted her glass. "That was then, and this is today. Them haters can kiss my sweet patootie! Cheers, girlie."

And we toasted.

After dinner, I wandered back out to the terrace. The air was thick and hot—this was "vacation weather," though, and I felt lighter and less scratchy now that I'd had a decent meal and cold, sweet sangria. I was even humming a Barbra Streisand song. *Me.* Humming, despite this being a memorial, despite the madness that I'd left behind. Despite all of that, a smile had crept onto my face and I was *humming* "The Way We Were." Mictlan Island had already changed me.

Evelyn sat at a poolside table. Two unopened bottles of water and a bag of potato chips sat near her hands. Her face reflected the pool light, but her eyes looked small and flat, like raisins in her head.

"Hey," I said with a smile. "You want company?"

She didn't respond.

I plopped into the chair across from her, then sighed long and loud. "This is incredible, isn't it? Being here, I mean." I tilted my face to a sky crammed with white sparkly pinpricks that people living in less-dense cities called "stars." "In L.A., we can only see Venus." I fixed my gaze on that faraway planet, then said, "When I was a kid, I wanted to be an astronaut, but I couldn't add or subtract to save my life. Carry the one? Go fuck yourself." I laughed, sangria wasted, and added, "I suck at math."

Evelyn was staring at my swollen wrist. "You should hydrate." She slid over a bottle of water.

I accepted the gift but shook my head and poked at my wrist. "Oh. Yeah. I guess it *is* a little swollen. But I'm not bloated."

She blinked at me. "You hurt yourself?"

I shrugged. "Something like that."

"Someone else hurt you?"

"Umm." Tears pricked at my eyes, but I blinked them back into storage. "Yeah, but I'm good, though. It's gonna get handled as soon as I'm back home."

"Your husband—did he hurt you?"

Her question punched me in the chest but made me laugh. "*Billy?* Oh, hell, no. He's an asshole, but he'd never raise his hands at me. It's just this family. There was a confrontation with one of them right before this trip, and . . ." I rolled my eyes, then twisted the cap off the water bottle. I took a gulp and shivered as the cold liquid extinguished the rising fire in my gut. "Another story for another time." I offered her a smile. "Thank you for caring, though."

We stared at the heavens in silence. Beneath us, the ocean crashed against rocks so violently that I thought by morning, we'd all be washed to sea.

I peeked at the older woman. Tears were streaming down her face and dropping onto that mess of a shirt. "You okay?"

She ran her hand across her cheeks, then sniffed. "I wanna go home."

I rubbed my thumb over the bottle top and sadness came to me like a butterfly slowly moving its wings, barely there but enough to change the world. "I'm a little homesick, too. I have a daughter. We're pretty close. You have kids?"

She shook her head.

"Are you married?"

Another head shake.

Poor lady.

"Now that I think about it," I said, "I'm a little homesick even when I'm home. Guess that's because so much has changed there, but—" I cleared my throat and sat up in my chair. "We're here now. Phillip's gone but not forgotten, and even better, he's gonna help make everything splendid, just like he did when he was alive. That's worth being away from . . . Where are you from?"

"New Mexico. My mother's there. And my dog Chachi, he's there, too, and I love them both so much."

I stood from my chair. "Well, on behalf of all mothers, then . . . you should get some rest. Brush your teeth. Say your prayers. Long day tomorrow. Sounds like Wallace has more guests coming. Enjoy the quiet while you can."

Evelyn closed her eyes. Her lips tightened over her teeth.

That flutter of sadness made me want to sit and be a comfort to her. But my eyelids weighed more than dark matter, and I could already hear myself snoring in the silence. Still, I had to offer her *something*. "If you need to talk, you can come to my room and hang out, okay?"

She looked up at me with grateful eyes. "Good night, Miriam. I'm sorry. For everything."

I squinted at her. *Sorry for everything?* This poor woman. Who hurt her so much that she apologized for being human? I patted her on the shoulder, then returned to my room. As I climbed into bed, though, I prayed that she didn't stop by, that she took her melancholy to her fancier room down the hall.

I just wanted to sleep. And I would sleep, like I'd never slept before.

An hour later, though, I awoke in my darkened room. Something—or someone—had nudged me awake. My heavy eyes skipped across the room—vanity, armoire, windows . . .

But nothing was there. No one was there.

I lay my head back upon the pillow.

Just my imagination.

Yeah. That's what it was.

Silly mind tricks.

9

Splat!

There it was again. Something hard, something fleshy, something smacking—

Splat!

Heart racing, I jerked up from my pillow and glanced at the clock on my nightstand—10:17 P.M. Those red numbers were the only light shining in the bedroom. Not for long. A flashlight beam played against the window.

Female voices whispered, "Miriam . . ."

A male voice said, "Come out and play-ay."

"Miriam . . ."

"Come out and play-ay."

I closed my eyes to hear them better but the sounds of Los Angeles—police helicopter, motorcycle engine, dog barking—kept me deaf.

Splat!

The window rattled.

My eyes burned and I pushed away the comforter. Then I grabbed my gun from the nightstand and—

My eyes popped open to bright morning sunshine. I found myself in a strange green bedroom not my own. *Where am I?* Panicked, I pulled the comforter—not mine, either—up to my chin. Above me, the crystal beads on the chandelier tinkled even though the windows were closed, even though no breeze eased through the room, and I watched those crystal beads with frightened eyes.

Where am I?

Mexico. You're in Mexico.

Pressure slowly lifted from my chest as my mind's eye replayed yesterday's tape.

Artemis.

Mictlan Island.

Phillip.

Phillip. He'd tricked me and five others into coming here. *Yeah. That's right.* That memory drifted like burning paper to join the other memories.

La Charon.

Shrimp scampi.

Sangria. Lots of sangria.

I sat up in bed, fully awake now.

Phillip's dead and I'm here. And his will . . . I may be rich two days from now, when I'm back home wherever home will be.

Panic? What panic? Not this girl, not anymore.

Smiling now, I selected wide-legged, white linen pants *(The baroness has a title . . . you have these slacks)* and a scoop-necked white blouse *(Mama found this in a little shop off the canals of Venice . . .)*. At the vanity, I pulled my hair into a ponytail, then bent to smell the perfect peach roses in the heavy crystal vase.

No scent.

I tapped the flowers.

Fake.

But the sky beyond my windows, and that color, the blue of sapphires and hyacinths? Not fake. That sky was my sky.

The aroma of frying bacon and onions, percolating coffee, and fresh-squeezed oranges rushed me as soon as I opened my bedroom door.

Javier, wearing black-and-white-checkered pants and a chef's smock, moved around the kitchen with ease. "*Hola,* Miss Mimi!"

I threw him jazz hands and smiled. "*Hola!* Where is everybody?"

"Wallace is out there—" Javier nodded back at the pool. "Desi's still sleeping. What's-her-face is, too, I think. And White Boy is choke-holding Frankie out on the front porch, ha ha. Breakfast will be ready in ten."

"Sounds great." I poured orange juice into a glass, then sipped. "This juice is delicious."

"*Gracias.*" He forced a potato across a mandoline, and seconds later, a pile of perfect potato slices sizzled on the griddle. "Sleep good?"

I shrugged. "Weird dreams—I forgot where I was for a minute. I miss my daughter."

"Your man's taking care of her while you're here?"

My man. "Yeah, he's taking her to Disney World."

He glanced at me. "You didn't want her to go?"

I shrugged again. "Mixed feelings about it. She'll be fine. I'm just being a mother. Gotta let go sometimes, right? I mean, if he can perform a root canal, he can manage a seventeen-year-old's schedule."

"True, but can't nobody love you like your momma loves you," Javier said. "I've only known you for a day, but I know can't nobody replace you, Miss Miriam."

Tell that to Billy, who was now replacing me with Ashlee, the anorexic-adjacent adulteress who kept a dirty house.

When I'd seen Morgan late Thursday night, I wanted to grab her, throw her in my Camry, and escape to Colombia. She'd stood at the living room's sliding door with her hands on her barely there hips. In that dim light, I couldn't tell if her skin had finally regained its healthy nutmeg coloring or if it was still . . . *gray.* She wore her favorite *schmatta*—a holey black leotard up top and my ancient *Purple Rain* sweatshirt worn as a skirt, its neck tugged down to those mere hips and the sleeves tied around her tiny waist. Because of Ashlee and Brooke, she hadn't stood at a barre for almost six months.

Yeah, Billy had chosen the woman who'd forced Morgan to forsake food for ballet. A woman with pointy bones, sharp edges, and severe right angles. She'd stolen my family and my house, and now she had my view of the mountains, and the entire world had a view of her nasty kitchen. I didn't have to enter the house to see those dishes piled high in the sink and pizza boxes tottering on the breakfast bar. Back on Thursday night, I'd glimpsed through the patio doors, wine bottles and dirty glasses on the granite countertops—countertops that I'd had put in along with the French door refrigerator and matching range top that I was *still* paying for each month.

When you've hijacked someone else's dream, at least keep that shit clean.

I'd left them there on that porch—*my* porch. Ashlee had wrapped one long alien arm around Billy's waist, then wrapped the other arm around Morgan's. They were *her* family now.

For now.

Just like Javier said: no one could replace me.

10

Wallace stood at the low iron fence that edged the backyard's terrace. His violet eyes glimmered with tears while his thin fingers worried the tail of his lavender linen shirt.

"Good morning." I handed him a glass of orange juice. "Breakfast is ready."

He thanked me and a teardrop tumbled down his yellow cheek. "This was one of our favorite spots on the island." He rubbed the scars on his hands as his gaze moved slowly across the horizon. "We'd visited six times together, and each time, this view took my breath away. Again, I resisted Mexico, wanting something more tropical, but this view. This view makes me stop and just . . . stare out in awe."

The bluest blue water. Sinless white and foamy waves. A clear view to the edge of the world. No smog. No planes. No skyscrapers. No tourists.

"I'd love to live here," I said. "Even as a caretaker."

"Is that a hint, doll?"

I said, "Bingo."

"We went through so much trouble buying this land." Wallace swiped at his eyes, then nodded. "It was all worth it. Yes, it was."

I squinted at him. "So, you and Phillip . . . ?"

"Bought it together. It's in his name, but I'm the one who brokered the deal. I'm the one who had the previous occupants . . . *evicted*, you could say. Phillip was a beast in court but a pushover everywhere else."

I gave him a sidelong glance, then stared at his scarred hands. "So no dead Native Americans haunting this place, right?"

"If I said yes, would you still want to be caretaker?" He tossed his head back and laughed. "No, this isn't *Poltergeist,* my dear. While some of the occupants may have lost their lives in this battle, it wasn't because of two gays from California wanting to build a vacation home. No, the government of Mexico expressed their enthusiasm in our interest and especially in our American money, which angered an unconventional businessman along the way. He was a squatter who could've paid for this land if he truly wanted, but . . ." He sighed and dabbed his knuckle at the corners of his eyes. "I miss Phillip—I thought I was prepared for his passing, but . . . it's scary how . . . *blank* I feel without him."

"I'm sorry." And I was.

Since Wallace wasn't ready to eat, I settled alone at a patio table closest to the kitchen and Javier brought me huevos rancheros, bacon, potatoes, and a carafe of coffee.

As I ate my perfect breakfast, I enjoyed the roar of the ocean. Watched lime-green butterflies and white gulls soar so high. Fluffy white clouds that towered into forever had started to fill my perfect blue sky. But they were the perfect clouds you had childhood dreams about, dreams about eating them with your hot cocoa and bouncing on one cloud after the other. I could've sat there all day. Stayed in that spot forever as Javier brought me food.

Maybe one day I will.

After closing my eyes and making a wish—*I wish to stay on Mictlan Island forever*—I pushed away from the table. I was, as my mother would say, full as a little tick. I glanced one last time at those flawless, marshmallow clouds that still crawled across the sky and whispered, "Please let Wallace say yes."

What if he did? Would Morgan come willingly? Would Mexican authorities let me stay?

I thought about this as I wandered the house and eventually found the media room.

The soundproofed walls muted Desi's squeals of delight back in the kitchen. "Breakfast?" she was saying. "I go to bed and there's food. I wake up and there's more food. Javi, you're my fairy food-father!"

I settled into one of the cranberry leather armchairs. Oversized. Baby soft. Plush. A perfect place to think about a tribute to Phillip.

What should I say? Something sweet, like, *I wouldn't be here without you.* Or something funny, like, *Really, I wouldn't be here without you—you tricked me, and now here I am in Mexico!* Or maybe something heartbreaking, like, *You looked past my faults to see the best in me, to see that my life was worth saving.* And as I stood before the others, I'd look up to the sky with tears in my eyes, then I'd point to the heavens and say, "You are magic, Phil Omeke. Pure magic." Or something like that.

"Crazy as hell, ain't it?" Frank had slipped into the media room, and now he plopped into a chair beside me.

"Ain't"? From *him*? Umm . . .

"Crazy, as in, Phillip dying?" I pulled my legs beneath me. "I had no idea he was sick."

"I sure as hell didn't, either." He ran his hand across his sweaty forehead, then wiped his hand on his shorts.

"I'm honored that Phil chose to invite me to come."

Frank sucked his teeth. "He *had* to invite me. I put Phil's ass on the map in Texas."

"How?"

"With my case," the banker said. "He had to do all

kinds of *Matrix*-Morpheus legal shit. They wrote new laws because of me." He pushed out his chest as though he'd discovered the shape of the sky. "I never thought I'd be meeting a bunch of ballers way out in the middle of nowhere, though. This is better than some stupid business meeting."

Hunh. So Frank was an undercover brother. He had stowed the ten-dollar words, and now he was just Frankie from around the way, droppin' *g*'s and embracin' "ain't" and "ballers."

I peered at him, for this and other reasons. Like: "Ballers? Who are we talking about?"

"Wallace Zavarnella and his buddies. Yeah, yeah, he's shady, but who isn't shady in real estate? Three more clients like him and I'm set for *life*."

"How is he shady?"

Frank sneered. "Like I'm gonna tell *you*."

"I know already. Just wanted to hear what *you* knew."

A bad bluff, because Frank snorted at me.

I whispered, "Is he wearing a *wig*?"

Frank flicked his pink tongue across his top lip, then moved closer to me—the air felt moist sitting this close to him. Like a giant cloud should have been forming over his head. "He's still sick. Cancer. The old white lady? I believe that's his nurse." He leaned back, then said, "We're having drinks around six thirty tonight. You should join us and maybe I can hook you up with my services, know what I'm saying? What do you do again?"

"You mean . . . for a living?"

Frank snorted. "Uh, *yeah*."

I cleared my throat. "Well, I have a daughter. She dances, so she needs me to drive her around the city for performances and auditions . . . so I've been home with her for a minute."

"She's what, seven, eight?"

"Seventeen. But then I'm, umm . . . I'm in marketing. Retail."

"Nordstrom? Saks?"

"Hidden Treasures."

"Used clothes and shit?"

"Luxury consignment."

"So . . . used clothes and shit from rich people?"

I scowled at him. "I'm incredibly successful—I'm the one who came up with the storytelling campaign where we took, like, a purse and created a story around it."

He squinted at me. "True stories?"

"Sometimes."

"So you lied to sell rich people's used clothes and shit to poor people?"

"No," I said with forced patience. "I turn a boring object into an objet d'art. That's called 'marketing.'"

He blinked at me. "What does your *husband* do?"

I glared at Frank's plump belly, at the buttons straining to keep his beige shirt from ripping apart. "He has a very successful dental practice."

Frank gawked at me as though I had swooped down from the sky to crap in his cornflakes. He stared at me a moment longer, then shook his head.

"What's wrong?" I asked.

"Just wondering why you're *here*. With *us*. I know Phillip did some pro bono work, but . . . you sleep with him or something?" He laughed, then said, "I forgot. Of course you didn't."

I lifted my chin. "Our relationship is none of your business. Let's just say that we were close."

Because this is what you do. Billy's constant lament skittered across my mind. The next word he'd always want to say but didn't was "lie." *This is what you do: lie.* Make up stories. Create something out of nothing. He'd said it back on Thursday night, after I'd told him about Prudence and her assaulting me. I hadn't imagined the way she'd looked at me, or how her combat boots had kicked the crap out of my arm. And I wasn't lying to Frank now about Phillip. He and I *had* spent a lot of time together. We *were* close.

Frank stared at me and said, "But not close enough to know that he was dying, that he was *dead*. What a pal."

"We weren't up in each other's house all the time," I said, my cheeks hot and nostrils flared. "We'd talk late at night for hours—"

"About your case."

"And *life*." Life before my case. Life after my case. And life after the *next* case. I cleared my throat. "He confided in me as much as I confided in him." More or less.

Frank cocked an eyebrow. "Not about *dying*, though."

Never about dying. Never about Wallace or anything related to his love life. Still: I meant *something* to him, because he'd invited me here, to his favorite place in the world.

"And what does your husband think about you coming to an island without him?" Frank asked me now.

I crossed my arms. "What does your *wife* think? Does she know that you have a thing for West Virginian widows?"

A slow smile crept across his lips. "That . . . that's nothing. Business—she inherited money from her dead husband, and of course, I'm just helping her decide what to do with it. I'm using my charm, know what I'm saying? Thinking three steps ahead. You know how we do."

I rolled my eyes. "Of course."

"You can't stand Wallace, but you'll kiss his ass for a million dollars."

"Damn right. I got bills. A daughter going to college soon. You have kids?"

He held up three thick fingers. "And they, too, are spoiled as hell and have expensive tastes. They have no idea."

"My daughter's mad at me right now. Same thing. People bully her—I handle it, talk to the folks, make sure it stops, and she thinks I've overstepped. But then if I *didn't* step, she and my husband would complain that I hadn't done enough." My stomach seized and I winced—the twisted ball of anxiety that I'd left behind on the tarmac back at LAX had found my gut. I fake-sneered at Frank and said, "See, now I'm stressed out again."

Frank laughed. "I can be one of *those* parents, too."

"Yeah?"

"I'm not buttoned up and bougie all the time." His mouth lifted into a lazy grin. "I got kicked out of the peewee football club for cursing out the coach."

My jaw dropped. *"You?"*

"And . . ."

"And?"

"I beat up the father of a boy who hit my daughter." Frank sank into the chair and let his head fall back against the pillow. "The little bastard refused to apologize to Janelle, and the dad, he was the biggest asshole I'd ever met, and . . . I just . . . I lost it. No regrets."

"Amen." I held out my fist.

He bumped it.

Solidarity.

"The girl bullying my daughter?" I said. "She left swastikas and frog stickers on Morgan's locker."

Frank gawked at me. "Your husband must've beat a few people's asses."

I snorted. "Billy is not that type of man. They could

burn a cross in the middle of his office, and he'd say, 'It's just a little fire.'"

"So you handled it, then?"

"Oh, hell, yeah, I handled it."

"And?"

"And me handling it led me to being here." I laughed and tapped the arm of my seat. "I'll be forever grateful to Phillip for coming to my rescue. Which is why I'm trying to think of something good to say for the memorial service tomorrow."

Frank stood from his chair. "I'll let you get to it, then. Morgan's gonna realize, though, just how badass you are. She'll be grateful that she has a mother who will get in Ignorance's face just for her."

I offered him a sad smile. "Hope you're right."

"I'm always right." He straightened up and squared his shoulders. "Now," he said in his pompous voice. "Time to mix with the hoi polloi and the great unwashed. See you around, Phil's Best Friend."

And just like that, the peace I'd found moments ago returned—but I still couldn't come up with a tribute. So I left the media room to find inspiration from the island's quiet. But Artemis had come alive. A flushed toilet. Heels clicking against tile. The rustling leaves of jungle trees. It was better noise, though, than car alarms, revving motorcycle engines, and firecrackers.

Even if he said no to caretaker, maybe Wallace would let me stay at Artemis a little while longer. That meant moving past the old man's insults and buttering him up to say, "Sure, doll, stay as long as you like."

Because I could thrive here.

I could start creating again.

I could begin writing my story about the disaster that was Brooke McAllister. Turn the narrative from Bully Mom to Bravo, Mom! There'd been nothing in the settlement that stated that I couldn't.

Here at Artemis, I could . . . *become.*

Even on the first floor of a mansion.

That didn't mean that I couldn't peek at life on the *best* floor.

Out on the terrace, Wallace napped in a lawn chair. Desi, lounging in a chair beside him, nursed a drink as she read a novel. Javier had cleaned the kitchen and had probably gone to capture urchins from the tide pools.

I trotted up the flight of stairs to the second level, then crept down a long hallway lined with framed photos of Artemis lost in fog, Artemis beneath bright skies, Artemis lit by the full moon. Frank had returned to his golden room, and he crouched with his hands on his knees as he gazed out the window. Like he'd run out of breath. His bed's headboard was cushiony and yellow, like the toilet seat in my grandmother's house.

I backtracked, passed the stairs, and came to a closed door. I turned the knob—locked. I continued down the hallway and stopped in front of closed double doors. According to Aunt Doris's video, this suite belonged to Wallace. I backtracked again, passing Frank's room to find the northernmost room on the second floor. The door was open, so I stepped across the threshold.

Eddie's bedroom had red walls and Asian-style lacquered furniture. The fancy couch held pillows that weren't for sleeping, and all of it looked like the decorator had raided the set of *The King and I.* The framed print on the wall wasn't Asian, though. It was that weird painting of the man screaming with his hands to his face and the red sky behind him, and all of it was wavy, and . . .

Wait.

Eddie had *two* views.

Both north- and west-facing windows offered views of the wilderness, and looked out to the Sea of Cortez and the dark speck that was Mexico.

How the hell had he landed a corner room on the higher floor with *two* windows?

What kind of upstairs-downstairs bullshit social experiment was *this*?

Wait.

The three large bags he'd carried on board *La Charon* now sat on his bed.

My fingers burned as I stared at those bags. Looking ... thinking ...

"Go on," I mumbled. "You're here now. You might as well."

I glanced back at the door, then back to the bags on the bed. *Go on.* I hurried over to the windows and glanced out—trees, the sea, no Eddie.

Where was he?

Somewhere in the house, a door closed.

Somewhere in the house, an alarm chirped.

Something gurgled through the pipes.

Then there was quiet.

I held my breath, tiptoed back to the bed, then tugged the zipper on bag number one.

Inside, there was a locked black case the size of a drill box. There was a yellow and green carton the size of the nicest Crayola set. *Shooting with the best.* 7.62mm. There was a locked black plastic case about forty inches long, and another box of bullets, this one black, for a 9mm. And there was a last box: TEC-9 20R gun magazines.

Damn.

I was right.

There *was* a wolf at Artemis.

Eddie was the wolf, and the wolf had a lot of guns. The better to kill us with.

11

Terror, cold and hard terror, crackled over me like ice.

Eddie had told a bald-faced lie on the boat about not having guns, but I was now standing over his bed, staring at bags of ammunition. I hadn't imagined the guns after all, *and* it was worse than I'd thought. Because in addition to the handguns, Eddie had also brought along a rifle. *A rifle!* Who the hell brought effin' assault weapons to a tropical island? In my head, in *my* world, a crazy man, that's who. A psychopath.

He needed to leave. Leave before he hurt or killed someone. Someone like me.

This time, I used my phone to take pictures—of the gun cases, of the box of bullets, of the assault rifle magazines. It took forever for me to focus the lens, snap six usable photographs, then zip up the black bag just as I'd found it. It took forever because my hands were now numb and cold, and had grown to be the size of catcher's mitts. Because my giant cold hands were now shaking like the rest of me. Because Eddie was planning to kill us. If not all of us, then at least *one* of us. And if he walked in on me right now . . . that *one* would be me.

Unless . . .

Maybe Phillip had wronged him somehow, and now Eddie planned to ruin his home-going by slaughtering his guests.

He probably had stowed a manifesto somewhere,

like most kooks did. Pages and pages of rambling, run-on sentences with poorly spelled words that went on and on about his hatred of blacks and gays and chem trails and Kenyan ex-presidents.

I had to tell someone.

Not Wallace—he'd been nothing but nasty to me. Mostly. Okay, he was less of a bitch this morning, but still, not Wallace. Not Frank, either—he was a kiss-ass Uncle Remus who cared more about vocabulary and Maseratis and the Dow Jones than survival. Desi wanted to sleep with the island's entire male population, including Eddie, so I couldn't tell her, either. And the other one, the gum chewer, Eden-Ellen-Evan—whatever her name was . . . no. She was . . . no. Back on the yacht, Javier had spoken up for me. He would listen to all that I had to say, and then afterward, he'd make me a mimosa. Yeah, I'd find Javier and tell him everything.

Now, though, I was somewhere I wasn't supposed to be—and I needed to leave. *Now.*

The hair on the back of my neck and on my arms stood as I crept out of Eddie's room to a hallway now longer than it was before. My shoes sank into the corridor's thick carpet, keeping me from rushing, slowing me down even though my heart beat a million times faster than its normal pace. Fortunately, no one popped up as I turtled down the hallway. Frank had even closed his bedroom door. Still, walking this slow was unbearable—inch, pause, inch, pause—but I couldn't risk calling attention to my being there.

Once I reached the stairs, I flattened all show of emotion on my face. Didn't want anyone asking, "Why are you rushing? What's wrong? Is something wrong? Something's wrong."

Down . . . down . . . down. I took each step as though land mines had been planted beneath each plank. Once I reached the foyer, I finally exhaled.

The front doors were open, and Ellen-Eileen-Evelyn stood out on the porch with her shoulders sloped and her head tilted to the sky. At the opposite end, past the living room, Desi and Wallace remained in their lawn chairs. The sun's light had softened.

Javier had returned to the kitchen and was now pulling a carafe of orange juice from the refrigerator. A bottle of Grey Goose vodka sat on the breakfast bar. "Miriam's in the house," he shouted. "Want seconds?"

I tiptoed into the kitchen. "No, thanks. So . . ."

"Know what? I don't think anybody's ever cooked in here. There ain't no grease splatters, there ain't no char . . ." He grabbed two glasses from a cabinet. "Hey, you seen my flask?"

"You dropped it back at the tide pool yesterday, so I picked it up. It's in my room. I'll bring it to you later."

"Dude, come look at this walk-in freezer." The chef beckoned me over to a steel door propped open by a wobbly-looking kickstand. He pointed to the floor and to puddles of melted ice covering the slick terra-cotta tile. "Guess I must've left the door open last night." He chuckled. "Don't remember—I was pretty wasted." A pulpy mess of paper towels sat on the edge of an icy pond—as if Javier had tried to wipe up the mess but had grown bored or distracted or overwhelmed before completing the job.

I peeked in to see the freezer's shelves crammed with cartons of ice cream, boxes of pastry shells, and bags of fruit. *Not enough food for that many people*—that's what Andreas had stated yesterday back in port. Standing there in the freezer's doorway, with my breath making tiny clouds and my eyes taking in shelves of frozen steaks, chickens, and turkeys? Yeah, there was food for days.

"I lucked out," Javier said. "All the meat's still frozen solid, not that I'm gonna use frozen meat. Nuh-uh, man. I found me some fresh fish in the fridge, and I'm gonna go out and dive in a minute, bring back some of them urchins and shit from the tide pools. Cuz Phillip, that dude loved him some sashimi." He bumped into the freezer door, knocking the kickstand up a bit. "Hey." He bustled over to the butler's pantry. "Are there limes? Maybe they brought over some limes, cuz if they did, then I can make some ceviche, and these cocktails with mescal, Tajín, and jalapeño, and . . . what else they got off in here?" He trundled back to the freezer.

Where was Eddie? I anxiously looked back at the living room, then took a seat at the breakfast counter. "Hey, Javier, so you know that guy in the Red Sox cap? Eddie?"

"What about him?" The chef grabbed a bag of frozen strawberries from the freezer shelf. His ass bumped the door again as he tossed the bag into the stainless steel sink. He ducked back into the freezer. "Whoa!" He slipped in the slush and landed on his ass.

The freezer's kickstand clicked up, and the heavy steel door slammed shut.

"Oh, crap!" I popped out of my chair as though a firecracker had lit in my pants and I pulled open the door.

Javier was struggling to stand because the soles of his flip-flops lacked treads. He'd make it into a crouch, but then he'd slip right out of it, banging his knees each time against the frozen tile.

My stomach pretzeled and I was already shivering, a native Angeleno who got cold at sixty-five degrees. "Just hold on. I'll help you up." I repositioned the kickstand on the slippery tile. It slid an inch . . . then held . . . held . . . but we didn't have much time before it slid and clicked away again.

"Okay, I got it, I—*Aye!*" Javier slipped again and his eyes squeezed shut as pain rippled from his knees up and across his bloated face.

Stooping, I inched into the freezer, no more sure-footed in my suede flats. But I inched . . . and I inched . . . and . . .

BAM!

The freezer door slammed behind me, loud, as though millions of doors were slamming at the same time.

Crap. I shuddered and stopped in my step. "It's okay. It's okay." I kept saying that—*it's okay, it's okay*—as I forced myself across the icy floor, as I wedged my shoulder beneath Javier's bulk, as I slipped his thick arm around my neck. "Okay. Try to stand. Slow, now. Slowly . . . slowly . . ."

Javier Cardoza was a big man, and if the smell of his breath was any indicator, he was also a drunk man— that meant "slow" was the only speed available.

The cold was chipping at my ability to move. His arm was squeezing my neck.

You know you can freeze in here, right? If he doesn't strangle you first, you'll freeze.

"Almost there," I panted, overheating now, as we inched closer . . . closer . . . to the door.

Your sweat will become ice and then it will freeze you to death. And then? You'll be dead.

"It's okay," I whispered. "It's okay." I said this even as my skin tightened. I couldn't die, not like this. I couldn't get sick, not like this. I didn't want to die. I'd get nothing from Phillip's will if I died.

My head filled with these mixed messages, but eventually positivity beat the most negative thought a person could think—*I'm gonna die*—and Javier and I finally reached that door. Every ounce of strength I had was now gone, and I wheezed as I twisted the freezer door handle.

No give.

You know you can freeze in here, right?

I whispered, "No, no, no," as my heart wobbled in my chest.

Javier's arm tightened around my neck. "One more time."

I twisted the handle again, then pushed it with my knee.

The door swung open. Warm air pulled us into its grasp and greeted us like a fretful mother.

Once we'd limped back into the kitchen, Javier kicked off his flip-flops and winced as he slumped to the floor. His left knee now resembled a strawberry cream puff—and so did his face.

Behind us, Desi and Wallace continued to nap in their chairs. They hadn't heard or suspected a thing.

"You okay?" I asked Javier between breaths.

Javier said, "No, but I'm about to be." He plucked a brushed silver pill case from his shirt pocket and popped it open. White powder. Not confectioner's sugar. He dipped his long pinkie fingernail into the small mound of cocaine, snuffed it, flicked at his nostril, then offered me a bump.

"No, thank you." I settled back into a cushiony high stool at the breakfast bar. "Feeling better *now*?"

"Oh, yeah. I think all this drama calls for a drink." The chef pulled himself to stand, then grabbed the bottle of vodka from the breakfast bar. He twisted off the cap.

"It's not even noon yet," I pointed out.

"Screwdrivers have orange juice in 'em. Breakfast of champions, baby."

"Eddie has guns," I blurted. "Lots of guns, and I have proof. Look." I plucked my phone from my pants pocket and found the pictures I'd snapped of the gun cases and the ammunition.

Javier took my phone, then swiped through the shots I'd taken. He grunted his indifference, then said, "Where the guns at? I only see ammo."

I blinked at him. "Why does he have ammo if he doesn't have guns?"

Javier shrugged. "You said, 'He has lots of guns,' and I don't see no guns. Don't matter anyway. We're here now."

"It *does* matter. Why the hell does he have boxes of this shit?"

Javier shrugged. "Don't know. C'mon, Miriam. It ain't like you trusted that fool before you saw them bullets. That dude is wound tighter than a yo-yo."

"Exactly. So?"

"So . . . *what?*"

"Don't you wanna know for sure if we should be scared? Don't you wanna know if he has something planned? A violent act of revenge or . . . or . . . if we're now targets in some Great White Hunter bullshit, cuz I sure as hell didn't sign up for *that*. And I'm not gonna be silent about it, either."

He smiled at me. "You're so dramatic. Ain't nobody paying attention to that nut. They don't care about *him* carrying guns around. If that's what it is, if that's what these rich fools want, crazy white boys with guns, then that's what they're gonna get, boom, boom, boom, no matter what you say, no matter what I say. If they want you gone, and I'm sure they do, you're gone.

"It's just like they did me. That's why I'm here. Paying my dues. Cuz see, they were trying to take me down, but Phil told 'em, 'Back the fuck up.' Cuz Phil was badass. You know what, though? Fuck 'em. I'm gonna show 'em all." He poured orange juice into two glasses, followed with generous pours of vodka. "They not gonna win. Nuh-uh." He shook his head as he offered me a screwdriver. "Here's to Phil O., baby."

We toasted. I sipped, coughed. "We need to do something about Eddie." I coughed again.

"Lightweight." His laugh filled the kitchen. "How you gon' do something about a crazy dude with a TEC-9 and you can't even drink right?"

"But he's—"

"Listen to me. Fuck him. If he pulls a gun or some shit like that? Run. I know you know about that."

"Yeah, but—"

"Don't wanna talk about him anymore. He reminds me of assholes I left behind at home. We're here to celebrate while we got the chance. Fate is fate. Hate is hate."

"Fine." I sipped more of my cocktail, unsure what to do next except enjoy the icy warmth of vodka slipping through my veins. "So how are *they* trying to take you down?"

Javier gulped a third of his screwdriver, then said, "You ever watch that show *Cook or Die*?"

"My daughter and I used to watch it together."

"I thought it was stupid at first. Walk the plank if the captains think your food tastes like ass. *Really?* But I went on anyway since Ofelia, that's my wife, wouldn't shut up about it, and I won the final challenge. My starter was reindeer pâté, the main course was herb-crusted elk chops, and for dessert, I made mangosteen sorbet."

"What's mangosteen?"

"It's this purple fruit kinda like citrus. Anyway, I won the damned thing, and I opened up my restaurant B.I.G., right off the Strip in Vegas? And anyway, my waitress, Trixie? She warned them fools that it wasn't for pussies, but they ordered it anyway." He shrugged, then guzzled the rest of his screwdriver.

I scrunched my face—had I missed a part of the story?

"Not my problem, man," he continued, his eyes shiny now as he poured more vodka into his glass, but then he drank straight from the bottle. "There's this thing called 'free will,' and the food's good, and ain't nobody else complained. The natives told me there's good fishing in these waters. So, that's for dinner, Miss Miriam, and y'all gonna love it and the world's gonna talk about how I impressed them fuckers on the island for Phil's going-away, and maybe I'll donate some of the money he paid me for this gig to the guy's family so they can shut the hell up and drop the suit. Just leave me the hell alone and lemme cook, you know?"

I stared into my cocktail. "Guess we all have our problems, huh?"

He pointed at me. "Not you, baby. Ain't nobody fuckin' with you and getting away with it."

I clinked my glass against his bottle, then drank. "I play to win, *amigo*. Phillip loved that about me."

"Hey." Javier's face darkened, and he leaned forward until it was mere inches from mine. "Some advice: stay the hell away from Eddie. That fucker's crazy. Shit get nutso 'round here, though, for real? Like I said: run . . . but run straight back here. My bag's in the pantry. Eddie ain't the only fool on this island—I got me a gat, too. Bought it off some *pendejo* before I hopped on *La Charon*. I don't go nowhere if I'm not strapped. Remember that, 'kay?"

I nodded, and the chair swayed beneath me.

"Good." Javier straightened, then flicked his hand at me. "Now leave. I got some cookin' to do."

I held up my glass, then tapped the breakfast bar. "You're on my team, though?"

"Hell yeah, I'm on your team." He winked at me. "Team Miriam all the way."

I wobbled away from the breakfast bar, lighter than I'd been all morning.

"Hey, Miriam?" Javier said.

"Yeah?"

"Stay sober, baby. Stay sober."

12

Stay sober.

Good advice from a drunk chef and owner of a black-market gun that was stowed near the boxes of bread crumbs and chicken stock, whose veins were filled with Florida orange juice, Russian vodka, and Colombian blow, the same man who'd mixed me two cocktails in nearly three hours.

Stay sober, indeed.

Screwdriver in hand, I shuffled out to the terrace with my shoulders loose, and with my knees weak and wobbly from the booze and the morning's dosage of Valium.

"Hey, girlie." Desi skipped over to me from the chaise lounge and pulled me into a hug. She smelled of cherry Laffy Taffy and baby powder again, and felt as smooshy as almost-set soufflé.

Wallace stood from the table and dropped a napkin onto his plate of untouched eggs and potatoes. "Miriam, would you like to come with us? We're strolling down to the docks to greet more of my guests."

Desi wiggled her nose like a bunny. "Say yes. It'll be a hoot."

Didn't really feel like sweating and hiking again, especially after just guzzling a screwdriver, but I'd do anything to make Wallace look favorably upon me.

And so, I joined the couple and trod the path we'd taken yesterday. Desi talked nonstop about her momma and her daddy, about Larry and how his accounting business was thriving before his death.

I was barely listening to her—mosquitoes had, once again, found me, the roving buffet, and so I focused my energies on slapping and scratching, clawing and panting.

"You're like an alley cat back there," Wallace said to me from the front of our short line.

"I should've kept my behind back at Artemis." Pebbles had found the insoles of my shoes and now rolled and scraped every part of my foot. A hike in suede Steve Madden flats? *(You are as stupid as they said you were . . .)* A hike wearing white linen Calvin Klein? *(You knew better than that. Who are you now?)* For those two decisions alone, I deserved to be miserable.

Each tortured step, though, brought us closer to the roar of the ocean and its cool breeze. I pictured myself running into the water to cool off and . . . and then more sand would fill my shoes, and it would rub and rub my feet until they became two size-six pearls. "How many people are you expecting?" I asked Wallace in an attempt to think about something, *anything* else.

"Twenty, total," Wallace said. "Phillip didn't want a three-ring circus. Just one big ring."

We broke through the jungle. Gray waves rolled in from the sea and crashed onto the white-sand beach. The boathouse had survived another day but it looked more slanted, more of an example of an obtuse angle than a working shed. Those fluffy clouds I'd enjoyed during breakfast now looked heavier, and grays and greens tinged their perfect bodies.

"That doesn't look good," Desi said, squinting at the sky.

Wallace didn't look up. Instead, he peered out at

the horizon. "*La Charon* should've been out there by now." He glanced at his watch, then walked onto the rickety dock. "They were supposed to arrive before one o'clock."

There was nothing out there in the shape of a yacht. Just that ocean and those clouds.

"Maybe there's weather back on the mainland," I offered.

He grunted and glared into the distance with his jaw clenching and unclenching.

Desi and I made "uh-oh" faces at each other, but we dared not speak. The wooden planks, though, groaned beneath our feet. *Exactly, planks. Exactly.*

"This upsets my plans for today," he said. "Fucking Mexicans—no offense. Raul and Andreas *are* Mexicans and they *have* screwed up my plans." He tossed me a fake smile that immediately slipped off his face. "The sky this morning was perfect. Raul checked the weather just two days ago, and the forecast . . ." With hands on his thin hips, Wallace paced the dock, gaze still trained on the horizon.

"There's a radio, right?" I asked. "You can call Raul and see what's happening, can't you?"

Wallace kept pacing, the planks beneath him kept groaning, and no one spoke for a very long time. Finally, he ran his hand along his sweaty forehead and limp wig, then dropped his arms to his sides. "You're right, Miriam. I should do that. Edward has radios. I'm sure Raul will have a good explanation— he's never failed us before. Really: the man's always come through, even in the most dangerous moments. Bringing over construction workers and supplies and whatnot." Wallace cupped his hands at his mouth, then shouted into the distance, "Sorry for calling you a fucking Mexican, Raul! You're one, not the other. Apologies, my friend."

Desi giggled. "Wallace, you are a hoot."

I said, "Yeah, a real hoot," then scratched the bite now welting on my neck. Were those guests in Phillip's will, too? If so, would they receive their share if they didn't show? Those questions sidled up to my lips, but I didn't ask, not with Wallace's smile gone again, not with his violet eyes hot like that, and his fists clenched into hard balls of fire and fury. Yeah, asking him about money would've been the end of me.

Eddie, bullet hoarder and secret assassin, met us at the porch. "Where's everybody else?" He almost looked relaxed, not rage filled at all—which meant that he didn't suspect that I'd visited his room and had poked around in his bags.

"No idea," Wallace said. "I need to use one of your radios to call Raul."

Eddie said, "Got it," then nodded. "I had this one case, boat was supposed to pull into the Boston Harbor around seven, right? It was one of those day-fishing boats that took weekend fishermen out to catch shit. Anyway, guy with a gun and a speedboat hijacked the fishing boat. Took everybody's cash, jewelry, all of that. The captain tried to be a hero, and boom, bad guy shoots him dead. Second mate? Tries to be a hero. Boom, dead. We get there, the *real* heroes, and the entire—"

"Edward, please." Wallace, pale now, squeezed the bridge of his nose. "More radio, less *Cold Case,* please."

Eddie pivoted on his heel, then both men charged into the house.

Desi plucked leaves from my dirty blouse. "You're a mess, girlie. Like you've been—"

"Cutting brush and walking in the jungle?" I asked as I scratched at the bites on my hand. "If you don't mind, I'm about to hog the bathroom."

Desi flicked her bite-free hand. Guess her blood wasn't as sweet as her perfume. "Take all the time you need. Hey—come to my room afterward. You can help me pick out an outfit for tonight. Maybe there'll be more men in this second group of people."

More men? I bit my lip, then smiled. "Didn't think of that."

"I'll even let you have first pick."

"As Wallace would say: Desi, you're a doll." I thought of telling her about the ammunition I'd found in Eddie's bags. I thought of pulling out my phone and showing her the pictures I'd taken. But Frank ruined that moment once he strolled out to the porch with two Bloody Marys in hand.

"For you, my dear." He offered Desi a glass.

She curtsied and said, "Aren't you sweet?"

He lifted the second glass to his lips and sipped.

I smiled, then mimed drinking from a glass he hadn't brought me. "Mmm, it's absolutely delicious, Frank."

Frank shrugged. "My apologies, Miriam. Didn't see you standing there."

Desi giggled, then tapped Frank on the chest. "You're awful."

Yeah, awful. The opposite of Javier, who had lined up glasses of Bloody Mary on the breakfast counter. I snagged one, thought about snagging a second, then guzzled half as I stumbled down the hallway to my bedroom.

Back in my quiet place, I closed the door behind me and placed the near-empty glass on the nightstand. So peaceful. So far from everything. Like the cops and their questions about Prudence's last visit to my house. It would be her word against mine, and neither of us had been upright in the last year. But I had video of Thursday night captured on my security camera, and even though I'd had problems playing the recording that night—*unable to connect to the internet* and then *No video available*—I was sure everything would come out right. And if I had only video without sound, even better. I could create the narrative, who said what to whom. Most important, Detective Hurley would see me on the ground. He would see Prudence kick my arm. That's all that mattered. One act of violence.

The room was cold, and goose bumps rose next to the mosquito bites on my skin. I stepped over to the thermostat—*sweet lord, it's sixty-two degrees, no wonder*—and clicked the red arrow button until the digital display hit seventy-five.

With one long sigh, I fell onto the bed, then studied the pictures on my phone that I'd taken of Eddie's boxes of ammo. Javier was right, although I didn't agree entirely with his conspiracy of rich men wanting us dead. But I played devil's advocate as I lay there, and I could easily explain away all of those weapons. Second Amendment, hunting island wildlife, personal safety, gun show. If I said something to the group again, Eddie would simply pull out his shooting instructor license, say that he was there because Phillip had taught him to shoot and that he wanted to perform a three-gun salute in the dead man's honor. And then, *then*! The others would mock me forever for crying wolf and Wallace would take back the money Phillip had left me and I'd never be invited to Artemis again.

I tapped each picture, then moved my finger to tap the trash can icon.

No. keep them. Just in case.

In case of what?

In case you need proof. After the smoke clears and everybody's dead, you'll have proof that you tried to warn them all.

Javier was right: I was so freakin' dramatic.

Still, I left the pictures in the album. Took long breaths

in and pushed long breaths out as I lay on the bed, eyes fixed to the ceiling. Other than the plane ride to Mexico, none of the last forty-eight hours had been expected—from Prudence's late-night assault and Billy's dismissal to finding TEC-9 ammo in a red-walled bedroom. All of this was bizarre—and made for great television. America would have been entertained and they would've rooted for me after all, had this been a reality-show competition. I would've been a fan favorite, invited to all-star seasons and . . .

My breathing slowed as I stayed in bed, as my mind wandered back to the mainland and to the people I'd left behind.

What was Morgan doing right now? Packing for Disney World? Watching YouTube and learning how to fix a new hairstyle or learn a dance move? Were she and Ashlee chomping spicy tuna rolls and slurping udon noodles at Sugarfish? Was she buying bath bombs the color of dreams? Did she miss me? Did she . . . ?

13

My eyes popped open. I'd fallen asleep.

Where am I?

My eyes scanned the ceiling of the dimly lit room, then slipped over to the damask-covered headboard, to my suitcase spilling clothes near the closet, to the cold dark fireplace and my cocktail dress draped across the chaise lounge and waiting to be worn. Something was scratching. Not a loud scratching, more like a mouse making a hole in the wall.

Where . . . ? I'm lost. Again.

"Artemis. I'm at Artemis." I swiped at drool on my lower jaw, then groaned as I turned over in the bed. My arms and legs were sore from traveling from one country to the next, from hiking jungle trails in Steve Madden flats, from Prudence McAllister's nearly lethal kick.

What time . . . ?

I found my cell phone tangled in the folds of the comforter: six ten.

The reception on the terrace started in a half hour.

I sat up in bed and looked out the window.

The sun had dipped somewhere in the west, leaving the jungle dark and making the light in my bedroom gray. All windows were closed—but a chill swept between the four walls, and the glass beads on the chandelier tinkled. And even though it was Mexico in July, I still shivered—the room's temperature was closer to fifty-eight degrees than seventy-eight.

As I moved toward the thermostat, I sniffed the air around me—a man's woodsy cologne.

Strange.

Had someone come to my room? Had someone stood over me as I'd slept?

I glanced at the door—it was closed—and then noticed the silver carpet . . . and the impressions left of shoes there.

Are those my . . . ?

I knew the answer before I could even finish the question.

Those shoe prints were bigger than mine, and had crossed over the pointy-toed prints made by my suede flat . . . *right?*

That scratching sound returned, this time, though, in my head.

It's the booze. It's fatigue. All of it's got you imagining things.

I shivered, then pulled the comforter around my shoulders. *Yeah. I'm imagining things.* I plucked the television's remote control from the nightstand drawer and aimed it at the sixty-inch monitor above the fireplace. The screen blinked on but remained dark. Of course—there could be no television without internet or cable service. So much for distraction.

The fireplace was natural gas, so I pushed the ignition button. No whoosh. No blue flame. No gas logs sat over the vents. Useless.

I took one last look at the carpet and those shoe prints—*just my imagination*—then shuffled across the room to the bathroom.

As high end as it was—with a fireplace near the tub and a pointless flat-screen television above the fireplace—the black-and-white tile reminded me more of a restroom in a California Pizza Kitchen than the bathroom at the Langham Huntington hotel in Pasadena. Hell, even a bathroom in the Embassy Suites. This was not a place to linger, to lose yourself in a novel or a crossword puzzle. Still, it was warmer than my bedroom. But then so were the polar ice caps and any place in Greenland, or even the freezer that had held Javier and me hostage for three minutes.

This fireplace worked, though—flames danced and dazzled as I stood before it to thaw out. I showered and scrubbed off dirt, caked-on makeup, and bits of bark and dried leaves. After I dabbed cortisone cream on my insect bites, I brushed my teeth twice. I slipped back into my igloo, determined to speak with Wallace about the room's broken thermostat. Couldn't handle two days of cold—that wasn't me being a diva, just a mammal from Southern California.

Perched at the vanity, I began the attack on my hair with a rattail comb, scraping and prying apart strands that had clumped together after the *episode* with Prudence McAllister. I won the battle by making a slick chignon, an elegant choice for a dinner party. I attacked my face next, skipping the ridiculous foundation that had stained my green silk tunic. I plucked my black Gucci dress *(Truman called you a swan, but you're more of a dragon . . .)* from the chaise lounge. The frock, cut from stretch crepe, was still tight around my middle, so tight that my toes were turning blue.

On my most challenging days, I wore a size 8. But the day I'd purchased this dress had been a good day, and so I'd asked the saleswoman at Neiman Marcus for a size 6. A tight fit, with "fit" being a loose description of the barbaric, primeval torture that had spread across my torso. The sales-bitch had cocked an eyebrow and confided, "You really need something bigger." I had snapped at her with "You can go now," then told myself that I'd wear three Spanx and eat four bags of spinach a day for the rest of June and July.

Yeah. Spanx and spinach.

Ashlee wore a size 0—I know this because I found her dress in Billy's suitcase during their sneaking-around days. I'd also be a size 0 if I'd hadn't had Morgan, if I chain-smoked Newports and lemon-juice-cayenne-pepper-cleansed every day.

But I didn't. And now, seated at the vanity wearing the Gucci dress *(allegedly flattening, supposedly flexible—it's a lie, girl, don't believe it)*, I tugged at the middle section's grosgrain bow to rearrange the shaper (one Spanx, not three as planned) now carving into my skin.

"It's all good, I'll be fine, it's okay." Light-headed and numb from the neck down, I slipped on my Louboutin spectator stilettos *(You're the type of woman who dismisses proper circulation . . .)* and waited for the dizzy spell to pass. As I sat there, I stared at the black-and-white framed photograph hanging on the wall above the chaise.

Sophia Loren was giving the stink-eye side-eye to Jayne Mansfield's tits hanging out of her dress. The picture had been taken at Romanoff's in Beverly Hills—I'd written copy for Hidden Treasure's winter catalog that featured replicas of Sophia Loren's dress. Sophia, so beautiful and classy that night, had been the opposite of Mansfield, who wore a flimsy, low-cut satin dress and looked like she'd just stumbled in from a brothel off Highway 66. It was obvious—Sophia wanted to stab the blonde in the face with a butter knife. But Mansfield had to do *something*—she wasn't as beautiful or as talented as *the* Sophia Loren. "Tawdry" had been her only solution.

Ashlee was the Jayne Mansfield in my life. All that spirally hair and those mile-long legs. And that email she'd sent. Ugh. Agreeing with me about Brooke, then smacking me on the nose about Brooke, bringing me close only to kick me in the gut. Talking to me like she was my moral better. *Who does she think she is? I* didn't have the affair with somebody else's husband. *I* didn't cause my brand of crazy to stink up our lives. And I would move on when *I* decided to move on. It had been *my* hard work and my salary and my perfect credit score that had put Billy through medical school. *She* was the one who—

Dizzy again, I closed my eyes. "Father God, help me." My prayer sounded small in the heavy stillness, like the prayer of a three-year-old lost in Buckingham Palace.

Maybe I should sleep it off. Maybe I should take off this dress. Maybe I should skip it all and go to sleep, wake up and start again, refreshed.

Hell, no. Not with Desi fluttering her eyelashes like that and speaking in hillbilly whispers, being the Appalachian Jayne Mansfield to my grown and sexy Sophia Loren. If I wanted to visit Artemis again and meet more of Phillip's fanciest friends, lawyers who would (hopefully) help me fight my legal battle, I needed to get up, wear the dress, mingle, and impress.

It was now six fifty. Time to join the others.

I spritzed my pulse points with perfume and glanced out the window.

Beneath the light of the moon, something moved over at the tree line. Couldn't tell, but . . . The tall grass moved and I kept my gaze on that . . . *There!*

In that tall grass, a teenage girl stood with her back to me. She wore a pink leotard and white track pants. Mist slowly curled around her legs and wind tousled her long black hair. She darted to the right and scooted up a twisty tall banyan tree with the speed and ease of a jaguar. She stood on the topmost branch, then lifted her hands to the sky. She held them there for a moment, then dropped her arms back to her sides. Then she took a step forward and fell from that banyan tree branch, disappearing somewhere in that tall grass.

I cried out and squeezed my eyes shut. *It's in your head, it isn't real, she isn't real, it's okay, you're okay.*

I forced my breathing to slow . . . forced the thoughts feathering around my mind to stop. . . . Finally, I opened my eyes, avoiding my reflection in the vanity mirror, avoiding the tall grass where the girl's twisted body lay crumpled. Instead, I stared at the small container of Valium that sat near my hairbrush. I stared at it forever, remembering the promise of a single tablet. No scratchy thinking. Easy breathing. No more echoes. No more ghosts.

Take one. You only need to take one.

But I shook my head and whispered, "No."

No. Even though two men had brought guns to Mictlan Island. *No.* Even though Brooke McAllister had followed me here to Artemis. *No.* Even though the shoe prints that had been left in the carpet *were* bigger than mine, even though those shoeprints *had* trampled over my shoe prints and had stopped at my bed.

I needed a drink. I needed a pill. But I couldn't surrender control to controlled substances. And I wanted to make Phillip proud. I needed to behave.

But those shoe prints . . .

And the ghost girl in the woods . . .

I needed *something.*

No.

Don't.

Stay sober.

14

And I would stay sober.

Since I'd been drinking throughout the day, I resolved to limit myself to one glass of wine and to kibosh any pill popping that night. Because bad things happened if you stayed drunk and medicated. I was a grown-up with self-control, not some ditzy young British heroine with low self-esteem and an even lower tolerance for prescribed meds, who awakened after an all-nighter next to a dead body.

I had issues, but being a ditzy-ass drunk wasn't one of them.

You'll be fine. It'll be great.

Beyond the courtyard, the trees rustled with the ocean breeze. Their slick leaves and flowers looked wet beneath a sky of soft purple clouds. Golden light from iron lanterns filled the terrace. The fire pit had come alive and danced with long, curly flames that gave off the most beautiful light.

The air smelled of vinegar, pepper, burned sugar, and the sea. All of it mingled with Desi's soda-shop perfume and Frank's cologne. Wallace was wearing a bespoke blue three-piece suit *(Power. Grab it. Now!)*. Desi looked lovely—she'd combed her bird's-nest hair back into tamed ringlets. She looked comfortable in her low-cut crimson dress *(Simple. Slutty. Elegant. They will never figure you out . . .)*.

She looked . . . lovely. Yeah. No hate. Honestly? I

wanted that dress. I wanted the freedom of breathing, of—

Frank's cologne. I sniffed again. Woodsy. Heavy. Familiar. I'd smelled that scent ... *Today,* after waking from my nap. Had *he* been the one who'd come into my room as I slept?

Maybe.

But why would he do that?

Made no sense. Just me being anxious. Just me being light-headed, damned dress.

I searched each face, looking for a woman who could be Aunt Doris sharing a drink with one of Phillip's friends. But I saw no one new. Had Wallace reached Raul on the radio? Had guests arrived but were too tired to attend a dinner party?

I ignored the flutes of champagne on the cocktail table and selected a glass of sparkling water. Perfect— and really, too much alcohol would have left me bloated, and there was no extra space for extra *anything* wearing *this* dress. And anyway, the Gucci's tightness made me weak-kneed and woozy, something already close to drunk.

Javier's appetizers had been arranged into black clay bowls and platters. Red things, things with tentacles, orange flower-shaped things on silver skewers. We all laughed uneasily as we studied the table. Desi slipped an octagonal-shaped thing onto a napkin and tiny red balls gushed from the creature and splatted onto her foot.

Desi whooped and said, "Those balls look like they came out of one of them bouncy-bounce rooms at Chuck E. Cheese."

I tried to hoist a seafoody ... *thing* onto my plate, and it exploded in purple-black goo. I "eeked," startled by the pickled creature's ejaculation.

Wallace chuckled and said, "I'm sure the squid's saying, 'That's never happened to me before.'"

And we laughed—all except for Eddie, who stalked the edges of the terrace. And Evelyn, who hunkered near the bougainvillea. She had combed her wiry hair away from her weird gray and blue eyes. Goat eyes, that's what they were. She wore a multicolored skirt *(Image not loading)* and a worn turquoise sweater with tiny holes in the wool *(Item discontinued)*.

Frank and Wallace picked up their conversation again. As Frank spoke, he lit Wallace's cigar with the most elegant gold lighter *(Its flame lit Fidel's famous Cubanos . . .)* I've ever seen. I joined them, content with nibbling round crackers loaded with ceviche. "That's a gorgeous lighter, Frank," I said, interrupting the men's conversation.

Frank ran his thumb across the scratchy-looking finish. "Cartier, eighteen-carat yellow gold."

"My husband smokes cigars," I said, "and he collects vintage lighters. Haven't seen a Cartier like that, though."

Frank pointed at me, reading my mind. "Not for sale. I received this piece from a very dear friend—I could never, ever part with it." He pointed again, then added, "At least, not for anything less than two thou."

"That all?" I asked. "I thought it would be worth more than that. I've seen some for five."

Wallace sighed. "*Anyway*, Frank, you were saying . . . ?"

"Oh, yes," he said, slipping the lighter back into his pocket. "Frogs."

"What about frogs?" I asked.

"Do you hear them?" Frank said.

"Like . . . right now?"

He rolled his eyes. "No, not at this very moment. One can't hear himself *think* in this noise. I mean, in the quiet. Frogs—they're croaking right beneath my bedroom window. It's somewhat *strange*."

I shook my head. "I'm from L.A. I don't think I'd know what a frog would sound like in real life."

He smirked. "I guess that kind of classification would take imagination."

"Or maybe," I said, "maybe I'm not that shocked animals make noises on islands. That frogs are croaking and birds are chirping and that it's all part of God's great plan." I shrugged, then offered an innocent smile before turning to Wallace and asking, "Where are your other guests?"

"Oh, *that*." Wallace rolled his eyes. "I *did* reach Raul on the radio, and he said that the weather kept them docked. They should all arrive tomorrow morning. So unfortunately, this will be a turnaround trip for them. Of course, I can't call any of them to apologize or to make arrangements for them outside that dreary little town, but they're rich, and some of them are very smart. I'm sure *someone* in the group will figure it all out."

Javier had entered the dining room. He wore a toque on his head and a pristine white chef's smock. He held Desi's elbow and guided her around the appetizers table, and for a second (okay, *many* seconds), I hated him for being with her, for betraying Team Miriam, and my stomach clenched at the thought of him telling her about my discovery in Eddie's bedroom. *Two-faced bastard.* "You see," he was saying to the widow, "the ink from the squid is salty, bringing with it a slight ocean-y taste."

Desi, uninterested in the properties of squid ink or Javier (ha!), kept her gaze tight on Eddie.

Maybe Eddie *left his footprints on my carpet.*

Red Sox had hiked past the swimming pool to reach the edge of the property, a drop-off that ended down,

down, down to the churning sea. He lifted a pair of binoculars with one hand and used the other to touch the butt of his gun *(gun!)*, now stuck in a holster on his hip. He paused in his step, stared out at something in the distance, then lifted the field glasses to study that something in better detail.

I clutched my neck and squeezed. *A gun!* Just like I'd said. I wasn't blind, I wasn't crazy, I knew it!

"Unclench, Miriam," Wallace said with a playful lift of his eyebrow. "Edward is security. The whole world didn't need to know that when you burst into the yacht's living room like Cicely Tyson on fire."

"Is he a police officer back in America?" Frank's question bristled with anxiety.

Wallace nodded. "Back in Boston."

"But what is he securing *right now*?" I couldn't exhale, I couldn't relax. Not with my pulse break-dancing in my chest. "Why do we need security? Are we in danger? This is just a memorial service, isn't it? Or . . ." My breath caught. "Or is this really Felix Escorpion's house?"

Frank said, "Who?"

"The leader of the drug cartel in Puerto Peñasco," I said. "Yesterday, the men back at port, Raul and Andreas, they told me about him and said that Escorpion has marijuana crops and opium poppies all over the island. Andreas said that Escorpion's men killed a bunch of Americans just last week." Or something like that, yeah.

"*What?*" Frank said. "Are you serious? Wallace, you brought us here—?"

"Miriam, dear, you are something else, aren't you?" Wallace sighed heavily, then turned to the banker. "Relax, Frank, and remember who you're talking to." He placed his hands on either side of his mouth, then whispered-called, "Wolf!"

I glared at the old man, then said, "So are you completely bald underneath there or not? Cuz honestly? It looks good. Your wig, I mean. Like ... you're ready to win it all back on a single throw in Monte Carlo. Like ..." I gazed at his hair. "Like ... your client just won the Nobel Prize in poetry but won't attend the acceptance ceremony and so you'll accept the award on his behalf. It's a nice wig. Really, it is. Now, if you'll excuse me." I sat my glass of sparkling water on Wallace's plate, then wandered back to the appetizers table.

You just can't help it, can you? I mentally kicked myself in the head—I'd just jeopardized my future. *Again.* All because I couldn't let shit go. All because I couldn't turn the other cheek. All because I couldn't let *him* win. On the other hand? My dress had loosened a *lot* since I'd gotten all that off my chest. At least.

Evelyn was also scuttling around the hors d'oeuvres table. She'd showered—I smelled soap but also something earthy. Like she had walked through a dairy farm to reach the terrace. She wore that gorgeous turquoise ring, oval cut with a silver band *(According to Aztec legend, the wearer of this ring ...).* It deserved a better hand than Old Goat Eyes.

"Having a good time?" I asked the nurse. "Haven't really seen you all day. Feeling better than last night?"

She groaned as she stared at the strangeness on her plate. "I don't like my food mixing." Her plump thumb was stained black with squid ink, and that purple-black goop had swirled into a dollop of sour cream.

"I hear that's good luck," I said, smiling. "Having ink on your thumb. Either that, or you just voted in Iraq."

"I wanna go home," she said, her eyes shimmering with tears.

"Then go home, Evelyn."

She grimaced at her thumb. "Can you help me? I don't know how."

I shook my head. "Sweetie, this ain't Oz, and I'm not Glinda. Just go to Wallace and tell him to call the boat. I'm sure they'll send somebody to get you. You'll have to wait until the morning, though, because it will probably be the same boat that was supposed to come today. Anyway, just ask Wallace, okay?"

She grunted, then sighed. "Okay." She stared at her thumb. "I don't know how to get this off."

I blinked at her. "Soap. Hot water. A little exertion on your part."

She sighed, then said, "Okay."

What was *wrong* with her? And this woman was a *nurse*?

Wallace and Frank retreated into the house, leaving behind a trail of rich tobacco smoke and arrogance.

I excused myself from Evelyn and followed in their wake. Desi joined me, and our heels clicked in time against the tile. A moment later, the seven of us stood around the table of deadly sins, board game edition. The chandelier and the stained-glass windows made chromatic shadows—crimson and gold and jeweled green and blue—against the walls and hardwood floor. No one spoke—perfect silence until Evelyn crunched a round of sourdough toast.

It was cold in here, and I shivered and wanted to return to the fire pit, my hot Latin lover for the night. "I don't like this . . . this . . . whatever it is." I flicked my hand at the table.

"I don't like that it's sittin' right in the middle of the house," Javier added. "All judgmental and shit. It's like bringing your grandma to a bachelor party at Caesars."

"Phillip always did have a strange taste in art." Wallace picked up the carved piece of a near-naked woman. "Lust." He sat the piece back on its panel, then tapped the green eye piece. "Envy." A man wielding a broadsword: wrath. The fat man eating: gluttony. The sleeping man: sloth. "A dollar sign," Wallace continued, "representing greed. And the mirror is pride."

Eddie snorted. "Today's art lesson brought to you by—"

"People who take shit way too seriously," Javier said.

"Like who?" I asked. "Herbalife salesmen?"

"Hipsters?"

"Wrestling fans?"

We laughed.

"Ladies and gentlemen," Wallace said, "please welcome Mictlan Island's very own comedy troupe—"

"We're just having a laugh, dude," Javier said. "Chillax, baby."

"Laugh if you want," Wallace said. "But if you look close enough . . . *ugh,* I really don't want to, but if you do, you'll see that this diorama reflects who we are: sinners. Take our lovely Mrs. Desi Scoggins, for instance."

Desi threw up her hands and shouted, "*Yes,* take me. Anybody! Take me, please!"

We laughed.

"You're a doll," Wallace said, shaking his head. "Mrs. Scoggins could be . . ." He moved his elegant, manicured finger along the table and stopped at the picnicking couple. But then he kept that finger moving until he plucked the half-naked woman carved piece from the tabletop. "Spooky. Just like that widget on a Ouija board. My finger just stopped at 'lust' and I didn't even tell it to."

I said, "Ha," then said to Desi, "You *are* a lusty so-and-so, even with clothes on."

Desi wiggled her nose. "You know it, girlie. I'm always butt naked in my heart." To everyone else, she said, "And I'm handing out free samples this coming Tuesday." Then she shimmied and bit her lip.

Frank chuckled. Eddie rolled his eyes.

"Mrs. Scoggins here was married up until . . ." Wallace squinted at the figurine. "I know it was a difficult time for you, but when did Larry die, dear?"

Desi blinked at him, then said, "It'll be a year in September."

Frank touched her elbow. "Oh, how awful. Heart attack?"

"No. Well, kinda. He had a bad allergic reaction to something." Her face flushed. Tension had tightened her twang—she almost sounded like a damn Yankee.

"Nuts," Wallace said with a nod. "In his mouth. Not being crude, but . . ." He chuckled, shrugged, then said, "Am I right, dear?"

Desi tried to smile at me. "See, we were hunkered down during a storm. There was a blackout, so we couldn't see nothing in the house. And earlier that day, I'd brought these cookies home—the girl at work had made 'em—and I hid 'em up on top of the fridge so that Larry wouldn't see them, cuz he was allergic to nuts. But with the blackout . . . I don't know how he found the tub, but he scarfed down seven cookies before realizing . . ." Her breath caught in her throat and her chin trembled.

I gasped. "Did you call 911?"

She shook her head. "With the storm, there weren't no emergency services makin' calls."

"And he died?" Javier asked.

Desi nodded, then swiped at her eyes. Her *dry* eyes.

"And here you are," Wallace said, slowly shaking his head. "Almost a year later and two hundred pounds lighter. I must say, death is the most effective diet available today."

"It's been nine months, to be precise, so he ain't *just* died," Desi spat. "I'm twenty-eight years old—I'm not ready to lock myself away in a creaky house with a thousand cats and never come out again. I'm too young to be a widow for the rest of my life." She looked back at me and said, "I'm living with my mistake—I shouldn't have brought them cookies into the house. They were just so damned delicious, and that's just me being greedy. Every day, though, I think about Larry and I wish . . . I wish . . . I miss him. I truly miss that man."

Eddie snorted, said, "Uh-huh, okay," then rolled his eyes.

Frank squeezed Desi's shoulder. "But Wallace, how does that make her a sinner? It was an innocent, and yes, imprudent error on her part, but a sinner all because her husband snuck and ate something he shouldn't have eaten?"

The older man shrugged. "Well . . ." He set the figurine back on the table. "Strange how those damn-delicious nutty cookies just . . . *happened* to be in the house right before one of the worst tropical storms in years. So . . . *strange*." He clamped his thin lips together to suppress a smile.

Oh, *snap*. He'd just accused Desi of murder.

"The D.A.," Desi said, "he couldn't prosecute me. *Wouldn't* prosecute me, since they didn't have a case. They couldn't prove that I tried to kill my husband, and so Phillip told 'em all to go straight to hell."

"*Tried* to kill your husband?" Eddie chuckled. "Waddaya, *stupid*? You *did* kill your husband. He's dead. In my business, that's what we call a 'clue.'"

Desi's face twisted, and she shouted, "I'm innocent, you small-dicked *bastard,* and I didn't come all the way here"—she turned to glare at Wallace—"to be accused of some bullshit I didn't do. Phillip knew how much I loved Danny, and he convinced everybody in the world that I loved that man to death." She pointed at Wallace with a trembling finger. "And if you're gonna keep bullying me and Miriam here, I'm gonna leave this island and tell the world how you bullied the lot of us when we're supposed to be mourning. You hear me, you mouthy old queen?"

Wallace blinked those cold lavender eyes at his newest target. "Just being honest, my dear. Sue me for slander. See you in court—you know where it is, correct? Oh, by the way, your dead husband's name was Larry. You loved *Larry* to death, not *Danny*."

I covered my mouth with a fist to hide a grin and stifle my laughter.

Eddie snorted. "Well, goddamn."

A twisted smile crept across Wallace's tanned face. "So, shall we eat?"

15

Shall we eat?

Wallace said this as though he hadn't just demolished a young widow by accusing her of killing her husband. But then, some people get very hungry after stomping someone else's head and heart until there's nothing but bloody pulp left on their shoes.

Shall we eat?

I said, "Yes, let's eat. *Please.*" A wonderful suggestion.

Still: poor Desi. We had just discovered that America's *sweetheart*, that America's *darling*, had come to Mictlan Island under a cloud of suspicion—and had just called her husband by some other man's name. And now her face had crumpled, and she was seconds from sobbing.

"I know his name," she whispered. "His *nick*name was Danny, and sometimes . . . sometimes . . . I know his name."

"It's okay, Dez." I hooked my arm through hers and whispered, "Remember why you're here. All for Phillip. Ignore Wallace. When it's time, we'll snatch his wig together."

She looked at me with pleading blue eyes. "You believe me, don't you?"

I nodded—a lie. This bitch had killed her husband and had probably slept around on him with some dude named Danny. I knew that like I knew Wallace Zavarnella was as bald as a buzzard beneath his wig. Arm in arm, I strolled beside Desi into the dining room. "I'm sure whatever happened on that awful night was an accident. I'm sure that Larry wants you to be happy."

She waggled her head. "He should've controlled himself—he wasn't supposed to be having sweets no way. That's why he was sneaking, not wanting me to catch him."

I said, "Um-hmm," then offered her an understanding smile. "You're here now, Desi, and I'm *positive* that Larry's up in heaven, wishing you were up there with him. Honestly: we all go a little mad sometimes."

She beamed. "Not you, girlie. I don't think you've *ever* lost control."

I threw my head back and laughed. "Desi, sweetie, I lost it right before I came here."

"Yeah?" Her eyes bugged. "What happened?"

"Thursday night," I said, "these assholes started egging my house." One part of their psych-ops plan to play with my head, to force me to go crazy. The FBI had "These Boots Are Made for Walking" and the squeals and squeaks of dying rabbits, and my bullies had . . . eggs.

Desi frowned and said, "Eggs? That's so hokey."

"Right? What is this, *Happy Days*? So once I thought they were gone and it was safe to go out, I went to look at the damage."

I'd tripped over the open suitcase on my way to check for damage. Sharpness had shot from my toes and seared a path up my calf. But I kept telling myself not to cry, that it was okay, that I was okay. I'd called out to Morgan. "Do you hear that?" But she didn't respond because she now lived full-time with Billy. I stood there, alone, holding my gun, surrounded by new furniture that my daughter would never sit on, standing in front of a television with a remote she'd never hog, frozen in between soft gray walls that she hadn't helped paint. *It's okay, I'm okay.*

"So I opened my front door," I continue, "and I'm holding Ripley—"

"Who's Ripley?" Desi asked.

"My twenty-two." Phillip had suggested the gun kind of casually, very 'Next time you're at the store, you may wanna pick up some toothpaste, coffee, and oh, get a gun.' So, I'd found You Gun, Girl, a store that specialized in women's defense, and purchased a twenty-two that I named after the heroine in the *Alien* series. Weird—I'd never been a gun type. I'd never wanted to buy a gun or even *shoot* a gun, but there I was, gun in hand, ready to blow somebody's head off.

"So I opened the door," I said now to Desi, "and this female shouts, 'This is for Brooke, *bitch*.'"

"Who's Brooke?" Desi asked.

I fluttered my hand at her. "My daughter's friend. Stop interrupting. So the female shouts, 'This is for Brooke, *bitch*.'"

And then something hard had struck my belly.

I'd gasped and grabbed my abdomen. Wetness oozed between my fingers. Ice-cold panic shut down white-hot rage. *Am I bleeding? Am I gonna die today?* I slipped in something wet and slick, and stumbled off the porch. The gun flew out of my hand and landed in the brown grass. My bare feet slid in more goop on the pavement. Something hit my arm. Something else struck my head.

More eggs. "Dripping from my hair, my neck and hands. My car alarm was going off cuz they'd thrown eggs at my car, too."

"Oh, no," Desi said, shaking her head. "No, no, no."

The alarm, the whispering and laughing, the sound of eggshells cracking against my property . . . Too much. Psych-ops were working.

"Splat splat, splat splat splat . . . Five eggs. Then ten eggs . . . and then I lost count."

"So what did you do?" Desi asked.

"I slipped on the ground, right? And then, *pow!* A kick. Sparks fly from my wrist to my shoulders, up to my ears and jaw . . . Then I laughed and I looked up at her and I said, 'You kick like a girl.'"

Desi giggled, then froze. "A *teenager* is doing this? *Kicking* you?"

I smiled and nodded. "Her name's Prudence, if you can believe that." Annoying ombre black-black and blue hair. Doc Martens boots. Nose ring. "But I'm not letting *Pru* get away with it, so I hopped up from the ground and I rushed her from behind. Knocked her to the ground, and her head hits the sidewalk. I pick up a rock, one of those fancy ones that line your garden, and I threw it at her boyfriend's Range Rover. I missed the window but hit the passenger-side door."

Desi gasped and covered her mouth with her hands. "You hit anybody?"

"Nuh-uh."

"And then?"

I pulled Desi closer, then said, "And then I grabbed another rock and I stood over her. And then I growled something Clint Eastwood-y, like, 'Come here again and I'll shove this rock down your throat.' Then I pretended that I was gonna throw the rock at her head. But I didn't."

I'd already prepared for this night by purchasing a video surveillance system. The moment Prudence had stepped onto my property, her fate had been sealed by three HD cameras. "And I had proof that she came to my house to harass me and to destroy my property."

Desi gaped at me in awe. "Why did she come? Why did she do this?

"Jealousy. Pure spite. They hate me and they especially hate my daughter."

Desi touched my shoulder and squeezed. "I'm so

sorry, girlie. And what the heck kinda name is 'Prudence' anyway?"

"I know, right?" I shrugged. "But I'm feeling much better now."

Thursday night, though, pain and humiliation had nearly crippled me. Yeah, I was feeling much better now, and I blinked back tears and smiled at Desi. "Don't know about you, but I'm hungry." *It's okay, I'm okay.* My mantra as Desi and I strolled into the dining room and joined Evelyn and the men. And I *would* be okay, once I learned my fate after Phillip's memorial service.

Desi's eyes widened as she took in the dining room. "This is just . . . two words. Gor. Jus."

The floor-to-ceiling windows looked out to dark woods—until all of it flashed white. A far-off soft rumble followed.

I stopped in my steps. "You guys just see that?"

No one else reacted to the weather. Only the woman from Los Angeles, where there were short-run, limited series' worth of weather. Thunder, lightning, rain were all guest stars. Winds—we did those. Fires and earthquakes, too. But this stuff outside? The flashing? The rumbling? Breaking news territory.

Another flash of uncontrolled electricity whitewashed the sky.

"It's just some rain on its way, girlie," Desi said. "It'll be over before it starts."

She was right—*relax, girl.* I caught my wan reflection in a large mirror hung on the northern wall. A rectangle-framed map of the world hung on the opposite wall. Bottles of bourbon and cognac sat alongside vases of peach roses on a buffet beneath the map. A three-tiered wedding-cake-styled crystal chandelier hung over the center of the blond-wood dining room table. More vases of peach roses served as centerpieces.

"It's like the dining room on a Disney cruise," Desi said. "Kinda reminds me of *Beauty and the Beast*."

The room was posh. Elegant, yes. But magical? Not so much. But whatever, she needed this, she needed enchantment, and so I said, "Just like it."

Desi pressed her hand to her chest. "Reminds me of my honeymoon cruise with *Larry*. Oh, *Larry*." She dabbed at her dry eyes again. "Oh, poor, sweet *Larry*."

Uh-huh.

Place cards told us where we would be seated for the evening. There were also gorgeous wineglasses etched with our names. I was assigned to the end of the table, with Desi to my right and Evelyn to my left, lording over an intellectual vacuum that rivaled *Jackass* and *Three's Company*. Wallace sat at the opposite end with Frank on his left and an empty chair on his right. There'd be better conversation down that way—more important, that side was closer to the roaring fireplace and farther from the cold draft now stinging my bare legs. I shivered.

"I'm cold, too," Desi said, rubbing her arms. "I think it's coming off the windows."

Eddie, standing at the windows, peered out to the dark wild. Moths the size of pteranodons had discovered the lights of Artemis and now beat against the windowpanes.

I tilted my head and listened . . . yeah. "You hear that? Sounds like squeaking."

"They're screaming," Evelyn muttered.

"Who's screaming?" I asked.

"The moths outside," she said. "They're death's-head hawkmoths. They're called that because they have marks shaped like skulls on their . . ." She bit and twisted her lips.

"On their *what*?" Desi asked. "Their furry little bottoms?" She giggled.

"On their thoraxes," Evelyn mumbled as she futzed with her turquoise ring. "They know a storm's coming."

"Edward," Wallace said, breaking the uncomfortable silence, "there's no Mexican cartel bursting through the doors tonight. Just a storm. And unless you're a god, there's nothing you can do about that. Please. Come join us. I'm sure you have great stories to tell. Hopefully, one about a hooker, a kitchen knife, and a can of motor oil."

"Very funny." Eddie marched to the table, then dropped into the empty seat with his jaw tight and his eyes trained on the windows. He was a red-faced, unsmiling man, the Mean Ex-Boyfriend who didn't cuddle, who didn't coo, who never told you that you *had* lost some weight. He was the Mean Ex-Boyfriend who always threatened that if he couldn't have you . . .

He met my eyes with his own hard blue ones. "You need something?"

I smiled, shook my head. "Just waiting to hear the story about the hooker."

"Not in the mood," he grumbled.

I said, "Okay," then turned to Desi, who was now dumping spoonfuls of sugar into her iced tea. I pointed at the blue gems in her ears. "Did Larry give you those?"

She touched her left earlobe, then shook her head. "Nuh-uh. My boyfriend Hoyt did. When he went over to Irahland, he picked them up. I know what you're thinking, and stop it right now. Me and Hoyt met during a *church* camp meeting and it was *strictly* platonic at first because I was still married."

"I thought you and Larry were deeply in love," I asked, squinting at her.

"We were, but like every relationship, we had our rough spots."

"How long were you married?"

"Two years. Anyway: me and Hoyt, see, we have so many things in common and he thought I was just about the smartest woman in West Virginia, and that made me feel so good, and I needed that at the moment, but anyway. Hoyt and me, we'd text and we'd email each other all day, you know, sending jokes and news stories back and forth, stuff like that.

"He'd take me to real nice lunches—he's wealthy. His family owns one of the last coal mines right outside of town. And they're turning it into a *clean* coal mine, so that's exciting. Well, finally, after all that, courting you could say, he asked me to go away with him one weekend. I just about lost my mind when he asked me."

I hid a yawn behind my hand. "Uh-huh."

"And he didn't wanna take me just anywhere. He wanted to take me to Newport News. So I said yes, and ohmygosh, lemme tell you—" She dropped her voice and leaned in close to me. "I have never been *touched* like that in all my life. And he touched me like that all weekend, and when he wasn't touching me, he was feeding me lobster and pouring me champagne."

Desi's eyes became dewy as her face flushed with Hoyt memories. "For a country girl, it was mind-blowing, but the weekend ended as weekends do, and we had to go back to our lives, and Larry didn't suspect a thing, not that me and Hoyt made love, cuz we didn't that weekend, that was later, cuz I still loved Larry with all my heart, but . . ." She tapped her earlobe again. "Hoyt sent me these the next week after our getaway with a note that said, 'Your eyes are more beautiful than these sapphires.'"

"Sapphires?" I laughed, shook my head, then laughed louder.

Desi's smile faltered. "I know—it's a little corny but it was sweet."

I caught my breath, then touched her wrist. "I hate to break this to you, *girlie,* but those rocks in your ears? They aren't sapphires. They're not even rocks. I can see all the lines and bubbles from here."

Her smile brightened, just as stars brighten when they're about to explode. "You're just joshin' with me."

I feigned a smile. "If that's what you wanna believe."

She wiggled her nose and rolled her eyes. But her hand brushed her earlobe again, then twisted the earring there, paused, twisted again, then that hand dropped back into her lap.

Fakes. She knew. A woman *always* knew.

The world beyond the windows flashed white again, and the chandelier's lights flickered. I counted to three before an earsplitting clap of thunder took my breath away.

Desi found a smile and tapped my hand, now clenched around a knife. She whispered, "Relax, girlie. This ain't hardly bad. I've seen worse, believe me."

Raindrops hit like BBs against the windowpane. First the moths came, then rogue electricity, and now rain. Would the glass hold?

Javier carried two bottles of white wine into the dining room. "I am pleased to share with you . . ." He filled Wallace's glass first. "A 2014 Chateau de Tracy Sauvignon." He sounded so professional, so responsible. Not high. Not drunk.

I leaned over to Evelyn and whispered, "I hope he cooked something *edible* for dinner. I don't know what the hell kind of appetizers were crawling in those bowls at the reception."

Wallace lifted his *Wallace* wineglass, swirled it, sniffed it, sniffed it again, peered closely at the pale golden liquid. Then he sipped, closed his eyes, smiled, nodded. "Reminds me of Central Park, summer of '83, Diana Ross in the rain. With Phillip. Our first concert together. We fell in love—"

"Hold up." Eddie blinked as his face reddened. "You and Phil . . . Phil was *gay*?"

I squinted at him. "Where the hell have *you* been?"

Wallace shook his head in awe. "What gave it away, Edward? Diana Ross? Or my impeccable table manners that require that I not ask my guests who they prefer to love?"

No one spoke as Wallace's eyes beat down Eddie's. "And once again, I question Phillip's loyalty to his clients."

Javier poured wine into the cop's glass, then Frank's.

I leaned over to Desi and whispered, "And the men get wine before us because *why* again?"

Javier trundled down to our side of the table. "Miriam?"

I nodded. "Yes, please."

Desi accepted wine, but Evelyn covered her glass with a hand and said, "I don't drink." Then she grabbed her *Evelyn* wineglass and pushed away from the table. "Maybe there's juice in the fridge."

No one responded. No one cared.

"I was just shocked, is all, Wallace," Eddie explained. "Some of my best friends—"

"Are gay?" Wallace asked in a bored voice.

"Hell, no," Eddie said. "Not in *my* neighborhood. They jack up gays where I'm from. They're cops now and their beats are in the South End, where all the gays hang out. You been there?"

Wallace squinted at the cop. "You are something else, Edward. Truly."

The rain was now falling steadily, and every time the world flashed white, I glimpsed trees bending and swaying, weak as dandelions against the gusts of wind.

I sipped from my *Miriam* glass—and like Wallace, I closed my eyes as the wine filled my mouth and slipped down my throat. It was the best I'd ever tasted. Apricots and pistachio and autumn, not summer. Not Diana Ross. No. Michael Jackson. *Bad.* 1987.

"Where can I purchase a few cases of this?" Frank asked. "I don't care about the price."

"Later, Franklin." Wallace lifted his glass. "First, let's toast to the man who has, for some strange reason, brought us all together—"

Glass shattered in the kitchen. A woman screamed.

Eddie jumped up from his seat and left the dining room table before anyone else could even stand.

Another scream.

Frank raced out of the room.

Desi darted from the table.

Was Escorpion here?

I, too, scurried to the kitchen to see Evelyn crouched on a barstool next to the breakfast counter now crammed with plates holding our first course. The tendons in her neck pushed against her skin. Her wild eyes and crazy hair reminded me of—

"Snake!" Evelyn screamed, pointing at the floor.

A tan snake with brown and gray splotches lay coiled beside a discarded Chiquita box near the freezer door. Shards of Evelyn's broken wineglass had landed on the creature's skin, making it sparkle.

What happened next happened quickly. A cleaver, a *WHAM!*, a chopped-off head, Eddie's hand, blood spatter, dead snake.

"Dude," Javier barked at Eddie, "you take that from my chopping block?"

Evelyn's knees buckled and she crumpled on the stool.

Frank caught her before she fell to the floor. "Somebody help me," he said, his face strained.

Eddie dropped the bloody cleaver onto the counter, then raced to catch Evelyn.

"Where should we take her?" Frank asked.

"Back to the dining room."

As Frank and Eddie carried the fainting nurse away, Javier glared at the snake corpse left on the tiled floor.

The storm sounded louder in here, with all the tile and stainless steel. Sheets of rainwater washed down the windows. Another flash of white caused the lighting to flicker.

I whispered, "No, no, please stay on," to the dimming lights.

"Ohmygosh," Desi said, fanning her face. "How did a snake even get in here?"

"Maybe it was in the banana box," I said. "Maybe it was hiding and then came out once the house got quiet again."

"Poor snake," Desi said. "It didn't hurt anybody."

"You need help cleaning?" I asked Javier.

"Nope. I've cleaned up worse." He smiled at me. "Don't be surprised, though, if you see this fucker in your frisée salad tomorrow night."

"Ha." I tried to grin, but part of me knew that he was serious.

He waved us off. "Go. Sit. It'll take me a minute to clean up the glass and the freakin' dead animal, but I'll have the first course out as soon as possible."

Desi let out a long sigh. "I think I need that wine right about now."

I gave her a lopsided grin. "Between the snake and the storm, I need *all* of the wine."

Lightning flashed. Thunder boomed. The kitchen went black—but only for a second—and then the lights popped back.

"Everybody okay?" Eddie called out.

I stood there, frozen and tense.

Desi smiled and shouted, "We're just fine!" She tugged my arm. "C'mon, girlie. Let's get you all the wine in the world."

Together, we returned to the dining room table.

Evelyn, flushed and flustered, was already seated in her place. Frank and Eddie, both sweating now, stood at the windows. Wallace hadn't moved from his seat and was now pouring more wine into his glass.

"I don't like snakes," Evelyn mumbled. "They scare me. They can kill you. They move so quickly. I was so scared. And I broke my glass. I was so scared."

She was stuck, poor thing, and I felt sorry for her. So I went over to the buffet and opened a bottle of bourbon. I filled a short tumbler with the brown stuff and thrust the glass at the terrified woman. "It'll help."

As she gulped, her skin reddened and the muttering about snakes and the trembling of her hands stopped.

"Is that better?" Desi asked.

Evelyn nodded—her goat eyes were clear. She patted her frizzy hair, then said, "I just wanted juice. I didn't mean to cause a commotion."

I waved my hand. "Whatever. I'm ready to eat."

Settled into our seats, we waited for the first course in between cracks of thunder and flashes of lightning. For the first time, Artemis was too warm and too stuffy for me, even with its high ceilings and windows. For the first time since stepping across the house's threshold, sweat pricked at my skin.

"Everybody okay?" Eddie asked again, breaking the quiet.

"Yes."

"Not really." (That was me.)

"Crazy night."

"Did you still wanna toast?" Desi asked. "In honor of Phillip?"

Wallace, hand covering his mouth, gave a curt shake of his head. "Later. This dinner party makes me want to take up smoking Parliament Lights again."

"Maybe you and Phillip should've chosen a less . . . rural location," I said.

"Says the woman who owns how many pieces of property?" Wallace asked. "Oh. Wait. None. And not that I owe you any explanation, but we *do* own homes in less rural areas. Artemis is just Phillip's favorite. This was his last trip abroad—he and our friend Seth spent days putting on the final touches."

"And you stayed home?" Frank asked.

Wallace nodded. "I was in the middle of treatment—I could barely travel to the bathroom without needing to vomit."

Desi giggled. "You let your man come to a romantic island with somebody else?"

Wallace sipped from his wineglass. "I admit that I was a *little* jealous at first. But I also knew Phillip—he didn't want to deal with my temper, first of all. And second, he wouldn't have had this beautiful estate without me."

"In other words," Desi said, "he knew which side his bread was buttered on?"

Wallace gave her a thumbs-up.

"But you kicked off the people who used to live here," I said.

Wallace rolled his eyes. "Again with that? It's how the rich stay rich, my dear. The mall that you enjoy on the first and fifteenth of every month? Someone used to live there. People like me gave you that Dress Barn and Payless shoe store. You're welcome."

Something flared in me, and I was moments away from blasting like a volcano and busting every window in that mansion. My mouth opened, but Javier bustled into the dining room. The fire in me died some, but I still felt its burn deep in my gut.

"Here we go!" He carried a tray arranged with the six small multicolored plates that had been sitting on the counter. "Our first course," he said, setting a plate before each of us. "Fugu sashimi with a citrus sauce."

Like the wineglasses, each plate had been personalized with our first name's initial scripted in gold across the surface. Our entire names had been printed in a smaller font alongside the date. They were plates you'd give as a wedding present to the happy couple or make for your child's first birthday party. And now, I guess, plates you'd purchase to commemorate a fancy dinner party on a private Mexican island. My *M* plate was sea foam green, and if I hadn't known, today was July 10. Adorable.

So. Fugu sashimi. The near-translucent fish flesh had been arranged into tissue-thin flower petals. A dollop of orange sauce sat in the middle of the arrangement and was surrounded by pink orchids.

"Javi," I barked, "what *is* this?"

The chef rubbed his hands together. "*This,* Miss Miriam, is the spotted sharpnose pufferfish. While it's not from Japan, this fish is the same as the Japanese puffer but caught out there." He pointed to the windows and the ocean beyond. "Mar de Cortés."

Frank plucked his orchids from his yellow *F* plate and set them on the linen napkin. "Is this the fish that can kill you if the chef doesn't prepare it properly?"

Javier clapped his hands. "Yes! Because of the tetrodotoxin in the liver and ovaries. So you're familiar with it?"

"I've traveled to Japan countless times," Frank said. "I'm close friends with bankers over in Tokyo who order it incessantly. Not for the faint of heart or the wallet, about $150 for an ounce." To the rest of us, Frank said, "To even *cut* fugu requires special knowledge and unique certification. I hope Mr. Cardoza here continues in this tradition of excellence in preparation, or this may be all of our last meals."

Frank, Wallace, and Javier laughed. Desi wanted to laugh, too, and her mouth lifted and fell, lifted and fell again because she didn't understand the joke. Finally, she simply smiled and twirled one of the orchids from her navy blue *D* plate beneath her nose.

I got the joke—not funny—and I folded my arms. "I'm not eating it."

"She doesn't put strange meat in her mouth," Wallace said. *"Anymore."*

"Ha, that's funny," Desi said, cackling.

"C'mon, Miriam," Javier said, smiling. "I've done this a million times. There's nothing to fear."

"Oh, no?" Wallace asked, lifting his wineglass. "Is that what you told Mr. Humphries right before he died in your restaurant?"

Javier's face darkened. "He didn't eat any fugu."

"Dead, dead, dead," Wallace said. "But what did you tell the world after he'd died, Javier? 'I didn't make him order it'?" The old man sipped from his glass, squinted at the chef, then said, "What? Did I say something . . . *offensive* again? Did I misquote you?" Wallace faked horror. "Oh, dear. Was I supposed to keep that secret? That Mr. Humphries died in your restaurant after eating something you prepared?"

With fake cheer, Javier said, "Fuck you very much, sir. Now, drop dead." He smiled at me. "Miriam, it's all good. Trust me. It's . . . Here, look."

Javier grabbed my fork, then jabbed a slice of fish from my plate. "In Japan," he said, "the chef is supposed to taste the fish to make sure it's safe for diners to eat. As a show of confidence, you know?" He dipped the fish in the citrus sauce and popped it in his mouth. "It's delicious. Oh, man. It's like heaven. Ooh . . . here it comes, the best part. The numbing effect. It's—" His face flushed, and his grin widened.

"It's *what*?" I asked.

"Is it normal," Desi asked, "that you're turning the color of strawberries?"

Javier nodded. "Mm-hm."

"Your face . . ." I said.

Javier's face tightened. Then the muscles in his face twitched. Tight. Twitch. Tight. Twitch. Uncertainty in his eyes—*what's going on, am I okay, is this normal, why?*—bloomed like a drop of blood in water.

Eddie said, "He doesn't look . . ."

Javier dropped the fork and slapped at his mouth. "My lip . . . tingle . . ." He lurched forward and an orange sea of vomit splattered on glasses and plates.

I hopped out of my seat and shouted, "No!"

Desi shrieked.

Javier slumped into my chair, and that twitching and stiffening in his pallid face moved down to his arms and his hands. His lips were puckering like a fish out of water, and he grabbed at his chest and clutched at his throat.

"Somebody do something," Desi squawked.

Lightning flashed. The chandelier lights dimmed— and this time, they didn't brighten again. Thunder boomed and all that energy razzed across my cheeks.

Javier's eyes glittered even as they rolled to the top of his head. Then his eyes crossed, squeezed shut, then repeated that cycle again and again.

My mind raced—*do something, save him, call the police, help him, Jesus, help him, is this happening, is he dying, help him*—but I couldn't move. I couldn't speak, even though there was so much to say. But my throat had closed and tightened and I couldn't . . .

Frank had also pushed away from the dining room table. "Is he . . . ? You okay, Javi?"

Javier didn't respond. His lips and throat kept making that suctioning pop-pop-pop sound as he gasped for air. His eyes kept glittering and rolling and squeezing shut.

The lights above us dimmed more, like the light found in romantic restaurants. But this was not romantic. Not with Javier's lips popping like that. Not with his breath pitching higher and higher and higher until . . .

Until there were no more high breaths and no more popping lips.

Excerpted from the *Las Vegas Review-Journal*
Thursday, January 3

CUSTOMER DIES OF STROKE
AT B.I.G. IN VEGAS

. . . Cardoza is the executive chef and owner of B.I.G., located off the Strip and known for excess in portion and exotic offerings.

"I didn't make him order it," Cardoza said. "He's a grown man. And I didn't tell him to eat the whole thing. Where does personal responsibility come in?"

Mr. Peter Humphries, 66, of Brooklyn, NY, suffered a stroke on January 2 after consuming a four-patty burger that also boasted smoked oysters, elk pastrami, twelve slices of Muenster cheese and two fried ostrich eggs stacked between two thick slices of Texas toast coated in Brie cheese.

Humphries is the second diner to die after a meal at B.I.G. In November, Rita Swanson, 70, died of a heart attack . . .

TWISTED

16

"Ohmygosh, ohmygosh," Desi kept saying. Her face had turned the color of marble.

"This isn't happening," Wallace, also pale, whispered. "This can't be happening."

"Do something," I was screaming. "Somebody do something. Help him."

Eddie said nothing, just dashed over to Javier, whose smock and face were soaking in a pool of vomit. He unloosened the buttons on the dying chef's top and then pinched Javier's nose. Just as he bent to place his mouth over Javier's, Evelyn scrambled over and yanked the first responder by his collar. The tendons in her neck were bulging as she yelled, "Don't do that!"

Eddie pushed her and shouted, "Get away!"

"He has poison on his lips, idiot!" Evelyn hollered back. "You'll die!"

Eddie's eyes bugged as he stared down at Javier's blue face. "But . . . he's . . . but . . ." Those same bugged eyes glazed as he realized that he couldn't safely save Javier from dying. And his excited breath left his body and his shoulders slumped just like his spirit.

"We should . . ." I swallowed, blinked, blinked again. "We have to do something. We have to call someone, call the police or . . . or . . ."

No one moved or attempted to save Javier Cardoza. Peppered around the dining room, we gaped at the chef's lifeless body now collapsed upon the dining room table. A sob burst from my chest as the shock of his violent end crashed into me. Dead, all because of fish? Fish that had been arranged like a flower on my M plate? Dead because he hadn't cut the fish right? Fish that I could've eaten? Fish that could've killed me? Realizing that death had been inches from my lips . . . dark spots swirled in between unfallen tears. And my chest . . . like my lungs were being squeezed between a vise and . . . *Dead right now—I could be dead right now.*

Desi hid her face in Frank's chest and keened like an abandoned cocker spaniel. Her sadness and snot soon covered the front of his guayabera.

Wallace had frozen in his chair. His hands gripped the arms so tightly that his knuckles looked like veiny quartz.

Meanwhile, silver rain beaded and trickled down the windowpanes, and expensive wine from our knocked-over personalized glasses trickled off the table and onto the carpet. Javier's last meal flecked the ivory chairs and the ivory tablecloth, hardening there, hell to scrub out. Only the vases of peach roses had remained unspoiled and upright.

Eddie had to do *something,* so he lifted Javier's wrist and placed his thumb against the chef's pulse point. He shook his head, more to himself than to us, then reached into his cargo shorts for a penlight. He shone light in Javier's right eye, then his left. Eddie shook his head again, then muttered, "Shit."

Lightning flashed on cue beyond the forest and thunder pounded the earth. Those screaming death's-head hawkmoths kept throwing themselves against the windows.

Desi blew her nose into a napkin, then muttered, "I'm not hungry anymore."

"Someone has to clean this up," Frank declared.

No one offered.

Eddie searched Javier's pockets and found the dead man's silver pill case. He opened the top, and white powder sparkled like magical fairy dust.

"What's that?" Desi asked, squinting.

"Cocaine," I said.

"How do you know?" she asked.

"Cuz he offered me some. Because *duh*."

Eddie dipped his pinky finger into the powder, then tasted it. "Yeah, it's coke. Bozo."

"Probably why he died so quickly," Frank said. "Not that he looked terribly healthy in the first place."

Eddie grunted, then pocketed the blow.

"We can't leave him here," Wallace said, finally speaking, finally releasing his death grip from the chair. "The heat will get him."

There was heat? For me, everything in this room had turned to ice again—flatware and wineglasses, the chandelier and the windows. All of it threatened frostbite and hypothermia, and I couldn't stop shivering.

Frank lifted Javier's feet while Eddie hooked his hands beneath the dead man's armpits.

"Please be careful with him," I said, tears welling in my eyes.

Eddie scowled. "Or, what? We'll break something? Too late."

I glared at him. "Not tonight, Satan. Not tonight."

Eddie flushed with shame. "We'll take him to the cellar. Or maybe the freezer—yeah, he'll be good there until the Mexican police come."

"So you're gonna call the police?" I asked.

Eddie said, "Yep."

"Will they come tonight?" I asked.

"Don't know. Probably not with the storm."

"Is it—?"

"Miriam," Eddie interrupted, "I don't know what's in your left pocket, and I don't know what number you're thinking, okay? Stop asking questions that I ain't got answers for, all right? Can we put him somewhere now?"

My mouth snapped shut, and I nodded.

Then, the two men duckwalked out of the dining room. Their shoes clomped in different rhythms as they carried the near-three-hundred-pound man to the kitchen.

Weeping again, Desi plopped back into her chair. Rings of sweat now darkened the underarms of her no-longer-perfect dress. Her hair had spiraled out of control, and her cries grew louder as if trying to force someone to console her. *Aw-roo! Aw-roo!* On and on, louder and louder. *Aw-roo! Aw-roo!*

All of it made my head ache and my eyes heavy. I heard my patience rip like new fabric, and I snapped, "Will you shut up?"

She froze in mid-*Aw-roo* and blinked at me. My words had been a rolled newspaper to her wet nose.

And for a moment, Artemis sank again into perfect peace.

"I didn't mean to . . ." I said to Desi. "It's just . . . This is . . ."

"I'll go get some paper towels and cleaner," Desi said stiffly.

"I'll join you," Wallace said, tottering behind her.

I stared at that large map on the wall and wished to be anywhere else but here. Then I glanced at Evelyn—she had quietly returned to her place at the table and was now chewing. Some of the pufferfish petals on her baby blue *E* plate were missing.

"Are you actually *eating* that?" I asked. "You're eating that *fish*?"

Her lips thinned as she stopped chewing. She waited a beat, swallowed whatever she'd been eating, then whispered, "I'm hungry." Her thick neck quivered.

Icy tears, not out of sorrow but from disgust, slipped down my cheeks. "You just saw him eat that shit and *die*. You have a death wish or something?"

"No."

"He didn't cut it right, Evelyn," I shouted.

She offered the weakest shrug in the history of shrugs.

"Why are you eating that?" I shouted again. "I don't understand. Help me understand." Because I *didn't* understand—unless she was eating the fish because she *wanted* to die. "Don't you *smell* that? Who can eat with . . . with . . . *vomit* everywhere? With freakin' *puke* all over the place?"

She dropped her gaze to the table. "I'm a nurse. The smell doesn't bother me."

"The 'killing Javier' thing—does *that* bother you? What about the 'he cut this shit wrong' thing—you're cool with that?" Her words had made me even colder and angrier, and every inch of my skin numbed. And my dress squeezed me, and I couldn't breathe, and worse than that, some of Javier's vomit had splattered onto my grosgrain bow. "Why didn't *you* try to save him?" I demanded to know now. "*You're* the nurse. Weren't *you* the one who was supposed to do CPR?"

"Good questions, Miriam." Wallace had returned to the dining room. He held a roll of paper towels in his hands, flawless yet fragile looking in his suit. His eyes were still sharp and a haughty mauve. "She *is* a nurse," he continued, ripping off sheets from the towel roll as if it had stolen something. He was smiling but he didn't mean it, not by the way he was strangling and snatching those paper towels. "Of course, she's killed just about every patient she's ever cared for," he said. "The cute little lady who collected teapots but couldn't remember her first name but somehow remembered Evelyn's name in her will. The other cute little old lady who owned mineral rights to a turquoise mine. And then there's the little old lady who wasn't cute at all, but was smart enough to hide a cheap video camera in a flower pot in her bedroom, which caught our nurse here and her secret needle poking air bubbles into the IV lines."

"IV . . . ?" I said to him. "How do you know about that? Who *are* you?"

"A Taurus," Wallace said, his eyes sharp as a razor blade. "A Democrat. Lover of sea salts from Provence and leather shoes from New England. I was also Phillip's confidant and confessor." He glanced at me and my skin chilled as though he'd cut me with just that look. "He told me everything as he lay dying, as he asked his Maker for forgiveness, especially"—he turned those glinting eyes back to Evelyn—"for defending *you*."

He tsked, then shook his head. "Poor, *stupid* Phillip. He just kept saving our nurse here, time and time again. We'd argue about the rest of you, but Nursie-Nurse here brought out the worst in both of us. Didn't know *why* he did, but he and I would fight about Nurse Pemstein at least three times a month. No matter—he's dead and she's still here, and her R.N. certification is *still* . . . valid. Unless New Mexico has finally taken *that* away from you. Have they, dear?" he asked. His grin turned into a sneer.

Evelyn sensed the danger. With raw-looking fingers, she tore at a hole in her sleeve with nails that had already been chewed down to the skin. "I didn't want Eddie to die touching Javier's . . . He could've died from the poison . . . Doesn't matter anyway—he's dead." Then she stared at me with those stupid goat eyes and breathed her raspy breath.

Empty, blank. Nothing there. Did she *feel*? Did she *wonder*? Could she only blink and chew and futz and mumble? Didn't she care that Wallace was moments away from ending her with just his eyes?

I shook my head at the red-faced woman. "Something's wrong with you."

"A mess," Wallace said. "One big nasty mess." He glanced at me and gave a slight shake of his head. "If it were up to me, *Nurse* Pemstein, I would've pushed you off the yacht on our way over here. I would've smiled as you drowned, then had Raul back up the boat and launch a missile at your corpse, you piece of shit." He pushed out a breath. "But Phillip wanted you all here. So there's nothing I can do except actively and loudly hate you."

Just as Evelyn opened her mouth to respond, another piercing shriek ripped through the halls of Artemis.

What now?

17

Before racing to the kitchen, I threw an uneasy glance back over my shoulder.

Just that quick, Evelyn had eaten another slice of fish from her plate. Brave or stupid, I couldn't tell, but my muscles tensed and I waited a moment to see if the nurse's arms would flail, if her mouth would froth, if vomit would shoot from her gut to puddle alongside Javier's. But she didn't flail and she didn't vomit—she just chewed and sat there and stared dumbly at her plate.

Why was she not flailing? Why was she not vomiting? How was it possible that Evelyn was still alive? Did she have four stomachs like a goat, with all four made of steel? Was she immune to tetrodotoxin or whatever the hell came from fish ovaries? The fish on my plate looked the same as the fish on Evelyn's plate. Maybe hers was a little less translucent? Had only one part of the fish—the part Javier had put on my green plate—been cut incorrectly? Would that have changed the flesh's opacity? Why was she even willing to take that kind of risk? Suicide—that was the only explanation. She wanted to die.

And that's what I thought as I entered the kitchen squinting—because I was still confused. And I continued to squint, because the kitchen was too bright. Golden light ricocheted off the stainless steel refrigerator and sink fixtures, off the perfect skin of the mangoes and papayas piled into ceramic bowls. The kitchen was so bright that astronauts could see it from space.

Javier's Crocs-covered feet, crossed at the ankles, vacation style, poked out of the freezer door. Eddie was skulking back and forth, hands clamped over his ears, his face red and twisted. His combat boots crunched pieces of the wineglass that Evelyn had dropped less than thirty minutes ago.

And Desi . . . she had been the screamer. Collapsed on the floor, she was hitting her fists against the tile, wailing at the tops of her lungs again. "He ain't had to die! Oh, lord, help me! Help Javi! *Aw-roo! Aw-roo!*" She hadn't been able to get attention in the dining room, so she'd taken her show on the road. Blanche DuBois meets Maggie the Cat meets John Travolta. One giant ham and cheese sandwich.

Aromas from the dinner that was supposed to have been eaten by now still hung in the air. Grilled lobster and shrimp sautéed in garlic. A platter of glistening asparagus speckled with minced red onions. A pan of melted butter congealing the longer it sat. Six bottles of wine lined up on the sink counter. Each dish was still edible. Each bottle of expensive wine was still drinkable. Nothing left behind obviously boasted cyanide as a key ingredient.

Frank kneeled beside the damsel and patted her shoulder. "It's okay, Desirée. I'm here for you. You're not alone." Beads of sweat trickled down the sides of his face and soaked into the collar of his shirt, now stiffening from Desi's snot and tears.

"I can't stay here," Desi said, her pleading raccoon eyes glued on Eddie. "Not with a dead man in a freezer. Oh no, no, no. *Aw-roo! Aw-roo!*"

Frank continued to pat her trembling shoulder and her messy hair. He kept cooing bullshit words about Javier not being in pain anymore and that there was nothing to fear and that help would come, don't you fret none.

Desi ignored the minstrel's ministrations as she thrust her hands out to Eddie. "I'm so *skeered*. I just don't know what to do. *Aw-roo! Aw-roo!* I'm so *skeered*. Help me."

I rubbed my temples. "Calm down, Desirée. Eddie's calling the police right now." I glanced at Eddie, who was gaping at the satellite phone in his large hand.

"The storm," Eddie said, shaking his head. "There's no signal."

Desi pulled herself to kneel. "Eddie, could you be a dear and walk me back to my room? I just don't feel safe no more." She wrung her hands and batted her gummy eyelashes.

Eddie glanced at me, and the corner of his mouth lifted into a knowing smile. He snatched the spray bottle of cleaner fluid off the counter. "Can't. I have to clean up the mess in the dining room." Then he marched past the kneeling woman, winking at me as he strode out of the kitchen.

Desi's face fell and her hands dropped to her sides. She lifted her face to the ceiling, then wailed, "I'm so *skeered*. Help me, Lord!"

"Sweet Desi," Frank said, taking her arm, "I'll walk you to your room."

"Can you make me a to-go plate?" she asked him, working those clumpy lashes again.

"Certainly." Frank darted here and there, plate in hand, taking a little of this, a little of that, and a bottle of wine.

"Don't forget forks," I said, smirking.

"Oh, yes." Frank plucked two forks from the cutlery drawer.

"And napkins."

He plucked four napkins from the breakfast bar.

Then Desi let Frank, whose hands were already filled with a plate, flatware, and a bottle of wine, help her stand. "I just don't know what to do," she said.

"I got you," Frank said.

"You got me?"

"Of course, I do."

"Can we go to your room?" she asked. "I don't wanna be so close to the kitchen."

Frank smiled and said, "Definitely. I understand."

Together, they shambled out to the living room.

Neither Wallace nor I spoke as Desi's performance went on the road again and up the stairs. After they were gone, the recessed lighting softened into a silky golden glow. Wallace sighed, then sank against the breakfast counter.

I approached the walk-in freezer and stared down at poor Javier, who was blue now. Someone had closed his eyes. "Is this . . . *real*? I just can't believe this is happening." His face had twisted and frozen even before the cold of the freezer had taken him. "He looks dead, like . . . like . . . and now he's . . . all because of *fish*?" So very cold, I clutched my elbows and asked, "Should we say a few words over him, or . . . ?"

"I didn't come here to bury *him*," Wallace spat.

"I know that, but——"

Scowling, Wallace swiped at the breakfast counter, sending a loaf of French bread and a basket of strawberries to the tiled floor. "This is bullshit. Bullshit." Then he sent a pile of paper napkins fluttering in the air. He closed his eyes and took deep, controlled breaths.

I turned away from him to gaze at Javier, alone on the freezer floor. My heart ached as I whispered, "Good-bye, Javi. May God be with you." Then I closed the heavy steel door.

"You never get used to it, do you?" Wallace whispered.

I glanced at him over my shoulder.

The anger had drained from his face, and he was now staring at the closed freezer door. "The dead, I mean. The ... stillness. My first was my twin brother, William. We were only twelve when he passed, and I remember pinching his face and ... His face ... it was so cold, so cold ... I thought, *This can't be him.* That's what I kept telling myself. *This isn't him, this isn't my brother.* He'd come to me in my nightmares, and he'd touch me, and his fingers ... his fingers were like icy stones, and his touch always left bruises on my skin, and ..."

He closed his eyes, then canted his head. "And then my mother and father, and now Phillip ... everyone I love ... they're all gone." He opened his eyes and stared at the closed freezer door. "If it weren't for William, we wouldn't be standing here right now."

I knelt to clean up the fallen strawberries. "What do you mean?"

"I was introduced to money once we received payments from William's life insurance policy." Wallace stooped to help me clean the mess. "After that, grief drove my parents to drink and to fight until their deaths, and I received checks after they'd passed. And I saved and I saved and I bought my first piece of land, and then ..." His gaze shifted from the berries in his hands to the freezer door. "Not a day goes by when I don't think about William."

"Wallace, I'm so sorry—"

He flicked his hand at my condolence like it was lint on his slacks. "Enough melancholy."

We tossed the berries into the trash can, then washed our sticky hands.

Hungry, I pulled the platter of asparagus closer to me.

Wallace peered at me but didn't speak.

I said, "What?"

"Close call, wouldn't you say?"

I didn't respond as I plucked an asparagus stalk from the pile.

"No comment?"

I shrugged, then crunched the head off an asparagus stalk.

"Guess the Fates will have to try again."

"Are you always this mean?"

"Dearest, I'm from New Jersey. In other words—" His eyes moved past me.

Raspy breathing. The near-silent gnawing of fingers against wool.

I turned to see Evelyn standing in the short hallway between the dining room and kitchen, twisting the shapeless sweater over her fingers. Silver tears shimmered in her eyes, and a sheen of sweat made her pudgy face shine.

"I see that you're still standing," I said to her. To Wallace, I said, "Guess who ate some of the fish?"

He gaped at me, then gaped at Evelyn, then back at me again. "Really? Why?"

"Wanna tell him why?" I asked her.

The pulse points in Evelyn's temples pounded. Her mouth moved, but she didn't speak.

"How is that . . . *possible*?" Wallace asked. "Do you want to die? Is that it?"

She didn't respond. Just twisted the sweater over her fingers.

"You know what?" I squeezed the bridge of my nose as an overwhelming sense of sadness came over me. I pushed away the platter of asparagus and wiped my hands on a kitchen towel. "I can't with you right now."

"That snake," she said. "It was poisonous."

I grimaced. "Yeah. And?"

"It almost bit me. If it had bit me, I could've died."

"But you ate the sashimi," Wallace asked, his hands in the air. "You could've died *then,* too. Different delivery system, same result, Nurse Pemstein."

After that snake scare, I'd given Evelyn a stiff drink, and I'd tapped her doughy shoulders. What else did she want? To be coddled like Desi? To be mourned like Javier?

"Mercy—is *that* what you want?" Wallace asked. "Like the mercy you failed to show poor Mrs. Mills?"

"Mrs. Mills was in pain," Evelyn said, now twisting the turquoise ring on her finger. "Mrs. Mills was dying."

I turned to Wallace. "Who is Mrs. Mills?"

"The sweet little old lady with the mineral rights," Wallace said. "The sweet little old lady who owned all the turquoise in New Mexico. The one who, for some reason, left said turquoise mine to Nurse Pemstein here. And then? That sweet little old lady died. I won't say that Nurse Pemstein *killed* her—I'm classier than that."

He paused, then said, "No, I'm *not* classier than that. Nurse Pemstein *killed* her. Or accidentally dropped a pillow on top of Mrs. Mills's face and then, somehow, accidentally pushed down on that pillow until the old lady stopped breathing."

"She was dying," Evelyn said again.

Wallace rolled his eyes. "Because if you keep saying it, I'll believe it? No, sweetheart. I don't buy the misunderstood, compassionate angel of mercy like dear Phillip did."

"They were all dying," Evelyn bleated. Her sweaty face became pinker. "They were dying and I helped them."

"I'm tired of all of this. Of all of you." He snorted, then regarded me with cool eyes. "You asked me a question: Who am I? Who are *you?* I'll answer that:

you're the woman who's *literally* gotten away with murder. Just like the Bumble standing next to you."

I pointed at Wallace with trembling finger. "I'm not doing this with you, old man. Phillip cared about me, wanted nothing but happiness for me. I *mattered* to him. You don't know the truth, won't acknowledge the truth of what I'm saying, and I don't feel like explaining it to you anymore." A knot sat in my belly and made it hard to breathe, hard to think. And I wanted to peel out of my ruined dress—the reek of Javier's vomit on my bow was making me sick.

"You skipped dumping the bucket of pig's blood on her head," Wallace said. "Thank goodness for that."

Drums pounded in my head as I spat, "Of course, you'd side with *Brooke.* How many swastikas have *you* painted on someone's locker in your life?"

He held my glare with one of his own. "None, but I've had a few painted on my stomach and carved into my left calf by vengeful, envious bullies like you."

I couldn't take it, so I reached behind me and pulled down the dress's zipper. Just like that, my torso relaxed and I could breathe again. "Have some *fugu,* Wallace. I'm sure Phillip saw you for who you were and would want you to have *all* of the fugu."

Wallace blanched and his smile died. "How *dare* you. You're not *fit* to mutter that man's name. Here you are, thinking that you've made it, that you're one of *us,* not realizing you're a Groupon guest, love. A coupon-clutching con who happened to travel in the same air as Phillip only because he had mercy on your soul and saved your wide ass from prison. You were *not* his . . . friend." In all the evening's madness, the glue holding his wig to his scalp had weakened, shifting the hair so that the part sat closer to his ear, comb-over style.

"We don't have to talk again," I said to him. "I'll

attend the memorial because Phillip requested my presence, *maybe,* but you and I? We're done."

He faked a sad smile. "Oh, no. And we'd never even gotten started. I have so many other guests coming tomorrow once the storm finally moves on—who will keep me company until then? Whatever shall I do?"

Evelyn reached to grab something off the breakfast bar, but her arm hit a roll of paper towels, which then knocked mangoes off the counter and onto the floor. She groaned and stared pitifully at the mess.

I scowled at Evelyn and said, "Maybe you should go to your room."

She pulled at a lock of brittle hair. "The lights in my room won't come on." She groaned as she kept tugging at her hair. "I don't know where the light switch is and the rain, it's raining hard." She swallowed, then said, "I'm still hungry."

I waved my hand at the food placed all around the kitchen. "Fine. Eat. Looks like Javier made a feast just before he dropped dead."

"Who's cleaning all of this up?" Wallace asked, plucking a papaya from the tile.

"You're not talking to me, remember?" I said, a hand on my hip. "I'm a guest, a coupon-clutching one. And I'm also petty. So. I'm gonna go call my daughter and make arrangements to get off this freakin' island. Good night."

I marched past both of them, wondering if Morgan would answer the phone.

If she only knew how close I'd come to death that night. Next time, she'd choose to spend the weekend with me. She'd love me harder and louder. And I wanted her to love me harder and louder, and the only way she'd do that would be if I called her. I'd cry as I told her the story of Javier's death, how the poisonous fish had been mere inches away from my lips until the chef saved me and—

"Making a phone call is impossible," Wallace shouted. "There's no service here, dearest. Remember? Also, if you leave the island, you forfeit anything the poor fool left you."

I stopped in my step. "Says who?"

"Says Phillip. It's a clause in his will. So you can either stay for the memorial or you can go back to Rikers or Pelican Bay or whichever prison you'll soon call home." He looked over his shoulder and out the window. "Although I doubt you'll even find a fishing boat to take you back in this weather. Your broom—does she work in the rain?"

"You are a total bitch," I whispered.

"And you, Miriam, are totally unworthy of Phillip's generosity. Why you're even here still confuses the hell out of me." He squinted at me and shook his head. "Phillip must've been out of his mind, which, given his brain tumor, becomes more and more obvious with every passing second I stand anywhere next to you. You—*this*—everything . . . this is all madness."

Yes. All of this *was* madness. Javier was dead because he'd eaten fugu off my plate. Fugu that he had wanted *me* to eat. And if I had trusted my new friend, if I had been the adventurous eater that Billy lamented that I wasn't, the body now cooling in the walk-in freezer would have been mine.

I laughed, then sighed. "I'll see you in the morning, Wallace. You throw a damn fine party."

Yeah. A damn fine dinner party.

18

Okay. I couldn't make a phone call, nor could I leave Artemis. Trapped.

I wanted to get as far away as possible from the smells, the spills, all of it. Quiet, I needed quiet. And pills, I needed a Valium. And so I hurried down the dark hallway, reaching my room in a rush. My heart tripped in my chest as my mind buzzed with questions, suspicions . . . even a little fear. Because Javier. Poor Javier. Why had he insisted on preparing fugu? Why not tuna tartare or crab cakes? Calamari or sautéed mushrooms? It hurt me to think it, but he was to blame for his death.

And Evelyn . . . she had eaten that poisonous fish, and yet . . . and yet . . .

Numb—I couldn't feel my feet or my hands. I'd just seen a man die right in front of me. I'd seen him twitching, gasping for breath, vomiting. And those images of Javier dying were now seared into my memory alongside memories of newborn Morgan in my arms and my dead father in his casket.

After closing the door behind me, I pulled myself out of that Gucci frock and threw the dress in a corner. Didn't want to see it, wear it, smell it, and I planned to somehow forget it once it was time to pack up and leave this place. I didn't mind the cold for the moment— maybe the low temperatures would revive those nerves Gucci had killed, and maybe the sweet stink of Javier's death vomit would freeze and die as well.

As I changed into boxer shorts and a tank top, I wondered: Had Phillip *really* included me in his will? Of course he had—he knew my situation. He'd held me many times as I'd cried. Had he written the requirement that I stay on the island until the end of the service? Didn't sound like the man I knew—he wouldn't have forced me to mourn. Not Phillip. Was Wallace playing mind games with me? Probably. How was I going to do this, put up with him, though? How long could I last? He was such a smug, pretentious . . .

Still: I wished I had his confidence. His ability to give not one damn about anyone or anything. Guess that pride came from privilege and power. Because who would he be without either? Who would he be without those strange eyes that made people gasp? Who would he be without the tailored suits and the expensive hair?

A gay Eddie?

Probably not. He didn't seem like the violent, strangle-your-wife kind of guy, like the ex-cop. Maybe Larry, Desi's dead husband? No—he was old but not clueless. Although that could be debated about Larry, since he'd married Desi. Maybe he'd be that coal-mining hick Hoyt, the one handing out fake sapphires.

I fell back onto the bed and stared at the ceiling.

A brain tumor. Hunh. Phillip *had* complained of headaches and had tripped on invisible things anytime we were walking together. He'd call me on the phone, having forgotten that we'd already spoken earlier in the day. He'd seemed . . . *out of it.* I'd taken his behavior as exhaustion—he was one of the best and busiest defense attorneys in the country. And later, I'd taken his silence and short temper as impatience and disinterest, not with *me,* of course, but with his other clients, a few of whom were now sharing living space with me. Through it all, though, he'd kept his sense of humor.

"I'm sorry, Phillip," I whispered.

I tipped my head to listen for his voice, just in case he'd heard me and wanted to say, "Attagirl, Miriam," like he always said. Or "You make me laugh," or "Maybe in our next life, we'll meet, and who knows . . ." So I listened, but there was nothing. Only the barely there groans of a big house settling into soft soil. Only the rain beating down on the trees and my heartbeat thundering in my ears.

Mr. A. Nansi. The name Phillip had chosen to fool me into thinking this adventure would be a reality-show competition.

Anansi. And now I remembered hearing all those Anansi stories during school field trips to the public library. Anansi was a spider in African mythology. A trickster who'd fooled others so that he could live the easy life. He had cheated a mongoose, a turtle, and a rabbit out of their baskets of food. He had cheated Death by trapping it in a spiderweb. He'd been so greedy for greens, beans, and sweet potatoes that he'd ended up with eight thin legs trying to steal it all.

Anansi. How clever.

Wait . . . Javier.

We each had bedrooms. In the video presentation, Aunt Doris had only shown the kitchen for Javier. He had been the help. The help always stayed in servants' quarters, unremarkable rooms the size of toy chests with dim lighting and talking mice wearing cute hats.

Where had he slept last night?

Why does that matter, Miriam?

Don't know.

I picked up my cell phone—no bars, no service, one voice mail. The message left by Detective Hurley. He'd asked about the "altercation" with Prudence. He'd wanted me to come to the station to answer a few

questions. Now that my attorney was dead, there'd
be no one seated beside me. Not good.

On Sunday night, I was supposed to head back to
Los Angeles ... unless I *didn't* head back to Los Angeles.

What if instead I took a plane to Colombia, as I'd
thought about so many times?

But then, what about Morgan?

Maybe I could fly to L.A., grab Morgan, then fly ...

*You're losing it. You're tired. It's been a long day.
You need a drink.*

My mind staggered from one thought to the next
half-baked thought. I still couldn't take deep breaths,
not with my grasp of reality slipping. I climbed out of
bed and stepped over to the vanity, ready to open the
tub of Valium that helped on occasions such as these,
occasions that found me confused or flabbergasted or
spinning heists from logic thinner than spider silk. The
drug sat next to the stainless steel flask that Javier had
dropped yesterday at the tide pool.

Stay sober.

What was the point now?

Drunk—that's how I wanted to be. Time flew if you
were passed out. Yes, I wanted to be drunk.

I inhaled, then slowly exhaled as I stood in front of
the cold window with my hands clutching my elbows.
Trying to, literally, hold myself together. Breathing
in ... out ... in ... *What is ... ?*

Way out past the live oaks and the dogwoods, a
green light flickered in the rainy darkness.

*Is it a rescue vehicle coming to take Javier back to
the mainland?*

Above me, a door creaked open.

Soft footsteps crept down the hallway.

Artemis groaned.

A lump rose in my throat as defeat and exhaustion enveloped me. *Phillip didn't leave me squat. I'm going to jail. I need to deal with it now or three days from now. Maybe I should get my ass on that boat or ATV or whatever that is with that green light.*

But what *was* it?

The green light continued to shine, but it never moved any closer.

My heart couldn't race any faster, and my freezing hands shook as I grabbed the Valium. After wrestling and fumbling with the childproof top, I finally pushed it off with a *phuff*.

No!

My mind screamed, high and piercing and long—but my mouth made no sound. The most silent distress call ever. Tears stung my eyes as my knees buckled and I collapsed against the vanity.

Inside the vial . . .

The tablets of Valium . . .

Gone. My pills were gone.

And now, the walls of a bedroom bigger than my biggest house boxed me in.

And out there in the hard stormy darkness, the green light blinked once, then disappeared into the inky night.

19

What?

I startled awake, and already my blood was racing through my veins.

A glance around the dark room told me that I was alone. A glance out the window told me the storm had passed, but now fog, thick and white, had taken its place. That green light hadn't flickered back on again, not that I'd be able to see it anymore. My muscles chilled, and I stretched my arms feeling as though I was breaking through soft ice. I had fallen asleep sitting up in bed, with the down comforter wrapped around my shoulders. I'd fallen asleep clutching my phone, and now I glanced at the screen: 1:26 A.M. A new day, a new—

Something had yanked me from sleep. *But what?*

The room smelled like eggs, sweat, and burned gravy. The room smelled . . . *warm,* as though someone had just left this space.

Somewhere in the house, a door closed.

Soft talking outside.

I tilted my head and closed my eyes to hear.

A woman. Whispering. Desi.

A man chuckled. *Frank?*

I crept over to the window and peeked out.

The jungle twinkled, a shiny black beneath the full moon.

A giggle. A "ssh."

I grabbed my jacket and sneakers from the suitcase.

Tiptoed out to the hallway, into the dark living room, bumping into the Bosch table in the foyer. I froze and stared at the figurines—something had changed on the panels, but I couldn't tell what . . . I shivered, then willed myself to back away from the table. I opened the front door but took one last look back—*what was different?* No time to figure that out, because two shadowy figures were disappearing into the wilderness.

The scent of wet forest and new mud wafted on thick white air.

Giggling. "Ohmygosh." Another "ssh." The voices had drifted from the north, from a path several feet away from the one we'd taken Friday evening to reach the house.

Hurrying to that soggy northbound trail, my shoes burped and slipped in the muck. I squinted to see a moving flash of white silk against dark trees. The fog kept me blind, wrapping around tree trunks and slithering up into the leaves. Cold dampness splattered around my ankles.

I didn't like it out here.

There they were. Desi, wearing a wispy nightgown that skimmed the damp earth, walking hand in hand with Frank, in track pants and T-shirt. They were hiking through a glade of banyans with branches twisting high to the moon and reaching down to the soft earth. Desi squeaked, "Ohmygosh, it's so dark," then giggled.

What was so dark? Something belonging to Frank or the nighttime jungle?

I tiptoed, making sure to stay hidden far behind them, making sure not to slip in the mud.

The trees became well-placed obstacles, showing up unexpected every few steps. The fog, the banyans, and the wet earth kept me slow.

My heart pounded and it took everything in me to not run to catch up. After darting for three minutes from tree to tree, a clearing appeared before me. I edged closer . . . closer . . . and stayed low to the ground.

Out on the exposed bluff, Frank held Desi in his arms. The features on his face, a shiny ebony now, were impossible to see. But when he smiled, the whiteness of his teeth mapped his eyes, his cheeks, his chin.

Desi looked hungrily up at him as he ran his thick fingers through her tangled hair. They kissed, a few quick pecks at first, testing . . . testing . . . and then they took longer kisses, greedier kisses.

Above me, past the fast-moving fog, thousands of stars bit into the black sky, weak competition against the moon's awesome light. Back here on earth, Desi pushed away from Frank, then let her nightgown slip off her shoulders. She had full breasts and a small potbelly. Frank slid his hand from her waist and wrapped it around her pale, thin neck.

I couldn't hear anything over the crash of waves against the rocks, over the knocking of my heart against my ribs, over the pounding of my pulse in my ears. But then, behind me, the undergrowth crackled. Snapped. Popped. I could hear that loud and clear. Someone else was here. Some *thing* else was here. My scalp bristled, and I gripped the trunk of the tree. My fingers dug deeper into the damp tree trunk and I pressed my face against the dark wood. *Breathe. Relax.* I forced myself to look back over my shoulder.

No one there. No thing there.

"Take 'em off," Frank croaked.

Desi wriggled out of her panties, then whooped as she threw them behind her and over the cliff. She cackled and danced around her new lover, giggling, then wagging her bare ass, a whiter, wider moon than the one hanging above us. Frank's gaze stayed on Desi's behind . . . until she stopped in her step, until his smile froze and his gaze shifted . . .

Right to where I stood.

Had I broken the spell?

I held my breath in case they could only see me if I moved.

Five seconds . . .

Seven seconds . . .

Ten . . .

"You're supposed to be lookin' at me," Desi snapped.

"All right, all right." He smiled down at his lover.

And I let out my breath little by little, in teaspoons.

She thrust her hand past the elastic band of his track pants, then drove her face into his.

I had stopped breathing again. Dizzy, I swayed on my feet, clutching the tree trunk again, this time for stability. My skin tingled—sex and fear and amazement and . . .

Wait. Wasn't Frank married?

My mind flipped back to earlier conversations, and . . . *Dallas, wealth manager, gold Maserati, secretary, root canal* . . . I couldn't remember. But he *had* to be married. A rich, middle-aged black man in Texas? Of *course*, he was. He was just being sly about it. He'd come here to get laid and to get paid. That's right—he'd told me all of that Saturday morning. All notions of fidelity had been banished now as his hands—*there, a gold wedding band, Celeste, his wife is Celeste*—grabbed Desi's ass, squeezed it, patted it like he'd pat a horse's or a cow's. *Good Desi, good girl.*

What did it feel like to be lusted after? To have a man risk his marriage just to be with you? Not that I wanted *Frank* . . . No. I mean, I'd had lovers surprise me with sunset dinners aboard yachts, intimate picnics staged in the middle of parks, a boyfriend playing my favorite song from his boom box while standing in front of my bedroom window, and other loud declarations of adoration here and there . . . more or less. But

I wanted to stand bare-assed and cold on a bluff with someone, *anyone* (but not Frank), with his hands discovering me, with his hands pleasuring me.

Frowning, I turned away from the two new lovers. I wanted to be desired again, pursued again, *taken* again. I wanted . . . fake sapphire earrings and weekend getaways to Newport News.

Poor Celeste. I didn't know her, but I had lived through a similar situation. Yeah, I had my own Desi Scoggins, who now lived in my house and enjoyed my view of the city and my fancy refrigerator.

But . . . what happened on Mictlan Island stayed on Mictlan Island—*for a price.* Frank would pay that price, just to keep me quiet. And Desi—what about Hoyt, the coal-mining baron who'd passed off blue plastic as precious stones, who had told her that those giant shrimp in Newport News were baby lobster tails? Did Desi want to break his heart? Did she want to keep this island liaison as much a secret as Frank?

Damn it. I wished I'd brought my phone to take pictures. *Next time.* There was always a next time. I chuckled to myself, then clamped my hand over my mouth as I slogged back to Artemis.

Yeah. Frank would pay to shut my mouth. Desi would, too. And by the time I left Mictlan Island, I'd have enough money to pay for another high-priced attorney.

Thank you, Phil Omeke. You *were* my only hope.

20

I couldn't open my eyes.

Something had pulled me from sleep, and now I couldn't open my eyes. My fingers touched thick crust that had hardened over my eyelashes, and I scratched at that crust, pinched the goop off my lashes. Scratched and pinched . . . scratched and pinched . . . There was so much.

Finally, *pop!* One eye pulled apart. *Pop!* Then the second eye opened.

Morning sunlight poured through the windows. Leaves rustled. The wind was up and a gust rattled the glass.

And I sneezed, sneezed again, high-pitched *eeps* that only dogs could hear.

I blinked and frowned at the dry yellow goop now stuck beneath my fingernails. *An allergic reaction to something?* Goop had swamped my eyes once after hiking with Madison through a field of poppies near San Diego—

Poppies. Back at Molinero Ocean Charter Services, Andreas had mentioned poppies and marijuana plants growing all around the island. Maybe in the dark last night, I had tromped over some of those flowers. I knew that I had touched trees, too, and had placed my face against their trunks. Maybe that's what . . .

The scream.

I'd heard a woman screaming—*that's* what had pulled me from sleep. *Had I dreamed that, or . . . ?* No—

my dream had been of Morgan and me jumping on a trampoline. We wore orange socks. I held an ice-cream cone in my hand and I had an ice-cream headache, even though I hadn't eaten any yet. Morgan and I had been laughing as we jumped higher . . . higher . . . We were so happy. We—

Another scream cut through the silence.

I froze in bed for a moment, then knocked the comforter to the ground. Who was screaming? Evelyn? Desi? I threw open the door and stepped out into the hallway.

The doors to both women's bedrooms were closed.

Back in my room, I blew my nose, sneezed again, pulled on the only pair of jeans I'd brought, and shoved my feet back into the pair of Pumas muddied from last night's trek.

I rummaged through my handbag and found the little bottle of allergy eye drops. Two drops in each eye, and I winced from the burn. I dabbed at my eyes with the tail of my shirt, then blew my nose again.

Eyes still burning, I crept to Desi's door and knocked. "You okay?"

No answer.

I knocked on Evelyn's door. "Is everything all right?"

No answer from Evelyn, either. Hunh. Maybe she had stumbled across another snake.

I'd heard a scream. But then, I hadn't slept well, hadn't eaten well nor medicated well in over twenty-four hours. Unless I had imagined . . . *No.* There were screams.

Someone else had to have heard *something*.

Wallace wore an apron as he moved around the kitchen with expert grace. He had cleared away most of yesterday's mess and was now mixing something in a bowl. A carton of eggs, a slab of bacon, a bowl of white mushrooms, and a stick of butter sat on the breakfast bar. Fresh coffee gurgled into a carafe.

Javier was dead, and we were having omelets for breakfast. The sun rose, the sun set. *On the next episode of Artemis* . . . A mean world, even on a private island in the middle of the ocean.

"Did you hear something just now?" I asked him.

Wallace's stirring slowed. "And good morning to you, too, Miriam."

"Sorry. Good morning."

"Are you okay? You're wearing . . . *denim*. And you look and sound absolutely dreadful. Like Mariah Carey in *Precious*. You know, a little tired, a little puffy. You've seen it."

I touched the bags beneath my eyes. "I *am* a little tired. And my allergies are acting up. Did you hear someone scream for help?"

"Scream? Like the boy who cried wolf? Like Henny Penny and that damn falling sky? Like any of those volcano movies where the disgraced geologist warns the village that the damned thing is gonna blow . . . Oh dear, Pierce Brosnan *had* been right, hadn't he?"

I sighed, then said, "Never mind. Probably the wind. Nature making noise. Eddie—have you seen *him*?"

Wallace nodded. "He's trying to reach the authorities again on the radio, I believe. I reminded him that *La Charon* would be here around eleven o'clock with more guests, and that he could just smuggle Javier on board. But he isn't listening, surprise, surprise." He tapped the whisk on the side of the bowl. "If you couldn't tell, I'm making omelets. Well, more like a frittata. Do you have any ingredient preferences? Anything for you, Miriam."

I blinked at him and said nothing.

He rolled his eyes. "Yes, I'm being nice to you. Being a bitch all the time can be terribly exhausting. How *do* you do it?"

I snorted but couldn't keep a small grin off my face.

"I eat a balanced breakfast every morning. Walk ten thousand steps a day."

"Ah. So. Frittata fixin's?"

"I'll be fine with whatever you decide." I shuffled around the kitchen in search of a small hallway that led to Javier's guest room. Only found that butler's pantry, a broom closet, and Javier's new home, a.k.a. the freezer. "Can I ask you a weird question? Where did Javier sleep on Friday night?"

Wallace's onion chopping slowed as he thought. "Probably near the media room. There's also a den or something over on that side. And there's a room upstairs next to mine. There are 179 rooms on this property. Hyperbole, darling." He leaned forward, then whispered, "It's a mansion. Anyway, does it matter now?"

I shook my head—no, it didn't matter. "We'll need to send his stuff to his wife back in Vegas, and it's just . . . I never . . . I just can't believe . . ." I shrugged. "Like . . . is Javier really . . . ?"

Wallace gaped at me. "Really . . . *what*?"

"You know." I bit my lip.

Sad realization washed over Wallace's face. "Oh, dear heart." He stepped over to the freezer and pulled open the door. "Behold."

Javier's solid-blue feet were now frozen into his chef's Crocs.

Wallace said, "Is that dead enough, dear?"

I nodded, then whispered, "Yeah."

Wallace closed the freezer door. "So, mushrooms? Bacon? Cucumbers for your eyes?"

There he is! Eddie, guns holstered, prowled around the swimming pool with a phone in his hand. His face was turned to the sky as he searched for visual confirmation that a satellite soared somewhere in the great beyond.

I darted out the kitchen door.

Wallace shouted after me, "No bacon, then?"

The sun was already high in the sky and the bright white light made me shield my face from the glare. It was as though no storm had passed through last night. The palms bent and swayed, and their fronds swished in the warm wind. The cries of circling gulls in the distance carried on the currents.

Sweat had darkened Eddie's Red Sox cap. His skin was as pink as the bougainvilleas that lined the terrace. He was muttering, "Can't . . . fucking . . . believe," as he jabbed his fingers at the phone's keypad.

I said, "Eddie—"

He startled and whirled to point the phone at my gut.

My hands shot in the air. "It's me. Don't shoot." If anyone could make a phone fire bullets, it would be *this* man.

He thrust his head forward, then pushed out air. "What?"

I eyed the phone. "Are . . . they coming?" Right then, my words were nitroglycerine.

"Is *who* coming?"

I slowly lowered my hands. "The police? You're supposed to be calling . . . ?"

He glanced at the phone. "Oh. Yeah. No reception. You stop me in the middle of trying to get reception to ask me that?"

"No. I . . . I just heard someone scream." I'd dumped the wind and nature theory just so that he wouldn't shoot me with his satellite phone.

A smile played at the corners of his mouth. "When? Where?"

I shrugged. "Maybe five minutes or so ago. I don't know where it was coming from, but I heard it. Maybe from the upstairs bedrooms?"

"Was it the wind?" he asked. "Sometimes the wind sounds like a woman screaming. There's a word for that, ain't there? 'Banshee'? One time, I got sent out on a call, right? Burglar alarm. Whoop, whoop, whoop, the damn thing's going off all crazy, and we go into the house, and it's the freakin' cat. The freakin' cat had knocked over this—"

"I heard a scream. From a woman. And since you mentioned it," I continued, "I heard glass break, too." *Yeah. Glass breaking.*

He studied me for a moment, said, "All right," then stomped back into the house.

As we passed through the kitchen, Wallace said, "We have to talk about all that needs to happen today."

Neither Eddie nor I stopped.

Heart in my throat, I was still uncertain if I'd dreamed that scream. But it was too late now to take it back. Too late to say, "Maybe not. It was probably the wind."

Eddie scaled the stairs two at a time.

I took those steps just as quick.

He turned left at the landing and barged into Frank's bedroom. Last night's dirty plates and cutlery were stacked on the nightstand alongside two empty water bottles. There was no glass on the carpet—not that I expected to truly find broken glass.

"Anybody in here?" Eddie yelled.

No response.

"It's looking like a freakin' cat," Eddie grumbled as he pushed past me.

I said nothing as we scrambled back to the landing, then down the hallway to Wallace's room.

Eddie stormed through the double doors, but I paused in the broad entryway. I'd never seen Wallace's lavender-colored bedroom in person. It was twice the size of my room, with a mirror that spanned nearly the entire interior wall. No art—just windows and smaller mirrors, some set in mosaic, others in heavy metal frames. Wallace's northwestern view . . . it was the greatest view of all. The ocean crashed and swirled against the rocks. Seabirds wheeled in the air as multicolored butterflies flitted over the canopy of dogwoods over there. Compared to Wallace's suite, my room was a weed-choked parking lot next to an abandoned train yard.

I'd find my better self with this view, with all this light and all this nature. And as I stood there, imagining greatness, Eddie threw open doors to the sitting room, the dressing room, and the master bathrooms, because Wallace had two master bathrooms.

A black-and-white framed photograph hung in a niche in the wall. In it, two twin boys around seven years old stood in front of a tree. Their brown hair had been cut into bowls. One boy was crying, wearing overalls with a giant hole in the knee. The other boy was smiling as though he owned all the candy in the world. His overalls were neat, his irises nearly invisible. I knew that smile—it belonged to Wallace.

My skin crawled as I stared at that picture, at that smile as little William cried . . . Guess Wallace had always been a callous jerk. He had probably pushed William down, then laughed at the hole in his twin's overalls.

Of all the pictures to hang, why had Wallace chosen this one?

"No one's here." Eddie darted out the double doors and raced down the hallway.

We passed the landing again, then rushed down to the end of the corridor to reach his room.

The bed was made and the black duffel bags were gone.

"Maybe the screams came from downstairs," I said, my mind frantic now.

"Or maybe you're just making shit up." His eyes and the vein in the middle of his forehead were bulging. "Yeah. I'm thinkin' that."

"No," I said, shaking my head. "I wouldn't outright lie, Eddie. I wouldn't, no matter what Wallace says. I heard a woman scream. And I heard glass breaking."

He studied my face and must've glimpsed my sincerity. "Fine." He hurried back toward the staircase.

Just stop. Just have breakfast and admit that the scream was probably the wind.

But I didn't stop. I followed him with my stomach complaining—the aromas of sautéed onions and frying bacon were wafting through the house.

Evelyn stood at the bottom of the staircase. Pale and glassy-eyed, she poked her fingers through the hole in her sweater, bigger now than it had been last night.

Eddie slowed in his step. "What the hell's *your* problem?"

She opened her mouth to speak but could only grunt.

Eddie sighed. "I don't have all day—"

"It's Desi," she blurted. "Desi's—" Her chin quivered as her lips clamped together.

Eddie popped down three more steps. "Desi's *what*?"

The nurse closed her eyes, then said, "Desi's dead."

21

"*What?*" Eddie and I shouted together. That one word made Evelyn flinch and hop back a step.

Wallace, a cup of coffee in his hand, stepped around from the kitchen. "It's not even ten o'clock yet—why are we already shouting at each other? We should all be preparing for Phillip's memorial. People are coming and everyone needs to pitch in and clean. Yes, even me, and I look *horrible* with a sponge in my hand."

I pointed at Evelyn with a shaky finger. "She just told us that Desi's . . . Desi's . . ."

"That Desi's dead," Eddie completed.

Wallace peered at the nurse, then whispered, "Why would you say such a thing?"

Evelyn, mute, gaped at me.

"What?" I asked her. "I can't hear you. Speak louder."

"Is this a joke?" Wallace asked.

Evelyn pulled at the hole in her sweater.

"Why aren't you *talking*?" Eddie screamed. "What the hell's *wrong* with you?"

No answer.

I charged across the living room to Desi's bedroom door. Wallace, Eddie, and Evelyn tromped behind me. I shouted, "Desi," then twisted the doorknob.

Locked.

"Move." Eddie pushed me aside and twisted the doorknob again.

Still locked.

He took a step back, lifted his boot, then kicked the space beneath the knob. The door flew open with a crunch.

A breeze drifted past open windows that let in a little light. The nightstand was crammed with an empty wine bottle, an ashtray, a dead joint with its butt smeared with red lipstick, a black cellophane wrapper for a Magnum condom, a pack of chewing gum, and a hard-back novel. Desirée Scoggins lay right in the middle of a bed big enough to sleep twenty people. She was na-ked and still. A pillow sat over her head; her right arm lay draped to her side and her left wrist had been tied with her blue scarf to the welded metal headboard.

"Oh." My leg bones disintegrated, and I leaned against the doorjamb.

Eddie said, "Hey," as he hustled over to the bed. "Hey, Desi?" He tossed the pillow to the floor.

Desi's eyes were bloodshot and wide open. A faint purplish tint of new bruising around her nose and mouth didn't shock me as much as the crusted blood between her teeth, on her cheeks, and in her ears. Blood also stained the wet sheets, which were pulled away from the top corners of the mattress. The stink of urine mixed with smells of sweat and sex, weed and fear.

Eddie untied Desi's bound wrist, then held the scarf out behind him.

I took the scarf. "Is she okay?"

He lifted Desi's wrist and placed his thumb over her pulse point. He waited . . . waited . . . then shook his head. He muttered, "Shit," then draped her arm across her bare, round belly.

"Maybe she passed out," I said. "Maybe she drank too much or . . . or . . . took a sleeping pill or . . . or . . ."

Frank popped into the doorway. He looked re-laxed in his T-shirt and khaki shorts. "Anyone making breakfast?" His eyes landed on the big bed. "What's wrong with Dez?" He squeezed past Wallace and Evelyn to enter the bedroom.

I grabbed his arm to stop him from moving closer, then shook my head.

"What's wrong?" he asked.

Words were catching in my throat, but I forced myself to say, "She's . . . gone."

He dipped his chin to his chest. "What do you mean, 'she's gone'?"

I whispered, "She's dead, Frank."

"No. That's ridiculous."

"I'm serious. She's . . ." Tears burned in my eyes as words caught and stayed in my throat.

Frank squinted at me, then turned to the others. "What the hell's going on? Is this another one of Phillip's practical jokes?"

I shook my head. "I agree, he went too far, but this . . ." I gazed at Desi. "This isn't a joke. She's not trying to fool us."

Wallace scooped the discarded pillow from the carpet and studied the blood now drying in the shape of Desi's face. Then he met the eyes of every living soul standing in the room. "Who did this? Which one of you . . . did this to her?"

No one spoke for a very long time, leaving the palm fronds to rustle and the surf to pound against the shore. The curtains lifted and twisted with that breeze. A perpetual nine o'clock, it never got any lighter or any darker in this room.

Finally, Evelyn whispered, "She was with Frank. They were together."

We all looked at Frank.

Frank lifted his hands and shook his head. "No. Nuh-uh."

"You *were* with her," Evelyn said, her voice firmer. "You were in this bedroom all night." She met each of our eyes. "And I heard them making . . . *sounds*."

Eddie crossed his massive arms. "What *kind* of sounds?"

Evelyn lifted her chin. "*Sex* sounds. Groaning and pounding and moaning, and it was so loud that I couldn't sleep."

Couldn't sleep? I didn't hear any groaning or pounding, and I'd slept fine right until that scream. *And broken glass, don't forget the broken glass. You heard it.*

Eddie, his face a shade lighter than rage-purple, clenched his fists. "What happened here, Frank? Things get a little out of hand?"

Sweat poured off the black banker like water off a melting glacier. Hands still out, he said, "She's lying. She's a nut, you said so yourself."

"I've never said that," Eddie said.

"*I* said that," Wallace pointed out.

My eyes skittered around Desi's swollen face. "Her earrings. Her earrings are missing. She had them on last night."

We all dropped our collective gazes to the carpet, then we scanned the nightstand, the windowsill, the bare parts of the mattress. No earrings.

"Maybe they're lost somewhere in her pocketbook," Eddie suggested.

"You take her earrings, Frank?" Wallace asked.

Frank, eyes large and frightened, looked to me for support. "Miriam . . ."

There was a welt on his neck, and a small drop of blood had soaked into the ribbed collar of his T-shirt. That's what I pointed to, that stained collar and that welt, and said, "You have a scratch . . ."

Frank touched the abrasion, then tugged at his

collar. "No . . . no, that was earlier . . . there were frogs croaking and I went out to kill—stop them and I . . . I . . . shaving . . . I was shaving."

"I also saw you last night," I said. "You and Desi left the house together. And I saw that she was wearing her earrings." *Probably.*

"You left the house to do what?" Eddie asked the banker.

"Would you like to answer that, Frank?" Wallace plucked the empty condom foil from the nightstand. "Or should we guess?"

"And then he stole her earrings," Evelyn said. "He tried to hide them, but Desi caught him and he killed her to keep it secret."

My heartbeat doubled, tripled, tripped over itself as I pictured Frank in bed, bent over Desi, his knees digging into the mattress, his hands mashing that pillow against her face. Spit was gathering at the corners of his mouth as her one free arm swung frantically in the air. How long had it taken to smother her? Five minutes? Ten?

Evelyn, jittery now, paced near the window. Her fingers gnawed at the hole in her sweater sleeve, and her jalopy breath rattled in her chest.

"Tell me right now," Eddie demanded. "Where are her earrings?"

"No clue. I am not a crook," Frank spat. "Nor am I a murderer."

With tears in his eyes, Wallace laughed. "There are only five of us alive on this island, and *I* certainly didn't do that." He pointed to Desi's limp body twisted in the soiled sheets. "Or *this.*" He held up the condom wrapper.

"I cannot believe you all are looking at me as though . . ." Frank's lips pooched and twisted. "As though I'm some kind of . . . of . . . no—I'm the fu-fu-

fucking president of a wealth management firm—I came to this island to network. But you and Phillip tricked me and . . . and . . . I will not tolerate such . . . such . . . *slander*. I'm not some . . . *convict*. Some . . . *monster*."

But there he was, stuttering and sweating like a guilty son of a bitch from the ghetto, caught red-handed and flecked with the blood of a white woman, a Richard Wright character come to life. And there *she* was, the white woman—lifeless and naked, filthy with blood and her own waste, staring at a ceiling she could no longer see.

Frank's eyes flicked at the door—he wanted to escape. Leaving, though, equated guilt, telltale heart bullshit that ignored the fact that *no one* liked being in a room with a dead person, no one liked being accused of murder. Still, he took that step.

I blocked the doorway. "You're not going anywhere."

He glared at me, then threw up his hands. "We had sexual intercourse. That's it. Nothing more. A man and a woman, two consenting adults, attracted to each other and acting on it." He whirled to face Evelyn. "And what in the fresh hell is your problem? Standing at the door, listening to us? You're disgusting." Then he pointed at me. "*There's* your murderer. The pettiest bitch on this island."

Eyes wide, I touched my heart, then said, *"Really?"*

"Black women hate everyone," Frank said, "especially white women who desire black men. You said that you saw Desi and me last night? You followed us, saw us out on that cliff, and that pissed you off, didn't it? Pissed you off so much so that you decided to take revenge on behalf of scorned black women everywhere."

I snorted. "Sorry—I'm not killing *anybody* over your round black ass. You were with her, Frank. I saw you. And this morning, I heard her scream."

Frank shook his head. "On my honor—"

"*Honor?*" Wallace screeched. "This coming from a man whose real name isn't even *Frank?* This coming from a man who stole millions from poor Americans who couldn't afford their homes, a man who forged signatures on sale agreements and then paid a gang member to assassinate his partner in crime while that partner in crime was getting a haircut? This coming from a man who can't even *behave* for a single weekend?

"Nothing about you is real," Wallace continued, his razor-blade eyes cutting Frank to bite-size pieces. "Nothing is real. Not that wedding ring on your finger. Not your fake wife Celeste. I doubt you're even human. You are the absolute worst, and Phillip's tumor cracked through his *skull* as he was defending you. I wanted to kick Phil's ass just to convince him to drop you as a client, but he wouldn't because he'd made a promise to you. Because *he* was an honorable man. Honor, Trey? You know *nothing* about honor."

"*Trey?*" I gaped at Desi's secret lover. "So you're a con? *And* you're a thief? You put out a *hit?*"

"*Two* hits," Wallace corrected. "Because then he had the gang member killed." He paused, then added, "Or, as he would say when he's not pretending to be a banker . . . *kilt*. Did I say it right, *Trey?* That you had him *kilt?*"

Frank licked his top lip as he glared at Wallace with the purest hatred available to mankind. "I won't even dignify that racist accusation with a response."

"Arrest him," Wallace ordered. "And when the boat comes, get him off this island."

Eddie grabbed Frank's arm.

"Let me go." Frank whipped out of Eddie's grasp. "Don't *touch* me."

"You're under arrest," Eddie said.

"Under whose authority?"

"Get on the fuckin' ground!" Eddie grabbed at Frank again, successfully this time, and draped his forearm beneath Frank's neck.

"Let me . . . go. Let me . . ." Frank clawed at Eddie's arm and rocked his body until both men were wrestling. As they fell to the floor, they bumped into the dresser and sent a ceramic vase flying to the ground and shattering into millions of pieces. They struggled over to the north wall, sending the framed Picasso print of a couple kissing to the floor. But then Eddie reached back and yanked a Glock from beneath his T-shirt. He held the muzzle against Frank's temple. And *that* changed *everything.*

Evelyn screamed.

I shouted, "Don't shoot him!"

"You killed her," Eddie howled, his eyes wild. "I know you did."

Frank's face was smashed into the carpet. His eyes were squeezed shut as he squealed.

"Wallace!" I shouted. "Call him off!"

Wallace watched the scuffle with a small, mean grin.

"Wallace!" I screamed again.

Finally, his voice calm, Wallace said, "This isn't how we do things, Edward."

Eddie pushed the Glock harder into Frank's temple. "It's how *I* do things."

"Edward," Wallace barked, "you don't want trouble again, do you? One death was easy to explain, but killing *two* black men in one year? Phillip's not here to defend you this time. We'll deal with Trey in a judicious manner. Stop. *Now.*"

Eddie calmed some, and his grip loosened around the weapon.

"Good," Wallace said. "Now, get him to his feet."

Eddie's breath came heavy as he pulled Frank up to

stand. The con's glasses remained twisted and broken on the carpet. Eddie's Glock had gouged its impression on his temple.

"You're under arrest, you sick bastard," Eddie spat. "I'm locking you in your room until the Mexicans come."

The bells in my head quieted, but my breathing and my pulse . . .

Eddie had killed a man before. And so had Frank—*two men*. And now, Desi was dead.

I couldn't do it—I couldn't stay in this house, on this island, not one day longer. No one was in charge. People were dying. Chaos reigned. I wanted to see my daughter again, and no amount of money was worth living one floor beneath Eddie Sweeney. Or Frank Clayton.

Hell, yeah.

It was time to go.

Excerpted from the *Times West Virginian*
Tuesday, September 23

WHITE SULPHUR SPRINGS WOMAN
LOSES HUSBAND AS A RESULT
OF TROPICAL STORM

More than fifty people have died as rescue teams continue to search for more missing residents after Tropical Storm Gretchen decimated large swaths of West Virginia.

The storm changed Desirée Scoggins's life forever when emergency services were prevented from reaching her husband Lawrence, 63, after an allergic reaction sent the retired accountant into anaphylactic shock. "All the phones were down and there was no one around to save him. The line just kept ringing and ringing."

Now, Desirée hopes to figure out how she will get through this. "I loved him more than anyone in the world. For him to die like this—over a cookie—is just nuts."

22

I planned to skip Phillip's memorial, scheduled for five o'clock. Instead, I would meet *La Charon* at the dock as it dropped off more of Wallace's guests. I'd say nothing to anyone about my plans because I was a grown woman and didn't have to explain *shit* to anyone. All sense of decorum and manners? Gone.

Because Desi was dead.

And Javier was dead.

And Artemis didn't have bars or reception or satellites.

"Sat phones don't *need* bars," Eddie growled as he paced the hallway outside of Frank's bedroom. "They're called satellite phones cuz they use—"

"Signal. Reception. Whatever," I said, hands thrown in the air. "Why aren't you reaching anybody? Do we even know for sure that there's a boat on its way?"

"Don't know." Eddie gaped at the clunky black phone in his hand. "This should be working . . . Must be a transmission delay. Nothing to freak out about."

"So now what?" Wallace asked.

"So *now,*" Eddie said, "I need to find an open space. And I need to be standing there when the satellite passes over."

But he couldn't do that *and* watch Frank at the same time. So, I was volun-told to be the first person standing guard outside Frank's bedroom. I glanced at my watch. *Crap.* It was almost ten o'clock and I needed to pack.

"Don't I need a weapon?" I asked. "Just in case he tries to escape, just in case he tries to kill another woman—me, in particular? You expect me to throw my shoe at him?"

Eddie glanced at my sneakers, then said, "Hold on." He jogged down to his bedroom.

Wallace asked, "Is a gun really necessary?"

I swiveled my head on my neck and placed a hand on my hip. "Fine. You stand here, then."

The old man rubbed his temples. "None of this was supposed to happen. Not today."

"Was it supposed to happen tomorrow, then? Next week?"

Wallace sneered at me. "Don't be obtuse, Miriam. It goes horribly with 'bitchy.'"

Eddie ran back to join us. "Here." He handed me a pistol that couldn't kill time and sure as hell couldn't kill a two-hundred-pound man. "I know it doesn't look like much," he said, reading my mind, "but trust me: it works. Just remember when you pull the gun out, do it smooth and fast. And *squeeze* the trigger, don't jerk it with your finger. Take your time in a hurry. Got it? Understand?"

I nodded.

"Listen to me, Miriam," he continued. "It's your responsibility, your *duty* to keep that bastard from escaping."

I said, "Got it."

"I'm trusting you right now," he said, squeezing both of my shoulders. "Believe it or not, I think you're good shit, all right? Don't disappoint me."

"I won't." Despite his assurances, though, the pistol felt weak in my hands. It felt hollow. Made from beer cans and beer tabs and store-brand aluminum foil, held together by Scotch tape and two jumbo paper clips.

"You shoot a piece before?" Eddie asked.

Ripley now hid beneath my pillow at home in Los Angeles after helping me scare Prudence McAllister and then joining me at Billy's back on Thursday night. "I have a twenty-two at home. I go to the range a few times a month."

"Good," he said. "So you won't freeze up when you have to pull the trigger."

When *I* have to pull . . . ?

I said, "I don't freeze," even though I didn't trust this peashooter to shoot anyone except me.

Eddie hurried down the hallway and down the stairs in search of a signal.

"I guess you're allies now," Wallace said.

I slipped the gun into my back pocket. "The enemy of my enemy and whatnot. So, have you heard from Raul or Andreas or anybody back at port?"

He shook his head. "They should be en route, even as Edward insists on trying to contact the authorities. A waste of time—we're already scheduled to head back tonight, and it wasn't like Raul planned to drop people off, head back to the mainland, then turn around and come right back again this evening."

I blinked. "So . . . he's gonna stay docked?"

"Of course," Wallace said.

My heart sank—there was no chance to escape Mictlan Island before tonight.

"You look troubled," Wallace said. "Bad allergy attack again?"

My head lolled on my shoulders. "I just can't believe this is happening. I'm just . . . I'm so sorry, Wallace. Phillip deserved a quiet weekend."

Wallace ran his fingers up and down his arm. "He worked so hard, never asked for much. And I couldn't even do this right." He squeezed his eyes shut, then tried to take a deep breath. "I'm going to lie down now. I have to at least *pretend* to be rested and relaxed before Seth and Drew and Leigh Anne and the others arrive. I'm a mess, the house is a mess, and two of my guests are dead. I hate all of you."

"And I hate you, too, Wallace. With all of my heart." I tried to smile to show him that I was kidding.

"Ha ha." But then his face turned the color of persimmon—anger combined with jaundice. "Don't come bothering me unless something crazy happens. Again." Then he shuffled across the hallway, touching the wall every now and then for stability, to ensure that he was still here, that this was not a dream.

The heaviness of exhaustion pulled at my eyelids, and my bottom half felt like it had been dunked and dried in concrete. I hadn't had a decent night's sleep since . . . since . . . July 2015. It had been a Saturday. Nothing special. Just quiet. I'd sat in my backyard with its view of Los Angeles, a glass of red wine in one hand and in the other hand a big book about a blind French girl during World War II. That had been a good night.

Besides being tired, my full bladder jiggled every time I blinked. I needed to pee, like, *immediately*. But Eddie was counting on me to stand guard.

I think you're good shit.

I rested my ear against Frank's door.

Silence.

What was he doing? Sleeping? Reading a novel? Planning his escape? Praying? Remembering? If Wallace kicked him off Mictlan Island right now, would he still get whatever Phillip had left him? Were all bets off now that he'd killed Desi?

I really, *really* needed to go.

My bathroom was just down the stairs. I wouldn't take long.

I'll go and come right back.

What could possibly happen in three minutes?

Toast burns. Pregnancy test results come back.

Frank escapes. But Frank had to know that if he tried to escape, Eddie would catch him. Then Eddie would hang him from the highest tree.

Because Eddie was the hanging kind.

Oh, well. When you gotta go, you gotta go.

Sunlight filled the downstairs bathroom, and the CPK-style tile work shone like glass. It was quiet in here and I could exist without being afraid of anything or anyone. Still, though, my head and heart ached like someone had kicked both with steel-toed boots, then poured acid into my ears. My entire body worried about the craziness on Mictlan Island. Two people had died in two days—and I had just been deputized to guard a murderer.

Me.

I was a mom. I hadn't gone to school for this. I wrote copy for used things and made notes like STET and CALIBRI/NOT CAMBRIA and INSERT SM HERE. KPIs and calls to action were my jam. This—guarding murderers—was not my kind of call to action.

And what the hell was I gonna do with a clearance-rack gun? It looked even flimsier sitting on the sink. Really: the liquid soap dispenser, with its stainless steel body, pointy spout, and slipperiness, looked deadlier than Eddie's gun.

I hated this place. I hated this place even though the sky beyond the bathroom's windows was a perfect blue and the waters were clear and soft and filled with God's most exotic creatures. I would have preferred Los Angeles, too hot and too loud and too crowded with its thundering airplanes and jammed freeways and police chases every third day. Other than the coyotes, the high pollen count, and the wildfires, there was no god in L.A.'s wilderness, not with its planned trails and decent cell phone reception. No one would die from eating fish in my hometown. Sure, lovers killed each other—like Frank had killed Desi—but at least there were cops to call, a few with itchy trigger fingers who sometimes ached to handle the problem right there at the scene. At least you weren't trapped on an island in a house with two dead people and a murderer afoot. At least.

Why couldn't Ashlee be here on Mictlan Island and I be happy at home with *my* husband and *my* daughter? I could almost taste that happiness—it was heavy, rich, thick like maple syrup. I'd tasted it before, not realizing that it was a rare and wonderful gift.

Beyond the bathroom's closed door, I heard Wallace whisper to Eddie, "Easy . . . Easy . . . Be gentle with her."

The two men were moving Desi. Guess Eddie had caught Wallace before he'd settled down for his nap.

I took my time in washing my hands and avoided looking at myself in the mirror. I feared that I wouldn't recognize my reflection if I *did* look—Artemis had changed me that much in just two days.

But I couldn't stay here forever.

I left the bathroom and hurried toward the staircase before Eddie spotted me away from my post. As I neared the foyer, I glanced at the Bosch table.

Oh, crap.

Because now I *saw.*

Two pieces were missing from the tabletop: the naked woman and the man eating cake. I counted the figurines. *Five pieces left.* On Friday night, there had been seven. With a shaky hand, I reached for the green eye figurine, but I stopped short just in case it was cursed. So I stared at the table a moment more, then carefully made my way up the stairs.

Who had taken the figurines?

Back up on the second floor, nothing had changed. Eddie and Wallace were probably still in the freezer, placing Desi beside Javier and the other slabs of frozen meat.

Frank's door was still closed.

I placed my ear against the wood to hear, then knocked. "You still in there?"

"Where else would I go?" Frank snapped.

I plucked the gun from my pocket, then slid against the wall to land on the carpet. I stared at the toes of my muddy sneakers, then up at a ceiling free of cracks, bumps, and water spots. My wrist, the one Prudence McAllister had kicked way back on Thursday night, was starting to ache again. I hugged my knees to my chest and let out a long, loud sigh. This day . . . This year . . .

"Miriam." Someone touched my shoulder.

I heard myself snoring and jerked my head up from my knees. I had fallen asleep, and the gun had slipped out of my hand to the carpet.

Wallace was crouched before me, and his violet eyes bore into mine. "Didn't mean to frighten you." He held out a sandwich and potato chips on a plate and a glass of iced tea. "I know you didn't get to enjoy my fabulous frittata—there will never be another one like it. So I made you this instead."

I stared at him, then I stared at the sandwich: a lobster roll made from last night's forgotten entrée. "You sprinkle it with extra poison?"

He winked at me, then said, "Of course, I did. It's to *die* for."

I took his offering, happy that he was smiling again. "Thank you. Hopefully, death by sandwich will be quick." Wallace had been right: being a bitch *was* exhausting. And actually, I thought Wallace was pretty funny. And Phillip had liked him, *loved* him, so he couldn't have been *that* bad.

After taking two big bites, my body took on solidity again. "Desi?" I asked, my mouth full. I offered for him to share my potato chips.

He took a chip and crunched it. "Desi's with Javier. Poor, poor thing." He helped himself to another potato chip.

"Why do you think Frank killed her?"

Wallace shrugged. "Maybe it was accidental. Maybe their game went too far. I've read about unfortunate instances like that, instances where sex gets away from you."

I said, "I guess," because I hadn't experienced uncontrolled, dangerous coupling, not ever. "So . . . the table downstairs. Have you noticed . . . ?"

"Noticed . . . *what?*"

"Some of the pieces are missing."

He peered at me, then laughed. "Oh, Miriam. And we were getting along so well."

"And why would I mess that up by lying?"

Wallace shook his head. He tried to wear a serious face, but the corners of his mouth lifted. Like me, he couldn't help himself from winning the point. "I apologize, sweetheart. So. Missing pieces."

"Yes, missing," I said calmly. "The gluttony and lust figurines. I'd noticed gluttony earlier and just now, I noticed Desi's piece. It's gone."

This time, Wallace frowned, and his eyes lost some of that sparkle. "Who took them?"

I shrugged, then bit into my sandwich.

"Did you?"

"No," I said, my mouth full. "I didn't."

He grunted and looked down the hallway toward the staircase.

I added, "I'm confused about something else, too."

He lifted his eyebrows. "Just about one thing?"

"Okay, I'm confused about a *lot* of things. Like you and Phillip."

He grinned at me. "You didn't know that Phillip was gay, either?"

I shook my head. "He never mentioned . . . you. And he and I . . . He and I . . ."

"Flirted?"

"All the time." *Well . . .*

"He flirted with *everyone,* dear. That's how he got people to trust him. Believe me, it was all an act. He didn't mean it." He squinted at me. "I take that back. If he'd *meant* it, if you had truly mattered to him, then it's not for me to dash your dreams. Just know, though . . . he was trained to mislead. Trained to be a listener, to understand. I was lucky that we found each other, and that we chose each other in this awful world."

He propped his chin on his knee and smiled wistfully. "Phillip and I both craved a connection, craved being together forever. To be the couple everyone says they don't want to be but secretly, they *do* want the house, the dog, the wedding bands . . . We were so close to that—no dog, but everything else . . . and now that he's gone, I feel . . ." He stared at the carpet as his mind searched for the word. "I feel . . . undressed . . . half done. Doesn't help that I haven't had a moment to mourn him properly, to give him the send-off he deserves." He plucked another potato chip from my plate. "Feel free to break into 'Wind Beneath My Wings' at any time."

I swiped at a tear that had tumbled down my cheek, then warbled, *"Did you ever know that you're my hero . . . ?"*

He gave me a sad smile, then said, "Lovely."

I dabbed at my eyes with a knuckle. "Whatever hap-

pened between Phillip and me . . . I didn't know he was
involved because I would've never . . . I'm sorry." Not
that we'd slept together. *Yet.* There had always been
the possibility, I'd thought, and if we'd had more time,
maybe we would've. No. Yes—we would've fallen into
bed together. I knew that for sure.

"Let's change the subject, shall we?" Wallace said.

"Like what you said about Eddie killing someone?
When?"

"When he was a police officer back in Boston."

My jaw dropped. "Is he the cop who shot the kid
who was holding a cell phone?"

"No. He wasn't that one."

"The mom, she was coming home from prayer meeting with her son in the car and the cop—?"

"No," Wallace said, shaking his head. "The black
motorist . . ."

I blinked at him. "Be more specific."

"One night, Edward pulled over a black motorist for
a traffic violation. That's what *Eddie* says, of course.
The situation spiraled out of control, as it always does.
Eddie shot first and killed the man right there on the
sidewalk."

"Again," I said, face warming, "be more specific."

"Edward claimed the guy had an Uzi, but the guy
didn't. And then Edward was acquitted of murder—"

I gasped. "And the people rioted. Orlando Jackson.
He was a high school football coach, and—Eddie's
that cop? I'm on an island in the middle of the ocean
with *that* cop? Wait—there was a woman, right?"

Wallace nodded. "Orlando Jackson was dating
Eddie's ex-girlfriend. Charlotte had just broken up with
Edward, so Edward hunted Jackson down, found him,
and the rest is history."

My pulse thudded in my head. "And where is Charlotte?"

Wallace studied his fingernails. "Edward won't say. Well . . . he *says* he has no idea, but you know how *those* types are. She's in the bottom of the Boston Harbor or divided between twenty trash bags dumped in twenty different landfills." He nodded at the door. "I don't know *what* Phillip was thinking, bringing *Trey* here. But then, Phillip did invite five of his most awful clients, so why not?"

Anger burst like lava in my gut. "I was *not* an awful client. I did everything he told me to. Do *not* put me in the same category as Eddie's racist ass."

He chuckled. "We obviously have different definitions of 'awful.'"

"Phillip agreed with me—Brooke McAllister had it coming. I didn't hunt *anyone* down."

"True. Still: your approach, my dear. Phillip told me all that you'd done, and to be frank, you were just . . . *mean*."

I tossed him a glare. "But it was okay for her to bully *my* daughter until *Morgan* developed depression and bulimia? Brooke was no Girl Scout—she lied to Morgan, stole her part in the recital. She—"

"Why are you always looking at what someone else did and not what you've done?"

"Was Brooke's behavior acceptable? Should I have let fate handle it as *my* daughter was dying? Was I supposed to turn the other cheek?"

"Again, being honest?" Wallace said. "I admire you sticking up for your child—especially since the teachers *weren't* doing anything. The social media campaign thing you pulled, though? A little over the top."

The lobster roll sat in my gut like an anchor. "I didn't think . . . I . . . I didn't mean . . ." A sob burst from my gut, and I tried to contain it by clamping my hand over my mouth. But it couldn't stay contained, and I wept there on the carpet as the old man next to me watched.

"You're crying," Wallace said, "and yet Philip successfully got you off on a misdemeanor and made the McAllisters look like the stupid bigots they were for trying to put you in jail. That's what you wanted, right? Freedom?"

I nodded. "But-but pee-pee-people ha-hate me."

"It's their right to hate you," Wallace said. "You can't take it back now, Miriam. It's done. You're free. Last I'd heard, Morgan hated you. But at least she can hate you to your face and not behind prison bars." He tapped my wrist. "Go rest—you need it for when the others arrive. I'll watch our friend Trey for now."

"But Eddie—"

"Is busy trying to make that damned phone of his work."

I blew my nose into the napkin that he'd included with my sandwich, then dried my tear-soaked face. "Are you still planning on going through with the service today?"

He shrugged. "Hopefully—don't despair, though. You'll get your prize right after his ashes catch the wind and drift away."

"You actually *have* him?" I asked.

"Of course. I carried his urn over in my tote bag. It's gorgeous. Or as Desi would say: Gor. Jus. The color of fire. I saw it and had to have it. I chose a matching blue one for me—icy blue—for when it's my time to shuffle off this mortal coil."

Wallace's tote bag. The one he hadn't moved for me back in Puerto Peñasco. And now that I replayed that scene in my mind, I saw that Desi had taken the seat on Wallace's *right* side. The bag with the urn hadn't moved from that chair on his *left*.

"So," he said as he stood, "go, dear. Have some quiet time. I'll take your dishes back down to the kitchen."

I sighed, then shook my head. "I came here because

I wanted to show the world . . . to show them that I'm not a monster. That I *do* have a heart. That none of this has been easy for me."

He tossed me a small smile. "And now that I know you, I truly believe that. You're a momma bear who was just swiping at a Nazi-wolf. And once this is all over, once we're back in the good ol' USA, I'll help you show the world that you deserve forgiveness. You remind me of me in many ways. Misunderstood. Cast as the villain before you even open your mouth. And from what you're telling me, Phillip had a soft spot in his heart for you.

"Tell you what, doll. You help me get through this memorial—keep people from wandering into the freezer and the rest of my guests from dying, and I'll introduce you to some people I know—people who owe me. They will do as I ask because they were you once upon a time, and I will tell them to re-create you. In the end, you will be forever grateful to me—that's your payment, and whenever I need a favor, you'll say, 'Certainly, Wallace,' because I'll be funding your resurrection. Good old-fashioned quid pro quo."

He chuckled, then added, "It will be the best apology tour ever devised. It will rival Hugh Grant's and Reese Witherspoon's. I promise."

FROM: Mimi Macy
TO: Morgandancer
SENT: 1:37 p.m., Sunday, July 10
SUBJECT: Good news from Mexico!
Hey, Mo-sweetie!

I'm emailing you even though you may not get this message until I'm back on the mainland, which should be soon. I'm packed and ready to leave. Yes, already. Can't believe that it's time to go. Just in case a bar pops up, though, and this message goes through, I just wanted you to know . . . all the rules here have changed. Long story short: I was bamboozled! But I'm still going to win. I've met someone. No, not like that. ☺ His name is Wallace Zavarnella and he's a real estate guy. He's also Phil O.'s husband (surprise, right??)—Phil died last month from a brain tumor, sad news! I was shocked speechless. Yes, me. Speechless!

We're actually here for Phillip's memorial service, and I'm supposed to get something he left me, thousands of dollars, I believe, and a referral to another lawyer. I'll find out for sure in another 2–3 hours, after the service. So soon, this will all be over. Also good news that Wallace *adores* me and he understands why I've done what I've done and that the McAllisters are out of control. He's promised to represent me (or something) against them. He said he'd also help me land a literary agent who will sell my book! He thinks I could probably get millions. Bestselling author, here I come! So. Even though there is no prize and this weekend won't be on TV, I will still win a few things that money can't buy. Freedom! Peace of mind! A new career!

Call it Fate that I landed here in Mexico. Whatever it is has changed our lives forever. In a good way this time. Ha ha.

I love you with every breath that I take.

Mom

P.S. There are no souvenir shops on this island. But I will find that purple sweatshirt if it kills me!

23

Wallace was now a member of Team Miriam, and that man's will was stronger than mine. *Good Morning America. The Wendy Williams Show*. Maybe he could sell my story, something that showed my side, the *truthful* side, like that documentary on Amanda Knox. *You think you know everything, but you have no idea.*

I left the Gucci dress in the corner of the room. Didn't need to shove something that didn't fit and that reeked of poisonous vomit back into my luggage. I glanced at my phone—the yacht would soon arrive. The memorial service would begin and end with Phillip's ashes released on the bluffs. Then we'd return for the reading of his will, and then I'd be out—the first person to set foot back on *La Charon*. Packed and ready to go, not one more minute spent at Artemis. I'd wait for the bad vibes to dissipate before asking Wallace's permission to return.

None of this had been expected. The real reason for our coming here. Javier's death. Desi's death. And Phillip . . .

This trip to Artemis had been his last big joke. Ha. Good one, Omeke.

Not that he'd meant for any of this to happen, either. Except that *now*, two people had died as a result of this strange gag, and those of us who were still alive had been left confused, terrified, and exhausted. Fortunately, all of this trouble and effort would be worth it, in the end.

How much had he left me? Thousands—he knew I needed thousands. *Several* thousands. Maybe a cool mil. It was obvious that Phillip was rich—he'd paid for all of us to come here. He hadn't charged me his full rate—I could've never afforded him. Wallace had called me a Groupon guest. Ha. He was right. Compassion—that's what I'd speak about at the memorial. *Phillip Omeke was the most compassionate man I've ever known.*

I zipped up my suitcase, then rubbed my eyes. They crackled like dried leaves beneath my fingertips. They were still a little swollen from the poppy-allergy attack, from crying, from lack of sleep, and from not drinking enough water.

I'm gonna be all right. It's gonna be okay.

I was ready to go home. Ready to start this New Start. To see my daughter and to plant the sunflower and wildflower seeds I'd bought last week. I missed Morgan so much that my heart and my gut ached. I missed her failed attempts at baking homemade cupcakes from scratch. I missed her rummaging through my clothes and picking out a neglected sweatshirt and making it new again. I missed her eye rolling and her impatient breaths and her actively ignoring me. Even the digital pictures of her on my phone had dog-eared and faded because I looked at them so much. She was my North Star.

Too much time had passed with her hating me, and that had been my fault. Jealousy and revenge had stolen away chunks of time, time I should've spent loving her and laughing with her. I wasn't perfect, but now I wanted to be—for *her*. I had tomorrow, and my tomorrow would beat out the sun and the sea as wondrous things. My tomorrow would inspire poets and pastors. The tale of the prodigal mother and her modern-day road to Damascus, her "blind but now I see" moment. I would deal honorably with Detective Hurley and the McAllisters and anybody else who had picked a fight with me. An expensive endeavor, but now that Wallace had volunteered to be my sponsor, I could afford it.

F. Scott Fitzgerald had it wrong. There *were* second acts in American life. Ask Robert Downey Jr. Ask Martha Stewart. And coming soon: ask me!

Who needed Valium? Not *this* girl.

Yes, Artemis was a remarkable house, a modern castle that I'd always dreamed about. As a place of relaxation, though, it had been useless. There'd been no time to enjoy the sauna or the tennis court. The walk-in freezer had become a high-traffic morgue and my neighbors here were worse than the dopehead and serial shoplifter who lived across the street from me back in L.A. As a place of reflection, though, Artemis had been a gift, a guru that had helped me find and see, feel and witness. Artemis was church. I'd learned my lesson, and now it was time to leave this place. And I could do all of this, thanks to Phillip Omeke.

I took in the magnificent chandelier, the soft green walls, and the view of the jungle beyond the windows. On the vanity, Desi's blue scarf sat bunched against Javier's silver flask and Eddie's cheap gun—*Wait* . . .

Where's Eddie's gun? It wasn't sitting where I'd left it, right by the—

By the . . .

Shit. While I had guarded Eddie's room, I'd fallen asleep and the gun had slipped out of my hand and . . . *I left it upstairs in the hallway on the carpet—*

A memory flashed in a corner of my mind. I saw it, that fuzzy memory. Then, I remembered more and saw all sides of it and what I saw made my stomach plunge to my feet. I squeezed my throat and groaned. "No. No. *No* . . ."

This morning, a scream had pulled me out of sleep. Eddie and I had searched the second floor, and had found nothing. On our way back down to the first floor, we'd bumped into Evelyn standing at the base of the stairs. She'd stood there, and she'd said to Eddie and me . . . she'd said . . .

Desi's dead.

That's what she'd said.

But the door to Desi's room had been *locked.* That's why Eddie had to kick in the door.

How would Evelyn have known, though, that Desi was dead unless . . . ?

Unless . . .

She couldn't have known Desi's state unless she had been in Desi's *locked* bedroom. The *locked* bedroom . . . the open window . . .

Shit.

Evelyn killed Desi.

Oh, hell. Evelyn . . .

But who could I tell? Would Wallace believe me now that he and I had called a truce? Eddie—he was crazy, sure, but he was also a cop, and he'd understand my logic. Frank, the last of the living, would believe me just to deflect suspicion off *him.* Yes. They would *all* believe me now.

Tell them. Right now!

I rushed over to the door and flung it open.

No!

A noose sat on the carpet, right at my feet. It had been crafted with silk scarves, just like the noose I'd fashioned for Brooke McAllister. She'd taken that noose and had used it . . .

A white note card sat beside the noose. A message written in thick black letters took up the center space.

I DON'T NEED THIS ANYMORE. YOU SHOULD TRY IT.

All feeling left my face, and tears burned in my throat and in my already-irritated eyes. I threw a frantic look up and down the hallway. No one was around, yet I felt that disturbed emptiness again, like phantoms chasing ghosts.

Doesn't matter. Grab your bag and go!

I grabbed the handle of my suitcase and shouldered my tote. *Screw it all.* I'd skip the memorial and wait at the dock. Let *them* figure out who did what.

I'd stepped across the threshold and over that noose and note card when a man up on the second floor shouted, "Stop!"

It was Wallace shouting.

Oh, no.

THE

JOKER

24

I was standing in the doorway of my bedroom, luggage in hand. I crumpled against the wall,
so dizzy that my legs were crisscrossing on their own.
Eddie's gun had disappeared from the vanity, and
someone had left this noose and this note—I DON'T
NEED THIS ANYMORE. YOU SHOULD TRY IT—at my
door. Wallace had shouted, "Stop!" and then Evelyn
had screamed, "No!" and then Wallace had shrieked,
"What are you *doing*?"

That's when I tore my eyes away from the noose on
the floor. That's when I pushed myself away from the
wall. When Wallace started shouting. Because Wallace
never shouted.

My mind careened away from all of this—the noose,
the note card, the two bodies in the walk-in freezer—
and raced into the wilderness, across the Sea of Cortez.

I kicked the noose away from my foot and ran, leaving my tote and suitcase in the room. I dashed down the
hallway and hurtled up the stairs to the second floor,
racing down the hallway and those framed photographs of Artemis in fog and Artemis beneath summer
skies. A wedge of sunlight shone from Frank's open
door and gleamed across the hallway carpet. Hands
lost in her hair, Evelyn paced and trembled in the spot
that Wallace was supposed to be occupying. Her fear
stunk up the hallway—musky and musty and solid.

"What happened?" I shouted.

She didn't speak. Just waggled her head.

I could hear water splashing and rubber soles squeaking against a wet floor in Frank's room. My stomach dropped—I didn't like those sounds, especially made together.

Impatient, I charged into the room. This bedroom was a poor Italian man's idea of how a rich Italian man would decorate. It was bright and well lit, gold and glass—from the pillows and tables, chandelier and fixtures, to the furry rug on the floor. Nearly every object boasted a lion or a Baroque cross—the dresser, the closet door, the curtains. If it couldn't shatter, then it had been mined from the earth, cut from ancient trees or woven on a flaxen-haired damsel's loom. Frank's broken eyeglasses and a small case of cigars sat on the carved walnut credenza alongside his Rolex watch and gold cuff links. Clothes were strewn everywhere, flung from the empty piece of luggage in the closet.

"I told you," Eddie roared from the bathroom, "get out of the tub!"

Water splashed. Those rubber soles squeaked.

I hurried to the bathroom and froze in the doorway. Lavender-scented fog hung in the gold-colored room. Wallace, standing near the toilet, was almost invisible in the steam that had whitened the mirrors.

Eddie stood over the spa tub's bubbling water, now tinted pink and brown. Frank was in the tub and Eddie's enormous hands were wrapped around his neck.

Seeing that chokehold made every hair on my body bristle. "What the hell are you doing?" I shouted.

Eddie startled and released Frank from his grasp.

"You killed him!" Evelyn shrieked from behind me. "You killed him. I saw you."

"I found him like this," Eddie was shouting over the roar of the tub's frantic bubbling. He was trying to stand, but he kept slipping. "I found him like this and I didn't touch him until . . . This is *his* fault. See, this son of a bitch—"

"Shut up." I edged toward the tub, trying not to slip on the wet tile. "We need to get him out."

Wallace blushed. "Are you certain you want to . . . ? He's naked."

I rolled my eyes. "I'm not Evelyn—I've seen a *dick* before."

"Can somebody find the clicker and turn this damn thing off?" Eddie shouted.

I hit the power button on the tub's inner wall. Calm. Quiet. Oil slicks gathered atop the steaming pink water.

"Let's get him out," I said.

Wallace didn't move from his spot near the toilet.

"Are you gonna help," I snapped, "or do you plan to just stand there and take notes?"

Wallace waited a beat, then crept over to the tub.

Eddie ducked his hands into the water and winced. "It's hot as hell. We should wait until it cools down some."

"Yeah, let's let it cool down some," I said. "That way he can be nice and real dead when we pull out his *corpse.*"

Eddie growled, then dunked his hands back into the water. He scooped out Frank's feet as Wallace and I each took one of Frank's arms. After several minutes of trying to lift slippery, dead weight out of the damn-hot water, we finally succeeded and laid Frank on the bathroom floor. Eddie glared at me. "There. He's out. Satisfied? Cuz now my hands are frickin' fried." He was a big man, an angry man, who now stood over a naked, unmoving black man. 1717, 1817, 1917, today . . . This was a timeless American image.

Frank's nose was swollen as though he'd been hit in

the face. *Oh. Yeah.* He *had* been hit in the face—in De-si's room by Eddie's flying fists. His skin was red and blistering. His feet were bleeding. The skin that had shed now floated, with a cigar also bobbing in the oily water. All of him had bloated like a frog trapped in a kettle of hot water. Just beneath the scent of lavender oil, there was also another smell. Boiled flesh.

I gagged and tasted stomach acid. *Keep it together, keep it together.* I took deep breaths, in, out, in, out. My nausea ebbed but my head still spun, and I knew I'd never enjoy the scent of lavender ever again.

Wallace kneeled beside Frank, then bent over to listen to the man's chest. He whispered, "His heart's still beating. It's faint, but it's still . . ." Wallace tilted back Frank's head to open his airway. Then he placed his open palm against the man's slippery sternum.

Eddie placed his hand atop Wallace's. "Let me do that. I've been trained—"

I slapped Eddie's hand until he snatched it back and tucked it beneath his armpit. "You've done enough," I spat. "Try calling for help again or go run down to the dock—it's almost two thirty, and the boat should've been here hours ago."

Eddie stuck his swatted paw beneath his damp Red Sox cap, then jammed out of the bathroom.

Wallace placed his left hand on top of his right. "Here we go." Then he started compressions to Frank's chest. *Push-push-push . . . another one bites the dust . . . push-push-push . . . another one bites the dust.*

I held my breath and prayed that Frank's heartbeat grew stronger, that he sat up, that he did something other than what he was doing now, which was . . . dying.

One hundred beats later, Wallace's face was glistening with sweat. He stopped, then bent over again to listen to Frank's chest. This time, he frowned, shook his head, and sat back on the slick bathroom floor. "He's gone."

Wallace, Evelyn, and I sat in silence, for hours, it seemed. Finally, I heard something boom and clap around me. Not thunder. Just my heart pounding at its new speed.

Wallace scooted away from the body and balled up near the toilet. His wig had slipped farther back on his scalp to show more liver-spotted skin and tufts of white hair that had survived cancer treatment.

And we sat and said nothing as Frank's body cooled.

Footsteps pounded up the stairs and down the hall-way. Not enough footsteps, though. There were not enough footsteps. Eddie, just Eddie, slammed into the bathroom. "No boat."

"What do you mean, no boat?" I demanded.

He caught his breath, avoided looking at Frank down on the tile. "The boat that was supposed to be here isn't here."

Wallace covered his face with his hands and groaned. "No, no, no."

"Could it still be on its way?" I asked, hearing panic in my voice.

Eddie shrugged. "I didn't see anything. Maybe they're running late cuz of the storm and all."

"Yes, that's right," Wallace said, light returning to his face. "It's sunny skies here, but they may be getting weather again on the mainland right now."

I blinked away my tears and squared my shoulders. Swallowed the nausea and bile swirling in my stomach. Forced calm into my voice before asking, "What happened, Eddie? With Frank?"

Eddie paled, and his eyes went wide, and his hands clasped and opened, clasped and opened. "All's I know is . . . he was in the . . . the tub . . . and he . . . I found him . . . He was trying to . . . And I . . . didn't . . . I tried to pull him out, but . . . he was heavy."

"He killed Frank," Evelyn whispered. "He was holding him down in the water. He was killing him—"

I held out a hand to shush her. It was hard enough trying to listen and think and breathe at the same time while listening to her bleat.

Eddie shook his head. "No. No, I—"

"I saw you," Evelyn brayed. "Your hands were around his—"

"Wallace," I said, "what happened?"

Wallace kept his eyes closed as he said, "I'd just awakened from my nap, and . . . and . . . I don't . . . I can't . . ." He covered his mouth, then hid his face in his lap.

In tears, Evelyn stood from the wet floor. "Murderers and death all around me. Murderers and death and I'm going to die, too, I know it, it's coming. Why should I live, why am I here?" She gazed down at me with those blue and gray eyes. "You see me—I *am* a waste of space, a bag of bones, not good for anything."

I frowned at her. "What the hell are you talking about?"

"If God let Frank and Desi and Javier die, then why does He spare me? You said so, you hate me and wish I was never born."

Stunned, I blinked at her, then said, "I'd never say anything like that to you."

Evelyn wiped her snotty nose on the sleeve of her sweater, and kept muttering, "A bag of bones, that's all I am. A boat *should* run over me and drown me. No mercy."

Two months ago, I had no idea I'd be standing in this bathroom, in this house, on this island, in Mexico. But then, that email came from Mr. A. Nansi, and oh, what good fortune, my luck had changed, and *finally,* something wonderful was gonna happen.

But now . . .

Where was the boat? Where were the Mexican police? Who would come for us? *Would* someone come for us? *Would* we leave Artemis? *Of course,* we'd leave Artemis . . . *We* . . . Not many of "we" were left, not many at all.

That Phillip. *Such a joker.* I'd said that less than an hour ago.

I'm so lucky. I'd said that, too.

Yeah. My luck had *definitely* changed.

Excerpted from the *Houston Chronicle*
Sunday, April 2

REDUCED SENTENCE FOR
MORTGAGE FRAUD

. . . saw his sentence reduced from 30 to 2 months for cooperating with authorities in the prosecution of his partner Montriece Carneckie.

Trey Porter, 49, a onetime real estate agent, joined with Carneckie in forgery and mortgage fraud over the last seven years. The scheme cost victims more than $20 million. The racket came to an end once a third partner, Alvin Alvinson, was murdered in a local Dallas barbershop. For cooperating in the murder investigation, Porter was given a reduced sentence.

"He was scared for his life," Phillip Omeke, Porter's attorney, claims. "Carneckie had threatened that he would come after Trey if he talked."

Prosecutors allege that Carneckie, Porter and Alvinson forced victims to pay thousands of dollars to save their properties from foreclosures on fraudulent loans, which were originally forged by the three men.

25

Yes, my luck had changed. But someone else had worse luck than me.

I stood there in the middle of the bathroom, staring down in disbelief at a dead man on a wet tile floor. Exhaustion and anxiety made me shake, and my organs knocked against each other in time to *push-push-push . . . another one bites the dust*. In that golden light, the steam made everything shimmer. Even everyday things—Frank's toothbrush, tube of toothpaste, razor, bottle of lotion—dazzled on the marble counter. None of it would ever be used again.

Quietly weeping, Evelyn trotted out of the bathroom, hands lost again in her woolly hair. A moment later, Frank's bedroom door slammed.

I turned to Eddie. "Why did you . . . ? Why?" My voice sounded raspy, weak.

Eddie stuck his right hand inside his shorts pocket, then pulled it out again. One of Desi's fake sapphire earrings sat in the middle of his palm. "While Frank was in the bathroom, I searched his luggage. This was in a pocket. He lied—he stole her earrings."

I squinted at him. "And so you *killed* him because—?"

"Are you nuts? I didn't kill him!"

"Your hands were around his—"

"That wasn't me killing him. That was me trying to help him."

"Help him? You're just like every other abusive asshole—"

"What did you just say?" he boomed.

"I *said*—"

"Play nice, girls!" Wallace perched on the toilet with his mottled hands gripping his knees. "We need to move him to the freezer."

My arms and legs were too weak to lift anything or anyone else. "What if we just lay a sheet over him?"

Him. Motionless. Lifeless. And his blood was now seeping around the floor's square tiles like grout.

"He was already like this when I got here," Eddie said to me. "I was trying to help him get out of the tub."

I rolled my eyes. "Get out of the tub, drown him, po-*ta*-to, po-*tah*-to, it's all the same, right? Tell it to the judge."

"All's I know is *this*." Eddie pointed at me. "*You* left your station. *You* were supposed to—"

"Wallace said he'd cover for me," I yelled.

"Wait just a minute." Wallace's violet eyes widened, and he touched his chest. "*I* said *what*?"

"You told me that I could go rest and that you'd stand watch—"

"Because I'm now Wyatt Earp? *Guarding*—that doesn't even *sound* like something I'd be interested in."

"No one was at the door," Eddie said. "I asked *you*, Miriam, to watch him, not Wallace."

My eyes scanned the wet, bloody tile as though the answer could be found among Frank's twisted boxer shorts and his eighteen-karat-gold Cartier lighter. "You're right, Eddie. You *did* ask me. I'm sorry." Was I going crazy, though? Hadn't Wallace agreed to stand guard? I had offered him the handgun and he'd said that I could go rest . . .

Didn't he?

That lighter . . .

I glanced back into the tub at that floating cigar, and I tried to smell past the stink of boiled man.

"Doesn't matter," Wallace said. "What's done is done. Frank is gone and there's nothing we can do for him now." He stood from the toilet seat. "*You* two decide what to do about him. *I* need to change out of these wet clothes and try to figure out where my guests are. Well, the ones who are still alive." He tossed a final look at Frank, clucked his tongue, then slipped out of the bathroom.

I closed my eyes and tried to slow the rush of my pulse. Tried to focus on the water's deep, dark plopping from the tub's spout. I even thought, *There's no place like home,* then quietly clicked my heels together just in case it worked for me like it had worked for the girl from Kansas. I counted to three, then opened my eyes.

There was Frank. There was blood. There was Eddie, standing at the sink, rubbing his hands across his face.

"Miriam," he said, addressing my reflection in the mirror, "I didn't . . . do this."

This. Frank lay there, dead, a *this* now.

I looked up to the ceiling to plead with a higher power, then noticed that the gold paint up there was a bit darker than the paint down here near the mirrors and door. I also noticed that a half-empty bottle of bath oil sat on the rim of the tub along with three thick votive candles with charred wicks. A matchbook sat on the toilet tank, a long way away from the tub.

"It's wicked strange," Eddie said. "I was thinking about those earrings, and so I came back to the house since the boat wasn't here yet, since I couldn't get a signal to make the call anyway. I ran up the stairs and came here, to his room, and no one was guarding the door. I rushed in, okay, and found his luggage, looked through it, and of course, I found the earring. And that's when I heard the splashing—he was in the tub. So I ran in, and he . . . It was hot in here, and I was a little pissed cuz he was taking a fucking bath when he'd just killed that girl, and I . . . I saw that something was wrong with him, and so I tried to pull him out of the tub but the water was so hot . . ."

I looked at that lighter again. At that cigar again. Could have been nothing. Could have been the reason for that darkened ceiling. I plucked the lighter from the wet tile. So elegant, even as it simply sat in my palm.

Eddie was still staring at my reflection in the mirror. "What is it?"

"Maybe the cigar fell into the tub, lighting the bath oil and burning Frank. Fire. Heat. That could explain his frantic splashing."

Eddie said nothing.

"When you came into the bathroom," I said, "what did you see?"

"I saw . . . Frank convulsing in the water, flopping around, making a mess. Could hardly see him, though, cuz of the steam. A lot of steam."

"Where was Evelyn?"

"Who?"

"The nurse," I said. "Where was she?"

He shrugged. "How would I know?"

"Do you know if Frank had used the tub before?"

Eddie shrugged. "Why would I know that?" He paused, then squinted at me. "What? You're a detective now? Everybody wants to do my freakin' job—"

"I'm asking because if he'd just run the water and assumed it would be the right temperature . . . Maybe the water was too hot to begin with? Like it was broken or . . . ?" A shrug with those questions—I didn't know nor did I believe any of this. Maybe a hot tub in a janky roadside motel would malfunction, but a Jacuzzi in *this* house, a mansion with a *name*?

Eddie scratched his head, then slapped his hand against his thigh. "You should've been here, Miriam. I trusted you, and you let me down."

"And I'm telling you," I said, "I wouldn't have gone unless Wallace had agreed to look after him. I know that I'm tired and a little stressed out, but I didn't put words in his mouth." I swallowed, then added, "And someone left a noose at my door. Someone also stole my Valium."

"Someone?" His eyebrows scrunched. "Like who?"

"Wallace? Or . . ."

"Just stop," he said, holding up his hand. "You just can't stop crying wolf. Are you gonna swear on your momma's grave next? Ask God to strike you dead if you're telling a fib? Demand a lie detector test? What?"

My skin burned as if it had just been lit with Frank's fancy gold lighter. I wanted to scream, *I'm not lying* and *I'll show you,* then drag him down to my bedroom, then shout, *See? I told you.* But I didn't scream. I didn't insist. The noose wouldn't be there. Not because it didn't exist, but because my role here at Artemis was Crazy Lady Who Made Shit Up, the Lying Liar Who Told Lies for No Reason. Because there wasn't enough drama with dead people and missing yachts, I had to go create more fantastical tales than the ones I'd tell years from now to my great-grandchildren on dark stormy nights.

"My girl Charlotte?" Eddie said. "She's a liar, too. Reminds me a lot of you. Just a white girl, a redhead, that's the difference. But she lied to my face as much as she breathed. You cheatin' on me, Char? Of course not, Eddie. You lyin' right now, Char? You're so paranoid, Eddie. You screwin' that guy, Char? On and on and her lying more and more . . . I couldn't stand it then, can't stand it now." His face tightened as he glared at me, as the veins in his temples bulged. "You're a lot like her. Drives me freakin' crazy."

My blood chilled, because his loathing of me was louder than that dripping water, louder than my banging heart.

Finally, he said, "Take it." He dumped Desi's single earring into my palm. "Once we find the other one, we can give 'em to her people. I'll go find something to wrap Frank in, like a tarp or something." Then, he stomped past me and out of the bathroom.

Oh, hell no. He wasn't leaving *me* alone with Mictlan Island's newest dead man. So I ran after him. "I'm going with you."

"Don't need you," Eddie said.

"I didn't ask permission." I squared my shoulders. "Either we look for a boat or a phone or whatever side by side, or I'll do it by myself."

Eddie's jaw tightened. "Fine. Keep up. Try not to die."

"Great," I said. "Try not to kill anybody."

He glowered at me, then forced himself to grin. "You're good shit, Miriam."

We hurried down to the dock—no yacht had been anchored off the pier. No yacht loomed far off in the distance. "You think pirates hijacked it or something?" I asked, my eyes scanning the horizon.

Eddie scratched his scalp, then dropped his heavy hand. "Maybe it's coming to the other side of the island. Let's go look."

We followed the shoreline—fine white sand became pebbles, and pebbles soon grew into rocks and finally boulders. The waves crashed violently here, churning and frothing, squeezing into skinny spaces between those slick stones. Up, up high was the bluff that had hosted Desi and Frank's midnight rendezvous.

"Hey, Eddie. I don't think a boat would come this way." My face and shirt were wet with perspiration and mist from the crashing waves.

The cop said, "I think you're right." He muttered a curse, then rubbed his jaw.

I stared at the large man, at his sunburned arms and strong mouth. Men like Eddie solved problems all the time. How to ship goods quickly between the Atlantic and Pacific Oceans. Where to find cheap labor to colonize stolen land. Then, men like Wallace stole those goods and purchased that stolen land at low, low prices. Men like Wallace kept secrets—and I thought he was actively doing that now. So I said to Eddie, "I think Wallace is keeping something to himself. This— none of this—seems right."

Eddie glared at me, then looked back to the sea. "Spit it out or save it for somebody else."

"I mean . . . this place. His job. Do you think he works for Escorpion?"

Eddie clicked his teeth as he thought, then ran his hand beneath his wet baseball cap. "I have my theories."

I waited a beat. When he didn't speak, I said, "You wanna share?"

"No, not really." He turned to me with flat blue eyes. "We should keep looking."

My legs burned from all the walking on the beach and slipping on wet rocks.

Eddie didn't slow down, nor did he look back to see if I had avoided being swallowed up in the surf or being eaten alive by a chupacabra. He kept moving, he kept his mouth shut, and he kept his theory of Wallace and this island to himself.

And because of his silence, I knew to trust a chupacabra or the angry ocean before trusting him or Wallace ever again.

26

Out here, way away from Mictlan Island's newest dead man, the air had freshness, and my lungs had to work less to keep me alive. Out here, way away from Frank, Artemis transformed back into the luxurious mansion that I'd first seen, the luxurious mansion with a media room and a swimming pool, a special place that pampered you and tricked you into thinking you'd done something in your life to deserve a butler's pantry.

After tromping around the island in search of a boat, Eddie and I determined that there was no way of escaping this place short of swimming the Sea of Cortez.

The cop and I parted ways at the base of the front porch. "I'm not giving up," Eddie said, his words tighter than his fists.

I ran my wrist across my sweaty forehead, then saluted him. "Good luck."

Wallace stood waiting for me on the second-floor landing. He had changed into a long-sleeved T-shirt, linen slacks, and pristine white sneakers. "Where did you and Edward go in such a rush? Is the boat here?"

"No boat. He's still looking."

"For?"

"Anything. Everything."

"I don't know what to do," Wallace said, wringing his hands. "I can't contact anyone on the radio—nothing but static now. A priest was coming, so who's supposed to lead the service? And . . . can we even have a service? It's just . . . just four of us and . . . This is a complete disaster."

I slipped my hands inside my jeans pockets. My fingers brushed against Frank's Cartier lighter and Desi's earring. I squinted over at the Bosch table. "I wanna check something. Come down."

"Really, Miriam," he said, taking one step—slowly, slowly—at a time. "Are you okay? I'm barely hanging on."

I snorted, then said, "I'm barely hanging on, too, especially since you sold me out. But I guess that's part of the fun." I approached the Bosch table with my stomach bubbling. I counted—one . . . two . . . Four pieces left on the panels.

Wallace said, "What do you mean by that? Since I *sold you out*?"

"You told me that you'd stand guard—"

"This again?"

"Yes, *this* again. And give me the gun."

"What gun?"

"I left it in the hallway when you told me that you'd stand guard—"

"This again-*again*." He turned to leave. "I'm going back to my room to stare at a television that doesn't work and pretend Kelly Ripa is as funny as she thinks she is."

I grabbed his arm. "No. Wait."

He glared at my hand as though it was made of toxic sludge. "Dearest, I suggest you don't go there."

I didn't let go.

His eyes hardened.

I squeezed his arm once to stress my seriousness, then released my grip. "Come with me. I have a theory."

"Can I not and pretend that we did?"

"I'm serious."

"Come with you *where*?"

I led him to Evelyn's bedroom and knocked on the closed door. "Evelyn, you in there?"

She didn't respond.

Wallace whispered, "Why are we—?"

I shushed him, then twisted the doorknob.

Unlocked.

An atomic bomb had exploded in her baby blue bedroom. Feathers from busted pillows dusted the dressers, curtains, and bedding. Cotton batting from the gutted suede chaise lounge spilled out onto the soiled shaggy carpet. Wads of wet, balled-up paper—spitballs—clung to the ceiling.

"What in the hell?" I whispered.

"Monsters lead such *interesting* lives," Wallace said as his eyes skipped from one mess over here to another mess over there.

I crossed the threshold into the room, stepping on matted this and crunchy that. My stomach dropped as the stink wormed its way into my nose. That stink . . . indescribable but close to the same stink found on farms. Old eggs, hay, sweat, and—

I'd smelled this before.

"Why are we in here, Miriam?" Wallace asked. "And when can we leave?"

My eyes scanned the filthy carpet and the flat surfaces. I spotted a dresser drawer that had been left open.

Inside: a clear baggie filled with pills stamped 2 DAN. Desi's second earring. A white and black plastic bottle. Eddie's gun.

I shivered, and that pressing feeling on my lungs returned. "*This* is why we're here."

"How'd you think to look in here?" Wallace said, squinting at me.

My mind struggled to land on a simple, believable explanation. "She just seemed . . . I don't know." I plucked the baggie filled with stolen tabs of Valium from the collection. "These are mine. She stole them from my room."

Wallace reached for the small white and black bottle and read the label. "Silver Cleanse Dip. Jewelry cleaner. Why do you think she has *this*?"

"Taste it and find out."

"No, you first." He shook the bottle, then read the label again. "Contains . . . oh, dear. Potassium cyanide." His eyebrows lifted in surprise. "Angel of Mercy Nurse Pemstein dropped some of this on your fugu last night, didn't she?"

I nodded. "While Javier was pouring wine, remember how she went to the kitchen for juice and then she screamed about the snake and we all rushed into the kitchen? We came back to the dining room and Javier served the fugu." My plate . . . she knew it was my plate because it had a whopping big *M* engraved across it—and if she'd missed *that*, my first name in smaller print sat beneath it. "That's why Evelyn wasn't scared to eat the fish on *her* plate. Javier . . . he'd cut the fish right. That's why she didn't die."

"And that . . ." Wallace pointed at Eddie's pea-shooter.

"I left it on the carpet—"

"But I didn't notice it," Wallace said, "since I went back to the kitchen and Evelyn must've . . . If Edward had asked you for it and you didn't have it . . ."

"He would've killed me." Those footprints in my carpet—she'd probably left those behind every time she'd look for something to steal from my room. And each time she'd entered and left, the room had felt warm and heavy, and smelled . . . eggs and sweat . . . *Had she left that noose?* No. She couldn't have known about *that*. Only Wallace knew, because Phillip had probably told him everything as he lay dying.

The old man rubbed his forehead. "For some reason, she's planning for every one of us to die. But if she thinks I'm dying by *her* hand, she's dumber than she looks, and I will tell her so. Where the hell is she?"

I glanced out the bedroom window and saw Evelyn sitting at a patio table on the lawn. She was eating from a bag of potato chips, *tra la la,* as though nothing dramatic had just happened in a bathroom on the second floor, as though she hadn't broken down in a pitiful mess, wishing to be run over by a swift-moving yacht.

Wallace stood beside me. "That's what psychopaths look like on a Sunday afternoon."

"We need to get off this island," I said, "and maybe, if Eddie can get the radio or the satellite phone to work—"

Wallace winced and stepped away from the window.

"What's wrong?"

He was tugging at his side. "I'm sore, and I'm tired from pulling what's-his-face out of that tub. Really: I can feel the cancer cells multiplying and the tumors gnawing and crunching away at the little bit of healthy tissue I have left." He took deep breaths in, then out, and shook his head. "But that doesn't matter right now. At this rate, with this woman roaming the house . . ."

I whispered, "The Bosch table."

"What about it?"

"Back on Friday night, you said that we were the embodiment of the Seven Deadly Sins. What if you're right? What if we're being punished, and once we're gone, our figurine . . . ?"

"Disappears." He nodded. "Maybe Evelyn is seeing to that."

I blinked at him. "But that's silly. Seven deadly . . . ? If Evelyn is killing us because . . . No. She doesn't know me. She doesn't know . . ." *What I've done.*

And anyway: Who would I be?

Lust? I'd been faithful to Billy during our marriage. Although I wasn't a virgin on our wedding night, I could still count the number of lovers I'd had on one hand.

But Desi. Larry and Danny and Hoyt and Frank and who knows who else . . . She had been strangled, left tied and naked in bed.

Gluttony? I liked food, but I never stuffed myself. I hated germy buffets and never took advantage of all-you-can-eat anything.

Javier had cooked and eaten and snorted and drunk. . . . He had died eating poisonous fish.

Greed? I didn't want thirty of anything, nor had I married Billy for his money. In fact, Billy *had* no money during our newlywed days.

Forging signatures, stealing, robbing, putting out hits . . . Frank had been boiled in his golden bathtub filled with oil.

Laziness? I'd only stayed at home with Morgan for three years, and then I went back to work. Even then, I never slept in and I kept a tidy house. I cooked. I did our taxes.

Pride? Okay. A little. But that wasn't a *problem*—I needed a very healthy amount of self-esteem to be black and female in America.

Envy? Anger? Well, yeah—again, it can be a bitch to simply exist, to *aspire,* but I wasn't *angry* about it. Nor did I begrudge people the fruits of their hustle. At least, not enough to *kill* someone.

More or less.

"Evelyn," I said. "She's stealing the figurines."

Wallace narrowed his eyes but didn't comment otherwise.

My face warmed. "It *has* to be her. Who else could it be?"

He held my gaze for a moment, then said, "I've been thinking about that since we discovered Desi this morning. And now with Frank . . . I just don't know."

"It's Evelyn," I blurted.

Wallace said, "Hmm."

"She screwed with the heating and made it so hot that Frank boiled. He tried to get out, but the tub was slippery from bath oil."

"And then, she ran down here on those stubby legs of hers and stole the dollar sign figurine."

"Is it gone?"

He tilted his head. "Is it?"

I narrowed my eyes—I didn't like his tone. "Yes."

He said, "Hmm," again, then shrugged his thin shoulders. "Say that Evelyn, for some reason, is doing all of this. Has someone directed her to kill us? Or is she doing it because she *wants* to?"

"Don't know," I said, "but I *do* know—"

"That we need to get off the island," we said together.

He leaned closer to me. His breath smelled sweet, but it was the sweet found in dark alleys and dank sewers. The sweet that told me something inside of him was dying. "Any ideas," he said, "on how we do that without using a phone? Without hopping on a boat?"

I shook my head. "No idea."

"Maybe we should ask our friend Evelyn about . . ." He pointed to the dresser filled with other people's things.

A grin cut across my face, and I snatched Eddie's gun from its spot. "Let's go."

Together, we shuffled past the foyer. I glanced at the Bosch table—the dollar sign *had* disappeared.

Outside, the air was a solid wall of moist heat. The sun cast everything in a sickly yellow light, and the leaves on the jungle trees swayed without sound.

The pistol was sticking to the skin near the small of my back, and I hoped that my sweat and body heat wouldn't melt the glue that held the weapon together.

"Wallace," I said, "we can't let her know right off the bat that *we* know that she had something to do with Desi and Frank. She'll run into the woods if it's obvious that we're coming to kick her ass."

"Agreed," he said. "Just follow my lead."

We snuck to the house's north end, then peeked around the corner.

Evelyn was still sitting at the small patio table on the edge of the lawn. Still shoving her hand into an open bag of Ruffles. Still stuffing her mouth with potato chips.

The green lawn lay like a carpet, and I stooped to touch the blades . . . which didn't give between my fingers. The grass was fake. *Fake.* All of it had been created in a lab somewhere in Taiwan. Were the only *real* things on this island the three dead people scattered around the house and the four who remained?

"There you are," Wallace said to Evelyn as he stepped around the corner. "Hate to interrupt your snack break, my dear, but it's time that we all have a serious conversation."

Evelyn stared at us. Her pitted face and raggedy sweater were grubby with potato chips, and her bloated fingers shone with grease and salt, bright pink and tender looking. "Conversation about what?"

"Believe it or not," he said, "I think you may actually have something worthwhile to contribute to finding a solution to this horrible situation. Shocked? I'm shocked, too. Tell me—"

"God is doing this to us," she said.

"Why?" Wallace asked. "For what reason?"

"As payment for what you've both done," she said.

"And what have *I* done?" I asked.

"The killing."

Wallace peered at me. "Miriam, did *you* kill Frank?"

I shook my head. "Of course not."

"Did you kill Javier or Desireé?"

"No."

"And I actually believe Edward," Wallace said. "He's a hateful person, but he wouldn't *boil* a man. He's a gun nut—his penis demands the use of blue steel." He turned his gaze back to Evelyn. "See, dear? Neither of us are sure what you mean by God punishing us for killing."

"Are there other people on the island?" I asked. "Maybe *they* did it."

"No," Wallace said. "This is Phillip's private island, and Artemis is its only residence. There are no other souls living on this abhorrent piece of land. But let's talk about Frank—how *did* he boil to death like that?"

Evelyn shifted her gaze to the bag of potato chips.

An overwhelming sadness settled over me—I would have to kill this woman. The sad part? I didn't mind. Not at all.

"Evelyn," Wallace asked, "do you have any thoughts on how Frank boiled to death?"

She bit her lip. "Maybe . . . maybe . . . the oil caught . . ."

"On fire?" I asked.

She nodded. "Or maybe . . . maybe . . . the water was too hot."

"But *how* did it get too hot?" Wallace asked.

Evelyn shrugged. "The thermostat?"

"Hmm . . ." Wallace rubbed his lips and pretended to be lost in thought. "Or . . . maybe we should start considering the possibility that something *supernatural* is happening here."

"Like ghosts?" I asked.

He nodded. "Really nasty ones, too."

I said, "Hunh," then wandered to the edge of the property as though lost in thought. Out there, the waves gleamed with sunlight, and the dark mass that was Mexico seemed as close to us as Saturn. I filled my lungs with moist, salty air, then turned back to Wallace and Evelyn. "Say that it *is* God doing this to us, as Evelyn suggested. Then . . . ?"

Wallace spread his arms, feigning hopelessness. "*Then,* we are meant to die here . . . unless either of *you* knows something that I don't know."

I smiled at the old nurse. "Like why you had Eddie's gun in your dresser drawer? Like why your hands look like you've scalded them in hot water, and why—"

"What's going on?"

I swiveled toward the man's voice but froze once my eyes landed on Wallace.

A red dot the size of an Indian bindi beamed on the old man's jaundiced forehead.

And Eddie said, "You move, you die."

27

My hands shot up and my pulse shot into the stratosphere.

"Hanging out without me? How rude." Eddie slipped from around the house with his TEC-9 aimed at Wallace's forehead. His eyes were hard and flat, shards of topaz.

"Edward," Wallace said, smiling. "Just in time."

Evelyn *eep*ed as she toppled out of her chair. The Ruffles bag fell to the ground and its ridged chips scattered across the pristine synthetic turf. She left them behind as she trotted toward the tree line.

Because it was so humid, the air now weighed thirty tons, and I had trouble keeping my hands up in the air. Beads of sweat trickled down my face, down my neck, across my body, making my damp shirt stick to damp skin. Eddie's gun, the wack one held together by spit, tape, and God's grace, still lived in the small of my back.

If I could reach for the gun and shoot Eddie before he shot us . . . But I didn't know for sure that the gun actually *worked,* that bullets would fly out of the muzzle instead of a red flag that said BANG. So I didn't dare move.

Wallace's chest had inflated with surprise—and it hadn't dipped yet to show that he had exhaled. He had stopped breathing, stopped moving, had frozen in place. All except for his hands. He had shaky jazz hands—probably because that red bead now glowing on his forehead had yet to move. "Edward, we were just trying to figure out—"

"Shut up," Eddie barked. "Where are they, old man?"

Wallace blinked. "Where are . . . *what*?"

Eddie inched closer to us. "My guns. They're missing. Where are they? What did you do with 'em? Who did you give 'em to?" He was one minute away from squeezing that trigger, shooting and shooting and shooting until no one remained standing.

Beep . . . beep . . . Sounded like a battery was dying. The high-pitched beep was coming from the satellite phone shoved into Eddie's back pocket. A green light—*a signal?*—flickered near the phone's antenna.

"Eddie," I said, "why would Wallace take your guns? To do *what* with?"

"You're right, Miriam." Eddie slowly moved the TEC-9 from Wallace to me. "Then *you* must've taken them."

"No. No. No . . . I've been with *you* most of the . . ." Fear had dried up all the spit in my mouth but I still tried to swallow. "The only . . ." *Gun you gave me is now hiding in my pants.*

"The only *what*?" Eddie shouted.

I flinched, and now *I* was the one suffering from jazz hands.

And the satellite phone kept beeping . . . beeping . . .

"The only *thing* we should be focusing on right now," I said, "is getting off this island."

He sneered at me. "Good luck with that, homegirl. We're not going anywhere anytime soon." He aimed the weapon back at Wallace, then said, "Right? You'd know this. Cuz you're a part of them."

Wallace hesitated before he said, "A part of *whom*? Of *what*?"

Eddie took deliberate steps toward Wallace until the

muzzle rested against the old man's forehead. "You're a part of the Escorpion Cartel. You're his lawyer, his number two."

"What?" Wallace and I both screeched.

"*You* directed all of it," Eddie continued. "The gun trafficking, the dope, the kidnappings. I know it. I know you. Seen you on TV, in the papers."

"*Me?*" Wallace asked. "Never."

The green light on the satellite phone flickered . . . flickered . . . and then it popped off. No more beeps. No more light. The signal was gone.

Standing this close to Eddie, I could see white powder dusting the tip of his nose. Had he snorted some of Javier's cocaine?

"Say something," the cop demanded with a twisted grin. "Explain yourself, asshole. Where's your witty comeback? You gonna tell us some random story about San Francisco in the seventies or about your little dog named Mr. Bigglesworth or some shit like that? Or are you gonna show the *real* you? Why don't you tell us how many *eses* are in your clique and how much *cocaine* you *hombres* brought into the U.S. last year? Which Wallace are you about to be right now, huh?"

Wallace's eyes bulged. His mouth opened, but then closed again. He shook his head, speechless for the first time all weekend.

I could feel the old man's heart pounding wildly in his weak chest. Mine almost matched its rhythm but couldn't—a TEC-9 wasn't mere inches away from *my* brain.

"So are you gonna come clean," Eddie asked, "or do I shoot you and spill it that way?"

"Edward," Wallace said, "I have no idea what you're going on about. Drugs? I don't even smoke *cigarettes* anymore. I'm just an old, washed-up cabana boy who married—"

"Answer. The. Question." Spit gathered at the corners of Eddie's mouth.

Wallace's eyes fluttered and any color he still had drained from his face. "I am not a part of the Escorpion Cartel—"

"Then who's running operations while Escorpion is rotting in a jail cell in Fort Worth? You, right?" Eddie's hand hardened around the gun's grip. "Answer me."

Wallace gulped. "Escorpion hates me. I kicked him off this island. We—"

"Who's running the cartel?"

Oh my god, I'm gonna die. He's gonna kill us.

Eddie's head jerked to the right. "What was that? You see that?" The muscles in his face jumped and twitched as he stared at the tree line, in the direction Evelyn had run.

Wallace and I also stared at the forest. Butterflies flitted above sycamores now swaying in a breeze that I couldn't feel.

Eddie grabbed Wallace by the arm. "Let's go. They're here."

My hands were skittish birds, fluttering from my hips to my arms, to my face, to my hips again, and to my arms again. "*Who's* here?"

"His friends." Eddie's eyes skittered from tree to rock to bird to butterfly. "They've been tracking us all this time." He tossed a glare at Wallace. "Just like you did when you killed the original number two. Surveillance cameras, tracking devices in cars . . . You *stole* the second satellite phone, didn't—?" His head jerked and his eyes hit the jungle again, harder this time.

I scanned the wilds but saw only the trees, those butterflies, the dirt trail that led back to the docks. There were rocks and ferns and tangled vines. But there were no bars, there were no satellites, there was no help and no chance. Past the woods, there was a sea connected to the biggest ocean on the planet. There was a boathouse that housed no boats. There was nothing. Except us. And Eddie. And he was paranoid and high and seeing things.

Somewhere in the tangle, a tree branch cracked, sending birds screaming to the sky. It echoed above the sounds of the jungle and the pounding of my heart.

They're here.

"What was that?" Wallace rasped.

We listened. No more cracking. Regular sounds again. Birds. Ocean. Wind.

Wait. *Stole the second satellite phone. There's a second phone?*

"Hear that?" Eddie's face was red and sweaty, and the vein in the middle of his forehead bulged, moments away from bursting. Would it burst? Could it burst? *Please let it burst.* He waited a moment, then nodded. "Yeah. Hear it?"

I didn't know whether to nod and agree, or to shake my head and say, "No." Because other than that snap, there were no sounds that weren't supposed to be. So I squeezed my eyes shut, wanting to hear; I opened my eyes, wanting to see, closed them again, wanting his paranoia to be real and not imagined, and wanting to fear something other than this man with a gun. This was my prayer: *Please let the danger be somewhere else, somewhere deep in the jungle and not here, standing a foot away from me.*

"Open your fucking eyes, Miriam," Eddie said. "Let's go."

I planted my feet firmly on that fake grass and folded my arms. "I'm not walking into the *woods.* You just said that Escorpion was here. Why the hell would I—?"

Eddie aimed the gun at me. "We can't get there from here. We need to move. So, move."

28

Can't get *where* from here?

Eddie wouldn't say where we were going—and he kept the gun pointed in my direction. So I moved.

With the TEC-9 aimed at our backs, Eddie forced Wallace and me to march into the jungle. The sun was lost up there in that weird copper sky. Twigs and dry grass crackled beneath my sneakers as we traveled on a smaller trail to the left of the main path we'd walked just two days ago (*or was that yesterday?*). And that monster that had tracked us on our first afternoon on Mictlan Island had found us again. It was big . . . and strong . . . big, strong, and invisible, and I smelled it. It smelled like sweating horses, dog shit, and sulfur.

I glanced at the men behind me. "I think we should go back to the house." My voice sounded as weak and as scared as I felt.

Wallace said nothing—his face was blank with shock.

Eddie's T-shirt and baseball cap were darkened with sweat. His eyes darted here and there, landing and staying in no one place for too long. "They're out here," he said. "I saw 'em. I heard 'em. You did, too. I got 'em good back at home. Fifty years to life. They vowed to come after me. They're trying to take revenge. *Venganza,* that's what they texted me. Got my partner Ryan first, though. Kidnapped him. Tortured him in some ghetto apartment. Beat him with bats, with rolling pins, wire hangers, understand? Ryan dies, okay, and then?

"*Then* they drain his blood in the tub, until there ain't nothing left. They toss him out of the window. He falls six, seven stories down into the alley. We find him an hour later, with a note stapled to his chest. *Tu eres el próximo.* 'You're next.' They're taking their time, though. Taking people around me first, one by one, taking Charlotte, just like I told the judge, cuz I don't know where she is, but they took her, and now they're leaving me for last."

Eddie watched me, then snapped his head to the right, hearing things I didn't hear, then stared up at the sun and the light filtering through the leaves. "Charlotte thinks she's quick, but I'm always three steps—" He cocked his head to listen, peered at the surrounding trees, then sniffed. "You smell that?" he whispered.

I stared at him for a moment before sniffing, too. I smelled growing things. Dying things. The sea. *Him.* That monster. One and the same?

Wallace didn't sniff, pant, or swipe at the bead of sweat trailing down the bridge of his nose.

"Go," Eddie instructed, pushing the back of Wallace's head with the weapon. "Keep walking."

The breeze was gone and the air was still even as weird warm mist rolled around our ankles.

"What do you know about dumbass Evelyn?" Eddie asked.

Wallace said, "I don't know *anything* about Evelyn."

"That bitch knows something," Eddie said. "She's never around. And she knew Desi was dead before anybody else did. She's your so-called nurse, ain't she? Bullshit cover story if I've ever heard one."

"Never met the woman until coming here," Wallace claimed. "I didn't hire her. I didn't invite her. Phillip did. She's *his* client."

"You won't admit it," Eddie said to Wallace, "but I know you're working with that hag. You and her, scheming with those Mexican scum. I bagged plenty of fuckers like you back home. Molesting and pimping little boys. Disgusting. You think Escorpion likes that shit? Hell, no. He's a *real* man. But you know what? I'll do him a solid. *I'll* take care of you. You'll die here before I do. Her, too. Yeah, you, Miriam. *Venganza*, motherfuckers."

No one spoke as we marched deeper into the forest. *Think! Think!* Where was the other satellite phone Eddie had tried to use, the one that was now missing? What was the emergency phone number in those emails inviting me here? I couldn't remember anything now. Each time my mind came close to landing on an answer—*it's in Evelyn's ... area code ...*—the answer spooked and flitted away like a startled sparrow.

Sleep—I needed sleep. That's why I couldn't think. That's why I couldn't remember. And my pills. Evelyn *had* taken my Valium, I *had* brought Valium to the island, right? When had I discovered them in her drawer? An hour ago? This morning? Yesterday?

Wallace—he'd slept throughout our time here. On the yacht. Last night in his room. I'd seen him napping yesterday in the chaise lounge on the lawn. *Right?* In a patio chair near the swimming pool? After breakfast? Why had he been so relaxed up until now? Was he really Felix Escorpion's number two? What was happening? *Why* was this happening?

We marched and marched, on trails and off trails, crisscrossing paths that we'd just left, passing Artemis's front porch three times. Marching and shuffling in circles. But I didn't speak or point out that we'd passed that same moss-covered trunk with its beautiful yellow fern three times already.

Finally, after an hour of this aimlessness, Eddie veered

to a path we *hadn't* taken, a path just a stone's throw from my bedroom window. That's when we came upon a weird-shaped banyan, with twisty branches that reached high into the canopy and twisty branches low enough to climb. Patches of red-black poppies grew in between the banyans. On the trail a few yards ahead sat a large, broken branch. Above it, up in one of those not-high, not-low branches, a pair of dirty black slippers swayed in the air. Connected to those slippers were a pair of unshaven, pale and plump legs. . . . a broom skirt . . . a ratty sweater . . . Evelyn's neck . . . and the rope that had broken it.

"Oh." I gasped and clamped my hands over my mouth. "Oh, no."

This hanging had been the crack we'd heard. And for several seconds, we stared at the still body without saying a word.

Finally, Eddie said, "Where the hell did she find rope?"

I gaped at the ex-cop. "Who *cares*? Did she hang herself? Or did someone do it to her?"

Wallace sighed, shook his head. "Doesn't matter."

"It does. Did someone kill her or—?" Something in me cracked just like that broken branch had cracked, and my knees gave and I collapsed on the dirt trail. Pressure was building between my ears, near my heart, and around my gut. I wanted to vomit and explode and suffocate at the same time. Through tears, I stared up at the dead woman's shoes, at her tongue clamped between her teeth, and then at the red-black poppies that could make the pain end. And then I was shrieking, shrieking even before I realized that those cries were mine. "No! No! No!" over and over again.

No to death. *No* to whatever it was that was now hunting us, haunting me.

Wallace knelt to comfort me, but I pushed him away and shouted, "We need to leave or we'll be—"

"Shut up," Eddie yelled, pointing that TEC-9 at me again. "Keep quiet or I'll . . . I'll . . . just . . . I'm thinking."

I swallowed my sobs, then looked back up at Evelyn hanging from the tree branch. "No," I whispered as I forced myself to stand. "I'm calling somebody. Right now. I'm calling . . . If that means finding a signal in the middle of the goddamned ocean, I'm getting off this island. I'm—" And then I ran back to the house, not caring if Eddie shot me in the head, not caring if the monster in the forest gobbled me up, not caring if the Escorpion Cartel found me and skinned me alive, drained my blood, then fed my jerkied body to their dogs. I didn't care about Wallace surviving or Eddie finally losing what was left of his senses. And as I ran, Artemis, white, pristine, and elegant, peeked through the sycamores, but never got any closer.

Bitch.

Didn't matter. I wouldn't stop running, even though my crying kept me blind, even though that straining and squeezing was now killing me cell by cell.

Because I was dead already.

TO: Morgan, Billy
    Call 911! I'm trapped
Today, 4:41 PM

TO: Morgan, Billy
    No 911 here. Mictlan island. House called Artemis 4
    people dead
Today, 4:49 PM

TO: Morgan, Billy
    Are you getting my messages???
Today, 5:04 PM

TO: Miriam
    UNDELIVERABLE
Today, 5:06 PM

TORPEDO, AWAY!

FROM: Mimi Macy
TO: Morgandancer
SENT: 8:03 p.m., Sunday, July 10
SUBJECT: Help!!

Dear Mo:

It's been three hours now and I haven't heard from you!! I'm not sure if that's because you are ignoring me or because you haven't received any of my messages. I've tried texting you but I know for sure that none of my texts have gone through. We were told that there's no wifi here but I'm still trying. So this email is like a message in a bottle tossed into the sea!! I hope that you get it. I hope that you read it in time and I hope that you do something to save me before it's too late!!

I'm not crying wolf!!

I'm not exaggerating!!

I'M IN REAL DANGER!!!!

Back on Friday, I came here to this incredible house with six other people. Last night, our chef died. He was poisoned. And then today, three more people died. Actually, I think they were KILLED by this sick, scary nurse who had murdered her patients before coming to Mexico. I think she poisoned the chef, and I think she strangled the woman from West Virginia and then, I think she boiled this black guy in the bathtub. We never got to find out for sure because she hung herself from a tree in the jungle. Or worse—someone hung her from that tree. I'm not sure, but we found a few clues that she did all of this, but that doesn't matter right now. Because right now, I'm on this island with a crazy cop and a drug dealer or something. *And* we found a field of poppies here. You know what that means??? Opium, heroin. Who's guarding it?? Someone has to be, and now that I know it exists, and they know that *I* know, they'll try to kill me!!

Just writing all of this sounds absolutely crazy. Like something out of a movie. Believe me: I know I make shit up sometimes, but right now, I'm not. This is all TRUE!!!

I haven't left my bedroom for almost three hours!! Not sure what I should do now. Except pray and wait—and I'm not sure what I'd be waiting for. Another boat with people was supposed to be here at eleven this morning for Phil O.'s memorial service, but it never came. We don't know if it even left the port or if it sunk in the storm. All I've done since then, since my last texts to you, is run, cry and stare out my window, out at the trees, waiting to die, regretting so much.

I was wrong to take revenge on Brooke. As the grown-up, I should've looked for better ways to deal with that situation. All that time, I kept saying that I was doing all of it for you—and in some ways, I *was* doing it for you. Because I'd do anything for you, Mo. But I know now that some (okay, all) of it was done out of spite, and done to satisfy my own needs.

I didn't want Brooke to get the best of me.

I didn't want her to win.

I didn't want her to avoid the pain.

I liked seeing her mocked and her reputation trashed.

I liked buying those scarves, and making that noose.

I liked sending it to her and suggesting that she use it.

But I didn't mean for her to actually use it, to actually slip the damned thing around her head, go into her bedroom closet and hang herself.

I didn't want her to commit suicide.

I didn't want her to die.

I wanted her to lose. That's all. To lose for once in her life.

I'm so sorry. That she died. That I pushed her toward her end. Most of all, I'm sorry that I hurt you. And that's the truth.

It took me coming here to this godforsaken island with these horrible people to realize how awful I've been and how truly awful Brooke's death was.

I hope I get the chance to make it up to you.

I hope for so many things.

Somehow, I know I'll see you again, Morgan.

Your love will bring me home. It always has. You are the best of me. You're the only person who will believe me, who knows I'm telling the truth. I need you now, Morgan. I need you to save me, or else you may never see me again.

Please, please send help as soon as you get this.

I love you so much,
Mom

29

The furious pounding on my bedroom door woke me.

It was Eddie again. "Open up now, you whore!"

A little after midnight, shocked that the noose and the card had remained there on the hallway carpet, I had tossed them out the window and into the bushes beneath the ledge. I had also slid the giant armoire and the chaise lounge in front of my bedroom door as a sound and violence barrier. The fancy furniture had muffled Eddie's voice and his fists, and had allowed me to sleep for a few hours without too much worry. But he was back, pounding and hollering again.

Still in bed, I stretched and my hand slipped beneath the pillow. My fingertips touched cold rocks or . . . What . . . ? I shot upright and tossed the pillow to the ground. There they sat.

Not cold rocks. They were the missing game pieces from the Bosch table in the foyer. The lusty wench. The cake eater. The dollar sign. And now, the hag.

Who . . . ? When . . . ?

Heart hammering in my chest, I grabbed the figurines, hopped out of the bed, and darted over to the fireplace. I reached in and ran my hands along the cold brick wall until I felt the short shelf there, the shelf where I'd hidden Eddie's lame pistol. I plucked the weapon from its spot, then hid the figurines there in its place.

"Open the damned door," Eddie demanded. He

paused, then calmly said, "We've done this before, sweetheart. It never works. You're weaker than me, we *know* this. And you get real loopy when your stomach's empty, right, babe? Yeah, you get a little punchy, but that's okay. We can fix something, a sandwich or whatever, and then we can talk this thing through. You're starving right now, ain't ya? Me, too."

Yes, I *was* starving. My stomach was gnawing at itself—Wallace's lunchtime lobster roll had been the only real meal I'd eaten since Javier's huevos rancheros breakfast yesterday. There was plenty of food in the kitchen—but I didn't want to break bread with Eddie. Oh, hell, no. I wanted this dude to go search for monsters and drug mules in the forest and never come back.

Wallace—I hadn't heard from the old man since I'd abandoned him beneath Evelyn's hanging corpse. Had Eddie successfully killed him? *Him.* Felix Escorpion's number two? One of Mexico's most feared? Wallace was many things, but not a drug dealer. He'd kicked people out of their homes, torn down historic buildings to replace them with malls and expensive condos. He and Phillip had purchased Mictlan Island from the Mexican government for just six million dollars. If anything, Felix Escorpion *hated* Wallace. Wanted *venganza* on the man who'd crashed his heroin operation.

I glanced at the clock on my cell phone—7:38 A.M.

Cold had taken up residence again in my feet, hands, and chest. I tiptoed over to the thermostat—fifty-five degrees. How was I freezing in the middle of the jungle?

I pushed the "up" arrow key, but the damn thing wouldn't move past fifty-five.

In my suitcase, I found the warmest outfit I'd packed: a fleecy yellow sweatsuit that Morgan had given me for Christmas. She'd saved to buy it: birthday money, random change, borrowed tens and crumpled twenties, and then she'd had Billy drive her around the city to find it. The sweatsuit was so soft and so bright, just like my Morgan, and now I rubbed it against my cheek and remembered the light in her face as I pulled back the wrapping paper that Christmas morning, the light in her eyes the first time I wore it, how she had elbowed me that morning and said, "You're fly for an old lady," and I'd said, "You're looking at *you* in thirty years," and then—

"Open up, bitch!" Eddie bellowed, kicking at my door.

I dressed as fast as I could, then shoved my feet back into the pair of mud-spattered sneakers. Last, I slipped the gun into the small of my back.

And Eddie kept shouting.

We need to talk about this.

I'm not gonna hurt you, I swear.

I'm still in love with you.

I promise I won't hurt you.

Char-baby, c'mon. Charlotte.

Charlotte? I spun farther away from the barricaded door. Had he thought he'd been talking to his *ex* all this time? Horrified, I gaped at the armoire that was rattling every thirty seconds from his kick or punch. The calm I'd earned from fitful sleep was now crumbling, like packed dirt loosening.

I closed my eyes and prayed, "Lord, if you get me out of this, if you let me make it home . . ."

You'll kill Billy and Ashlee just like you said you would?

Back on Thursday night, I'd sped west on Slauson Avenue after my "thing" with Prudence McAllister. I had parked in front of the house that should've still been mine. Morgan had been standing in the French doors as though she'd had a premonition that I was coming.

"It's late, Miriam." Ashlee stood on the porch. She peered at her watch, then glowered at me with big doe eyes. "What's wrong now?"

Solomon Burke's soulful voice drifted from the living room and out the front door. *I'll give you my everything . . .* Billy's favorite song was playing on the stereo.

I ran my fingers through my hair but they caught—tangles made by the egg Prudence had thrown at my head as I'd lain on the ground. "I'm not going away until I talk to Billy."

Ashlee sighed, then said, "Hold on." She left me standing on the porch. *My* porch just two years ago.

The neighborhood hadn't changed since I'd been displaced. The California ranch next door still boasted its grand piano and grander lawn. The Mediterranean's porte cochere still harbored an aging Jaguar. The Remmicks still had that breathtaking view of the Pacific Ocean on one side and the skyscrapers of downtown Los Angeles on the other. Billy always bragged about his view of the Santa Monica, San Gabriel, and San Bernardino Mountains.

"Mimi, why the hell—?" Billy filled the doorway even though he was a slight man. Just forty-eight years old, he was now completely gray. Of course, he'd blamed me for his hair color. "What happened?" he asked.

"Long story." I offered a weak smile to match the quaver in my voice. "Are you gonna invite me in?"

"That wouldn't be a good idea."

I snorted and heat burned my upper lip. "Says who? Ashlee?"

"No. Says Morgan—she wants you to leave."

I glanced back to the living room windows and to my seventeen-year-old daughter, who wore a sweatshirt that had belonged to me in 1984. "I was attacked to-night," I said, my gaze still on our daughter. "They came to my house again and this time, they *assaulted* me."

"Okay. Who came?" Billy asked, rolling his eyes.

"Prudence McAllister, Jake, and Cecily."

Freckled Cecily Pritchard, seventeen, with hair the color of fire and lemonade, had stood on the sidewalk. She'd been Brooke's best friend and Morgan's, too, once upon a time. All three girls had met on the first day of kindergarten and hadn't separated until ballet and middle school and boys forced their breakup. Until sixth grade, Brooke, Morgan, and sometimes Cecily spent vacations in Hawaii and Mexico with each other's families. The trio rode their first roller coaster together, learned how to swim and plié together. I drove Brooke to her first dance class, then drove her to every class after that until sixth grade. I taught Cecily how to make French toast and gave her lunch money anytime her mother forgot. I treated those girls like my own anytime we traveled—anything I gave Morgan, they also received without hesitation.

But then a seismic BFF shift occurred, and soon, Cecily was out and Brooke was in. I noticed this change once Brooke and Morgan bought those necklaces with pendants that said BEST on one and FRIENDS on the other. It had never mattered that Brooke was white and Morgan was black. Sisters from other misters, they'd always say. But soon, Morgan got the lead in both winter and spring recitals. Cute blond soccer team captain Dylan then asked Morgan to junior prom instead of asking Brooke. Brooke started hurling the words "nappy" and "ashy" in Morgan's direction, and then the swastikas and Pepe the Frog stickers came. Despite all that Morgan had done, all that *I* had done, Cecily and Brooke put goddamned *frog* stickers on my daughter's locker?

Last year, I did something about it, to make the abuse and harassment stop, and the rest was history. I pleaded with Cecily's and Brooke's parents to intervene. When the adults refused and the girls' behavior continued, I posted pictures and videos on Facebook, Twitter, and Instagram. I talked to teachers and college counselors, dance instructors and volleyball coaches. And I had proof.

And now Billy was smirking. "You're telling me that three rich white kids—"

"Jake's not white—"

"Two and a half rich white kids drove to a bad neighbor—"

"Because it's black, it's a bad neighborhood?"

Billy sighed. "Drove into a *black* neighborhood *again* after being told to stay away from you, but they drove there anyway to egg your house and beat you up?" He gaped at me. "And that's a believable story to you?"

My lips flattened against my teeth as I growled, "It's not a story. Prudence, that little bitch . . ." I held up my wrist. "She broke it."

"You go to the emergency room?"

"I'm on my way," I lied, "but I already know that it's broken. Fractured, at least."

"At least." Billy shoved his hands into his pockets, then leaned against the doorframe.

Morgan glared at me from her spot in the living room and shook her head.

Ashlee appeared behind Morgan and wrapped her long arms around *my* daughter's shoulders. She whispered in Morgan's ear, then together, they left the window.

"Miriam," Billy said, "why are you *here*? What do you *want*?"

I stared at the two-year-old scar on his cheek, made

by one of my fingernails. The crushing in my chest made it hard to speak—no words came even though my mouth moved.

"Did you call Phil?" he asked.

"Not yet."

"You call the cops?"

"Not yet."

"Why not?"

I threw up my hands and squeezed shut my eyes. "Because . . . I didn't feel like going through all that tonight. Because I should be home, resting for my trip tomorrow. Because Jake's dad will simply do the powerful lawyer thing, twisting it so that *I* was the one who egged my own house and magically contorted enough to break my own wrist. He did it before, he'll do it again. Once I get back from Mexico, I'll send copies of everything to Detective Hurley, and to Phillip, and they'll arrest her ass before she can hurt me again."

Billy ran his hands over his face, then let out a long, loud sigh.

"I have video of them attacking me," I said.

He almost smiled, which meant that he smirked. "Let me see it."

Shit. I fumbled for my phone. Tapped the security system's app. *Video not available at this time.* "I think I have to . . ." I closed out of the app, then opened it again. *Video not available at this time.* "Give me a minute."

"When was the last time you took a Valium?" he asked.

My mouth moved again, but instead of speaking, I shrugged. And we stood there in silence until my larynx thawed, and I blurted, "The video, it's here, I swear."

His brown eyes softened. "If the kids did, indeed, come tonight—"

"I'm not making this up. I really do have video this time. It's just not playing for whatever reason."

"If something truly happened tonight," he continued, "you should call the police, just to be on record, and then you should call your lawyer. After you've taken care of business, you should really take something to calm down. That's why Dr. Sandoval gave you a prescription. There's no shame in that, Miriam."

I pointed at him with my trembling injured hand. "Don't do that. Don't act like you care. I know you don't."

Billy pinched the bridge of his nose. "You're right. I *don't*. Nor do I believe you. Because this is what you do."

We stood there in silence again.

He appraised me, his pity barely hiding his scorn. Judging my egg-stained tracksuit and my stiffening hair, my midforties gut and my cracked iPhone. "What is it that you want me to do? What do you want me to say?"

"*Excuse* me?"

"This." He waved his hand at me, then at the sky. "All of this is staged. You manipulated this to get me to do . . . *what*? Don't act surprised. I know you—we were married for eighteen years. What do you *want*, Miriam?"

"I wanna see my daughter."

"She doesn't wanna see *you*. Respect that."

Sweaty and shaking, I sipped the jasmine-scented night air as egg crackled and dried across my skin. *Enough!* I struck my thigh with my healthy fist, then shouted, "Respect? Even though you're letting *her* disrespect *me*? Even though you're letting *her* treat me like shit? Even though—"

Morgan slipped behind her father. The loose tendrils

around her head resembled a corona. Her coloring *had* returned, even though her green eyes still looked flat, lifeless.

"You know I love you, Mo," I said to her. "I love you more than anyone in the world."

Morgan rolled those cold green eyes. *My* eyes.

"Maybe," Ashlee said, "you should've thought about that—"

"Did I ask you anything?" I demanded, head cocked.

"You brought this on yourself," Billy said.

"I was protecting our child."

"By persuading another child to kill herself?" Billy screeched.

"I was acquitted—I didn't kill her."

Billy glared at me, his nostrils wide.

Morgan hid her face in Ashlee's knobby shoulder.

Anger and sadness swirled from my gut up to my heart. "I leave tomorrow." My knees hitched as I backed off the porch. "And life's gonna be different when I get back. And you'll see: you were wrong about me, about them, about everything. You'll see that . . ." My voice caught in my throat. "But it'll be too late."

"Okay. Fine. We'll take that chance." Billy's gaze wandered to the neighbor's house across the street, then down Corning Avenue. "Have a safe trip, Miriam. Get some rest. You need it."

My head was spinning and I tasted sour milk and bile. Ripley was hidden in my jacket pocket, and now my hand brushed against the gun's wooden grip.

That's when I decided: *as soon as I get back from Mexico, I will kill Ashlee and I will kill Billy.* I wouldn't fail this time. I wouldn't flinch. I had come so close to it on the night I'd found them together and he had sneered at me, and she had flashed that cold smile at me, and I had launched myself at Billy like a jackal, spitting and clawing until his blood and skin had dirtied my fingernails. That night, at Ashlee's dumpy apartment in San Pedro, I would've shot both of them dead if I'd had a gun. But that night, I didn't have my gun.

So close. Billy and Ashlee had no idea that death had been seconds away, that I'd spared them. On this night, though ... Once I returned from Mexico, I told myself, I'd handle them the way I should have. And if that meant someone got hurt, so be it.

But that was then. This was now, and *now,* I didn't mean it. Not any of it. That night, I'd been angry and hurt and ...

"Let it be, Char, all right?" Eddie said. "I didn't mean to call you a whore. You know I'm not so good with words, honey. You know I go off sometimes. On everyone, not just you. I just wanted to scare you, is all. My bark is worse than my bite."

He chuckled, then added, "Although my bark is a son of a bitch. 'Member that time we got into it on the paddleboats? You really thought I was gonna knock you over into the water and you was scared cuz you can't swim. You didn't drown that day, did you? That's cuz my bark, sweetheart. I'm all talk, Char."

It was too early in the morning for his brand of crazy.

I scanned the room. Soiled cocktail dress. Stiletto heels. Bottle of perfume. Rattail comb. The baggie of Valium I'd reclaimed from Evelyn's dresser drawer. None of them were good weapons. Especially if Eddie had been snorting Javier's—

Gun. My head jerked—in the kitchen, just a day ago, Javier had told me ... *something something* ... bag in the pantry ... *Gat* ... *bought it off some* pendejo ...

Tears of joy flooded my eyes—a real gun existed just rooms away.

"I know what you're thinking," Eddie continued. "I didn't drown you, but I did all kinds of other shit to you. Did more than bark. But you know what, Char? You forced my hand."

To get that pistol, though, and to find food, I needed Eddie to leave my door. Right then, I was Wendy in *The Shining* and Eddie was Jack, and we were just as deserted on this island as Jack and Wendy at the Overlook Hotel high up in the Rockies. Wendy had made it out, though. Yes, she had made it out and Jack had frozen to death. All I needed was an ax, a blizzard, and a garden maze. Or Javier's gun.

"You cheated on me!" Eddie was now shouting. "What did you expect me to do? And you cheated on me with that *nig*—? With *him*? What the *fuck,* Char? He mouthed off at me, so yeah, I pulled his ass over when I saw him that night. And he disrespected me *again,* so damn right, I was gonna react. Fuck him. And you know what? Fuck you, too, ya fuckin' skeezer. You think you're scared now? You think you're scared *now*? Just wait. I got something planned for you, sweetheart." This time, Eddie's kick made the armoire tip forward a bit.

Get him away from the door.

I lurched over to the vanity and popped a Valium, and then another Valium to make up for lost time. That's when I spotted the crystal vase filled with fake roses. I tossed the flowers to the carpet and picked up the vase. A Waterford, the finest crystal in the world. I opened the window, letting in jungle-wet air. The sun sat high against the blue sky and its light glimmered down upon the rich green of the trees and high grass. It was a perfect day for destruction.

I used all of my strength to throw the vase out the window.

The crystal piece sailed high for a moment, catching enough light to form prisms in its belly before landing in a great crash at the start of the thicket.

I heard Eddie gasp, and then I heard his heavy silence.

Soon, footsteps bounded down the hall, then echoed against the hardwood floor in the foyer. The front door slammed.

I closed my eyes and imagined him staring out from the porch, surveying the wilderness with his weapon ready, seeing nothing . . . nothing . . . then . . . *that!* That's when I saw him, in real life, race toward the jungle. He stopped before the trail, knelt, and plucked a shard of crystal from the dirt. He peered at that fragment, then looked back at the house.

I ducked beneath the window before he saw me. I rubbed my sweaty palms against my pants as I counted to thirty. At thirty-one, I peeked over the windowsill.

He was now standing with his back to me. Staring . . . staring . . . He tossed the glass to the ground, then raced into the wild.

Now!

I pushed the chaise and armoire away from the door. Held my breath and peeked out from my room. Nothing to my left except Desi's wonky door still hanging from its hinges. Nothing to my right except Eddie's grimy Red Sox cap abandoned on the carpet. Shadows crept along the cold walls, and the heavy silence was broken only by my breathing.

Go now!

I didn't look at the table in the foyer—didn't want to see which piece would go missing next. Instead, I crept to the kitchen. The Valium was already working like a flatiron that had just smoothed frizzy nerves. And as I crept, I didn't fret; while I hurried, I wasn't harried. All good. Just chill. *Boom-shaka-laka.*

The kitchen smelled like a Nuyorican bodega on an August afternoon. Food Wallace had used to fix a frittata that no one had eaten still sat on the breakfast counter along with Javier's dinner remains. Ice cubes clattered into the refrigerator's bucket, and I froze. Had Eddie heard that noise wherever he was?

I had to move *now,* and so I scurried past the dining room. The stink of chaos and vomit and old fish and death made me gag. As I stepped into the butler's pantry, my stomach growled—my brain had told it that my eyes were now drifting across cartons of crackers, jars of olives, boxes of cereals, dried noodles, dried beans, and canned broth. So orderly in here. Everything stacked just so. Neat. Sensible. And yet, steps away, bodies, cold bodies.

Business first. Javier's black duffel bag sat beside a pallet of bottled water.

I pulled at the bag's zipper with twitchy fingers.

Bam! A gunshot reverberated through the jungle.

What the hell? My heart staggered in my chest for a moment before it was pulled back into its pleasant drugged hug.

He'd be here any minute now.

Which he? Eddie or Wallace?

Didn't matter. *He'd* be charging past the saplings, crashing up the porch stairs, banging into the house to find me here . . .

Any minute now.

I rummaged through the duffel bag. Bottles of rum, a baggie of weed, packets of rolling papers, an extra chef's smock, and a black gun case that looked just like

Eddie's gun case. *Yes!* I pushed the clasps, and the case opened with a *pop.*

Oh *shit.* No . . .

Oh *shit.*

The gun case was empty.

30

The gun case couldn't have been emptier.

No!

Javier had told me . . .

A gat . . . bought off some pendejo . . .

Eddie must have found it and taken it.

For a minute or two, I couldn't move. I just stooped there in the pantry, staring at that empty gun case. I stood finally, eyes still on Javier's bag, mind too relaxed, muscles too far from tense. The Valium was doing its job. *Maybe taking two wasn't a good idea.*

Disappointment poked at me, but I didn't freak out. Couldn't freak out. Medically impossible to freak out.

What now?

Thinking . . . thinking . . .

I still had Eddie's lousy popgun that I didn't trust.

Oh, well. If that's the only weapon I have . . .

Back on my knees, I sorted through Javier's black bag. I kept the rum and dumped out everything else. I packed bottles of water, mangoes, and skinny loaves of French bread. In went cans of tuna, a jar of mayonnaise, and crostini just in case I needed to hole up again in my bedroom. Then, with Javier's bag over my shoulder, I backed out of the pantry.

Time to head back to my room.

I paused as I passed the refrigerator. Six newspaper clippings sat beneath six magnets that I hadn't noticed before.

The article beneath the cactus magnet: WHITE SUL-PHUR SPRINGS WOMAN LOSES HUSBAND IN TROPICAL STORM.

Under the Mexican flag magnet, the clipping CUS-TOMER DIES OF STROKE AT B.I.G. IN VEGAS included a picture of Javier standing in front of his restaurant.

An iguana magnet with REDUCED SENTENCE FOR MORTGAGE FRAUD sat beneath the flag.

There was BOSTON POLICE OFFICER NOT CHARGED and NEW CLUES IN FIFTY-YEAR-OLD DOUBLE MURDER beneath a pair of matching maracas.

The last article—NO FELONY CHARGES FOR MOTHER IN BULLYING CASE—sat beneath a lime-green butterfly magnet.

Who had put these here? Evelyn? Wallace?

On numb feet, I crept back to my room without anyone jumping out at me from the shadows. Before closing the bedroom door, I whispered, "Eddie?" He could've snuck in during my adventure to the kitchen, but a quick glance in the closet and under the bed told me that I was alone. With a heavy sigh, I dropped Javier's bag on the bed. My wrist throbbed as I slid the armoire and chaise back to barricade the door, then hid the gun in the fireplace next to those Bosch figurines.

Take a minute. Think. Eat.

I perched on the bed, tore back the mango's peel, ripped into the sweet, soft flesh, then gobbled a hunk of French bread. I guzzled a bottle of water and I listened to my blood sizzle and my bones harden. The room moved out of shadow as the sun found its place high in the sky. I stayed on the bed. Ate more bread and another mango, dozed off a few times, startled awake to find myself still alone in the room. This could not be my plan—hide until someone found me. But my body didn't want to leave this spot. Indeed, popping two Valium had been a mistake.

And so I lay there, and I slept, and I dreamed of Prudence McAllister kicking me, of Morgan pushing me down a flight of stairs. I dreamed that I sat on a white-sand beach, sobbing uncontrollably, never being rescued, the tide swallowing up the beach with each surge of waves.

Sweating and panting, I sat up in bed. The shadows had returned, and the sky had turned a bruised blue-gray. I looked at my phone—it was nearly five o'clock. The drug had worn off, along with the hope that *La Charon* was now anchored at the tiny boathouse. Too much time had passed. Either the yacht had capsized or Escorpion had killed Raul and Andreas. Either way, the boat wasn't coming. I was stranded.

My throat tightened and horror banged at the door protecting my calm. *You can figure this out. Do not give up. You're a fighter.* Hope sizzled through my blood like caffeine, and I said, "Okay," and hopped out of bed.

At the fireplace, I ran my hand along the short ledge and found Eddie's gun. I could use it now, knowing that my knees wouldn't give, knowing that I wouldn't accidentally shoot myself. Then I crawled over to the window and peeked out at the darkening jungle.

No Eddie.

Was he still alive?

I saw movement—a flash of bright skin, a pale face turned sideways. A gun pointed stick-'em-up style. Eddie, capless behind that TEC-9, skulked from the house to the forest.

Fear crackled and clicked down my spine.

What had he been doing all this time?

He would remember me. He would think of Charlotte. He would come back with more threats.

My cell phone was still in my back pocket, and I

pulled it out: no bars, no reception. I needed to find that second satellite phone.

Maybe Evelyn had stolen it, like she had stolen everything else.

I pushed aside the chaise and the armoire again and opened the door. I hugged the hallway walls and inched toward Evelyn's bedroom. So dark, so quiet until something somewhere clicked and a fan pushed cold air out from hidden vents. As I moved closer to Evelyn's room, then stepped across the threshold, I heard flies, hundreds of flies, buzzing near the windows and around the pile of clothes near the closet. My skin crawled—there was no reason for there to be so many flies unless . . . *Had something died?*

I peeked closer at the pile.

A brown snake lay atop the clothes. Unmoving. Broken. Now being consumed by flies . . .

Heart pounding, I pawed through the dresser drawers, pushing aside socks and skirts and raggedy bras.

No phone.

Evelyn's turquoise ring sat atop the dresser. It was as beautiful up close as I'd imagined. Silver band, classic oval shape. What a story it had. *A blood-crusted talisman worn by the killer nurse who'd killed three people in less than two days on this one island. There were other bodies scattered throughout New Mexico . . .* I reached for it, paused, then snatched back my hand.

That ring was also cursed.

Evelyn's ancient turquoise suitcase sat in the closet. It was the hard-shell kind, the kind a great-aunt purchased from Sears & Roebuck before her flight back to Mississippi on PSA.

I pushed apart the right and left latches.

Ker-*chunk.*

The top popped open, and the scent of body odor, onions, and wet wool coiled around my head. I could taste the funk, and it mixed with all that water I'd guzzled and the mangoes and French bread I'd gobbled. Nauseous, I pawed through the skirts, shirts, and sweaters, swallowing the bile now burning up my throat. My hand struck something hard and rectangular.

The other satellite phone!

My heart soared as I hugged the phone to my chest, as I tried hard to ignore the low buzzing of those flies around my head. I turned on the power button and the green indicator light flickered. I punched in Morgan's cell phone number, then held my breath. There was a *beep-beep-beep* followed by a woman's automated voice telling me that the call couldn't be completed as dialed. Fine. Okay. What now?

I stood and glanced out the window. My breath left my lungs.

It's her!

The girl in the tattered pink sweatshirt stood in the swimming pool with her back to me. The tattoo on her neck peeked past her thinning black hair. She lifted her skinny right arm and pointed one crooked finger to the sky.

The phone vibrated in my hand and the green light near the antenna flickered weakly.

I hurried back into the hallway. My steps slowed as I reached Desi's bedroom. Nothing had changed. Dim light, no light. A strange, heavy smell. Spilled and aging blood. The sheets and comforter were still twisted messes on the ground. The pillow sat on its clean side. Her nightgown lay on the chaise, still waiting to be worn.

Back in the living room, I looked beyond the glass, past the terrace.

The girl was still standing in the pool.

I took a few steps toward her, and the phone vibrated again and the green light brightened.

Closer . . . closer . . .

I stepped out into the cool air. The smell of chlorine was as crisp as the scent of salt and sea. Gulls, millions of them, circled in the distance. Down here, though, were empty deck chairs, empty poolside tables, no flip-flops left near the Jacuzzi, no dog-eared novels or forgotten towels. It was as if the seven of us had never been here.

Brooke McAllister stood in the middle of the pool, still, unmoving.

I nudged off my sneakers and rolled up the legs of my fleece bottoms. Stepped into the water and ignored the cold. Didn't care that the bottom of the pool felt as slick as snot. I waded to the western edge, right where the property ended and the cliffs began, high above the rocky shore where the waves crashed against each other and ate away at Mictlan Island. I keyed in "0–1" and then Morgan's cell phone number again.

Ring-ring, ring-ring . . . Click. "Hello?" My baby's voice.

"Morgan," I shouted, fighting madness. "I need you to send help—"

"Mom, is that—?"

Then silence. Hard, deathly silence.

Terror banged in my gut, and I screeched, "Hello? Sweetie? Morgan?"

No answer. Just that hard, deathly silence again. She was gone.

"What the *hell* are you doing?"

I gasped and whirled around.

He had finally found me.

31

"I thought you were dead."

Wallace and I said that to each other at the same time. He stood on the terrace behind me, his toupee flapping wildly in the wind, his body as thin as grass. Any other occasion, we would've laughed, pointed at each other, and said, "Jinx!" But this was not that time.

"Where *were* you?" I climbed out of the pool and slipped on my sneakers.

"I hid in a tiny cubby in the media room," Wallace said. "There are hidey-holes all around Artemis for storage and taking cover during hurricanes. I just never thought that I'd have to use one. But I did, because Edward has completely lost his mind. I'd tell him to go home and take a pill, but I think he's already high as hell on something."

"Javier's cocaine," I said. "Eddie found it in Javier's pocket, remember?"

Wallace closed his eyes, nodded. "So what's the plan?"

Show Wallace the phone, and ask him to help find the best spot to make a call? Or keep the phone a secret from a man who had lied about why we came here?

"Miriam," Wallace prodded.

I pulled the phone from my jacket pocket. "I found the second satellite phone. Evelyn had hidden it in her luggage. But my calls aren't going through."

"Because, dearest . . ." He pointed at Artemis. "The

haunted mansion is blocking the signal. We need to find an open space."

My shoulders slumped for only a second before I remembered. "I know a place."

Moments later, he and I crept through the glade of banyans, on the same path that Desi and Frank had taken on their midnight rendezvous. Soggy leaves and mud made our shoes squelch, but the cries of birds masked our noise. I kept glancing up, expecting to spot another pair of legs dangling from the branches, or men with AK-47s watching us from on high. But I only saw branches, millions of fallen purple-brown seedpods, pale pink flowers and tangled vines, red birds that flitted from twisted limb to twisted limb, and butterflies that soared toward the sun.

Every ten steps, I stopped to listen. To the birds sing. To the dull roar of the ocean. I especially listened for the clamor of crazy that now clattered off Eddie like gongs, clarinets, and electric guitars. I could feel Wallace's heartbeat pushing between the blades of my shoulders, churning against my own sweat and my own fear.

"Where are we going?" the old man whispered. "I fear that I can't keep walking on like this. My back is killing me."

"We're going to the bluffs. We're not too far." I glanced at him over my shoulder.

His face was quivering with pain. Perspiration poured off him as though he'd just climbed out of the swimming pool. His long-sleeved T-shirt and linen slacks hung off him—all that sweat had stretched his clothes two sizes bigger.

"Do you have meds on you?" I asked.

He winced, shook his head. "But we can always make homemade morphine, right? Poppies, poppies everywhere. You have a mortar and pestle?" He tried to chuckle.

I stopped walking. "If you need to head back to the house, you should. I'll be fine."

"And miss this great adventure?" He flicked his hand, then shook his head. "You may need me, doll. I'll rest when—"

"You're dead?" Eddie slipped from behind a tree with his gun aimed at Wallace's chest. The thick scar on his forehead cut into his face like the Colorado River through the Grand Canyon. His pupils, as large as nickels now, pinwheeled in his bloodshot eyes.

That crazy that I had tried to listen for lurched out of him like electricity, sizzling, dangerous, and unpredictable. And with all my sweat, a current could easily jump off him to electrocute me. But my anger ignored my anxiety, and I shouted, "Kill us already, you sick bastard."

Eddie said, "Such a drama-mama. Relax, darlin'. I'll get to that." He snapped his fingers at Wallace. "You. Stand over there."

Wallace, hands up, mischief and humor washed out of him, took two steps away from me.

"More," Eddie said.

Wallace obeyed and took a few more steps.

I could barely hear myself think over my thundering heartbeat. *What now? What should I do?*

Eddie's gun! It was still hidden in my waistband.

The cop pivoted away from me. "Didn't think you'd end like this, right, Escorpion?"

Escorpion? He'd said earlier that Wallace was Escorpion's number two. But *now* he was The Man?

"Did you think you'd die like your hero, Pablo Escobar?" Eddie asked. "In a blaze of bullets? Mourned by millions?"

Wallace blinked. "*Now* who's being a drama-mama? Not that there's anything *wrong* with that." He paused and his features shifted and hardened. "I'm not Pablo, but I can sure as hell give you anything you want. What do you want? Money? Power? Women? Ask for it and you got it, it's yours." His voice had flattened, and his tone had lost all campy "extra." Now he sounded like Wally from New Jersey, trying to make a deal. "We can talk this out, Eddie. C'mon, I'm a magic man. But I can't do my magic if I'm dead, understand?"

I could feel the gun beneath my T-shirt, that hard metal throbbing against my right kidney. As Wallace talked about all that he could do for Eddie, I slowly reached down to my side and very . . . very . . . slowly pulled the gun from my pants. The pistol felt stronger today—maybe because I had now placed all of my hope into its manufacturing. Praying that it wouldn't make noise, I clicked off the gun's safety.

I didn't hear a thing. But Eddie heard everything, and his head swiveled like an owl's.

My skin felt loose except in the space between my breasts. There, in that space, I was stitched tightly together by a heavy, heavenly hand. I tiptoed closer to Eddie until I stood less than a foot away from the back of his head. "Drop the gun."

He looked over his shoulder but wouldn't meet my eyes. "Or what? You'll shoot me?"

My hands tightened around the grip. "Please drop the gun."

Eddie chuckled. "Stop fucking around, Charlotte. I ain't got no beef with you. Put down the gun, honey, before somebody gets hurt."

"Put your gun down first, honey," I said.

He smiled. "No way. See, I'm killing this fake son of a bitch today."

I shook my head. "I can't let you do that."

"C'mon, Char. He's the reason we're all dying, sweetheart." Eddie nodded at Wallace. "I guess he's got you fooled, too, huh? The prissy, funny gay thing—it's an act. He's nothing but a thug. A snitch. You can't hide anymore, fucker."

The old man looked so tired now. The sparkle in those lavender eyes was eclipsed by exhaustion, age, and sickness. They were no longer the eyes that had scrutinized my face and eggy hair back on Friday afternoon.

"I don't care," I said, my voice quivering. "We'll handcuff him, baby. We'll call the cops and they'll take him to prison. You don't want anything else on your record, right?"

"You think the Mexicans are gonna help?" Eddie snorted. "Those same cops are gonna build a tunnel from his jail—" He swiveled and pointed his gun at me.

BAM!

Red mist sprayed across the copper sunlight. Red mist sprayed across my right hand, and some of it splashed my neck and face.

A meaty redness bloomed in Eddie's right eye, and he dropped to the forest floor like a six-foot-tall sandbag. He didn't move again.

Take your time in a hurry.

I wore pieces of him—he'd found new skin, a new home. I stood there, my hand vibrating, suspended in time, holding a gun that hadn't shot a *BANG!* flag after all, holding a gun that had actually shot a real bullet. And now, I couldn't hear anything else except the *BAM* of that single gunshot. A perfect sound.

Excerpted from *The Boston Globe*
Friday, March 3

BOSTON POLICE OFFICER
NOT CHARGED

The court ruled that Edward Sweeney acted lawfully when he shot and killed Orlando Jackson, 33, in Boston, Mass., in November and will not face criminal charges for his use of force, a district attorney said on Thursday.

Officer Sweeney believed he faced an imminent threat when he pulled over Jackson for a routine traffic stop. The officer spotted a gun in the man's lap. At the time, Officer Sweeney was not wearing a body camera that would have recorded the incident.

The controversial decision to not prosecute Officer Sweeney raised fears of protests in Boston. Some community activists said the shooting was caused by race—Sweeney is white and Jackson is black. This is the second police shooting involving Officer Sweeney. After the shooting of Jackson, he had been placed on indefinite administrative leave. . . .

32

    I tore my gaze from the old man to stare at the dead man lying at my feet. A single bullet had penetrated his orbital socket, leaving behind busted eyeball, bloody pulp, and glistening bone—and all of it now oozed down into the jungle carpet. Bigger, blacker flies than the ones in Evelyn's bedroom had heard that gunshot and smelled dead flesh, and they now descended on Eddie's unmoving body.

"You *shot* him." Wallace gaped at me with horror and fascination.

"I . . ." I licked my salty, dry lips and tasted copper. Eddie's blood. Tears burned in my eyes and I prayed that he hadn't had HIV or hepatitis or anything that could kill me days, months, years from now. "I . . . I . . ." Tried to swallow the boulder lodged in my throat, but it wouldn't budge.

"You . . . *killed* him," Wallace said, still fascinated.

"He was going to shoot . . ." My words stuck again and my pulse quickened as the realization of what I'd done filled my head. *Killed him. I killed him.* I glanced down at my yellow sweatpants, now flecked with blood. My tennis shoes were flecked with blood. My T-shirt—blood.

I had killed someone. Straight up. No nuance, no sussing out meaning. I'd held a gun and I'd pulled the trigger and my defense attorney was no longer around to explain it all away.

Slapping away the fat tears rolling down my cheek, I

lifted my chin. "Self-defense. I did nothing wrong, and I'd do it again. I had to protect you." My heart shuddered at my mouth's bravado, at hearing words similar to the ones I'd uttered just last year to my daughter, to Detective Hurley, then to Phillip Omeke.

Don't let your mouth get your ass in trouble. Too late.

I held out my left hand, and said, "Wallace, wait—"

He flinched. "Don't come any closer."

I chuckled and rolled my eyes. "C'mon. You know I'm not gonna hurt you. We're getting off this island." I grabbed the second satellite phone from my back pocket. "Let's look for a clear spot, all right? Just like we'd planned. Come on." Talking to him like he was six years old. I started toward the bluff, refusing to look back at Eddie—there was nothing I could do for him to make it better.

But there's something he could give you.

His gun. That other satellite phone. So, I turned back, and said, "Hey, Wallace—"

Wallace was bent over Eddie's body. He pried the TEC-9 from the dead man's grip, then plucked the other satellite phone from the dead man's pocket.

I forced myself to smile. "I was just about to do the same—"

Wallace pointed the gun at me. "Hand me the gun and the other phone."

"What the hell are you—?" I aimed Eddie's gun at Wallace and pulled the trigger.

Nothing this time. Worse than a *BANG!* flag, the gun had now jammed.

Wallace shook his head, then pulled the TEC-9's trigger.

BAM!

The shot echoed through the trees, sending birds bursting into the sky in a cacophony of tweets. I shrieked as dirt near my left foot pocked and drove gravel into my calf.

"I don't want to shoot you, Miriam," Wallace said. "I've grown quite fond of you, actually, but I *will* kill you. So give me the other phone. *Now*."

I squinted at him—his eyes were hard as amethyst again. The bitch was back. I held out the phone and asked, "Why do you need two?"

Wallace snatched the phone from my grip. "The gun."

I handed him Eddie's gun and said, "I thought we were working together to get home."

"You just tried to *shoot* me. And do you think I'm blind? Do you think that I haven't noticed those missing figurines?"

"I . . . I . . . Evelyn must've taken them. She probably—"

"Evelyn did this, Evelyn did that. Blame the old goat since she's hanging from a tree and unable to defend herself. That's pretty low, even for you."

Because this is what you do.

"I'm not letting you steal my game piece, Miriam. As you would say, not today, Satan. Not today." Wallace moved away from me, then sprinted back the way we'd come.

I finally looked down at Eddie—he still hadn't moved. "I didn't mean to," I whispered to him before racing back to Artemis.

For someone old and sick, Wallace had made great time, and now his toupee had left his head. It was hanging on by strands of white hair still tacky with glue.

"Hey," I shouted, "why are you running from me? You have the guns! You have the power!"

"Who says I'm running from *you*?" he shouted back.

"They know I'm here. I'm the one who ruined everything for them."

But I didn't care about "them," whoever *they* were.

I only cared about going home.

I only cared about using one of those damned satellite phones.

Artemis, named for the goddess of the hunt, shimmered at the end of the trail. Wallace stumbled up the
porch steps and dropped the satellite phones and Eddie's TEC-9. Both phones landed near the old man's
foot. The gun skidded far across the porch. Wallace looked at the weapon, looked at the phones,
then looked back at me. Decisions, decisions . . . He
grabbed the phones, then ran into the house.

Seconds later, I bounded up those steps, grabbed the
TEC-9, then also stormed into the house.

Wallace had just reached the second floor, and his
breathing sounded like a truck driving through glue.

"Give me the one of the phones," I shouted up to
him, "and I'll leave you alone. I just wanna call—"

He disappeared down the hallway.

I took the stairs two at a time and reached the landing as he reached his bedroom's double doors.

"Wallace, wait!" I tore down the hallway as he
slammed the doors behind him.

I twisted one of the knobs, expecting it to be locked.
No—the handle turned and the door flew open.

The last rays of sun were catching every mirror and
piece of glass in the room, blinding me with light. I
blinked from all the flashes, then squinted to make
out the white leather sofas and wing chairs, the crystal chandelier and the fireplace. The bedroom looked
empty. The windows were closed—he couldn't have
jumped. The black-and-white framed picture of the
twin boys was gone from the wall niche. Phillip's fire-
colored urn had now taken its place. I glimpsed my

reflection in those mirrors—standing that far away, I saw no bloody evidence that I'd shot and killed Eddie.

"Wallace?" I said now. "Where are you?"

I peeked beneath the bed and found a pair of slippers. No Wallace. I threw open the closet door. Ten suits hung on the racks. Three pairs of expensive-looking loafers had been stuffed with cedar blocks and placed into wooden cubbies. No Wallace.

"You forced me to shoot," I shouted. "You have no reason to hide from me. The pieces on the table—I didn't take them. Why would I lie about that?"

"You're really asking that question?" His voice was muffled, but he sounded close—he had ducked into another secret hidey-hole like the one in the media room. "And you still aren't listening: I'm not hiding from *you.*"

"I just wanna go home." I squeezed the bridge of my nose, then sighed. "I don't care who you are or what you've done. We survived this, you and me. We're fighters. I just wanna see my kid again."

He didn't respond.

I leaned against the wall and forced my breathing to slow . . . slow . . . After five minutes of inhaling and slowly exhaling, my mind cleared and I could think again. "Wallace," I said, "we will survive this—you have to believe that."

"My brother William . . ." He paused a beat, then said, "He'd find this ironic."

"He would? Why?"

"I'm now the one who's scared. He was always frightened of me. I did terrorize him. I never liked weak people, and he knew that, and so he tried to stay as far from me as he could. For that alone, he was the smarter one."

"You never told me *how* he died."

"I could blame poverty."

"He was malnourished?"

Wallace said nothing for a few seconds, then said, "Something like that."

Where is he hiding? Keep him talking.

"Wallace, how did William die?"

"There was a ground well on our property," he said. "We were always careful around it."

I edged my way around the closet and found the spot where he sounded closest.

"Sometimes," he continued, "we forgot the well was there. William forgot once—he was running away from me at that moment, scared of what I had planned to do to him that afternoon. He was running from me and he fell into that well."

"How long did it take for help to come?"

Silence, then, "Help *didn't* come."

My blood turned icy and my lips clamped together. "Why not?"

"I wanted to see what would happen if he stayed down there. I said nothing as the entire town searched for him, and I didn't tell my parents or anybody that I knew where he was, and . . . I have his picture here with me."

"You told me a little about life insurance after his death. You received a payment."

"Not after *his* death. After my parents'."

"They died, yes."

"They were murdered."

My body trembled and I was cold again—because of the vents and because of the words Wallace had just spoken. I didn't want to hear any more. Didn't want to *know* any more. I squeezed my eyes shut and tried to shove his story away from my active thinking. "I don't care about your past," I said, voice cracking, "just your right now. *Our* right now. Just where we'll be tomorrow this time."

"You'll kill me. Everyone wants to kill me."

"I don't!" I shouted. "I don't wanna kill you. Where *are* you?"

"You can't hurt me here. No one can hurt me here. Phillip had these little safe rooms built for moments like this. He told me so, right before he died. He told me that this closet was the safest place in the house, on the island.

"It wasn't supposed to be like this. Escorpion, he must've had everyone killed on the boat. He must've, and that's why they're not here. He's coming for me."

"No one's coming," I said, even though I believed that Escorpion had murdered the crew of *La Charon*. "Hey, Wallace. Island fever—that's what you have." I touched a wood panel, and my sweaty fingers searched for a button, a lever, or a seam. "Wallace, please. Raul, the skipper of the boat? He gave me his cell phone number. He told me to call him if something went wrong. And something's gone horribly wrong, wouldn't you say? Please: let me call him. He's not dead—I'd bet my life that he's alive. And when I contact him, I'll stay out on the cliff or at the boathouse until he comes. You can have Artemis all to yourself. And if I see Mexican gang members, I'll run back and let you know. Then I'll hide somewhere. I'll hide in the media room."

"You have Raul's phone number?"

"Yes."

"What is it?"

"Doesn't matter—you need an open space to make the call, remember?"

Silence, then: "I'm not sharing this space with you. You can't come in here."

"Fine. That's absolutely okay with me."

Silence again, then: "Did you steal the figurines off the Bosch table? Did you help Evelyn kill Javier, Desi, and Trey?"

My mouth formed "no," but I stopped myself from speaking. *Strategy, Miriam. Appear remorseful, promise never to do it again. Do whatever it takes to survive.*

"Did you take the—?"

"*Yes.*" I closed my eyes and placed my forehead against the wood panel. "But . . . I . . . I didn't kill . . . I didn't . . . I'll give you the gun—I don't want it. The phone, I just need one phone."

He said, "Leave the weapon on the closet floor. Wait in the hallway. Count to fifty. I'll take the gun and I'll leave you one of the phones. Then, you can come back at fifty-one once I'm safe again."

"Sounds good." I sat the TEC-9 on the cream carpet. "Okay. It's on the floor." I stepped back and watched the panel. "Tell me when to start counting."

"I just need to find the button to open the . . . open the . . . oh, dear."

"What's wrong?"

He didn't speak.

"Wallace? What's wrong?"

He said, "Miriam, I . . ." and then, "Oh, no."

Excerpted from the *San Francisco Examiner*
Monday, June 15

NEW CLUES IN FIFTY-YEAR-OLD
DOUBLE MURDER

DNA may help investigators solve the 1967 murders of Lottie and Ricardo Zavarnella, both 45 years old at the time of their deaths. For nearly fifty years, investigators had no solid leads or suspects in murders that shocked the then-small farm town of Fresno, California. Until now.

The couple's bodies were discovered by their surviving son Wallace, then 20, on Christmas Eve. The husband and wife had been stabbed to death and dragged to the undeveloped land behind their home. The Zavarnellas' second son, William, died eleven years before in an apparent accident—he'd been reported missing but was found dead two days later. He had stumbled into a ground well and suffered a broken neck.

"We recently received a critical piece of evidence in the mail," Fresno County Sheriff Arlen Bassett says. That critical piece: the knife possibly used in the murders. Investigators in 1967 never recovered the murder weapon, and now forensic experts hope to find the DNA of the murderer on the knife's handle or blade— even after fifty years. Depending on factors like sunlight, water and heat, DNA can last up to a million years.

"In stabbings like this," Sheriff Bassett says, "not only are the victims grievously injured, the suspect is injured, too. He or she loses their grip on the handle due to the blood, and their palm slides down to the blade."

As a result, the suspect's blood would mingle with the victims', leaving behind crucial DNA. And according to Bassett, it is difficult to thoroughly clean a knife—blood can become lodged in the wood handle as well as the edge of the blade or between the blade and the hilt.

"All we need now is a Q-tip and we can start building a DNA profile. We may have our murderer after all this time."

33

Oh, no?

What did Wallace mean by that?

I stood there in the closet, gaping at wood panels and screaming, "What? Tell me. *What's wrong?*"

"There's a letter here," he finally said. "Right next to the control panel, and . . ."

"And what? What does it say?" My lips were now completely numb.

After several moments of silence again, Wallace read:

"'Sweetheart. This is not a joke. By the time you read this, my brain will have eaten itself alive. I take comfort in knowing, though, that I'm still smarter than you, even after death, because you are here on this island, in this cubby, because of me.

"'I knew you'd find yourself in this safe room—I was all too happy to plant the idea in your head. Who are you hiding from, I wonder, because there has to be someone stronger than you, so strong that you needed to hide.

"'I loved you. It's hard to say that, to admit that I loved an evil man. A conniving man. A man who took so much from me, took so much from so many. A man who denied me happiness and freedom.

"'I was a fool to love you, but when I stopped loving you, you wouldn't let me go. You threatened me. You reminded me that you've hurt people who loved you before. That you'll hurt me—and that I'm no different.

Sadly, I'm just one more domestic abuse story—except you only just admitted to the world our true relationship, you only admitted to the world that you and I were partners and lovers, only because I was dying, only because *you* were dying. Every day, over the last two years of my life, I've thought about your denial. And as I prepared to die, I thought about your denial while I cleaned our attic and closets. I found the knife, the weapon you used to kill your parents. You will deny this, that you killed them, but science will uncover the truth. That's why I sent the knife to the sheriff in Fresno. You killed them. You also killed William. All for money.'"

I whispered, "Shit," then rested my forehead against the cool wood panel. Wallace was a murderer. A cold-blooded . . .

"'Don't worry,'" Wallace continued to read. "'You aren't the only one I will take with me as I die. I'm also punishing those clients who made my last year alive completely miserable. Miriam, Javier, Trey, Desirée, Edward, Evelyn—they are six of the worst human beings I've ever had to save. Because of me, they didn't die in jail, killed by time or needles filled with poison, and now as I lie dying, I regret that. There is a price to pay. For all of us.'"

The old man groaned.

I tasted salt from tears that had slipped down my cheeks.

Wallace read on. "'Joseph Conrad wrote, "The belief in a supernatural source of evil is not necessary; men alone are quite capable of every wickedness." Evelyn, the most miserable wretch of all, the evilest of them all, the one who destroyed any chances of my going to heaven, didn't want to come to Artemis, and I know she didn't want to do as I asked once she arrived. But she came and she did as I asked because if she hadn't,

I would've had her beloved dachshund Chachi killed, and then her abhorrent mother Nancy chopped into pieces and spread across the Mojave Desert. So Evelyn poisoned. She strangled. She boiled and burned. She didn't have to worry about you because I knew that you and the three who survived would simply take care of each other.

"'My final instruction to that hopeless creature: hang yourself from the strongest branch. Yes, I told her to do that, and on my last trip here, I left the rope and the jewelry cleaner to be used in the food in what would be her room, and I also left figurines on the table for Evelyn to take once each of you perished. I wrote her instructions to increase the temperature on the Jacuzzi tub's thermostat. No one will mourn a nurse who killed at least three of her patients. Good riddance.

"'So, congratulations, my love—'"

Wallace choked back a sob, and then another. Then he forced out, "'Don't bother with scattering my ashes. You won't be leaving this closet, since you loved hiding in one for most of our relationship. Don't torment yourself about Escorpion taking revenge for stealing his land. He won't find you. But you *will* die here. That's for certain. Your cancer, like mine, will slowly eat at your liver and then chew through your stomach and the rest of your insides until there's nothing whole and nothing healthy left.

"'Hallelujah.

"'See you in hell, my love. There, we will be together forever, you and I—just like you'd threatened every time I talked of leaving you. This is the end of all things, my love.

"'Phillip

"'P.S. There *was* no Saturday boat coming for the memorial service. There were no other guests. All of that? Fiction. The truth: this weekend was reserved just for you and the six. As far as my will is concerned? I lied about that, too. You won't receive a penny—not that you'd be alive to spend one dime—and neither will anyone who may somehow make it off this island alive. Project Angel Food and the California Association of Black Lawyers, however, are about to hit their end-of-year fund-raising goals. You will not be acknowledged in their annual reports.

"'P.S. I hope it hurts.'"

34

"Help me!" Wallace was now banging on the closet panel.

I don't know how long he'd been banging, because my ears had just heard the most bizarre, the most horrific thing. Wallace had allowed his brother to die and had murdered his parents. He'd hidden the murder weapon in his attic all this time. And Evelyn—I had been right about her. But Phillip—I'd been wrong, so wrong, about him, about how he'd felt about me. I couldn't believe that he'd brought me here to . . . *die*.

No will. No inheritance. No memorial service.

Set up. I'd been set up. To *die*.

And Phillip had hated Wallace—and he'd hated Frank, Javier, Eddie, Desi, Evelyn, and me so much that he'd brought us all here to *die*.

Wallace would suffer the most by slowly dying in a safe room.

"Oh, no," I said, my face warm and my belly swarming with foamy nausea. "No, no, no."

Phillip had lied to me about our relationship. Where I thought there was love, there was simply loathing in disguise. I'd told him my fears, my secrets, and he'd plotted ways to . . .

I hunched over—couldn't breathe, couldn't—

"Miriam," Wallace was shouting, "what the hell are you doing out there? Help me! Call Raul!"

"How?" I barked back. "You have both phones! And

I lied—Raul didn't give me his cell phone number. I just said that to convince you to come out of the closet."

"Oh, no, please no." Then he started to shriek and wail.

My own eyes burned with tears. "Let's think. Let's . . . Maybe there's another phone somewhere."

"I can't die here, Miriam," he said between sobs. "I can't—"

"I'll be back. I'm gonna search the house." I ran out of the closet and back into the room of mirrors. I tossed the drawers, searched the nightstand and the two palatial bathrooms with the sunken tubs and the breathtaking views of the sea, searching for something . . . searching for anything . . . but finding nothing.

Don't give up.

I dashed out of Wallace's room, jammed down the hallway past Frank's room, and burst into Eddie's lair. That dangerous red and black lacquer décor made my shoulders hunch. Like there were hidden guillotines and ninja stars waiting to decapitate me.

Eddie's cargo shorts—all khaki—and his T-shirts—all black—sat ordered in the dresser drawers. His socks—all white—were rolled into balls. His boxers—all light blue—sat in neat squares.

I slid my hands through the order in search of something . . . anything . . . finding nothing but leaving a mess. I tasted sweet mango, blood, and stomach acid, and I screamed like the screamer in the painting that hung over Eddie's bed. I collapsed at the black glossy desk that overlooked the jungle. Somewhere out there, Eddie lay dead on the ground with a hole in his eye, all because I'd killed him.

Nauseous, I placed my forehead against the cold slick wood and tried to catch my breath. But I couldn't catch my breath and my stomach tightened, so I shifted my head to breathe. That's when I spotted a handheld radio sitting in a dock—Eddie had used one yesterday to reach Raul back on the mainland. But Wallace had tried again with no success. There was another pistol—Javier's—as well as the chef's pill case that Eddie had confiscated. I flipped open the top—not much coke left. Eddie *had* helped himself. I dropped the container back on the desk and stared at that radio.

Did it still work? Couldn't hurt to try.

I grabbed the pistol and the radio, then raced back to my bedroom. I snatched Desi's scarf from the vanity—it could be a flag to wave—then grabbed Frank's gold lighter and Javier's rum-filled flask—tools needed to start a signal fire. My eyes scanned the room and landed on the chaise that I hadn't relaxed on, the empty armoire that had never held my clothes, and the bed I'd slept in but never peacefully.

This had been the worst vacation of my life. The thought of leaving a one-star review on a travel website made me crack the thinnest smile. *Don't eat the fish! There are dead people everywhere. Nothing but bad vibes. Nice terrace, though.*

My legs burned as I sprinted out to the hallway. Desi's scarf, so blue, so long, trailed out behind me like a banner—until it snaked around my left leg and its tail slipped beneath the sole of my shoe. So slippery, that silk scarf, and right before I reached the staircase landing, I slipped and crashed to my knees, *thisclose* to tumbling down the steps. The radio, flask, and lighter flew out of my hands and my chin banged against the floor so hard that I saw stars. I waggled my head to clear my vision, but there was no time to think about the pain zigzagging around my face. I wrapped the long scarf around my wrist, told myself to be careful, to not trip again, pulled myself to my feet, then grabbed the radio, flask, and lighter. I tapped the small of my back—the gun was still there and it hadn't gone off.

Down in the foyer, I slowed some just to glare at the table of seven sins and three of the remaining game pieces—envy, pride, and anger. *Fuck you, I'm not dying today.* I'd return with a lit twig and burn it—and Artemis—down to the ground, forever and ever, amen. Now, though . . .

I rushed out the front door, not noticing the pretty lilac flowers on the dogwoods or the lime-green butterflies or anything.

Maybe there's something useful in the boathouse.

I raced down the jagged path back to the dock and burst into the tiny hut that smelled of rotting wood and seawater. I swiped my brow with Desi's scarf as I looked around the little room. Bare. Not a rock, not a rusted tin can, not one thing existed between those four pitiful walls.

I was out of breath by the time I reached the windswept bluff where Desi and Frank had stood once upon a time. So loud with the waves crashing over the rocks, with the seabirds crying out. Every time a large wave hit the land, the ground vibrated beneath my feet. I didn't fear slipping off, though, because I'd stood on bluffs like these before. Rancho Palos Verde. San Pedro. Malibu. Big Sur. I was a child of Southern California, land of fire, earthquakes, and bluffs carved by the Pacific Ocean. I knew cliffs and just how far to go.

I wiped my sweaty forehead with the damp scarf again, then powered on the handheld radio I'd found in Eddie's room.

There was a crackle and a burst of static.

I mashed the key on the radio's side, then said, "Hello? Anybody there?"

White noise.

I twisted a knob and switched channels. Static again, but not as much as before. "Hello?"

No answer.

I glanced at the enormous sky, so blue and so for-ever. *You're out there. Hear me. Please.*

I keyed the radio again. "Hello? Please. Someone?"

Fizzfuzztchetttshhee . . .

Out there! Way out there! Something man-made was racing across the sea.

Fire! They'd come closer to the island if they spotted fire!

I scrambled around the bluff and the edges of the jungle to collect leaves and branches. The heap came to my knees. Frank's Cartier lighter was filled with lighter fluid and the sky was dry. *Good.* I sprinkled rum on the pile, then selected a branch. Held the lighter to it until the twig caught flame. Then I held the lit twig to the rum-soaked pile. Fire flickered here . . . fire flick-ered there . . . and soon all of the heap burned bright, and soon after that the fire grew and black smoke bil-lowed in the thick air.

Bravo, Mom! You go, *Miriam!*

I smiled and hopped with glee. Then I gathered more brush to keep the flames alive.

How long had I been standing there?

What was Wallace doing right now?

Was there food in his hidey-hole? Was there water? An emergency toilet?

Way down there, the foamy water churned, and the tops of the rocks were barely visible.

Way out there, the boat had changed direction and . . .

Is it coming this way?

Yes, it was! White foam trailed behind the boat.

I whispered a prayer of thanks, then stepped closer to the cliff's jagged edge. The boat was far out but still charging toward me. I glanced at my phone—ten min-utes to nine o'clock—then glanced ahead at the dusty orange moon rising over Mexico, then glanced back at the setting sun and at the mellowing sky of golds, reds, and purples. A perfect sunset. A perfect moonrise. Darkness was coming—the fire would burn brighter in the dark.

That last email from A. Nansi—Phillip Omeke in real life—told me that there would be times I'd cry and times I'd celebrate. Which time was this, since I was now doing both?

The wind bit at my face but the fire kept me warm. I unraveled Desi's long blue scarf in the air, another signal, and I hollered, "Help!"—not for the people in the boat to hear but as cathartic release.

Could they see the fire? Could they see the scarf? Could they see *me*?

I yelled, "Help! Help!" until my throat grew raw. I jumped. I screamed. My arms tired, and I dropped them to my side. Distressed, I rubbed the edge of the scarf between my fingers.

Doubt had set in—doubt *always* set in.

That *was* a boat, right? Not a mirage? Or was that a whale breaching the surface? A sailfish like the ones that had accompanied us as we sailed over on Friday afternoon?

I waved Desi's long scarf again, although a bit unsure now. I jumped. I screamed. Even if I was hailing a watery phantom or a sea creature, it still felt so productive. With the scarf trailing behind me, I ran back to the edge of the jungle for more wood. Bigger fire—I needed bigger fire! After dumping the wood onto the blaze, I ran back over to the cliff—

Just like it had in the hallway, the tail of Desi's long scarf slipped beneath the sole of my sneaker. And just like I had in the hallway, I stumbled forward. This time, though, I caught myself before falling to my knees, but I was still moving fast, still moving forward because of the silk scarf beneath one shoe and because of the pebbles and loose dirt beneath the other shoe and because my exhausted limbs and my exhausted mind had been beaten up over the last three days and couldn't work together to successfully upright my body before—

Too late. My forward momentum launched me off the cliff, and the hard ground disappeared, and I hung in midair.

I screamed, "Ahh!" as my mind screamed, *No!*

I had slipped, I had fallen, I was falling.

Shit.

I twisted my body until I saw the sky and the black smoke and the swirling ashes . . .

No.

No!

Why is this happening?

Stop this from happening.

Desi's scarf. *That fucking scarf.* I had slipped on that—*please, God, help—!*

The crash into the sea came and the world turned white and every nerve in my body shrieked. And then the world and the pain faded and I felt nothing. No hurt. No fear. I tasted copper and salt and teeth. Waves crashed over me, and water filled my eyes and mouth. But I broke through to the surface and saw sky again. And I saw that fat, dusty moon. And the fire, I saw that, too. And I floated on my back as pain and numbness fought over me.

As I floated, I thought about Prudence McAllister, how she had stood over me on Thursday night, how foamy spit had gathered in the corners of her mouth. Her last words to me . . . What had been her last words to me?

Couldn't think. It hurt to breathe. Like . . . it was like . . . every bone in my body had broken and now, every bone in my body had filled my lungs.

The sweatshirt. I'd promised Morgan that I'd bring

her a sweatshirt. There'd be enough time to buy it at the airport or . . .

Pain burst around my heart and my arms numbed.

This is it.

I'm almost there.

Wallace will have to find his own way home.

35

The blue scarf caressed my ear as it dipped beneath my head and pulled me down into the water.

It wanted to kill me.

I could have let the scarf go, but I'd won it. It was mine.

I was alone, drifting in the warm waters of the Sea of Cortez, floating on my back. Numb. My arms and legs felt so far away . . .

It was the first time this week I was truly resting. The first time ever that I'd floated in the ocean.

So many firsts.

My cracked lips parted. "I don't like it here."

Jagged rocks poked through my T-shirt and scraped the skin on my back. Salt water dribbled into my mouth, and I swallowed it, knowing that I wouldn't die from thirst. Not tonight. The sea tasted alive, tasted like tears. Morgan's tears. She had cried so many times, and I'd held her, wanting to cry, too, wanting to cry now, but no, I didn't. I wouldn't. Crying would be admitting that they were right. Crying would frighten me into accepting the hurt. I didn't feel hurt. No, not at all. I had to resist. Resistance was like the coral now scraping against my back and my arms and my neck. Resistance hurt. Resistance protected.

I blinked—salt water was burning my eyes.

The big sky had darkened into oranges and purples, juices and bruises, dragons and sunsets.

Pretty. So pretty.

I should've climbed out. Should've swum to the shore to join the others back at the house. If I stayed in the ocean, though, I'd still . . . join the others back at the house, just meeting up on the other side. No difference. Not now. Not anymore.

A wave crashed over me. Pain burst and banged near my eyes. The world brightened, and I winced, and then the bright world spun. Dizzy, I closed my eyes.

Morgan, swaddled in her nursery blanket, smelled of sunshine and love.

Mother held my shoulders, so proud of me, then tapped the honor society pin on my collar.

Daddy had stopped running beside me as wind stung my face, as the spokes on my bicycle's wheels click-click-clicked as I rode faster and faster down Duncan Avenue.

Bright light shone above me and made me close my eyes. Desi's scarf wrapped tighter around my wrist, pulling me down as something behind my heart slipped past my ribs, through my skin, and drifted toward the light.

There she stood, way up on the cliff, prettier than the sky. Her dark hair blew across her face. Those dark welts on her neck looked like tattoos. She'd torn a hole through a pair of pink tights. Had slipped them over her head and slipped her arms through the legs. Ballerina forever. There she stood, the fairest of them all, way up there, looking way down here at me. Always looking down . . .

The edges of my vision brightened and my lungs pinched my chest.

"I'll see you in hell," I whispered to the girl.

And there, you and I will meet the Devil together.

Excerpted from the *Los Angeles Times*
Wednesday, February 11

NO FELONY CHARGES FOR
MOTHER IN BULLYING CASE

A Los Angeles mother on trial for cyberbullying a
17-year-old girl who later committed suicide was convicted Thursday of misdemeanor computer charges. The
jury convicted 46-year-old Miriam Macy of accessing
computers without authorization, punishable by up to
one year in prison and a $100,000 fine.

Prosecutors alleged that Macy's taunts over social
media, followed by a package containing silk scarves
fashioned into what prosecutors claim was a noose,
led the teen girl to end her life.

"She's an evil woman," said Phoebe McAllister,
the girl's mother. "She went too far. Who was the
adult?" When asked about allegations of bullying by
her own daughter, McAllister claims it was all a mis-
understanding. "Girls are, by definition, awful to each
other. Brooke meant no harm when she painted that
swastika on Morgan's locker. And anyway, Morgan's
black. Swastikas shouldn't mean anything to a black
family. Some of our closest friends are black."

Earlier, prosecutors sought to charge Macy with
murder. "The girl died because of [Macy's] actions," ar-
gues Fatima Eggleston, who prosecuted the case. "So,

no, I'm not satisfied with the jury's decision." Eggleston also alleges that Macy posted unflattering pictures of Brooke across social media. She also emailed potential universities and colleges several pictures and screenshots of Brooke wearing White Power regalia, writing the n-word on lockers and leaving frog stickers that are symbols of the "alt-right" on desks. Eggleston points to Nazi materials that were found in Macy's car. "She planted a lot of these things to fan the flames."

"Morgan Macy was a victim of terrorism," defense attorney Phillip Omeke states. "While [Miriam's] approach makes us uncomfortable, she did what many parents would do—protect her daughter at all costs. The [materials] recovered from Miriam's car are totally irrelevant. There is proof that Brooke McAllister engaged in despicable, white supremacist behavior. I am proud of Miriam's devotion to her family and applaud her bravery. I'm satisfied with the court's rejection of a murder charge."

"Brooke was a child," Eggleston states. "We've all made mistakes in our youth. Mrs. Macy humiliated a minor and she should be punished for it. That's why the family will proceed with their civil case." Attorneys also alleged that Macy had associates assault Brooke in a shopping mall parking lot during the busy holiday season. Bystanders reported that the unknown assailants kicked Brooke in the head and shouted, "This is for Morgan, [expletive]." There are uncorroborated reports that Macy drove the car the assailants used to escape. Macy denies her involvement.

Phoebe McAllister recalls the afternoon her daughter died. "I just had this awful feeling that she was past her regular depression. I don't know, call it mother's intuition. And then my oldest daughter, Prudence, called me and said, 'Bebe's on her account, live, and she says she's gonna do it.' And she did do it, right in front of the world."

"I believe Miriam Macy," one juror who requested to remain anonymous stated. "Brooke was a white supremacist in the making. She dished it out but couldn't take it. Yes, Miriam should've handled it another way and she should be punished for that, but to send her to jail for *murder*? That's ludicrous."

McAllister's older sister Prudence disagrees. "Brooke wasn't perfect, but Miriam is evil. She may have avoided getting locked up, but this isn't over. I don't know how, I don't know when, but she'll get hers in the end."

EPILOGUE

Raul Molinero said nothing as he pulled the woman onto *La Charon*'s deck.

Andreas climbed out from the sea. He glanced back at Mictlan Island, at the fire burning so bright in the night sky. "Is she alive?" Andreas asked as he clicked off the boat's bright searchlight. "She's broken up really bad. And the fish got to her a little."

The older man shone a penlight in the woman's bloody right eye, then her bloody left eye. He moved his wet hand over his mouth, then shook his head. *"Ella esta muerta."*

Andreas sat with his back against the couch and stared at the lifeless body. "We should've come sooner."

Raul grunted.

"Think anyone else is alive?" Andreas asked, nodding back at the island.

Raul thought about Mictlan Island's secret past for a moment. The truth and the rumors. And how the rumors *were* truth. He thought about all the bad things that had happened on that piece of land since Felix Escorpion's drug operations had been halted, since the famous attorney Philip Omeke had completed construction of Artemis a year ago. He thought of the time before that, about the bodies Escorpion had buried all over the island, beneath those twisted banyan trees. He thought of all the people—before they later became bodies—he had ferried over to meet their end without hesitation. He'd done it to please his boss. To settle scores. To stay aboveground.

Anyone alive? Raul said, "No. They're all dead."

"So . . ." Andreas cleared his nose, then spat on the polished wood floor. "What do we say?"

Irritated, Raul glared at the kid. "We did our job, just like Mr. Omeke wanted. We came on the day and time we were told to come. We found her like this, in the water, floating, dead. The end."

"The end." Andreas nodded, then ran his hand through his wet hair. He stood, then limped to the ladder that led up to the communications room. "I'll call the coast guard."

Raul watched the kid disappear up to the second deck, then prayed, "Lord our God, receive our supplications . . ." After reciting the novena, Raul slipped his fingers over Miriam Macy's eyes. He had noticed them Friday afternoon back at the office.

She'd had such pretty eyes.

Green like the Sea of Cortez.

ACKNOWLEDGMENTS

I wanted to see what would happen if I took seven Americans to an island and revealed their secrets—and had them pay the ultimate price for that. Cruel, yes, but that's entertainment. Thanks to Jill Marsal, my brilliant and supportive agent, who also wanted to see what would happen, too. Thank you, Kristin Sevick, my awesome editor, who helped me abuse my darlings. My family has always supported my career and my nature and I want to thank you Mom, Dad, Gretchen, Terry, and Jason for being my support. David and Maya Grace, my travel buds and my loves, thank you for adventuring with me and sending inspirational texts and pictures of people doing and saying stupid stuff. My pages are stuffed with your donated lunacy. To readers everywhere, thank you for picking this up and always giving me a chance to make you breathless.

Read on for a preview of

AND NOW SHE'S GONE

RACHEL HOWZELL HALL

Available in Fall 2020 from
Tom Doherty Associates

FORGE A FORGE HARDCOVER

1

She had to do it.

She had to glance in her rearview mirror.

Because a black SUV was rolling up behind her.

Closer . . .

A black SUV with the green Range Rover medallion on the left side of its grille.

Closer . . .

The truck stopped inches away from her car's rear bumper.

The sound of music reached her first—Notorious B.I.G., "Hypnotize."

Shit.

Maybe her worry was irrational. It wasn't like she was on an abandoned road. She was on the west side of Los Angeles, and there was a sports equipment store over there. And a Taco Bell over there. There were storefront windows that promised *Pho! Massage! Comic Books!*

Didn't matter, because right at that moment, she was the only woman in the world.

But the man behind her wore familiar-looking aviator sunglasses and—

This truck could be his.

Shitshitshit.

Whenever she spotted a black Range Rover, the hair on her neck and arms shot up like straw. In this city, that meant she was a scarecrow four times a day.

She was trembling now, panic sizzling through her

blood. She fought it, shallow breath by shallow breath, until she could take deeper breaths, until her fear huddled in that safe place behind her bladder. She kneaded her mind to remember any tiny detail that would tell her this was not the truck. Like ... A yellow pine tree air freshener hung from the mirror. Like ... A white scrape on the fender's black paint.

No luck.

She was boxed in—car to the left of her, car to the right, cross traffic and red light before her. In the crosswalk, an old lady inched from one curb to the other curb.

What if he tries to open my back passenger door as I'm sitting here?

The doors were locked.

What if he tries to break a window?

Then she'd ... blow the red light, try her damnedest not to hit the old lady in the crosswalk, but if she had to hit her ...

No. She wouldn't let him walk up on her again like that.

The driver removed his sunglasses.

Those eyes ...

She squinted at the image in the rearview mirror. "That's not him."

Those eyes ...

Too small. Too spaced apart.

He was not the man who had promised to kill her.

Not this time.

2

Los Angeles was a city of skies—and everyone in the city now sweltered beneath a dirty-blue sky. Later in the evening, that same sky would turn rose quartz and then, in the morning, Necco wafer orange. Because the marine layer, exhaust from cars and refineries, and brush fire smoke reflected the sun. It was a murder sky, killing four million people slowly . . . slowly . . . molecule . . . by molecule.

But Grayson Sykes wouldn't die on this eleventh day of July because of that killer sky.

She planned to end her day with dollar tacos and strawberry margaritas with her coworkers at Sam Jose's. They would talk about Zadie's upcoming retirement, Clarissa's upcoming bachelorette party, and Jennifer's "thing" with her husband's chief mechanic.

Gray had no wedding and she was far from retirement. "I just won't eat heavy tomorrow," "Are you serious?," and "I did my steps today"—those were her happy hour lines. The quartet would eat, drink, and laugh; they'd cast lustful glances at men who should've been home with their wives, who should've been working out at the gym, who should've been at the office preparing PowerPoint presentations on midyear fiscal numbers.

Now, though, Jennifer Bellman sat in the lobby of the smoked green glass and metal building where Rader Consulting was located. Just a hop, skip, and jump away from the magnificent Pacific Ocean, Rader

Consulting did it all—from pets to cons. Looking for lugs in all the right places, squeezing into spots where cops weren't allowed to go. No warrants? *No problem*. Need info? *Got it right here*. From background checks to finding long-lost boyfriends. From simple internet searches and deep, dark web dives to, *ahem*, other methods.

The blonde was pretending to read the two-week-old *People* left on the coffee table. One of the primary skip tracers at Rader Consulting, Jennifer sniffed, snuffled, and clawed to find missing deadbeats and debtors. Men saw the hair, the boobs, the blouse that framed those boobs, and they never took her serious enough to keep their traps—or their flies—closed.

Gray asked, "Why are you sitting down here?"

Jennifer bit her bottom lip. "There's a new tech titan on the third floor. Tall, Slavic hotness in a Hugo Boss suit. He needs to know that I exist." A gossip, a ditz, a flirt—thrice-married (and still married) Jennifer could be all that and worse.

The "worse" now walked beside Gray to the elevator bank. "Where'd you go?" she asked.

"Pharmacy."

"No offense, but I don't know *why* we celebrate one hundred percent linen."

"You lost me." Gray pressed the Up button.

"Your *pants*, honey." Jennifer *tsk*ed Gray's wrinkled white linen slacks, then batted her baby blue eyes. "What's that dog with all the wrinkles in its face?"

"A Shar-Pei?"

Jennifer clapped. "That's it! Wrinkles everywhere, like your slacks. They're cute, though. The dogs, I mean." Jennifer and her perfect blonde bob and her perfect high breasts bursting from her floral print Chico's dress. So efficient, Jennifer Bellman. So eager to climb and so eager to please.

Not really. Jennifer Bellman was a fifty-year-old rottweiler in cocker spaniel cosplay.

The two women entered the elevator together. Gray's eyes burned—Jennifer wore enough perfume to scent a small country. At the end of the day, Gray always smelled like marshmallow and vanilla.

"Oh," Jennifer said. "Nick's been drifting through the building looking for you."

"He texted—he just gave me my first *real* case."

Jennifer clapped. "No more looking for lost Chihuahuas! Cheating husband?"

"Missing girlfriend."

The elevator doors opened to the second floor.

"You're gonna need help," Jennifer said. "I'll be right there to guide you. My first bit of advice: when all else fails, cry. Tears make people feel sorry for you, and they'll tell you anything you need to know just to shut you up."

White-haired Zadie Mendelbaum stood at the breakfast bar clutching a soft pack of Camels and a bottle of Dr Pepper. A career of squinting at records had frozen her face into a mask of narrowed eyes and an upturned nose. She also had a pack-a-day habit and exquisite hobbit-size hands. She'd worked at Rader Consulting since its establishment, seven years before, and was always proud to boast that she was "employee number one."

The old woman reminded Gray of one of her foster mothers. Naomi Applewhite also had a Dr Pepper addiction, but she smoked hard-pack Newports while sucking peppermints. Gray had stayed with Mom Naomi for seven months. Two weeks before starting eighth grade, Gray had been snatched out of that depressing Oakland apartment by Child Protective Services and placed into a girls' home. No explanation given. Whenever Gray smelled smoky mint or cloves-black licorice-almonds, she thought of Naomi Applewhite. Which, now that she worked with Zadie, was all the time.

"Went on break without telling me?" Zadie followed the two women into Gray's office.

Gray dropped her purse onto the credenza. "About to start my first missing person case."

"Congrats, honey," Zadie said. "How you feelin'?"

"Excited. Nervous. Nauseous."

"Like a virgin at a prison rodeo?" Jennifer asked.

"Never been to a rodeo," Gray said. "So . . . *maybe*?"

"You'll do fine." Zadie pointed at the pile of books on the corner of Gray's desk. "Looks like you've been studying."

For two years, Gray had worked as a contractor for Rader Consulting, writing reports, transcribing recordings, and *much, much more!* Now, though, she wanted to be a private investigator. She'd read handbooks, attended community college courses, shadowed Nick for two weeks, and watched YouTube videos featuring investigators on the job. She'd even immersed herself in mysteries written by Hammett, Chandler, and Mosley. Nick promoted her, placing her on his license until she'd be eligible to apply for her own in three years. And then he'd given her a case: finding Cheeto, a stolen Chihuahua.

"Sounds simple," Gray said. "Find the guy's girlfriend. I shouldn't fuck it up too much."

"You obviously haven't met you," Jennifer snarked.

Gray plucked a sheet of tissue from the box on her desk. "I have, and I'm actually the best report writer here." She cleaned her tortoiseshell glasses but kept her gaze on Jennifer.

Jennifer offered a saccharine smile. "Totally different skill set. But you'll see that."

Zadie clicked her nails against the Dr Pepper bottle. "I'll always remember my first missing person case. . . .

He woke up on Saturday, stayed home while the wife and kids drove to synagogue. He fed the dog, opened the front door. He took his kayak out in the marina, where he 'drowned.' But really, he swam down shore for three miles, where he'd hid dry clothes and a new life and a new name behind a fucking drug dealer's boat."

Gray and Jennifer eyed each other.

Zadie had just described how her husband Saul had disappeared thirty years ago.

"Well, women disappear all the time," Jennifer said. "Some *intentionally*."

Because she'd grown tired of her man, had grown tired of his hands, of that job, of those freaking dishes that kept filling the sink, dishes that no one touched even as its stink wafted through the house. If she wasn't taking the kids with her, she kissed them farewell, took out the trash one last time, and just . . . *left*.

Natalie Dixon, a woman Gray knew once upon a time, had disappeared like that.

Unlike the men who disappeared, women left their egos behind along with their keys, photo identification, and unpaid electric bills. These women may have wondered about their past lives—*What are they doing back home? How are they living without me? Did somebody finally wash those damned dishes?*—but they rarely did more than wonder. They never visited old haunts. They never searched their names on Google or checked their Facebook pages. Unlike most men who vanished, women rarely got caught. They just wanted a new beginning.

Natalie Dixon had also longed for a new life and hadn't wanted to be found. Guilt had gnawed at her spirit, Gray recalled, and that prickly sensation of millions of eyes had pecked at poor Natalie Dixon, and she always worried that the wrong pair would pick her from the crowd.

"Two, three days, tops," Gray said. "That's Nick's estimation."

"I would say use sex appeal to help you," Jennifer said, eyes on her coral-painted fingernails, "but that won't work. Fortunately, you have a great personality. You can talk about books and . . . and . . . movies and . . . politics. Oh, and comic books. Improvise. Make shit up."

Gray cocked an eyebrow. "I'm good at making shit up."

"She's better than you at that, Jen," Zadie said.

"Doubt it," Jennifer sang, with a twisted grin. "I'm a *supreme* liar—Oh!" She pointed at Gray. "Think I'm a bitch now? Skip Sam Jose's tonight and see how evil I'll be tomorrow morning. I can't do Clarissa alone."

Zadie rolled her eyes. "That girl does nothing but yak, yak, yak."

"I'll let you know about tonight," Gray said.

Jennifer slapped Gray's desktop. "Nuh-uh. I've dated enough black men to know that 'I'll let you know' means 'I'm not showing up.'"

Gray laughed.

"You'll see your ex-*marine*," Jennifer sang.

"*Former* marine," Gray corrected.

Hank Wexler was the new owner of Sam Jose's. Two weeks ago, the square-jawed jarhead with blue eyes and thick salt-and-pepper hair had claimed that the blue-inked Hebrew letters tattooed on his left forearm were Gray's name. Back then, he didn't even *know* her name, not that him not knowing had kept Gray from licking tequila salt off his skin. An hour later, she and Hank had made out in his office—it was like they'd known each other in a former life, so making out so soon was okay. He had tasted like whiskey sours and Juicy Fruit gum. That had been a good night.

"No flaking," Jennifer said now, as she glided out of Gray's office.

"Scout's honor," Gray shouted. "Have a margarita waiting for me."

3

   Dominick Rader, founder and CEO of Rader
Consulting, was not at his desk.

Gray, though, had enough information to start
working.

It was two o'clock, and traffic pockets filled with a
trillion cars mixed with bursts of highway freedom,
and sometimes, *sometimes*, the speedometer on Gray's
silver Camry crept toward forty miles per hour. *Zoom-
ing.* She rolled down the sedan's windows, then turned
up Angie Stone on the stereo, lamenting not being able
to eat or sleep anymore cuz of love.

Right then, Gray felt "L.A. fly," a near-native alone
in her car beneath that weird-colored, murder sky with
those white plumes of smoke to the north, to the east,
and to the west of her. One woman in the second-
biggest city in America, disappearing in a heartbeat
from block to block. No one and everyone knew her
in Los Angeles. Some called that a weakness, like color
blindness or fallen arches. For Gray, that six degrees
of anonymity was Marilyn Monroe's mole or Barbra
Streisand's nose.

She kept north until she pulled into the garage for
UCLA Medical Plaza, a city unto itself. Anchored by
the university, the plaza spanned nearly seven hundred
thousand square feet and was filled with outpatient
centers, hospitals, and research facilities.

Cardiologist Ian O'Donnell worked in UCLA's Ur-
gent Care department, and Gray met the eyes of patients

waiting to see someone about their lungs, their hearts, their mucus. Battered chairs hosted bloody men with bruised knuckles. Diabetics waited for insulin shots and children clutching blankets barked coughs that sounded like gravel trucks. The waiting room stank of phlegm and unwashed bodies, but the carpets were clean and the lights were bright.

At least.

Gray pushed her eyeglasses to the top of her head. She crossed and uncrossed her legs as though she needed to pee. She ignored the tingle and yanking near her belly button—her body knew she needed to be here as a patient—as she scanned the waiting room in search of threats.

Runny noses and runny eyes made her clench. She couldn't get sick again—not even a cold, because colds sometimes masqueraded as stealthy pneumonia with its filled lungs and hacky cough. And then pneumonia led to health questionnaires that requested information she didn't want to share with staff here or at sketchy clinics that passed ibuprofen off as penicillin.

"Next." Behind the registration desk, a black woman beckoned Gray to step forward. She pushed an admissions form toward Gray. "What's going on today?"

Questions, even though she had dry eyes and clear lungs.

And a missing appendix. And minor abdominal pain. And possibly a fever.

"Actually, I'm not here for a medical visit," Gray said. "I'm here to see Dr. O'Donnell on business. I was asked to come by this afternoon." She scribbled her name on top of the admissions form, then pushed it back.

The clerk said, "Okay, have a seat over in the chairs. He may be tied up, though. As you can see, we're busy today."

Since Gray would rather wait near blood than perch close to viruses she couldn't see, she selected a seat near an old man holding a saturated bloody towel against his forearm. She winced at him to show sympathy, then found her phone in her purse.

It was time to create a new phone number for this, her first major case as a private investigator. She used Burner, an app that allowed her to generate as many phone numbers as she needed while keeping her personal phone number private. Nick Rader had a number. Jennifer, Zadie, Clarissa, and her coworkers had a number. Utilities, taxes, her apartment's management office—those shared the same number.

That virgin-at-a-prison-rodeo nervousness crackled through her, and she grinned as Burner generated a new number for the Isabel Lincoln case.

Yee-haw!

She pulled intake forms from her leather binder.

Isabel Lincoln had been missing since May 27 and her birthday was just a day away. She had brown hair and brown eyes. Tall at five nine. There was a butterfly tattoo on her left thigh.

A heartbreaker. That's what Gray's father, Victor, would say about pretty girls like Isabel Lincoln. Big, innocent eyes. Sweet, innocent smile. Long ponytail and *Vogue* cheekbones. The kind of girl you married. A Mary Ann. *You're not a Mary Ann*, Victor would tell Gray. *You're . . . the Skipper.* No-nonsense. Reliable. Resourceful.

Gray reread Isabel's race as listed on the intake form. *White?*

Isabel Lincoln was not "white." Mixed, *maybe*. High yellow, definitely. Isabel Lincoln was as white as Halle Berry.

The second intake form had been completed for a dog with curly chocolate-blond hair. The Labradoodle, named Kenny G., belonged to Dr. Ian O'Donnell and had been with Isabel on the day she disappeared.

"Gray Sykes?"

Gray looked up and over to the door that separated the waiting room from the treatment areas. That voice belonged to a tall, sun-kissed god with dirty-blond hair and swimmer's shoulders that strained beneath his blue scrubs.

"Dr. O'Donnell?" When he nodded, she floated over to him with her hand out to shake. Something quickened and fluttered in her belly—he'd knocked her up by simply standing there.

His eyes pecked at her short, boy-cut hairdo, her Rubenesque hips, and her Victorian bosom, and then his eyes glazed and he stopped seeing her altogether. He finally accepted her hand. "You can call me Ian. I was expecting . . ."

"Nick assigned your case to me."

"Ah. Let's talk in my office."

Past the double doors, past the bleeding and asthmatic, and past the beeping machines, Gray finally landed in Ian O'Donnell's office. It was a clean, ordered space with folders placed on the corner of his desk and pictures of patients pinned on a corkboard. Near the desk phone, there were pictures of Ian holding Kenny G., a picture of Kenny G. wearing a doggie surgery cap, and then another picture of Kenny G., romping on the beach.

Gray sat her bag in the other guest chair, then noted the one picture of Isabel. In this shot, the sun was setting at Isabel's back and her face was hidden in shadow. Gray could barely see Ian's one-and-only.

Did the nurses they'd passed—the ones who'd gazed at him as though he lit the skies each morning—did *they* believe that Isabel was his one-and-only? *Had* she been his one-and-only?

According to the good doctor, yes, Isabel had been. They'd been so happy. They'd rarely argued. They had plans, ambitious plans—a wedding, then a honeymoon in Barcelona and Pantages Theater season passes.

"I really thought we were happy." Ian was pinching his bottom lip, and it now looked cherry red and bee-stung. "I just want her to come back home. I want her to just . . . *talk* to me, you know, and explain why she left this time. And why she pulled my dog into all of this."

"You think she's alive and well?"

His hand froze mid–lip pinch. "Of course. The police would've found her and my dog by now if something had happened, right?"

In her mind, Gray shrugged. "Did you contact the police?"

"Yep. End of that week she disappeared. June first."

Gray wrote "June" on the pad, but then the pen stopped writing. She scribbled. No ink. Her pen was dead. She offered Ian an apologetic smile, said, "One minute." She reached for her purse and her nervous hands knocked the bag to the ground. Wallet, hand sanitizer, chewing gum, coins, all of it, clattered out and around the linoleum floor. Gray dropped to the ground and shoved spilled contents back into the handbag. The doctor's stare burned her back and she wanted to cry as she hurried with the cleanup. And, in all of the ruckus, she neglected to find another pen.

Slipping back into the chair, she said, "Sorry," then pushed out a breath. She'd have to remember as much as she could.

He was staring at her. "All done?"

"Yes." She was boiling inside—heat jumped off her skin like flares off the sun.

"Are you okay?" the doctor asked. "You look a little—"

"I'm good, thank you. So . . . June first. What did the police say?"

"They said that she broke up with me, that the text message she sent proved it."

Gray ran her palm across her sweaty hairline. "And what did the text say?"

He swiped around his phone, then set the device before her.

The text had been sent on Monday, May 27:

LEAVE ME THE FUCK ALONE. YOU CAN GO STRAIGHT TO HELL. WE ARE DONE!!!

Gray nodded. "Yeah. Reads like a breakup."

"The cops said that I pissed her off enough that she decided to take the dog, and unless there was evidence of foul play, they had no reason to look for her. I could report Kenny G. as stolen, but they said that reporting could backfire. They think she'll get tired of the dog and will bring him back. They obviously haven't met Kenny G. He's a keeper."

Gray held up a hand. "Let's back up. You said, 'Left this time.' She do this a lot? Leave?"

"Are you going to write any of this down?" he asked, eyeing her.

Gray's cheeks burned. "Umm . . ." She pointed to the cup of pens near his computer monitor. "May I?"

He nodded.

She scribbled as much as she could in five seconds. A bead of sweat trickled down her temple but she didn't swipe it.

Ian O'Donnell bent to open a small refrigerator near his desk. He pulled out a bottled water and twisted the cap. "I think you need this."

She caught that bead of perspiration with a knuckle, then reached for the small bottle. As the cool liquid slipped down her throat, the craggy, cranky places in her smoothed and cooled.

Refreshed, she dropped the empty bottle into her bag. "Thank you."

"It's hot out there." He leaned back in his high-backed chair. "So, Isabel leaving . . . Whenever we're in a rough patch—if we're arguing or her friends are being jerks or whatever—Iz—that's what I call her—Iz just gets in her car and leaves. Since we've been together—it would've been a year on the fourth—she's walked off about two or three times. She's gone for a few days and then she comes back, ready to be a grown-up again."

"Where does she usually go?"

"Palm Springs. Vegas once."

Las Vegas used to be a great disappearing town, before the casino owners installed all those surveillance cameras, before sorority girls Snapped and Boomeranged and selfied, sometimes catching random, taggable folks in the background. It was damn near impossible to hide in Vegas now.

Gray asked, "Is it possible . . ."

No ink coming now from the nib of the borrowed pen.

She wanted the earth to gobble her up for good. Since the earth refused to move, she lifted the binder some, so that Ian O'Donnell couldn't see that the words she wrote on her pad were now invisible. "Is it possible that Isabel just didn't want to come back this last time?"

The doctor's green eyes flared. "We have a future together. I'm a nice guy, and . . . and there's her family. I don't think she would've left them to get back at me. No way.

"She's selfish, that's her problem. Thinks only about herself, and part of me wants to . . ."

"Part of you wants to . . . what?"

He pinched his lip.

"You don't think she wants to come back," Gray said. "Why, then, does she need to be found?"

He turned a sad pink. "Because I want my dog."

"Are there other folks I should talk to?"

Isabel's parents, Joe and Rebekah Lawrence; her best friend, Tea Something; her coworkers Farrah, Beth, and Nan; and Pastor Bernard Dunlop.

"Oh," the doctor added, "and one time, this guy Omar texted her while she was in the shower. I took down the number but never called it. Don't know who the hell *he* is."

"Did you read Omar's text message?"

"Nope. Her phone was locked."

"Could you send those numbers to . . ." Gray offered her new phone number, and Ian O'Donnell texted contact information for everyone except the Lawrences.

"I've never met her parents," he said. "Tea's been my go-between in this craziness."

"When was the last time you talked to Tea?"

"I saw her about two weeks ago. She still hadn't seen Iz."

Gray held up the intake form. "On here you describe Isabel as being white. I'm looking at her and I'm . . . not seeing that. Which means that other people won't see that, either."

"She's biracial. She prefers to check that box instead of the other box."

"The . . . *other* box?"

Ian waved his hand. "I don't see color. She's *human* to me."

Gray's nerves jangled, and she was almost certain that her eyes had crossed.

He cocked an eyebrow. "What?"

Gray jammed her lips together.

"Iz and I . . . we're post-racial, and really . . . Do

you act this way with all of your clients?" He sighed at her just like the white boys she'd dated back when Public Enemy and Air Jordans had crossed color lines.

"What questions should I ask her to prove that she's Isabel and that she's okay?"

Ian O'Donnell rubbed his chin as he thought. "What was my first car? What was my first gift to her? And . . . what am I allergic to?"

Ian, Ian, Ian—even in Isabel's proof of life.

"Did you and Isabel live together?" she asked.

"We were talking about her moving to my place, but we hadn't done it yet."

Probably because she smelled the crazy on him and didn't want it to get into her favorite coat. Hard to get the stink of nuts out of wool. Gray had lost many a good outfit that way.

"I helped pay her rent, though," he said. "Since her credit's shot, I hold the lease."

"Where does she live?"

"Some neighborhood. I don't know. I don't go over there a lot. Never went over there before we started dating." He then recited Isabel's address on Don Lorenzo Drive.

"That's off Stocker Street," Gray said. "In Baldwin Hills."

"Sure. I don't know that part of town."

"Tina Turner had a home there. John Singleton, Tom Bradley, Ray Charles . . ."

"Wow," he said, unimpressed. "Anyway, I can meet you there later today."

"Awesome. So, where do you think she went? The desert or the Strip?"

He lowered his chin to gaze down at her. "If I knew that, I wouldn't be asking you for help, now would I?"

She thought of his single nice gesture toward her, the

gift of water. One small bottle. Though she was fake smiling, she wanted to lunge across the desk and drive his cheap, dry pen through his golden cheek.

He frowned at her as though she were a child. "Her friends probably think I've done something to her. I haven't *touched* her. I haven't *seen* her, and I would never, ever *hurt* her. Like I said, I'm a nice guy. We're a typical couple. Yes, I'd get mad. Yes, she'd get mad. I'd scream, she'd scream, we'd both scream.

"Our last argument, though? She told me that she hated me, that she'd kill me if she could get away with it, which was unbelievable. I know she didn't mean it, but goddamn, it hurt, hearing that. And then, to take my *dog* on top of that?"

There was a knock on the door, and a cute blonde nurse with Michelle Pfeiffer eyes poked her head in to say, "We need you, Dr. O. It's getting crazy out here."

Ian O'Donnell offered Hot Nurse Pfeiffer a ready-made smile. "I'm almost done, Trin."

A moment passed after the nurse had closed the door. Then Ian's eyes and Gray's eyes met—his now shimmered with tears while hers remained as dry and flat as all of Los Angeles. Those dry and flat eyes doubted that they were looking upon a man madly, deeply, truly in love.

Because weren't men all madly, deeply, truly in love before they were no longer madly, deeply, truly in love—minutes before they shot up classrooms, sanctuaries, dental offices, or bedrooms? Boyfriends and husbands, baby daddies and one-night stands were always madly, deeply, truly in love. Bloody love. Crazy love. Love-you-to-death kind of love.

Gray was a skeptic, a cynic, an agnostic of love. She believed more in yetis, chemtrails, and human-meat restaurants than in that four-letter word. "Here's your pen," she said now, dropping the doctor's nonworking writing utensil back into its cup.

Ian O'Donnell stood from his chair. "I'd like a report from you at the end of each day. Nick promised that in my contract. Even if it's just a couple of sentences, I want to know your progress. Who you've talked to. What they said. Et cetera."

Gray closed her binder with a pop. "Certainly."

"No excuses. Every day. Do you understand?"

Ian O'Donnell. The hero, the god, the man who healed people every day. The man who probably always got what he wanted from women. He'd expect nothing less from Gray.

Yeah.

He had no idea.

Forge

Award-winning authors
Compelling stories

. . . .

Please join us at the website
below for more information
about this author and other great
Forge selections, and to sign up for
our monthly newsletter!

. . . . www.tor-forge.com . . . .